MIDSUMMER'S

BOTTOM

ALSO BY DARREN DASH

THE EVIL AND THE PURE

"The book flaunts the grim panache of a London crime saga, and all the characters are engaging, no matter how despicable they are. Not for the faint of heart, but this novel's character studies and ever shifting plot will excite fans of English noir." **Kirkus. Recommended read.**

"*The Evil And The Pure* is a deliciously dark delight; a gritty, realistic look at the depths of human depravity. The twists and turns have you reeling with shock. A glory to read. 5/5 stars." **Matthew R Bell's BookBlogBonanza.**

"A thoughtful and enthralling examination of a society that is seedy, corrupt and painfully uncompromising. Few writers can so easily and powerfully communicate the complexities of people dragged into a world of darkness and despair." **Safie Maken Finlay, author.**

"I found myself brilliantly horrified and captivated as I read and was taken along on a dark journey with a range of dangerous, sick and even innocent characters." **Chase That Horizon.**

SUNBURN

"A well-written and disturbing piece of fiction. The plot reads like an international horror movie, enticing the reader with a series of detailed and comedic chapters before exploding into a vision of blood-chilling gore." **Books, Films & Random Lunacy.**

"This demonic masterpiece does not fail to disappoint even the biggest of horror fans." **Crossing Pixies.**

"The elements of classic horror are very much present here. *Sunburn* held me firmly in the moment, demanding my full attention right to the very last page." **Thoughts Of An Overactive Imagination.**

"Like the *Hostel* films, they have a lot of set up and then shizzle hits the fan... and then hits it again for good measure!" **Dark Readers.**

AN OTHER PLACE

"This is, by far, the best book of 2016, possibly the best book of this decade... the bastard love child of Kafka and Rod Serling, throwing in a dash of Ray Bradbury for good measure. 5/5. Just brilliant. " **Kelly Smith Reviews.**

"*An Other Place* sees an imaginative writer at the top of his craft. It brings to mind *The Twilight Zone*, yet even Rod Serling himself would have struggled to come up with an alternate world so completely off-the-wall and yet oddly meaningful as Dash has here. 9/10 stars." **Starburst.**

"Its luckless hero moves from ghastly scenarios to even ghastlier scenarios with such horrid reliability that his story reads like extreme black comedy. 4/5 stars." **SFX.**

"Lewis Carroll, L. Frank Baum, and Brett Easton Ellis may have written some weird stuff, but *An Other Place* tops all of it, both in terms of re-readability and overall scope." **Dread Central.**

"This book really did blow my mind... each page turn was both chilling and thrilling in equal measure... the conclusion left me with goosebumps. 5/5!" **Rachel Hobbs, author.**

"Dash's surreal tale has its share of unsettling moments. There's also an abundance of intriguing peculiarities. An often baffling tale, but its protagonist's wry commentary is undeniably entertaining." **Kirkus. Recommended Read.**

Midsummer's Bottom

by Darren Dash

MIDSUMMER'S BOTTOM

DARREN DASH

Leabharlanna Poiblí Chathair Baile Átha Cliath
Dublin City Public Libraries

HOME OF THE
DAMNED LTD

ACT ONE

1.[I](i)

A glade in Feyland. Enter OBERON, the king of Fairies.

OBERON: Puck! thou vile worm, thou squat, unseemly wart!

Hide no more! Show thy face, or I do swear —

Enter PUCK, a Fairy.

PUCK: Good king Oberon, hold thy royal tongue;

Honest Puck is here: my lord, I have come.

OBERON: At last! Where hast thou been, foul, tardy sprite?

PUCK: Chasing the day through the dark of the night.

OBERON: Didst thou not hear thy master's noble call?

PUCK: I heard it clear as a harpy's shrill bawl.

OBERON: Then why didst thou not come? It is the sworn

Duty of my subjects, upon hearing

The voice of their lord and king, to make haste!

PUCK: But time turns only once, and Puck loathes waste.

OBERON: Is it a waste to heed Oberon's cry?

PUCK: It is, my lord, when Puck is on the spy,

All senses fixed on a young maiden fair,

Fingers like snakes in her long golden hair,

Slyly unknotting her fierce Viking braids,

And then to her beau, to polish his blade;

Like two grey shades these many months they walked,

Marching in time, but chastely set apart;

Tonight, pray thanks to Puck's ministrations,

They dance as one to love's wild vibrations.

OBERON: I would hear more of this another time,

But it will have to wait. Know you the day?

PUCK: Days are for mere mortals to weigh. I know

Of centuries, and have seen decades flow,

But days? How may one, immortal as sport,

Concern himself with a timespan so short?

OBERON: You speak the truth of Feyland; but you lie.

PUCK: Lord, how can acknowledged truth be a lie?

Your logic is absurd, even to I.

OBERON: In the depth of summer, Goodfellow, truth

Is a jester dressed in shrouds of madness.

PUCK: You do not mean... it cannot be... oh gods!

OBERON: 'Tis true, Puck: Midsummer has come again.

PUCK: Curse the forces which measure time like dust,

Impris'ning us in this temporal crust.

OBERON: Yet, even in Feyland there must be law.

We cannot choose Time and then draw it from

Our scabbards only when we so desire.

PUCK: I swore we should not make a pact with Time;

We sold our souls when we dotted that line.

OBERON: As I recall, you were instrumental

In aligning our fate with Time's champion.

"It will afford good sport," you said in jest,

And urged us to regale Will with our tales.

PUCK: I was mad. My lord, you should hate poor Puck,

Yet you stand, smiling, as though I brought luck.

OBERON: My hatred of you has oft' known no bounds,

But today I harbour more hope than hate.

My queen and I have hatched a cunning plan.

PUCK: To free us from the tyranny of Man?

OBERON: Of all men, no, our destinies are tied,

But from those of the glade we might slide free.

PUCK: My lord, in truth, I've always held you high,

But if this works, I swear to paint the sky

In overlapping shades of green and red;

Across the horizon I'll etch your head!

OBERON: Rejoice not yet, good Robin of the night,

For much must be done to win the good fight.

My lady and I boast two fine, wise heads,

But wickedness makes for a sharper threat.

We have need of you, impish, roguish Puck,

To shake loose our chains and unpick the lock.

PUCK: I sense devilment in my lord's fine words,

There's a timbre to your voice, long unheard.

Shall we raise hell again, my noble king,

As we once did before Time reined us in?

OBERON: If your wits have not been softened by Time,

Perhaps we'll again shine as in our prime

And cause havoc. Come now, we must away.

This night slips all too quickly towards day.

Time is passing. We have much to discuss.

Exeunt.

1. [I] (ii)

Del Chapman's finger paused deliciously over the ENTER key. To either side, men and women were drearily tapping away their lives, chained to keyboards like slaves, faces illuminated by the sickly bright glare of soul-sucking computer screens.

Del pitied his colleagues, for this would be their life's lot. They'd sit here, or in similar pits, until death or retirement, counting the minutes in every slow-passing hour, dreaming of weekends, a week's holiday at Christmas, a fortnight in the summer, scrimping and saving for an annual trip abroad that would largely involve sheltering from a merciless sun and drinking watered-down cocktails.

Del had been here a mere three months but it felt like a decade. How could people move so docilely towards old age and dotage? They should be fighting the advance of time, not embracing it. It was one thing to accept defeat, but to never raise a fist in anger or test the walls of the cage...

Three months! He'd only accepted the job to experience work first-hand. He had often spoken with scorn of the rat race. In pubs he would mock his friends and implore them to broaden their horizons, until one had responded with a tetchy, "You can't knock our way till you've tried it."

And since Del always liked to acknowledge a good point well made, he decided that he *would* try it. After ten years of blessed idleness, living off the good will of his friends and scamming the gullible or picking pockets (only ever from those who could afford the loss), he'd *put his talents to good use* and sold his soul – temporarily! – to the horned devil of paid employment.

A week had been more than enough – shaving and showering every morning, dressing in clean clothes and making sure his shoes were polished, soporific daytime radio humming in the background as the drones bitched about how they were underappreciated and underpaid – but he'd persevered, so that no one could claim he hadn't given it ample time. He was young and could afford to waste a few months of his precious life.

But the day had come to move on. A quarter of a year had passed while he decayed in this timeless, meaningless subworld. Summer was upon Limerick – not that you'd know it by the grey skies – and to stay longer would mean emerging in autumn or winter, and that thought was too depressing to countenance. Del wanted to run free through the city streets – naked if he wished – and not have to worry about frostbite.

It was time.

He hadn't handed in notice or told anybody of his decision. It was easier this way and more fun. He'd impressed during his time here and been granted increased responsibilities – his boss said he had a magnificent future with the company – so his sudden departure would create a satisfying measure of chaos.

He'd put in a lot of overtime these past few weeks, working on a personal project. Del was a wizard with computers, and viruses were his speciality. He bred them like a mad scientist breeding destructive bacterial strains. Few things in life afforded him more pleasure than setting loose a virulent bug on a neatly ordered digital universe — *Go, baby, go!*

He'd been decently treated by his employers. He liked his co-workers and didn't want to cause them harm. But they needed help. Del Chapman was no Spartacus, but in his own way he was a freedom fighter, constantly pressing for the rights of the individual.

These slaves were probably beyond help but Del was determined to at least open their eyes to the possibility of freedom. Every computer in the building was networked. His virus would speed through them and crash the entire system in a matter of hours. There would be no way to retrieve lost information. The company would recover (and maybe pay for some decent anti-virus software next time round) but it would reel from the blow for several weeks. Employees would be laid-off or rested. With so much free time on their hands, perhaps one or two of the braver souls might lift their nostrils and sniff the air of true freedom.

Del's finger descended and the virus sprang from the traps, its fangs glinting, tearing from one terminal to the next, spreading its deadly disease at the speed of communication.

"Run free," Del muttered, both to the virus and his career-shackled colleagues.

He rose and tapped his neighbour's shoulder. "Call of nature. Back in a minute." His unwitting victim nodded without looking up from his screen, terrified of missing some magical electronic symbol. Del smiled as he considered the consternation in the man's face when the computer began creating psychedelic mazes from which there was no escape.

He left his coat and personal belongings behind, including the keys to his flat. He wouldn't need them. It was a warm day and the world was full of belongings. He could accumulate more if he wished. The world was always quick to offer its gifts to those who had no genuine yearning for them.

*

At a hundred and forty-eight kilometres an hour and rising, Del streaked through the night, headlights slicing a path through the darkness, Metallica exploding from the car's state-of-the-art speakers. Behind, a police car trailed him, siren blaring. The officers had tried cutting him off but now were content to tail him, sure that he'd eventually take a bend too fast and skid or overturn.

Del had *borrowed* the car, a sporty BMW, taking a set of keys from a manager's coat on his way out. He'd driven round the outskirts of the city, making an entire circuit, bidding it adieu. The world was enormous and it was time to explore. He'd had his fill of soggy, boggy Limerick. Time to bow out and head in the general direction of... *away.*

A couple of officers in a patrol car had clocked him breaking the speed limit during his farewell lap and he'd been playing a merry game of chase with them ever since. He didn't know how the game would end but he was sure he wouldn't be caught. Almost every rogue falls foul of the law in the end, and Del had resigned himself to an eventual spin on the prison wheel, but he felt in his bones that the day of paying his dues wasn't yet upon him.

Del's zigzagging course through Limerick's countryside warren of minor roads hadn't taken him far from the city, regardless of his speed. A glimpse of a road sign told him he was a mere eleven kilometres distant.

"Time to lose these suckers," he growled, checking his rear-view mirror. The pubs would be closing soon and Del was thirsty.

Del trained his gaze on the zipping-past scenery. After a while he spotted the outlying trees of a forest and slowed while looking for an entrance. Finding one, he took the corner neatly, then accelerated viciously. He sped down a twisting road for a kilometre before spotting a small dirt road on his left. Hastily reducing speed, he backed into cover, then cut the lights and rolled down the windows.

For a few seconds there was quiet. Then the wail of the approaching cop car. His stomach tensed – could his gut feeling have been wrong? – but relaxed again as the car roared by and continued on into the depths of the forest.

They'd never find him now.

Del switched off the engine, leant back, shut his eyes and sighed happily. He'd wait a few minutes, then bomb it to a pub in time for last call. A few pints, then he'd be far away by dawn, leaving everything behind — his job, his past, even his name.

He didn't react when the passenger door clicked open, thinking that the noise was just the cooling of the engine or a low-hanging branch brushing against the roof. But when he looked over a minute later, he was stunned to notice a small figure in the seat next to him.

"Who the hell are you?" Del gasped.

"A friend I am, for all that I may seem;" came the unexpected response. "Have you never espied me in a dream?"

"What?" Del asked stupidly, confused by his guest's cryptic answer.

"Full explanations will, in time, unreel;

For now, I would advise you take the wheel."

"Listen, weirdo," Del began, "I don't know who you are or why you're talking that way, but this is my car and –"

The engine roared to life and the car lurched into reverse. Del cringed away from the wheel, then grabbed on for dear life. He slammed a foot down on the brake — no response.

The figure to Del's left spoke again.

"The time has come to lay control aside.

Sit back. Relax. Unwind. Enjoy the ride."

"Who are you?" Del yelled, jerking on the wheel. "How are you doing this?" The car didn't react to his savage jerks, and instead of careening wildly into the bushes, the BMW stormed back along the dirt road, picking up speed.

"My name and purpose will in time be dealt;

Till then you would do well to fix your belt."

Del stared at the small man – still shaded by the dark forest night, impossible to identify – then at the road in the mirror. He hadn't strapped on a belt since he was a child – anarchists have no time for safety constraints – but now he gulped, reached behind and drew the strap across.

Del watched the speedometer climb to a hundred. One-twenty. One-fifty. He couldn't understand how they were making such headway on so poor a track, or how a connecting dirt-road could be so long.

Del was about to risk another question when they burst into a clearing. He just had time to spot a van directly behind them and scream — then they were ploughing into the van, filling the night with fiery sparks and the screeches of tortured metal.

*

Del must have passed out, because when he next looked around, he was lying on damp grass beneath a crooked tree. He sat up and groaned. It took him a few seconds to realise he wasn't in pain. He checked his arms and legs twice, to make sure he wasn't injured, then shakily rose to his feet.

The BMW had made a crunching mess of the van, which lay capsized, windows smashed and sides caved in. The police car which had been chasing Del was there, and had been joined by an ambulance. As Del watched, a couple of paramedics prised a body from the pulverised van and laid it on a stretcher.

"Please, no," Del sobbed, stumbling forward. Had he killed a man? He feared so. Nobody could have crawled out of that wreck alive. Del Chapman loved chaos but abhorred violence. Had the cruel fates played an awful trick on him? Had he become an unwitting killer?

"The human's bones and organs are all firm.

He will sleep and suffer no further harm."

Del turned slowly. The small man from the passenger seat was standing behind him. He was even tinier than Del had first imagined, no more than four foot six. He was dressed in an odd, purple suit, and had curiously-shaped features, angular and sharp.

"He's alive?" Del asked suspiciously and watched the paramedics carefully load the stretcher into the back of the ambulance. There was no sheet over the man's face, which was a positive sign. The police were examining the van and car.

"For two whole weeks he will but sleep and dream;

Then, as new, he will return to the scheme."

"How do you know that?" Del asked.

The little man smiled.

"I know, for he was cloaked with grand fey luck,

As are all who stand protected by Puck."

Del shook his head. The small man either didn't want to make sense or couldn't. Either way, Del had had enough of him. He stepped forward and raised his hands high. Though he'd often fled from problems of his creation, this time he meant to do the decent thing.

The police didn't see him.

He coughed politely. When nobody responded, he took several steps forward. Now he was standing in the headlights of the police car. They *had* to see him.

But they didn't.

There was a tap on his shoulder — the little man again.

"To their eyes you cast no visible light;

To them, you're but a shadow of the night."

Del frowned. "You mean I'm invisible?" he asked incredulously.

"Invisible, indeed, and mute to boot."

Del waited for the second, rhyming line, but this time there was none. In the ensuing silence, he decided to test the stranger's assertion. "Hey!" he yelled. "I'm over here! I'm the one you want!"

Neither of the policemen raised an eyebrow. Del strode up to them, waving his arms and yelling, but to those in the forest he had no substance. They couldn't see or hear him.

He reached out and brushed the back of a paramedic's neck as he closed the door of the ambulance. The man shuddered and rubbed the touched flesh, then looked around at the dark forest with unease.

"C'mon, Joe," he called to his mate. "This place gives me the willies."

"Bloody townie," his colleague laughed. "Afraid of your own feckin' shadow." But he climbed into the ambulance and strapped himself in. Though he'd never admit it, he too had been unsettled by the otherworldly atmosphere.

"This is unreal," Del sighed, falling to his haunches, watching the ambulance depart. "Did I die in the crash? Am I a ghost?"

Behind him, the little man laughed uproariously.

"By the gods — he thinks himself a spirit!"

"I don't know what *you're* laughing at," Del sulked. "They didn't see you either. If I'm dead, so are you."

"The day of harvest is not on us, friend;
We both have far to go before the end."

"So how do you explain our vanishing act?" Del sniffed. "I know the law's supposed to be blind, but this is stretching things."

"Friend Chapman, you are shrewd for a mortal,
But mankind stalled at wisdom's first portal.
Come: we'll find two toadstools and tell stories."

The small, odd-looking man offered Del his hand. Del studied the wiry fingers for a moment, then wearily took them and let himself be led away from the flashing lights, into the dark-knit heart of the forest.

*

The toadstools were enormous, like something out of *Alice in Wonderland*. The little man hopped onto one and dangled his legs over the edge of the cap. Del tested another to determine its firmness, then propped himself against it.

Del was beginning to come to grips with the situation. One of the bonuses of swearing allegiance to the forces of chaos is that it prepares you for anything. He wasn't sure if this was reality or a dream, and if reality, how such marvels as invisibility, walking away unscathed from car crashes, and giant toadstools had come to pass, but he was content to roll with the crazy scene.

"Settled?" the little man asked. "Ready?"

"You can speak normally?" Del grunted.

"When dull scenes call for words deliver'd prime,
    Flexi-Puck can dispense with rosy rhyme."

Del grimaced. "You're back to the couplets. Could we get along without them? It's hard for me to follow you when you're talking in verse."

"You will have to rise to the occasion," the small man replied with a grin, then launched into his tale.

"Know this first: I am the infamous Puck,
    Servant of mischief, chaos and sly luck.
I hail from Feyland, realm of magic dreams,
    Where Oberon's king and Titania's queen."

"Those names sound familiar," Del mused, scratching his head. "Was there a movie about that place?"

"My lords and I in light myth are held dear,
    Glorified by the wordsmith, Will Shakespeare."

"That's right." Del clicked his fingers. "*Midnight's Dream*, the one about the guy with the head of an ass."

"*A Midsummer Night's Dream*," Puck corrected him with a

wince. He shook his head and returned to the narrative.

"The story, as related, is most true,

Though playful Will did add some sections new.

We sought to have the ancient legends told,

To spread the mirth of Fey across the world.

'Twas a mistake, a grave and foolish act.

If we'd but known the price it would exact!

We ne'er anticipated such a run:

We thought the tale would set with sev'ral suns.

We assumed the play would have its fine day,

But then would just as swiftly fade away.

We were fools, as we now most sadly see,

To shackle ourselves to Earth's history,

For, though we knew it not when we did sign,

We'd chained ourselves eternally to Time.

Part of the pact we made with brash young Will

As we sprinkled Feyland's dust on his quill,

Was to always by his spry version stand,

Lending our presence to each show, each land."

"I'm not sure I understand," Del said, unwittingly adding to the rhyme. "You're telling me you helped William Shakespeare write a play?"

"*Help* is not the word we would choose to use,

For we were much more than a simple muse.

We opened his eyes and led his frail hands,

That play was ours. The unkempt mortal man

Was but a vessel we used to create,

Or so we believed, dumb to our true fate."

"You mean *you* wrote it?" Del couldn't keep the scepticism

out of his voice.

"Not directly," Puck answered, too despondent to work his words into verse. "The Fey do not know how to write. We never bothered to learn — we had better things to do."

"I can dig that," Del nodded.

"But we as good as wrote it," Puck went on. "We visited Will at night and relayed our tales. We dictated the plot and were responsible for most of the puns. It was our play, not his — or so we thought." Puck kicked at the toadstool. "What we did not realise was that by aligning ourselves to the realm of man, we ensnared our spirits in its mortal mesh. Part of the pact we made was that we – Oberon, Titania, myself and the others mentioned in the play – had to attend every performance. *Every. Performance.* 'Twas the wordsmith's idea. Will was a sly fox, almost as cunning as good Puck."

"I get it," Del said, nodding slowly. "You and your buddies let Shakespeare write a play about you, and in return you had to agree to attend all the shows."

"The way Will put it, it seemed an honour," Puck said bitterly. "Though human audiences would come and go, we would always be on hand to judge each acting troupe. He made us think he was doing us a favour."

Del couldn't see the dilemma. "So what's the problem?" he asked.

"The *problem*," Puck responded gruffly, "is we have had to suffer through every version of the play these past four centuries. Four hundred years of watching the same play. Can you even begin to imagine how torturous that is?"

"Isn't it a good play?" Del asked innocently.

"It is great!" Puck shrieked. "But no play can stand up to four hundred years of repeated viewing. It is not too bad when a remarkable group of actors get their hands on it, but most of the fools are amateurs. They mangle the lines and make mockeries of the characters. They overact, add comedy routines and sometimes perform revisionist versions." Puck shuddered.

"Can't you close your eyes and plug your ears?" Del suggested.

Puck's nostrils flared.

"After four long cen'tries of butchered verse,

We believed we could be hit with no worse.

Over time one becomes numb to the pain:

Wounds prickle so long, then never again."

"You've reverted to rhyme to punish me, haven't you?" Del asked.

"Yes," Puck agreed. *"Close your eyes and plug your ears!"*

"I was only trying to help," Del protested, but Puck ignored the weak apology.

"Then, as we grew accustomed to our state,

A fresh set of fools set our teeth a'grate.

They were no worse than many clowns before;

Indeed, to some, they seemed as shining stars.

The curse lies not in their limitations,

But rather in their grim dedication.

Ev'ry midsummer – nineteen without fail –

They stage their paltry show and cause us hell."

"They can't be *that* bad," Del interrupted.

"They are," Puck assured him. "Bumbling, untalented, clumsy, mismatched. I could go on and *on*. In truth, they are not the worst — just annoyingly consistent. Most amateurs stage it and move on. Not these devils. They return year after year, a performance every midsummer's eve. We have grown to dread them. It takes a lot to shake an immortal entity, but these humans – to use one of your mortal phrases – scare us shitless."

Del made a small choking sound and turned his head away.

"Are you laughing at Robin Goodfellow?" Puck asked indignantly.

"Who's that?" Del gasped.

"Me."

"I thought your name was Puck."

"I am known by many names," Puck replied.

"I'm sorry, but it's ridiculous. I mean, an immortal fairy, scared of a bunch of actors. Why don't you sprinkle some magic dust on them and send them packing?"

Puck sighed miserably.

"Would that we could, but it's part of our pact

That on matters like these we may not act."

"What would happen if you did?" Del asked.

"We would be punished."

"By who?"

"A force that bears no name."

"Sounds nasty." Del thought on the imp's words some more and a frown slowly developed. "What does this have to do with me?"

Puck brightened and returned to full, flowery verse.

"For nineteen years my poor kind have suffered

As through the play the damned mortals stuttered.

We believed there could be no bless'd relief
And so resigned ourselves to sullen grief.
But, of late, in their sev'ral moments spare,
My lord and lady have scented the air
For trace of a man with some fey-like glee,
A wry human imp, as Puckish as me.
They've scour'd the land for a creature of night,
One who revels in havoc and delights
In the destructive chaos he ignites,
With whom a Puck could strike a bonding light.
They sought, not for one endowed with evil,
But one as shrewd as a cunning weasel,
One who –"

"Hold it," Del interrupted. "I get the picture. You can't interfere with these actors directly, but if you found a human who shared your anarchic mindset, you could send him among the actors and get him to ruin their show. Correct?"

"Friend Chapman, thou art a sage."

"The greatest sage of any age," Del sang sarcastically. "But you're out of luck. I'm no actor. I've never been on a stage in my life."

"On stage you would never have to set foot:
These actors perform in nature; a wood."

"In a forest?" Del glanced around at the trees and it clicked. "*This* forest?"

"Aye."

"You mean the world's worst actors are *here*? In *Limerick*?"

"Not the worst. Merely the most annoying,
The most frustrating and the –"

"– most cloying," Del finished.

"Not bad," Puck complimented him. "You learn quickly."

"You needn't think you can flatter me into doing this," Del warned the fairy, who made innocent moon-eyes.

"'Tis not Puck's way to issue pleas to hearts,

He is by far more playful in his art.

Consider, mortal, the game to be had

By tricking these clowns and turning them mad.

Puck can in your two hands great power place,

Provide a full bag of tricks that would grace

The most magnificent witch's boudoir.

All you need do is embrace this keen hour

And place your trust in the hands of this Puck."

Puck leant across and for the second time that night offered Del his hand. Del hesitated longer this time before deciding whether or not to accept it.

"I wouldn't have to harm anyone?" he asked.

"Not a hair on their head, nor a crack in their bottom."

"I'd just have to mingle with them and create a little chaos?"

"'Tis not the wish of the fey folk to hurt,

Merely to escape this accursed fort."

Del liked the notion but wasn't sure he was the right man for the job. What did he know of acting or plays? "How will I infiltrate their ranks?" he asked. "Won't they spot me for a fraud? I can't act or memorise lines. How am I supposed to –"

Puck cut him short.

"We have more answers than a pope has pray'rs,

But night draws on: we must seek them elsewhere.

If you trust good Puck, then lend him your hand

And he will lead you to magic Feyland,

There to meet his lieges at a ball,

Who can explain the ins and outs; the all."

"You want me to go with you to Feyland?" Del looked around nervously. "Is it far?"

"The leap of a mouse. The length of a dream."

"How do I know you'll bring me back?"

"Feyland can hold none but those who choose it."

"I've only your word for that."

"Aye, and 'tis the word of a merry sprite,

The ignoble Puck, liar of the night.

But it is all I can offer.

Take it or leave it as you will."

"I'll probably regret this in the morning," Del muttered, "but..." He drew breath, then ploughed on.

"Very well, Puck, I shall take your hot hand,

But if the sport proves not most fitting grand,

I'll slice off that hand and hoist it up high

And make you sorry you told such a lie."

"*Verrrry* good," Puck purred. "We will make a sprite of you yet. Come. Midsummer draws nearer by the minute. We must away."

The two joined hands and the branches of the forest drew together above their heads. When they parted, all that remained in the glade was a pair of wilting toadstools, which quickly rotted into the earth with the rising of the sun.

1.[I](iii)

Anna Devlin lay on her side and watched her husband snoring, fascinated by the way the early sun had pierced a chink in the curtains and illuminated his scraggly nostril hairs. As he took a deep breath, Anna gently laid the tips of two fingers to the base of his nose. When he exhaled, the short stiff hairs blew out and tickled her flesh. She touched the fingers to her lower lip, then lifted the sheets.

Terence was a fitness freak – a *life addict*, as he preferred to put it – and his stomach and chest formed a cage of taut, rippling muscles. Anna ran a finger along his abs, smiling as they twitched. She leant over and slowly kissed his left nipple, feeling the beat of his heart through her lips. Terence hated her playing with his nipples when they made love. He was such a prude.

She wondered if most men were as conservative in the bedroom as her husband. She wouldn't know. Terence had been her first, her only. They'd met twenty years earlier, when she'd been a schoolgirl and he'd been her teacher. Although attracted instantly to one another, they'd kept the romance on hold until she'd completed her studies. A whirlwind affair had followed and, six months out of school, a week after her eighteenth birthday, they had wed.

Anna often wished she'd waited a few years. There was so much she'd missed out on, boyfriends, college, a job, the simple struggles of life. She felt she wasn't a complete person, that she'd traded the depths of maturity for an early marriage and security.

Terence yawned and rolled towards her. His eyes opened when he bumped into her, then closed against the morning light.

"You left the bloody curtains open," he groaned, shading his eyes with a hand.

"*You* closed them," Anna replied defensively.

"I always leave them ajar," he grumbled. "How many times have I told you? You can't depend on me for the practical things. You know my head's away in the clouds more often than not. It's up to you to…"

She turned on her side and tuned out while Terence launched into the first of the day's lectures. After twenty years, it was too late for regrets. Anna had made her bed and was determined to lie in it. But as Terence droned on, she couldn't stop the thought from flitting through her mind — *if only I'd waited.*

*

Ingmar buttered toast while Don riffled through the morning's newspaper. Dance music throbbed in the background, the volume low enough not to bother Don, high enough to be audible to Ingmar as he swished through the kitchen preparing breakfast. "Four slices of toast or six?" he called.

"Six," came the instant reply.

"Maybe you should limit yourself to four," Ingmar suggested.

Don lowered the paper and frowned. "I always have six slices of toast."

"I know," Ingmar said, "but with the play so close, and your stomach… well…"

"What's wrong with my stomach?" Don asked indignantly. He glanced down at his bulging belly. "That's latent muscle."

Ingmar sighed. "Remember the trouble we had fitting you into your costume last year? I have problems enough, without having to wonder how big you'll be."

"I'll be the same size I always am!" Don roared.

"Alright." Ingmar knew when to give up. "Six it is."

"It'd be different if you let me eat meat," Don grumbled. "If I'd sausages and rashers to round out a meal, I wouldn't have to rely on the damn bread so much."

"You know where meat leads," Ingmar chided him. "Clogged arteries and bad breath."

"So you keep telling me," Don grunted. He laid the newspaper aside to make room for the plate. He picked up the top slice of toast and bit a huge chunk out of it. Ingmar noted the bulging of Don's chubby cheeks with disapproval but said nothing. He'd try and get the older man to come on some walks with him over the next couple of weeks. Those, coupled with plenty of sex, would hopefully knock him into shape.

"It's so peaceful here, isn't it?" Ingmar commented, spreading a delicate dob of marmalade across his thin slice of toast. (Only sixty calories a slice!)

"It's like a graveyard compared to Dublin," Don agreed, munching busily. "How did you sleep?"

"Like an angel," Ingmar said.

"It took me ages to drop off," Don said. "I always have trouble adapting to the quiet."

"You should try playing music," Ingmar said.

"No point," Don said. "I wouldn't be able to hear it above your snoring."

"I don't snore," Ingmar protested.

"Then there must have been a pig in the bed with us last night."

The two men smiled fondly at one another, then tucked into their meals.

Ingmar Van Dorslaer had first come to Ireland from Germany as a student. He'd enjoyed himself and, years later, had returned. He'd only meant to stay for a few weeks, but had made friends, landed a job and settled into the Irish way of life. Now here he was, twelve years later, a convert of the Emerald Isle. He even sounded Irish most of the time, though his German accent occasionally surfaced if he was nervous or feeling stressed.

The track came to a close and the next kicked in. Ingmar drummed his fingers in time with the beat. He was a DJ who loved his tunes. When he wasn't behind a turntable, he spent his nights on the dance floor, bopping away to the sounds of the age, keeping abreast of the latest developments and crazes.

Don wasn't so keen on music. They'd met at a disco, and Don pretended to maintain an interest, but he lacked Ingmar's passion, and trance certainly wasn't his thing. He liked songs he could click his fingers to.

Ingmar finished his toast and picked up a magazine. He opened it to the fashion pages and ran a critical eye over the lanky models. "Look at the muscles on him," he tutted, pointing to a photo of a film star. "He used to be cute. Now he's all bulging biceps. He still has legs to die for but he eats too much meat, I can tell. A healthier diet, less time in the gym..."

Don didn't even glance at the photo. He had no interest in other men. A noble quality, yet it irritated Ingmar. On the one hand, it was nice to have a considerate, thoughtful lover. On the other, Ingmar occasionally wished he'd hooked up with someone more adventurous, who shared his own, varied tastes. They'd had many arguments over the years, when Ingmar's eyes – and other parts – had strayed.

"That's a good song," Don remarked — high praise indeed.

"It's new," Ingmar told him. "A friend sent it to me. Some young French band."

"Which friend?" Don asked.

"Otto," Ingmar said, picking a name at random.

Don frowned. "I don't recall you mentioning an Otto before. Where's he from?"

Ingmar rolled his eyes. Time to start inventing again. One day he'd run out of stories, and where would that leave them? What sort of a relationship would it be if they had to – God forbid – start telling each other the truth?

*

"'I do entreat your grace to pardon me.

I know not by what power I am made bold,

Nor how it may concern my modesty

In such a presence here to plead my thoughts;

But I beseech your grace that I may know

The worst that may befall me in this case,

If I refuse to wed Demetrius.'"

Kate Pummel laid her copy of the play aside, stared at herself in the bathroom mirror and stretched the skin of her face, checking for wrinkles.

"'The worst that may befall me,'" she chuckled, then adopted a deep, masculine voice. "The worst, Hermia? They'll lock you up in a nunnery with a bunch of mad penguins, or lop off your head and use it as a football."

People had been so brutal in the past. Imagine having to face a life of celibacy or execution for betraying the wishes of your father. Kate's dad had wanted her to study law. Would she have had the courage to face the habit or the chopping block if his word had been sacrosanct? Thank God she lived in saner times.

Kate would play Hermia in two weeks. This was her second year with the company. She'd played a fairy last time. The role of Hermia was a big step up but she was ready for it. She'd come a long way, though there was further still to go.

Kate took five deep breaths, letting her head tilt backwards, then forwards. She rolled it slowly to the left, then the right. Then she addressed her reflection. "Kate Pummel, you're a beautiful woman, in the prime of her life. Your height is perfect, your shape ideal, your poise remarkable, your diction delectable. You are talented and ambitious. You will be one of the greatest actresses the world has ever seen. You will succeed. You cannot fail. It's only a matter of time."

This was her daily pep talk, and it went on in this manner for five minutes. The routine had seemed corny when she'd first tried it, but now it was an integral part of her life. Confidence, she'd learnt, was essential to the go-getting actress.

Kate had wanted to be an actress since the age of eight, when she'd played Mary in the school Nativity play. She'd been *bitten by the bug* and there was no cure for that disease. Her life since then had been devoted to performance. She wasn't sure how far she could go, but she believed in aiming for the top.

She stepped back from the mirror and stretched gently. She'd put her back out some years before, and was anxious not to repeat the accident. It wasn't so much the pain she feared – a good actress needed to experience pain, to add to her range – but the incapacitation. If she had to ditch this play because of a sore back, she'd simply die.

Kate had spent three years studying drama, then three on the road. She'd travelled most of Ireland, playing wherever offers took her, often without pay. She wasn't precious. She'd have a go at anything, from a walk-on part to a teenager or a wrinkled crone. She regarded every role as a learning experience. Plus, the travel allowed her to build up a network of contacts. Most of her gigs (as she referred to them) this year had come about because of associations formed over the past two.

The phone rang downstairs. The signal here was dreadful, so she wasn't relying on her mobile, and had shared the landline number with all her contacts, asking her friends and followers to use that if they wished to get in touch. (So far, very few had.) After a final stretch, she trotted down.

Kate was supposed to have been staying with Don and Ingmar, in the cottage they rented every year, but at the last moment a member of the company had pulled out and this two-storey house became available. It was too big for a single person but Kate wasn't complaining. Most actors had to crack Hollywood before they could revel in luxury like this.

She paused by the phone, to get her breath back. There

were few worse mistakes an actress could make than answer a phone out of breath, gasping and wheezing. What if it was a producer or director at the other end?

"Good morning," she sung brightly, picking up the receiver. "Kate Pummel speaking."

"Hi," came the soft reply. "It's me."

Kate relaxed. She knew the caller. No need to be on guard. "You're early. I was exercising."

"I couldn't wait any longer. I dreamt about you all night. I wish I could have slept over."

"Don't be silly," Kate giggled. "I know how things are. I'm not going to ask for the impossible."

"I'll manage to stay some night. I'll think up an excuse."

"I don't want you jeopardising your position," Kate said. "After all, there's plenty we can do in the daylight, as we proved yesterday afternoon."

Her caller chuckled lewdly. "That was wicked, wasn't it? You were no sooner in the door than... But I couldn't keep my hands off you. It had been four months."

"I know," Kate lied — unlike her lover, she hadn't been keeping track of time.

"Was it...?" There was a stifled laugh.

"...as good for me as it was for you?" Kate asked, smiling.

"That's so corny. I can't believe I came out with it. Forget I asked."

"The answer would have been *yes*," Kate said teasingly.

"Really?"

She could picture him beaming and had to bite down on a hand – not too hard, she didn't want to leave marks – to cut short the giggles.

"I'll try to come over after rehearsals," her caller said. "It might be tricky, but – So!" he boomed, changing tack abruptly. "Eleven o'clock start. You'll be there?"

"Your wife came in, didn't she?" Kate asked.

"You betcha," came the merry answer. "Eleven, then. See you!"

The line went dead.

Kate replaced her receiver and stared at the phone in silence. Getting involved with a married man, and a colleague to boot. The one thing she'd vowed never to do, especially at such a critical juncture. This play could be a big step forward. It was her meatiest role to date. She might get noticed by a critic or talent scout. It was crazy to risk all that for a meaningless fling.

But she couldn't help herself. She'd felt attracted to the older man the first time they'd met, and when he'd made a pass, she hadn't been able to resist. She would have been happy to let the affair stand as a one-off, but he was eager for more, and the attention tickled her fancy.

What a mess. Oh well, things would sort themselves out, as they invariably did. All she had to do in the meantime was pray that his wife didn't find out and have her ejected from the play and the house.

*

"Who were you on the phone to?" Anna asked.

"Diarmid," Terence replied smoothly. "Making sure he didn't forget what time rehearsals start."

"Oh," Anna said and wandered away again.

Shit! Had she believed him? Did she suspect?

Terence Devlin ran his fingers over his bristly beard — barely more than stubble — and opted to believe his wife was ignorant of his extra-marital shenanigans. He'd drive himself mad if he started suspecting her of suspecting. Second-guessing was the game of demons and fools.

Terence jogged up and down the stairs. Normally he'd be in the middle of an early workout — he put in a couple of hours a day, seven days a week — but the pressures of preparing for the play meant he wouldn't have time to tend to his body over the next two weeks. One of the drawbacks to directing. Never mind — he'd snatch as many spare moments as he could for a spot of impromptu exercise.

After a few minutes of jogging, he paid his morning visit to the toilet. His insides were as finely-tuned as his exterior and he concluded his business briskly. As he washed his hands, he studied himself in the mirror.

"Looking *good*," he murmured. He patted his lean stomach and grinned. Not bad for a man in his late forties. There weren't many his age who'd held their shape. That was how he was able to attract young beauties like Kate Pummel, when other middle-aged men had to resort to manual techniques, ladies of the night or — worse still — rely on their wives.

Terence blamed Anna for his affairs. Kate wasn't the first young lady he'd seduced. (In Terence's mind, even a fumbling, drunken, one-night fling was an act of great, romantic seduction.) If Anna hadn't let herself go to seed, he wouldn't have to seek solace elsewhere. She'd been a magnificent teenager. His star pupil. Legs like steam pistons, able to run all day and still have enough left in the engine for a night of hot, steamy sex. (Once she'd graduated, of course. Terence hadn't been fool enough to risk his job by sleeping with a student.) He'd struggled to keep up with her during the first years of their marriage. Now a lame turtle could outpace the lazy, oversized cow.

Anna blamed the children. "Pass a pair of nine-pound babies and see how *your* body fares," she often sneered. But Terence didn't buy that. It was easy to make excuses. She could have won the battle of the bulge if she'd fought harder. Did she think it was easy for him? His regime would test a man half his age, and some days he felt like it would kill him, but you had to punish yourself to reap the rewards.

Rewards such as yesterday's rendezvous. How many other men pushing fifty could bring a virile young woman to the throes of three consecutive orgasms? Only a man in Terence's condition could weave sexual magic that intense. (It never occurred to Terence that, of all the women he'd seduced, the only ones he'd driven to orgasm were *actresses*.)

Terence pressed closer to the mirror and examined his roots. His thatch had started to grey in his early twenties. Rather than let it dull naturally, he'd resorted to the cheap tricks of chemistry — dye. At least his beard had retained its original colour. There were a few swaths of grey among the black, but a hint of grey in your beard was a sign of distinction and maturity.

"Are you going to be in there all day?" Anna asked.

He jumped — he hadn't heard her enter. "Haven't I told you to knock before barging in?" he howled.

Anna snorted. "After all these years of marriage, have you anything to hide?"

"It's not about hiding," Terence snapped. "It's about privacy."

"You're a big kid," Anna sighed, tugging down her knickers and taking a seat.

"Do you mind?" Terence asked indignantly as she began to tinkle.

"No," she smiled.

"You wouldn't behave this way if the children were around."

"But they're not," Anna said, finishing and flushing. "There's only you, and around *you*, I'll behave any way I please. Aren't you the one always telling me we should be free to express ourselves?" Pulling up her knickers, she blew Terence a kiss, then sauntered out, leaving her husband to clench his fists, grind his teeth and swear obscenely but in silence.

Once his nerves had settled, he pushed all thoughts of Anna and Kate from his mind, trotted to his study, locked himself in with his notes, and settled down to the serious business of finalising affairs for this year's performance by the Midsummer Players of the Bard's immortal *A Midsummer Night's Dream*.

*

Don Magill plugged in his electric razor, switched it on and ran it over his head. When he was through, he slid a hand across the smooth pate and smiled — there was nothing as sensitive to the touch as a freshly shaven scalp.

Don unplugged the razor, then eased his six-foot frame off the edge of the bed and opened the window. He took a couple of deep breaths before strolling out to see what Ingmar was up to. He found him in the kitchen, strapping on a pair of jogging shoes. "You're not going for a run this early, are you?" he asked.

"The early bird..." Ingmar replied.

"Bollocks to birds," Don grouched. "What am I supposed to do all morning if you're off running?"

Ingmar smiled. "You could come with me."

"Nuts to that," Don sniffed.

"Have it your own way." Ingmar stood. He was only six years younger and two inches shorter, but he looked like a schoolboy compared to Don. A *sexy* schoolboy, Don mused, in those shorts and vest.

"We've got practise at eleven," Don reminded him.

"I know."

"I'm not taking you if you're sweaty and smelly," he warned.

"I'll be back in plenty of time to shower and change," Ingmar promised. "I'm only going for a short jog. You should come." He gave Don's stomach a loving pat. "Might get rid of some of that."

"I don't need to get rid of any of *that*," Don replied snootily. He turned away in a huff but relented when Ingmar pecked his cheek. "Be careful on the roads. The potholes are treacherous."

"This isn't my first time here," Ingmar reminded him. "I'm familiar with the terrain. It's not like I'm a *virgin*."

They grinned, then Ingmar waved and took to the road. Don watched him power away from the cottage and only shut the door once his lover had disappeared from sight behind the encompassing trees.

"Then there was one," Don muttered. He glanced around sneakily then retreated to the bedroom. Ingmar's case was under the bed but Don's was perched high on the wardrobe, out of the smaller man's reach. Don hauled down the case and lugged it over to the bed.

They'd packed together the day before, in their small Dublin apartment, but Ingmar had taken a phone call at one stage and, in those free minutes, Don had seized his chance.

He removed the trousers, T-shirts, socks and underwear from the top of the case, then his carefully folded suit. Beneath that lay the bottom flap, one corner of which Don now slowly peeled back with the tips of his chubby fingers.

He located the package and slid it out. His mouth was watering but he made himself wait while he repacked the clothes. When the case was safely in place on top of the wardrobe, he let himself out, sat down at the kitchen table and tenderly unfolded the layers of greaseproof paper.

The three slices of ham were dry and crumpled, but to Don's meat-starved eyes they could have been prime slices of a proud farmer's prize-winning pig. He sniffed the pungent pork — unpleasant, but he'd scoffed more off-putting morsels, one of the occupational hazards of sharing his life with a dedicated veggie.

Don bit into the first slice and almost wept — heavenly!

This was Don's eighth year with the Midsummer Players.

He wasn't that fond of his colleagues or the play, which he felt was one of Shakespeare's lesser works. He came for the break, the fresh air and no goddamn students.

Don was a drama teacher. He'd decided, many years ago, that he'd never make it as an actor, so he'd settled for teaching. There were worse ways to spend a life, he supposed, but he found it difficult to imagine many.

Fourteen years of preaching to acting wannabes, seeing them enter his class full of hope and confidence, watching as their inadequacies were dragged to the surface, their dreams dashed by a series of blown auditions, poor performances and negative reviews. Don believed teachers suffered more than their pupils. The students could admit failure, shrug it off and get on with new lives, but the teachers were stuck with the pain, faced with fresh waves of stage-fodder, year after year after year.

Don shivered as he considered his latest crop. Of his nineteen students, perhaps two would make it as character actors in theatre or TV. The rest...

Don needed regular retreats from the pain. Two weeks in Limerick each June. A week in Scotland every October, with a band of old chums. Three blissful weeks at Christmas, when he and Ingmar trekked across Europe, performing two-man shows to pay their way and endear them to their continental neighbours.

And those were just the recurring holidays. There were also many one-offs. He'd often drop everything in order to fill in for a sick actor in Wexford or help a pal in Mayo stage a hastily-chosen play. Once he'd jetted off to France to star in a nudist colony's production of *Mother Courage*. A controversial piece — all the actors kept their clothes on.

He always structured his holidays around work. He couldn't handle idleness. He had to be doing something creative. He craved invigorating roles which kept him busy and let him forget about those poor, doomed dreamers in Dublin.

While the travels across Europe were the highlight of most years, Don always enjoyed his Limerick gigs. He looked *great* compared to the rest of the Midsummer Players. Occasionally a guest performer would bring a touch of quality to proceedings, but the constants – Terence, Anna, Felix, Nuala and Diarmid – were awful. Don felt like Olivier or Mark Rylance among them.

Ingmar wasn't much better than the others, but he only came to please Don. If they ever broke up, Don was sure the German would leave the world of sawdust and tinsel behind without a second thought.

If they ever broke up.

The thought worried Don enough to make him lay the third slice of ham to one side. Was their relationship in trouble? Don wasn't sure. There hadn't been any major rows lately but he knew from experience that quiet lulls often preceded a sharp, sudden split.

It had been rocky from the start. Ingmar had made no secret of the fact that he didn't believe in monogamy and wanted to be free to fool around. Don hadn't liked it but his heart had left him with no other choice than to agree to his lover's terms.

How many men had there been since? Only one serious lover, a Londoner who'd nearly whisked Ingmar away forever. But the opportunities for quick flings were boundless. A DJ who spent his nights in one club or another... How was Don to know what he was up to? Hire someone to follow him? He'd rather see their affair end than live like that.

Still, he couldn't stop worrying or imagining. When Ingmar said he was nipping down to the shops and didn't return for hours... where was he? When he came home from work, too tired to talk, had he just been spinning tracks or had he been playing hide-the-sausage during an extended dance mix?

Don sighed, folded the slice of ham in two and popped it in his mouth. Anyway, he could relax for the next two weeks. They were stranded in rural Limerick, surrounded – as eight years of research had led him to believe – by determinedly straight farmers. Ingmar could be nothing *but* faithful out here in the Sodom-free forest.

*

It was Felix Hill's thirty-third birthday. Not that anybody cared. Nuala, his wife, only celebrated old pagan rites. He hadn't told his work colleagues, as they rarely shared personal information. And his friends in the Midsummer Players were too involved with the machinations of the play to focus on anything else.

Felix sighed. "Happy birthday, Mr Hill," he mumbled. "I hope this year's as enjoyable and profitable as the rest."

Hah! He'd been stuck in a dead-end insurance job for seven years, ever since relocating from the North to marry Nuala. He hadn't been setting the world aflame as a twenty-six-year-old, but at least he'd been able to dream. Now he was thirty-three, growing stale at work, married to a woman fifteen years his senior, paying off a mortgage, killing time until the day came when he could retire, survive on a paltry pension, then die.

Some life.

The killer was, it was his own fault. *He* had fallen in love with an older (twice divorced and once widowed) woman and let her persuade him to up stakes. *He* had gone cap-in-hand to the insurance firm – run by one of Nuala's ex-husbands – and begged for a job. *He* was –

A fist hammered the bathroom door. "Have you shaved it off yet?" Nuala roared.

"No," Felix replied.

"Hurry up. I want to smear your chin with oil and rub it between my breasts. Hurry, Felix. Mummy's *waiting*!"

Felix grinned foolishly as he listened to her clump away. Oh, he moaned about her, and there were mornings when he'd wake and look at her hardening face and wonder what he was doing in the same bed as her. And there were days when he'd stand next to her six-foot-one frame and feel he'd married a mythological she-warrior. And there were times when her husky voice caused his teeth to grind.

But for all that, he loved her. She was his, and there were moments when all he wanted was to spend the rest of his life gazing up into her dark brown eyes, holding her, feeling the beat of her heart and the rise and fall of her lungs.

"Cheer up," he told himself. "There's no cake, but there'll be plenty of rumpy pumpy." Nuala had a high sex drive (even after three husbands) and she always treated him to extras on his birthday.

Felix tugged morosely at the wiry hair on his chin. He hated shaving off his beard, but Demetrius – the character he played – was a young, dashing nobleman, and though Felix could pass for a man of twenty-one without the beard, with it he looked forty. So, every midsummer, he scraped his face naked.

He took one last fond look at the beard – it would be two months before it was back to anything like its present shape – then picked up a pair of scissors and carefully clipped away at the bushier patches.

He spent ten minutes on the beard with the scissors, then took a moment to study himself. He looked like something out of *Deliverance*. There was no going back now. He ran hot water and let the basin fill, then lowered his face and dampened the bristly hair. He took his tube of shaving gel from the shelf, squirted some into the palm of his left hand and rubbed it in. He checked his razor, positioned it at the top left of his face and let it slide.

He considered his relationship with Nuala while shaving. She was a writer of (bad) romantic fiction which she released under a number of pseudonyms. His mother had been a fan and she'd dragged Felix to one of the author's signings. He had gone only to look after his mother, but had fallen for the charms of the busty, towering woman in the chair, who'd spent much more time chatting to them than he'd expected, since so few fans had turned up. Nuala – she'd insisted he call her by her real name – had asked him if he could recommend a bar in Belfast, and he'd gulped, summoned up all his courage, and said that he could escort her to a few places if she liked. She'd seduced him that very night, he'd visited her down south a few weeks later, and things had developed swiftly.

He winced as the blade nicked the skin to the right of his mouth. Christ, he hated shaving! He ran the razor through the water, angrily sloshing it from side to side, shaking loose foam and bristle. What fool had first come up with the idea?

One day Felix would tell Nuala what he thought of the Midsummer Players and their stupid play. Every year they put on the same show, and every year they were just as awful. Hell, most of the Players didn't even want to be there. Anna did it because she was married to Terence. Nuala was involved because her second husband had been the group's director, the *genius* who'd dreamt up the project. Ingmar was there because of Don. And Diarmid... Well, Felix wasn't sure about him. It was hard to tell, since he said so little, but he didn't seem to revel in his annual exposure to public ridicule.

Only Terence and Don were genuinely committed to the play. Every so often, somebody new would blow in with an appetite to equal theirs – such as Kate this year – but they always moved on. Bloody Terence and bloody Don. If not for them, Felix would be able to keep his beard.

"Ow!" He'd cut himself again, this time on the chin. He licked a finger and applied some spit to the wound. He'd stick a piece of tissue on it later if needed.

Felix focused and got on with the job of completing the shave as cleanly as he could. There would be plenty of time to muse on the follies of the world later. Two weeks. A long, wearying, theatrical bloody fortnight.

*

Diarmid's fingers began moving the mouse pointer towards the BUSINESS folder in his bookmarks toolbar. He paused before completing the action, torn between conflicting desires, then grimaced and switched his laptop to standby. He mustn't look. There was the play to worry about. He had to put work behind him.

But it was difficult. Diarmid Garrigan lived for his work. He was a banker, and no place seemed as sweet and womblike to him as his tiny office in the central city bank. There he could sit alone, connected virtually to the world, cut off from actual physical contact, free to float in the wonderful online universe of finance. Two weeks away from that was torture.

Yet they were weeks he *had* to take. He spent the other days of his legally required holidays working from home. If he had a choice, that was how he'd spend this fortnight too. But he *had* to be part of the Midsummer Players. He'd never been able to explain it, not since first seeing them perform as a sixteen-year-old.

He'd cycled out to the woods that night with a girl, one of the few times he'd tried dating, before he decided he wasn't cut out for a life of social interaction. His expectations were low. He knew that he would have to sit through two and a half hours of fairy-related crap. As he stared around the clearing, he shivered, and for the first time in his life he began to wonder if the possibility of sex was worth the troubles it involved.

But to his amazement the play spun a web of wonder before his eyes. He hadn't been able to follow the ins and outs of the plot but that didn't matter. It was the way the fairies intermingled with real people, the magical names of the characters – Oberon, Titania, Puck, Peaseblossom – and how they expressed themselves. He sat entranced, even during the interval, unable to exchange the simplest of words with his date, who stormed off in a huff at the end of the show, insulted at having been snubbed by a nerd.

Diarmid hung around after the play, hovering at the edge of the glade like a lonesome sprite. Terence noticed him and came to see if he was alright. "Well, young man," he said amiably. "What can I do for –"

Diarmid bolted guiltily. He raced through the forest, snatched his bike and set off for home at a furious pace. It was a fifteen-kilometre cycle, and he wasn't the fittest teenager, but he covered it in record time, even overtaking his *girlfriend* along the way, despite her mammoth head start.

He spent the next twelve months trying to forget the play but he couldn't get it out of his system. He bought several copies of *A Midsummer Night's Dream*, each with a different introduction and notes. He tracked down critical appraisals of the play, accounts of past performances and stage instructions. He watched films of it online and made two long treks up-country – skipping school on one occasion – to see amateur productions. He couldn't get enough of it.

He made the front row for the Midsummer Players' next show and sat enraptured, eyes ablaze, silently mouthing the words along with the actors, craning his neck to follow each performer as he or she entered or exited, not wishing to miss a moment. He was blind to the clumsiness of their delivery, the way they mangled the lines and warped the author's intentions. He saw only the magic, the wonder, the *fairies*.

He grabbed a front-row seat again the next year. He was eighteen by this time and had recently started at the bank which was to become home. Terence, recalling the strange youth, cornered him after the show. "Hello," he said, extending a hand, which Diarmid gingerly shook. "I was watching you watch the play. You really seemed caught up in it."

"I... I... was," Diarmid wheezed.

"You like *A Midsummer Night's Dream*?" Terence asked.

"It's muh-muh-muh-marvellous."

"Why, thank you," Terence beamed, taking the compliment for himself. "By the way, I'm Terence Devlin, the director."

"I... I'm..." Diarmid took a deep breath, then burst out with a mess of jumbled-up lines. "*I am that merry wanderer of the night And sometime lurk in a gossip's bowl In very likeness of a roasted crab And slip I from her bum, down topples she, I am that shrewd and knavish sprite Called Robin Goodfellow.*"

Terence blinked slowly, taken aback, while Diarmid stood shivering, wishing he could flee. Then the director wrapped an arm round the young man's shoulders. "M'boy," he wheezed, in imitation of W.C. Fields, "I think you and I should have a little talk." And he'd led a dazed Diarmid backstage to meet the other members of the company.

Terence kept in contact with Diarmid and asked if he wanted to become part of the Players. They needed people working behind the scenes, helping with the costumes and props, pairing off with the actors to help them memorise their lines. Diarmid would be doing them a great service if he volunteered.

Diarmid jumped at the chance, and for two years, plain service was his lot. If he'd had his way, it would have remained so. But fate intervened in the third year — a freak virus took out three of the cast the day before the show. With nobody else to call upon, Terence persuaded (bullied) Diarmid to step into the breach in the role of Puck, his logic being that at five foot six, he was ideal for the part.

That night had been the most wonderful and terrible of Diarmid's life. He'd thrown up several times before the show, to the point where he looked worse than the virus victims. He was sure he'd forget his lines or mistime his entrances or trip and make a fool of himself.

"But Diarmid," Anna had laughed, "you're playing the patron saint of fools. It would be in character."

Somehow he made it through the performance. He was sweating and vomiting by the end – offstage thankfully – but he made it. In fact he gave such an agitated performance that Terence enlisted him as a permanent addition to the cast, despite his desperate pleas to be left out.

"Look," Terence said gruffly, knowing it was the only way to treat the younger man, "stick with us as an actor or go your own way."

And that had been that.

He'd played most of the male roles since. Each time he was as nervous as the first. It never got any easier. This year, because their numbers were low, he was playing both Bottom and Lysander, a monumental task. He'd be on stage, in one important role or the other, for the majority of the play. He was dreading it.

Yet he had to go on. There were forces at work which Diarmid couldn't fathom, drawing him back year after year to Shakespeare's piece of whimsy, forces which caused him to buy a house in the woods to be close to the glade, forces which took no notice of rumbling stomachs and sleepless nights.

He sighed unhappily, flicked the laptop back on, and went surfing the web for tales of financial derring-do.

Fourteen days of practise. A fortnight sharing his life with eight other humans, having to talk to them and laugh at their jokes and break bread with them and... The horror! The horror!

Shaking his head, he told himself to look on the bright side. Fourteen days from now, it would be over, and he could return to work and lose himself in the maze of finance for another twelve months. Two short weeks and everything would be back to normal.

Until next year.

*

"Don't forget to brush your teeth every night... Yes, I know you're sixteen and don't need to be told, but... Yes, I know... I *know*, but I'm your mother, it's my job to worry. I hope you're being nice to your grandparents... I know they are... I *know*, but they're your grandparents. I'll ring again soon. Give Terry my love... Yes, and Granny and Grandad... I miss you too... Bye."

Anna hung up with a wry smile. She complained about her sons for fifty weeks of the year, but every time they sent the boys away, she missed them like crazy. She would have let them stay, but Terence needed a free house to focus on the play. He wasn't just an actor, he'd remind her. As director, he had to worry about lighting, props, costumes, bookings, advertising...

It was a load of precious, self-serving cobblers. The play *was* time-consuming, and as director Terence *did* have more on his plate than the others, but after nineteen years, how stressful or challenging could it honestly be?

Anna listened to the unusually silent house, a frown darkening her features. She hadn't minded in the past. The break from the kids had been a novelty, and they'd had fun — Terence had been more attentive to her needs in those days. They'd often raced through the house at night, stark naked, making love in random rooms. That didn't happen any more, not since Terence started sowing his wild oats.

She knew about his flings. She'd tried lying to herself when he'd come home late from school, and gone to several conventions without her. She'd told herself he was working hard for her and the kids, striving to get ahead. But inside (not so deep down) she knew what was really going on.

And now there was Kate. Anna had seen the looks they'd exchanged last year, the way Terence brightened whenever the young woman's name was mentioned, how he'd fought to give her the part of Hermia, the extra time he'd said he would have to spend practising with her. There was something between them, Anna was sure. She just didn't know how serious it might be, whether it was another of his meaningless affairs or if this would prove to be the killer.

She'd been expecting *the killer* for years. The affair which would develop. The woman who'd steal Terence away for good. The wicked bitch who'd force her to snap and kick the bastard out. Would Kate be the fatal vixen? Was the writing on the wall at long last?

Anna was prepared. She'd consulted a lawyer, opened a secret bank account and squirrelled money away. When judgement day arrived, Anna would be ready. The split would be fast and clean.

Anna rolled up the bottom of her T-shirt and prodded the layers of flab. She used to think this was why Terence treated her badly – *How could any man be loyal to a lump like me?* – but had come to disregard that negative thinking. She'd watched enough talk shows to know that women who blamed them-selves for their husband's infidelities were fools. Her size had nothing to do with it. There were plenty of men who'd love a wife of Anna's proportions, who wouldn't make her feel like a fat slob, who'd consider her a Rubenesque beauty.

The children were the only reason she'd stayed. Anna would sooner gouge her eyes out than see her boys hurt, so she'd stuck with him, hoping he'd mend his ways, hating the idea of putting her children through a divorce.

But she was done placing their needs before her own. They were big boys now. She'd make things as easy for them as she could, keep it civil and grant Terence all the visiting rights he craved, but children had to face pain too. Nobody could pass through life unscathed.

She lowered the T-shirt and let her thoughts drift to the play. While she'd no affection for the foolish work, it had become a key part of their lives. She was sure she'd miss it when they broke up and she moved on. Would it be this year, she wondered? Was this going to be her final flirtation with fairies? She had a feeling it might be, so she was determined to put in more effort than usual, to do the play as much justice as she could this time round. After nineteen years of poor-to-awful performances, she felt she owed it that much.

*

Nuala's pen sped across the page as though the world was running out of time and her words were to provide its epigraph. Her head was down, her tongue glued to the roof of her mouth, and her face twitched furiously as she scribbled. In the story, Reginald Llewellyn Gogarty was launching a desperate rearguard defence, delaying the king's troops while his lover, Lady Andretta Bojeur, fled by the rear window. He was exhausted − before the sword-play he'd had to scale a cliff, and there'd been a struggle with a wild horse, which he'd had to wrestle to the ground and break − and the tip of his sword dipped. The king's men grinned, sensing victory. Reginald dedicated his final thought to his beloved Andretta and prepared to die. Suddenly, the woman who gave his life meaning was by his side, sobbing, telling him she'd rather die with him than survive his death alone. Seeing the danger she was in, Reginald's guard rose and he laid into the startled troops, driving them back down the stairs, fighting like a man possessed. Which, of course, he was — a man possessed by love.

"*Possessed by love*," Nuala mused, wiping a shaking forearm across her chin. "A good title. I wonder if it's been used before?" She scribbled a note, reminding herself to check, then flexed her fingers and rolled into the final chapter of her latest bodice-ripper.

Nuala Shay – she had kept her maiden name through her four marriages – knew the book was no *Gone with the Wind*, but it wasn't half bad. She'd been in the writing game a long time and knew the difference between a good yarn and a passable bit of tat. This was one of her better efforts. It had started as a routine sequel to an earlier novel, but the Llewellyn Gogarty character had taken over the story. She'd meant to kill him off at the start of the second half – he was supposed to be a temptation for the beautiful heroine, before she returned to the arms of her original beau, the dashing pirate, James Bloodshot McStay – but that plan had fallen by the wayside. Now, not only would he survive, he'd also win the girl. The irascible James had been called away, leaving the path conveniently clear for the renegade king's champion. In the next sequel, Nuala would play the two men off against each other. Sparks would fly and who knew how it would end? Certainly not Nuala — she never planned more than a book ahead.

Nuala had been directing the actions of twinkly-eyed pirates and beautiful damsels for sixteen years. She hadn't been imaginative as a young woman, but Martin – her second husband, the man who'd founded the Midsummer Players – had encouraged her to develop her artistic talents. At first she'd channelled her energy into acting, but bringing somebody else's vision to life didn't excite her, and following failed forays into the realms of painting and music, she tried her hand at prose.

To her surprise, her first novel – a crass love story about a nurse who falls in love with an older patient dying of cancer, who turns out to be a millionaire with a dashing adult son – was picked up by a publisher and sold enough copies to merit a sequel. She'd penned forty-three books since – almost forty-four – each of which had found a niche on shelves across the land.

Her books, published under a series of pseudonyms, hadn't been bestsellers, and most had passed unnoticed by the critics, but she had plenty of fans. Nuala could offer only simple pleasures, but what was so bad about that?

She slowed as she ambled through the last few paragraphs. Reginald and Andretta leapt hand in hand through an upstairs window, and landed on an irate woman's fruit barrow. Reginald thrust some coins at her, then threw a small sack of gold into the air. The marketplace erupted. The king's troops were trapped in the mayhem, allowing Reginald and Andretta to slip away. Andretta made playful mention of James Bloodshot McStay, saying it was time she returned to him. Reginald silenced her with a kiss. She resisted, then melted into his arms.

Nuala hovered over the book a final moment, wondering if there was anything else she needed to add. She decided that was as good a place as any to leave the pair and so – slowly, reverently – she signed off with the customary, *The End*.

She slammed her pen down and sat back, feeling like a

queen. The book had been bothering her – she'd feared she wouldn't finish it before rehearsals began – but here she was, book in the can and a whole two weeks in which to do nothing but prance about in the countryside. Wasn't life perfect?

There was a knock on the door. "Enter!" she commanded.

Felix stuck his head in. "We'd want to be getting ready," he said. "It's a quarter to eleven."

"Give me a minute," she replied.

"How's the book going?" he asked.

"Finished," she smiled.

"That was quick," he commented. "Did you just slap on an ending?"

"I did not," she snapped. "I've never rushed a book in my life. I wouldn't cheat my readers."

"Not half," he chuckled. "I remember *The Seventeen Trials of Andre Delarious*. You got to trial number nine, ran out of ideas, and re-named it *The Nine Trials of...*" He ground to a halt. Nuala was regarding him stonily. "Sorry. Didn't mean to interrupt. Just letting you know the time."

Nuala growled softly as her husband withdrew. Felix bloody Hill. Why on Earth had she married him? A Mummy's boy who'd attached himself to a suitable substitute when the old dear came to her natural end. Nuala had known as much going into the marriage. So — *why?*

"Because I was at an all-time low," she sighed, answering the question aloud. "My books were selling poorly, I hadn't attracted a handsome man in ages, I felt old, useless, unwanted. He came into my life at a vulnerable moment and, fool that I was, I settled for him."

She closed the A4 pad and sighed again. Poor Felix. He'd been so innocent. She was the first celebrity (she just about qualified for that status) he'd ever met. He'd been delighted when she talked to him as an equal. When she made a play for him, the sap never stood a chance.

Why didn't she set him free? She'd abandoned two previous husbands. Nuala Shay was a woman who brooked no nonsense. She was stern, not just in appearance – at six-one and built like a wrestler, she came across as an Amazonian – but in spirit, not a woman to be held back by the shackles of petty males.

So why was she still with Felix? He wasn't much to look at, a mere five foot four in his bare feet, though he always wore platform shoes, which brought him up a few inches. He had a pleasant face but hardly striking. And that beard hid...

The beard. Damn it all to hell. That was why he stuck his head in — he'd been fishing for a compliment and some nookie. She'd told him she was looking forward to seeing him bare-cheeked, so he'd ventured into her den like a little boy with a new insect he wanted to show off, and she'd cut him down.

"I'll make it up to him later," Nuala grumbled. "I'll wear the police uniform and play strip-search. He goes gaga for that."

It annoyed her that he depended on her so much. She couldn't respect a man who didn't stand up for himself, who let his wife bully him. Why couldn't he be strong-willed and independent, like... like...

Nuala's eyes narrowed. She rose and tiptoed across the room, opened the door a crack and listened. She could hear Felix moving about upstairs. She closed the door and returned to her desk, picked up the phone, hesitated, then dialled.

*

"Hello — Kate Pummel speaking."

"Hi, Kate," came the (barely) feminine response. "Only me."

"Nuala," Kate said. "You just caught me. I was on my way out. What's up?"

"Nothing much," Nuala said. "Just ringing to remind you of the time."

Kate smiled. "Thanks."

"What are you doing tonight?" Nuala asked. "Up to anything exciting?"

"I'll probably make an early night of it. First days of rehearsal are hard. I'll be a wreck come nine o'clock. A hot bath, a glass of wine, some relaxing music, then bed."

"Sounds lovely," Nuala sighed. She cleared her throat. "Would you mind if I popped round? I thought I might bring a bottle of bubbly to celebrate the start of things."

"Sure," Kate said, "as long as you don't mind leaving early. Is Felix coming?"

"Felix?" Nuala paused. "I'm not sure he can make it. I'll ask him" – the hell she would! – "but I think he's made other plans."

"That's a pity," Kate said. "Tell him Terence will be here, if that makes any difference. You know how men hate being stuck with two women and no –"

"*Terence*?" Nuala interrupted.

"He said he'd come by to see how I was settling in. Anna will probably be with him" – the hell she would! – "so if the two of you want to come and make a small party of it..."

"Oh." Nuala's disappointment was evident but she made a brave effort to shrug it off. "No problem. I might nip in if I get a chance, but I'll probably be tired too. Maybe I'll leave it for another time."

"No worries," Kate said. "Always delighted to have you and Felix over."

"Yes. Well. I'll let you go. I have to make tracks. Don't want to be late. See you, Kate."

"Bye, Nuala."

Kate hung up and frowned. Was it her imagination or did that giant of a woman have a crush on her? She'd noticed the way Nuala had spent a lot of time around her the year before. She'd thought it was just a friendly veteran trying to make a new girl feel at ease, but Nuala had called several times over the last twelve months, trying to arrange a play that the two of them could take on together. Was she...?

No, Kate was surely imagining things. She'd asked Terence about Nuala and he'd given her the whole story, the four marriages, the trashy romantic novels, her infamous affair with a news anchorman. Nuala was most likely sick of the same old faces – she'd been with the Players since the start, the only surviving founder apart from Terence – and eager to befriend a newcomer.

Kate checked to make sure she had everything. A copy of the play. A writing pad and several pens. Two bottles of mineral water. A scarf. A bag of low-fat crisps for lunch. The keys to the house.

She opened the door but stood shielded by it a moment longer, trembling. She knew the cast members from last year but that didn't prevent the nerve-worms. She was always like this at the start of a production. She'd be OK once she lost herself in the role, but right now, on this gloriously sunny morning, she was as jittery as a schoolgirl entering class at the beginning of term.

"Come on, Kate," she told herself. "You're beautiful. You're talented. You're a professional. You'll be fine. Better than fine — you'll be magnificent. You'll take this play by storm and give the world a Hermia it will never forget."

That was better. She felt the worms receding, driven back by the positive vibes. There was the long walk to the glade still to come, and the awkward period of standing around and chatting as the others arrived, but she was over the worst of it. She was in control now. She was ready.

Swinging back the door, she strode forth into the sunlight like a proud Valkyrie heading out to conquer the world, calling to all in her path, "Challenge me if you dare!"

*

This was it. The moment was upon him.

Diarmid switched off the telly and stood listening to its insides sizzling. His stomach was sizzling too, but it wasn't serious. He'd taken things easy over the last couple of days, eaten plainly, drank lots of warm milk. He wasn't going to be sick. He wasn't. He wasn't.

Diarmid felt an almost irresistible urge to dash to the phone and ring the bank. Had the market crashed? Had the economy crumbled? Were customers pounding on the doors, demanding their money? He should ring, just to check.

He didn't. If he let one excuse delay him, he'd invent another. The bank was safe, the market stable, the economy fine. He was merely stalling, the way he did every year.

Diarmid stood by the telly a moment longer, head bowed, cursing the day he'd cycled out here to impress a girl. Then he stormed from the room and out of the house. He didn't lock the door behind him. He hadn't time to waste on such trivial concerns. He had a play to prepare for.

*

"Come on! I knew you'd be late. What time was that for a jog?" Don slapped the shower curtain while Ingmar washed the last of the suds from his hair.

"Quit whining," Ingmar snapped. "I had it perfectly timed, but I told you what happened. I ran into a little old lady, knocked over her bag of shopping, had to stop and help her pick up everything."

"A fishy tale," Don snorted. "More likely you ran into a tall young stud and –"

The curtain swished aside and Ingmar jabbed Don's chest with a finger. "Vun more vord," he warned, his accent slipping, "and I am troo vith dis sham show."

"What do you mean?" Don asked, startled.

"I'll qvit!" Ingmar roared.

"You can't quit," Don yelped. "How would I explain it to the others?"

"Screw dem!" Ingmar's face was red. "I put up vith dem becoz of you, but if you start accuzing me of cavorting every time I leave the house, I'll –"

"I wasn't accusing you," Don whined, eating humble pie as rapidly as he could scoff it down. "I was just upset. You know what a stickler I am for punctuality."

"Punctuality *balls*!" Ingmar snorted, stepping out of the shower, dripping on the floor. "The next two veeks, I vant peace and quiet and nutting else. No more 'Vhere vere you?' No more 'Vot are you up to?' No more –"

"OK," Don said soothingly, handing Ingmar a towel. "I won't pester you again. Only, please, get dried and dressed as quickly as you can. We won't say any more about..." He trailed off, his attention turning to Ingmar's rippling muscles. "God, you're hot when you're wet."

Ingmar burst out laughing. "Idiot," he said, fondly stroking his lover's cheeks. "Get my clothes. We can salvage a few seconds if you help me dress."

"True," Don mused. "Although, if we're going to be a few minutes late in any case, it wouldn't matter if we *dallied* a while longer."

Ingmar shook his head. "You're something else. First you bite my head off for being late, then... Go!" He flicked his towel at Don's rump. "We can play when we get back."

"I'll hold you to that," Don grinned, then turned and headed for the bedroom. Ingmar was right. There'd be plenty of time for playing later. Right now, they had other priorities.

*

Nuala washed her hands, ran a comb through her short dark hair and slipped a kimono on over her underclothes. She checked in the mirror to make sure her face was fine, then dabbed a few drops of perfume behind each ear. Perfect.

"Are you ready?" she asked, entering the bedroom.

Felix was pulling on his platform shoes. "Just a minute," he said gruffly.

She ran a hand over his bare chin. "Does Feely-weely forgive Mumsy-wumsy?"

"Cut it out," he growled, shoving her hand away.

"Don't be mad at Mumsy-wumsy," she gurgled. "Mumsy-wumsy luvs her Feely-weely. She's sorry she hurt his feelings."

"Don't treat me like a child," he snapped, but she could see the corners of his mouth twitching.

"Mumsy-wumsy has a pressie-wessie for Feely-weely," she said, caressing his chin with both hands this time. "Does he want to know what it is?"

"Go on then," he said grouchily.

"It's..." she whispered. "A..." She bent over. "Sur..." She grabbed his legs, yanked and sent him sprawling backwards on the bed. "Prise!" she yelled, dashing out the door. "Got to catch me to make me tell."

"Come back," Felix shouted, laughing as he struggled to his feet. "You know I can't run in these things. Hoy!" He took off after her, jogging awkwardly in his platform shoes, calling for her to stop.

Nuala teased him as she ran, while he pretended to be enraged. She could have easily outpaced him, but slowed before they got to the glade, to let him catch her. Whereupon, with much giggling, friendly punching and pinching, an *advance* on the *surprise* swiftly followed.

*

Terence and Anna sat together in the study, listening to the grandfather clock tick away the seconds. Terence was reading a paper, while Anna flicked idly through the pages of a long historical novel. Neither was taking much notice of the words. They were both secretly watching the clock.

In earlier times, they'd spend these last precious moments gabbling about the play, their friends and the fortnight to come. Anna would sit on Terence's lap and he'd squeeze her waist to convey the excitement that his words could only hint at. Even when their marriage started to fail, the warmth of this magical time had united them, if only momentarily. But now even that was gone. There was nothing of the bonding fire of love between them any longer. Not even a spark.

Anna's eyes focused on the clock. She let the second hand run all the way to the top, then closed her book. "We might as well be going."

Terence glanced at her as if he hadn't a clue what she was talking about. Then he looked at the clock and made a small humming sound. "I suppose it's time," he sniffed. "Are you ready?"

"Yes."

"Then," Terence said, folding the paper carefully and laying it to one side, "we'd better be off. You have the keys?"

"I thought you had them."

He made a show of checking his pockets. "So I do. Righty-o."

Terence stood, opened the study door and politely gestured for her to proceed. He always liked to play at being a gentleman, even if the only audience was his couldn't-care-less wife. Anna took the cue and passed leisurely before him. Then, side by side, but never touching, they strolled towards the awaiting meadow... and the play.

1.[I](iv)

Viewed from above, the glade was an almost perfect green rectangle, parting the forest like some strange emerald pool. The grass was long at the moment, strewn with weeds, but it would be mowed before the show. Trees lined the sides like silent sentries.

On a fine June morning, the air at one edge of the glade shimmered and an arched, rainbow-coloured gateway to Feyland formed. Moments later, a solitary human stepped through. From the fey side of the portal, a cunning creature spoke.

"You know your task. You have your actor's mask.

Are there any questions you wish to ask?"

The human thought a moment, then shook his head. "No. I'll suss things out, then get back to you."

"All the fine folk of Feyland bid you luck,

But none more so than I, your mentor, Puck."

"Mentor!" the human snorted. "The *mental* Puck, more like."

"Would that I could stand firm and plead my case,

But the cast now descend upon this place.

Until the setting of the sun: fare well!"

With that, the gate to Feyland closed, leaving the human stranded in the summer-scented world of the mortals.

*

Del Chapman stretched and sniffed the air. His nose wrinkled. Bright, fresh and lovely a day as it was, it appeared foul following his spell in the land of the fey. This world couldn't match the scents and tastes of Feyland, where every molecule had been moulded by the supple fingertips of magic.

Del bent and felt the springy grass beneath his feet, still damp with the morning dew. He raised his wet fingers to his lips. The dewdrops couldn't compare with the contents of Titania's wine vats, or even the common brew of the lesser fairies, but it was the taste of home, and for that Del was grateful. He'd had enough of perfection. There was only so much traipsing merrily through the gentle lands of the beautiful people that a merchant of chaos could take.

A couple entered the glade. They didn't spot Del until he rose and waved an arm in welcome. They paused, startled by the sight of the stranger, then returned his gesture. Del hurried across.

"Hi," he beamed, shaking the man's hand, then the woman's. "You must be Terence and Anna." He knew perfectly well who they were. He had been observing all of the Players through a magical globe of Oberon's in the lead up to his return. It was the fey equivalent of a video camera, but one that could follow a person in the human realm anywhere, and it had granted him all sorts of useful insights into their personal lives. "Del Chapman. Pleased to meet you."

"Del...?" Terence asked uncertainly.

"Chapman."

"I'm sorry," Terence said. "Have we met before?"

"I'm a friend of Michael's," Del explained. Michael Finnt was the man whose van he'd smashed into all those weeks ago. (Only last night in Earth time.)

"Oh," Terence smiled. "Is Michael with you? I was expecting him yesterday."

"I'm afraid Michael can't make it," Del said.

"Can't...?" Terence gasped. "But he said... he promised... What are we going to do without him? Where the hell is he? He can't do this to us. I'll sue for breach of contract. I'll –"

"Terence," Anna said, laying a silencing hand on his elbow. "You don't *have* a contract with Michael. He was doing you a favour, remember?"

"I don't care," Terence huffed. "We had an agreement. What are we supposed to do now, conjure a Puck out of thin air? I can't believe this. The selfish –"

"You'll have to forgive him," Anna said to Del. "He's a little dense this early in the day."

"No problem," Del smiled. "I'm a sluggish starter myself."

"What are you talking about?" Terence snapped.

Anna faced her husband. "Do you think this gentleman came all the way here just to deliver a message?"

"Well, I –"

"Michael has a phone, hasn't he?"

"Well, yes, but –"

"So, if Del isn't here to pass on a message, he's here to...? Think hard."

Terence frowned, then slowly smiled. "You're here to play Puck!" he shouted.

"Very good," Anna muttered sarcastically.

"I'm here to offer my services," Del said modestly. "I'm only an amateur, not half as good as Michael, but I know the part – I've studied at the feet of a *real* master – and I think I can do a decent job."

"This is marvellous," Terence beamed. "I thought we were sunk. We've had so many problems this year. Sorry I barked."

"That's OK," Del said. "I should have made myself clear from the start."

Behind them, Diarmid and Kate entered the glade.

"Morning all," Kate yelled. "I ran into this young fellow on my way. Anybody know who he belongs to?"

Diarmid blushed and gave her a shy dig in the ribs.

"Good morning, Kate," Terence boomed. Then, to make it look as if he was equally pleased to see both of them, he added just as loudly, "Morning, Diarmid. Wake up on time?"

"I was up at seven-thirty, the same as always," Diarmid answered quietly, gaze flicking to the stranger.

"Old habits die hard, eh?" Terence chuckled. "How about you, Kate?"

"I was up with the birds," Kate replied. "Good morning, Anna. How are you?"

"Fine," Anna said, her voice devoid of any emotion. "Good morning, Diarmid."

"Anna." The banker smiled fondly at the plump, attractive housewife. Anna had been kind to him down the years, helping him through his panic attacks when the day of the play rolled round, ready to lend a sympathetic ear and a sick bag.

"Kate, Diarmid, this is Del Chapman," Anna made the introductions.

Del shook hands with the newcomers. "I'm here to fill in for Michael."

"Is he OK?" Kate asked. "I've met Michael a few times, though he probably wouldn't remember me."

"Actually," Del said, "he's mentioned you. Said you were a promising actress."

"Really?" Kate nearly exploded with pride. "That's very flattering, I'm... Gosh. What do you say to praise like that?"

"You gulp down his juice and get off your knees," Terence muttered jealously.

"What was that, dear?" Anna asked.

"Nothing," he said quickly. "Here's Felix and Nuala."

The company turned to greet the author and her toy-boy husband.

"Morning," Nuala bellowed.

"Good morning," Felix said. He looked flushed and there were twigs and bits of bush stuck in his clothes, but nobody passed comment.

"Who's the new boy?" Nuala asked as she strode towards the group.

"This is Del Chapman," Kate said, sticking an arm around her new best buddy. "A friend of Michael's. I think I've heard of you," she said to Del. "Didn't you play Billy Pilgrim in a musical version of *Slaughterhouse Five* a few years ago?"

"Guilty," Del grinned blithely, inwardly thinking, "Slaughterhouse *what*?"

"Oh, I meant to go to that," Nuala squealed. "It was supposed to be a howl."

"I didn't realise you were so experienced," Terence said, nodding thoughtfully. "That was a large production. And to play the lead... very impressive. Mind you, there's not much singing in *A Midsummer Night's Dream*."

"How come you're doing *this*?" Felix asked, shaking Del's hand. "This is hardly a suitable platform for a star."

"I'm no star," Del laughed.

"All the same," Felix continued, "most of our guest actors are game youngsters or washed-up have-beens."

"Now, now," Terence growled. "We're a long-established company with a fine reputation. This isn't the first time we've attracted a major name."

"Really," Del said, "I'm not that big a –"

"Bullshit," Felix snorted. "This is a Mickey Mouse show and everybody knows it. If *Billy Pilgrim* here is so hot, what's he doing slumming it with us?"

"Felix," Nuala growled, "I thought we discussed this after last year's debacle."

"I'm not trying to offend you, Del," Felix said. "I'm just surprised. This is a very amateur production. Most pros run for their lives if they get within sniffing distance of us."

"As a matter of fact," Del said, "the Midsummer Players are well known on the rep circuit and positively spoken of."

"Are we?" Terence asked, blinking.

"Absolutely," Del said. "Michael was chuffed when you invited him to perform with you. He saw it as a significant feather in his cap."

"That's odd," Nuala smiled. "We've been begging him to come for years. He owed Terence a favour and this was supposed to be the payback. He seemed quite reluctant to get involved."

"That's just Michael's way," Del said. "You know how actors are, never wanting to appear keen to take a role. Besides, he had a lot of... Oh, here come another two. The last of the company, if I've got my numbers right."

All eyes fixed on Don and Ingmar.

"Hello there," Don shouted. "Isn't it a glorious day?"

"Magnificent," Terence replied. Then, glancing at his watch, he shook his head. "You're late."

"Sorry," Don smiled. "Call of nature." He looked at Del curiously.

Kate made the introductions again. "Del Chapman, meet Don Magill and Ingmar Van Dorslaer. Del is this year's guest star. He'll be filling in for Michael. You're probably familiar with his work, Don — he was in the *Slaughterhouse Five* musical a few years back."

Don's face was a blank. "The name doesn't ring any bells. Who did you study with?"

"Nobody," Del said. "I prefer to learn from people than actors. Mind you, I've had fruitful dealings with a few of your past students. They speak very highly of you — they say you're the best in the business."

Don cackled. "Students will say anything if they think it might improve their grades." He caught Ingmar's eye and grinned smugly. "Actually, I think I *have* heard of you. Weren't you in a Galway troupe's production of *Cat on a Hot Tin Roof* a while back?"

"Meow," Del replied, to everyone's delight. *Cat on a Hot Tin Roof...* He'd heard of that one, but had no idea what it was about.

"My, my," Felix said archly. "Your credentials increase by the minute."

Del studied the small Northerner with narrowed eyes. He was the only one who sensed something *off* about Michael Finnt's replacement. Del would have to be careful around him.

"What is wrong with Michael?" Ingmar asked.

"Yes, what happened?" Anna asked.

"An accident," Del said glumly. "A car crash."

"No!" Diarmid gasped.

"Is he alright?" Kate exclaimed.

"Is it serious?" Nuala wanted to know.

"We'll have to go see him," Felix said. "Which hospital was he admitted to?"

Del coughed uncomfortably. Puck had assured him the actor would be asleep for the next two weeks but Del had seen enough of the imp to know his methods weren't the most reliable. He'd rather not take any unnecessary chances.

"He's fine," Del said. "It was a minor crash. He'll be..." He coughed again and cast his gaze to the floor as if burdened with guilt. "Listen," he said, lowering his voice for dramatic effect, "if I tell you something in strictest confidence, will you promise never to reveal a word?"

"Go on," Terence said eagerly. "You can trust us."

"Yes, Del," Kate said, giving his arm a soft squeeze. "You're one of us now."

"Scandal," Nuala beamed. "Spill the beans. What's the rogue been up to?"

"Well," Del said, improvising wildly, "you know about Michael's *penchant* for younger women?"

"Yes," Kate squealed, to Terence's disapproval.

"He's recently been seeing a lady who turned out to be quite a bit younger than he believed. Radically younger. *Lawfully* younger."

"Oh my," Anna gasped.

"Heteros," Don sneered. "They're all the same — slaves to lust."

"Yes," Ingmar sighed, his eyes misting over.

"The police aren't involved, are they?" Kate asked.

"No," Del said. "The girl's American, and only a month or so below the legal level. She's with her parents, due to return to the States in a couple of weeks. Her father is fuming but doesn't want to get involved in a case which would delay their return home. Still, Michael thought it was best he keep his head down, in case the father had a change of heart."

"So he's gone into hiding," Nuala chortled.

"Which hole did the fox bolt down?" Terence asked.

"I'm not sure," Del said. "France is lovely this time of the year, so maybe he's gone to study a few Gallic plays."

"Gallic fillies, more like," Don commented.

The group discussed Michael's possible whereabouts, the members glad to have such a juicy titbit to break the early tension. They were more relaxed now. Even Diarmid was getting involved in the conversation, asking Del questions about his previous performances.

Del fielded most of the queries with alarming simplicity. He said he didn't like discussing past shows, which everybody understood. And he hated name-dropping, which – of course! – was a complaint shared by the others. So that effectively ruled out all references to show business, neatly robbing the troupe of the chance to expose his glaring lack of knowledge. All that was left was his personal history, which he invented at great and colourful length.

Finally, after twenty minutes of milling around, Terence

distanced himself from his colleagues and clapped his hands. He stood poised in the glorious sunrays for a well-timed moment, before speaking.

"Friends," he said in a stage whisper, "it's time. The summer draws towards the day of its equal cleaving. The voice of the Bard murmurs at the porthole of reality, demanding to be heard. It's time to put reason aside and immerse ourselves in the waters of the Fairies. Friends, colleagues, fellow dreamers…" He raised his hands high and bellowed, "Let the play commence!"

*

The play, of course, was a long way from commencement. They didn't even touch it that first day. Instead Terence put them through their paces on a series of improvisational routines.

"Each actor's body is a tool," he told Del, "and one must learn to master its use before applying it to a particular task."

"Del's a professional," Kate said. "I'm sure this is old hat to him."

"Please," Del said quickly. "I want to be treated like everybody else."

"Don't worry," Terence grinned, "you shall be." He addressed the group again. "We'll start with a few stretches."

Terence was a natural when it came to physical education, since it was what he did for a living. That, however, was a secret which none of the Players (with the exception of his wife) knew. To them he was Terence Devlin, English and History teacher. In fact he was Terence Devlin, P.E. instructor, who occasionally took a Civics or Religion lesson if one of the other teachers was indisposed.

He was terrified of the truth coming out. That was why he hadn't accepted a position with a nearby school. He drove almost sixty kilometres to work every morning, and back again in the afternoon, just to keep the true nature of his job a secret from his closest friends.

There was a five-minute wind-down after the workout, during which everybody walked around the glade, taking deep breaths, letting the blood recede from their faces. There was no talking during this period, which was Diarmid's favourite part of the day. He knew the acting exercises were next on the list, and sooner or later he'd have to take centre stage, as everybody did in turn. He wished there was a way around it. After all, he knew every line of the play. He'd have rather worked in the bank these two weeks. But this was how Terence ran things and there was no arguing with Terence.

The director called them back together. "Time to explore."

"This will be fun," Kate said to Del. "We –"

"Kate!" Terence barked. "If you *wouldn't* mind paying attention, we'd all be *most* grateful."

"Sorry," Kate blushed.

"Now," Terence said, keeping an eye on Kate and the newcomer. "Here's where we begin to test our bodies. We're going to communicate with our limbs. We've been through this plenty of times, though some" – he glanced at Felix, who had the good grace to look sheepish – "have been less inclined to participate than others. So we all know how it works."

"Del doesn't," Kate said.

"I'm sure Del knows plenty," Terence sniffed.

"You lead, I'll follow," Del said merrily. "I'm a quick learner."

"We'll start with flight," Terence said and a happy sigh swept through the troupe — they *liked* flight. "Be birds," Terence cooed, flinging his arms wide and arcing his neck in what he believed to be the manner of a swan.

The Midsummer Players followed their director's example and, one by one, flapped their arms up and down, some slowly, some quickly. They hopped and floated about the glade, twitching their heads in clumsy imitation of the creatures of the sky, chirruping and whistling as they went.

Del was momentarily stunned but soon overcame his shock and joined in the fun. He pretended to be a stork carrying a newborn baby and walked around with his back hunched and his teeth clenched, as though gripping the babe by the neck.

Nuala tried a few different stances but none felt right. After a minute or two, she turned to Terence and wiggled a hand above her head.

"Yesss?" Terence asked, remaining in character, hissing slightly as a swan would if it could talk.

"Is there any chance I could be a butterfly instead of a bird?" Nuala asked.

"Go wherever your muse takes you," Terence said gravely.

Nuala lowered her arm. She was glad he was in a reasonable mood. Some years he was a stickler for rules. Once, when they were pretending to be planes, she'd asked if she could be a helicopter, and he'd roared abuse at her for ten minutes.

Nuala lay on the ground, picturing herself as a tiny caterpillar in a cocoon. She'd been dormant a long time and now the day of ascension was upon her. She could feel the wings rippling along her back. (She shook the kimono a few times to simulate the sensation.) But the cocoon was restricting her. She was a prisoner. She had to break free.

Nuala gritted her teeth and arched her back sharply, grunting with the effort, then ripped away the walls of the cocoon. She stretched on the grass, feeling the warmth of the sun as though for the first time, thinking as a butterfly. "Sun. Trees. Breeze. Wings." She rotated her left arm, then her right. "A small bound." She jumped forward a half step. "Frightening. The rush of air. Leaving terra firma, rising to become part of the heavens. A celestial being. Free!" Her head rose. Her arms/wings stretched forth. And, finally, she flew.

After flight came automobiles. Everybody had to pretend to be a car, bus or lorry. (Nuala chose to be a tank.) They roared around the glade, changing gears, mimicking engine growls, speeding up and slowing down.

Kate pretended to be a sports car which had been appropriated by joyriders. They were steering her across the country at lunatic speed. She tore around the rim of the glade, then slipped amidst the trees, which she treated as human obstacles. The joyriders wanted to hit the people but Kate – as the car – was fighting them.

She exhausted herself careening around trees, until at last she ran out of gas and fell back into the glade, panting and sweating. There was a burst of applause — the others had concluded their role playing and were watching her.

"Eight out of ten," Ingmar roared.

"Nine," Nuala shouted.

"A perfect ten," Terence yelled predictably.

"Thank you, thank you." Kate got to her feet and took a bow. "You're too kind." She pretended to weep.

"No tears yet," Terence warned her. "Is everyone ready to continue?" There was a round of affirmative grunts. Kate hurried over to be part of the gang again. "OK," Terence said. "This time we'll be Vietnamese children running from a posse of napalm-laying jets."

"What age are the children?" Don asked seriously.

"Four years old," Terence replied. "They don't know how cruel the adult world can be." He paused, jaw quivering at the horror of it all. "Today they'll find out."

*

Lunch came and was welcomed by everybody. As the days progressed there would be times when they'd work through lunch, unable to tear themselves away from the material, but it was best not to push themselves to breaking point this early.

They sat around the glade, eating and drinking, naturally forming into smaller groups. Kate sat with Don and Ingmar, discussing Dublin and its buzzing nightlife. She'd spent a few months there this year and had roomed with the two on a number of occasions. There was much to catch up on.

Felix spent the break with Diarmid. They said little, which was fine by the Northern man. The Players rambled on too much. It was nice to sit back and listen to the sounds of the meadow.

Nuala joined Terence and Anna. They'd been friends for many years, shared a long history, and had much to talk about. But did they discuss politics? The great social and economic evolutions of recent decades? Changing attitudes and people? No — to Anna's exasperation the elder two focused on the stupid bloody play.

After a while Terence excused himself and popped over to see how Kate and the boys were getting on. Anna watched him trying to ingratiate himself with the trio, wrapping an arm around Kate's shoulders, giving Don a friendly dig in the ribs, passing a comment about Ingmar's tip-top condition. He could be Mr Sociable any time he wanted. Except with his wife.

Nuala caught Anna's eye and shrugged. She would never come out and criticize Terence (he had been a great support when Martin died), but the shrug was her way of signifying that she knew what the old goat was up to and didn't approve. Anna smiled and laid a grateful hand on the huge woman's knee.

Del spent the break circling the glade, drifting from one group to the next, getting to know his compatriots, exchanging short tales and jokes, surprised by how easy it was to fit in.

He avoided Diarmid and the suspicious Felix as long as possible, but finally sat down between the two. "A busy morning," he grinned.

"Uh-huh," Felix said, studying the lean, brown-haired man. (Who was taller than him, of course, like almost everybody else. Damn this world and its bloody giants.) "You're something of a celebrity," Felix sniffed. "What companies have you played with? Where? When?"

Del let his head hang with shame. "You saw through me from the start, didn't you?" he said, surprising the pair. "I fooled the others but you had me pegged from the beginning. I knew I couldn't get away with it."

"With what?" Felix asked softly.

"It was a lie," Del whispered. "I *was* in *Slaughterhouse Five* but I was on stage for all of three minutes. I've played bit parts in loads of productions but never a lead role, or even a key support."

"I don't understand," Diarmid said. "You're *not* a professional actor?"

"I'm nothing but a professional wannabe," Del sighed.

"So how come Michael sent you in his place?" Felix asked.

"He didn't." Del lowered his voice further, so the two men had to lean in close. "When Michael realised he couldn't make the play, he rang a friend and asked him to take his place. That guy's a competent performer, who'd have done the Players proud. But Michael didn't have time to meet in person, and he's rubbish with emails and Facebook, so he entrusted *me* to pass on the information, where to come, where he'd be staying, the rehearsal dates and so on. I was supposed to go with a folder to his friend's house and –"

"But you didn't!" Felix gasped with delight.

"No," Del said. "I saw my chance and, fool that I was, took it. I told the friend he didn't have to come, that Michael was able to make it after all."

"I don't believe this," Diarmid groaned.

"*I* do." Felix chuckled wickedly. "But given your lack of experience, how did you think you'd get away with it?"

"Well, from listening to Michael..." Del glanced at the other Players. "I don't think I should continue."

"Continue! Continue!" Felix's face was alight. "He said we were useless, didn't he? So bad that a fake could slot right in and seem at home. So rotten, in fact, that we probably wouldn't even notice the fake ourselves. Right?"

"He didn't think *all* of you were bad," Del said. "He had good words for you and Diarmid."

"Don't make me laugh," Felix laughed. "Diarmid just about passes muster –"

"Thank you," Diarmid smiled.

"– but I'm not meant for this acting lark. Nor are most of the others. We're as poor a crew as you could hope to find. We suck."

Del had anticipated Felix's disillusionment but he hadn't expected so venomous a response. It was rewarding but a tad surprising.

"If you feel that way," Del asked, "why put yourself through the ordeal?"

Felix looked over at Nuala. Del followed the smaller man's gaze, then nodded understandingly.

"And you?" he asked Diarmid. "Do you feel the same way?"

Diarmid shook his head. "I love it. I *have* to be in the play. For me it's an addiction."

"I guess this is it then," Del said glumly, rising. "I'll reveal the truth to the others before I do any real damage. Maybe Terence will be able to find a proper replacement. I'll tell him –"

"Hold on," Felix said, grabbing Del's arm and hauling him back down. "Let's not be hasty. Maybe you *can* have your shot at fame."

"I don't understand," Del said, though he knew only too well. He could hear the tumblers whirring inside Felix's head. The man was stuck with a play he hated, forced to return indefinitely for the love of his wife. He'd thought there was no way out, but what if someone truly atrocious found his way into the group? A ham who'd been turned down by every company in Ireland? What if the fraud got through the next two weeks and took to the stage? They'd had plenty of stinking reviews over the years, but what if this amateur was so woeful that every critic was offended? It could result in a violent reaction which might prove too much of a blow even for people as thick-skinned as Terence and Nuala.

"I like to root for the underdog," Felix claimed. "You saw an opportunity and grabbed it. That takes guts. Having come this far, it'd be a shame to fall now."

"You mean you won't grass me up?" Del tried hard not to chortle.

"If Diarmid is prepared to hold his tongue, so am I," Felix declared.

"How about it?" Del asked.

"I'm not sure," the banker mumbled. "It wouldn't be fair on the others. They put in a lot of time and effort. I wouldn't like to scupper their show."

"Neither would I," Del exclaimed. "I don't want to harm the production. All I want is a chance to shine. Is that so wrong of me, to want to succeed just once?"

Diarmid chewed his lip. He knew he should go straight to Terence and reveal the treachery, yet he sympathised with Del. Despite being a banker, Diarmid was a kind man who wished nothing but the best for his fellow humans. It was in his hands to make or break Del and he hadn't the heart to destroy the newcomer's dreams.

"Here's what I'll do," he decided. "I'll keep quiet for the time being –"

"Yes!" Del hissed triumphantly.

"Good man, Diarmid," Felix grinned.

"– but my continuing silence depends on how you perform. If, after a couple of days, I don't think you're good enough, I'll ask you to confess to the others. If you won't, then I will."

"Fair enough," Del beamed.

"I was going to add the same stipulation myself," Felix assured them. (The hell he was!)

"You two," Del sighed, crocodile tears sparkling in his eyes. "I don't know how I'll ever repay you guys. I... Oh, give me a hug." Before they could slither out of his way, he was hugging the life out of them.

Across the glade, Don nudged Ingmar and nodded at the embracing trio. "A lot of man love going down over there," he joked.

"My, my," the DJ purred, raising an eyebrow. "This could be more interesting a fortnight than I'd anticipated."

1.[I](v)

The day drew to a close shortly after six o'clock, which was an early finish for the Midsummer Players. Terence believed in pushing his troops hard, but it didn't do to push *too* hard — there had been premature burnouts in earlier years.

It had been some day, Del reflected wearily. After lunch they'd embarked on a series of dramatic exercises, improvising scenes from famous plays and *baring their souls* by *confronting their inner demons*. They'd had to laugh, mimic terror, be reflective, merry, angry, bewildered. And, of course, they'd had to cry. Ye gods, how they'd cried!

Spurred on by Terence, each had stepped into the figurative spotlight to gnash their teeth. Some were natural bawlers — Diarmid, Ingmar and Kate could produce tears on tap. Most of the others needed *encouraging*, which was shorthand for bullying and teasing. Terence was good at that. He'd stand imperiously, hands on hips, and lash into his victim, sneering and jeering. He called Felix a deformed dwarf. Don was a talentless, pot-bellied poof. Anna was fat, ugly, useless.

No one told the belligerent bully to take a hike, even Felix, normally so waspish about his height. They only stood, heads bowed, willing tears to come. When they eventually gushed, everybody would cheer, gather round for a hug, and offer words of comfort. It was extraordinary.

When it was Terence's turn to sob, the Players took turns at goading him but their insults weren't as cutting as his — "You stink as a director!" was about the harshest it got.

Nuala and Del were the only two who couldn't cry. Nuala was incapable of producing theatrical tears. Terence made a half-hearted attempt to break her, but though she screwed up her face and howled like a banshee, her eyes remained dry and he soon abandoned the task.

Del was a different matter. Terence didn't know the newcomer well enough to attempt a full-frontal assault. He made a few probing passes – "You're a terrible actor." "You have no talent." – but he felt uncomfortable striking at random.

"We'll try again in a couple of days," he told Del. "Don't worry — we'll claw down your inner walls before the fortnight's up. Another week and you'll be wailing like a cold and hungry baby."

Del shivered as he mopped the back of his neck with a towel. Still, he'd known what he was letting himself in for. Oberon and Puck had been crystal clear. This was exactly as they'd described.

"How do you feel?" Terence asked, tapping Del's shoulder.

"Good," Del lied. "You go at it like rabid wolves, don't you?"

"No other way," Terence smiled. "Most of us are part of the regular workforce. We've limited time to devote to our theatrical craft, so we have to take things at a violent run. By the way, what's *your* brand of poison?"

"Jack Daniels," Del replied promptly.

"No," Terence laughed. "What do you do for a living?"

"Oh," Del smiled. "I'm into viruses."

Terence blinked. "As in chemical warfare?"

It was Del's turn to laugh. "No. Computer viruses."

"Ah." Terence grinned sheepishly.

"So," Del said, "where do I bed down? Is there a decent B&B nearby?"

"We wouldn't stick a valued member of our company into a B&B," Terence huffed. "You'll stay with Anna and myself. We've plenty of room."

"You're sure?" Del asked. "I don't want to impose."

"We'll love having you," Terence insisted. "You'll be company for Anna. I have to spend a lot of time out of the house, with the play and all. I'll feel better knowing there's someone there to look after her." (Someone to divert her attention while he was off canoodling with Kate, was what he really meant.)

"If you're sure..." Del said.

"It's decided," Terence declared, then dragged Del off through the forest, discussing the play the entire way home.

*

Anna prepared a simple meal for them. Terence ate lightly at the best of times, and with the play so close, he didn't want anyone beefing up, as he felt it made them more sluggish. She risked her husband's disapproval by telling Del she could cook chips and a fry if he liked, but he said whatever they were having was fine by him.

Terence was ready for a long chat afterwards but Del excused himself and went for a walk. "I'm psyched," he said. "If I don't get out and calm down, I'll be awake all night."

Terence told him he was free to come and go as he pleased. The back door was always open — crime was virtually unheard of in this part of the world.

"What do you think of him?" Terence asked Anna, watching through the window as Del slipped into the forest.

"He seems nice enough," Anna shrugged.

"Yes," Terence hummed. "Polite, honest, modest. But what did you think of him as an actor? He didn't make a big impression on me."

"Maybe he's nervous," Anna said.

"That's probably it," Terence agreed. "I hope he gets over it soon. I don't want him dragging us down. If he can't keep up, we might have to cut him."

Anna squinted. "I thought we were stretched to the limit."

"We are," Terence said, "but we can juggle the roles even further if necessary. In theatre, if a director's brave enough, anything can be achieved." His chin jutted out smugly and it took all of Anna's willpower not to drive a bunch of fives hard at it.

*

Del hurried to the glade. When he reached the clearing, he coughed three times, clapped his hands twice, and farted once. There were other ways to summon the fairies, but few more vulgarly amusing.

The portal to Feyland appeared, broad and arched at the top, engraved with finely detailed deer, lightning bolts and flowers. The doors opened — magical music, sensuous light, delicious smells, warm breezes, laughter. Then a small figure slid through, the doors closed and disappeared, and there was only the dark of the forest again.

"You came," Puck noted.

"Did you doubt me?" Del replied.

"You humans are as strange as Puck is fair;

Your oaths have all the thin substance of air."

"Suspicious little so-and-so," Del grinned. "How about a couple of toadstools? I've been on my feet all day — I'm knackered."

Puck crooked his middle fingers and a pair of toadstools swiftly sprouted. Del wished he could do that. Puck had promised to teach him, but not until after the play. The imp didn't want the human getting sidetracked.

"How went the day?" Puck asked as they took their seats.

"Not bad," Del said. "We danced a lot. Acted like idiots. Pretended to be birds. Laughed and cried. It was a lot like Feyland actually."

"The Midsummer Players you have all met?" Puck asked.

"Yes."

"And a fitting plan: have you formed one yet?"

"I'm getting there," Del said.

"Perhaps you should take up Oberon's scheme,

Twisted, it was, as a monk's sultry dream."

"No," Del said firmly. In disregard of Puck's earlier vow, Oberon had asked Del to stir up hatred and set the actors at each other's throats. Del had refused.

"But a day you've spent in their company;

In truth, do we not deserve to be free?"

"I understand your position," Del said. "Twenty years watching these clowns... Brrr! But, hopeless as they are, they're a nice lot. Terence is pig-headed, Ingmar's vain, Nuala's... well, Nuala. But I like them. I'll do my best to sabotage their plans and disband them, but not violently."

Puck snarled with exasperation and leapt up on his toad-stool.

"We argued this at length, both night and day,

Whilst you dawdled in the land of the fey.

If you have a plan, put it to the test,

Our applause will last years if it proves best.

But if your wits do deal an empty hand,

Will you follow Lord Oberon's own plan?"

"No," Del answered stubbornly.

Puck sighed.

"As I feared, you're besieged by mortal flaws;

I think you can't contribute to our cause.

'Twas a false hope. We shall cast it aside

And take our punishment in our sad stride."

Puck hopped off the toadstool and clicked his tongue. The portal to Feyland reappeared and he headed towards it.

"Wait," Del said. "Don't give up on me yet. Maybe the task is too great and I'm doomed to fail, but I'm not without ideas. I have plans, ill-formed though they are. Let's discuss them and sort something out."

Puck hesitated, then faced the human.

"My precious time I do not wish to waste;

If your words are weak I will make due haste

Rather than stay and have you numbly baste

My tender ears with your thick, futile paste."

"Have it your own way," Del sniffed. "Just don't come crying to me when midsummer rolls round and you're forced to bear witness to another performance by the Players."

Puck winced.

"A valid point. I'll listen and I'll stay.

Go ahead, good Chapman, and make my day."

"Have you been watching Clint Eastwood movies?" Del asked suspiciously.

"I know not this Clint of the Eastern wood;

Is he a force of darkness or great good?"

"Forget it," Del smiled. "Let's put our heads together. I'm sure such cunning creatures as you and I can conjure up something artful and mirth-filled."

Puck stood undecided a moment, then returned to his toadstool and this time leant against it. "Speak," he said bluntly. "What have you in mind?"

They passed the better part of the next hour discussing the Midsummer Players. Del had spent some of his time in Feyland covertly observing the Players through a precious crystal globe of Lord Oberon's which allowed one to eavesdrop on any party in the human realm. (He'd tuned out whenever things had got sexual — for all his mischievousness, he was no voyeur.) This, combined with what he had seen of them today, had allowed him to detect brittle undercurrents running beneath the surface jovialities which he believed he could tap into.

"The bonds between them could easily snap," he said. "Terence and Anna don't get along, and sparks will fly if she finds out that he's been fooling around with Kate. Felix and Nuala snap at each other a lot — I should be able to play on that. Don and Ingmar are promising too — from what I overheard while keeping tabs on them, the former believes in fidelity, while the German has a roving eye."

"His eyes in his sockets are not fixed firm?"

"I mean he has an eye for the boys," Del clarified. "Diarmid seems to be the only one not at potential loggerheads with any of the others. I'm sure, if I had more time, I could turn them against one another like tomcats fighting over a she. The only real problem is, we're working to a tight schedule. If there was just some convenient way of bringing passions swiftly to the boil..."

Puck's gaze turned thoughtful.

"We could, on their foul heads, magic dust spray

And turn their desires our own wicked way."

"Magic dust?" Del frowned. "Like Oberon gave you in the play?"

"The very same."

"It would make one of them fall in love with another?"

"Nay. The Bard at that point chose to construe

A device more suited to comic woo.

He took the facts of Feyland's magic dust

And gave it – as he said himself – more thrust."

"I wish you wouldn't speak in riddles," Del complained. "Does this magic dust exist or not?"

"Exist the dust does, but not in the form

Laid down on page by the emperor worm."

"The...? Oh, Master Shakespeare." The fairies had a score of unflattering names for history's grandest playwright.

"Tell me more about this dust," Del urged.

"There is a dust, in plentiful supply,

Which, when anointed on a human's eye

May make its way straight to the beating heart

And all sensibilities drive apart.

Thus one who desires but also denies

Will embrace romance and abandon lies;

Lust which for years has been kept under wraps

May have its wild way, at long last untrapp'd."

"This is fabulous," Del exclaimed. "Why didn't you tell me this in Feyland?"

Puck shrugged.

"In Feyland the dust's as common as wine.

Besides, unless there's previous design

Before the appliance of the said dust,

It affects the human not. The heart must

Hold in advance the flames of hot desire;

There must exist the kindling for a fire.

Dust may unleash what will has held within,

But lust may not be sparked where love is thin."

"You mean," Del said, struggling to decipher the imp's words, "if a person has a secret crush on somebody, the dust causes them to act on their feelings, but it can't make a person fall in love with someone they feel nothing for?"

"Aye."

"That's a pity. Still, it's an angle." Del sighed. "If only we had a stooge."

"I understand you not," Puck said.

"We need a cat to stick among the pigeons and stir them up."

"I fear that you have lost me in the dark.

You believe a feline might aid our lark?"

"I'm speaking metaphorically," Del said. "That dust of

yours wouldn't be any good at the moment. Apart from the obvious chemistry between Terence and Kate – which hardly needs magic dust to bounce it along – I don't think anyone has designs on any other Player. We need someone to turn their heads and tweak their libidos, heat their inner juices and drive them to fits of lust and jealousy."

Puck shivered ecstatically.

"Stirring terms. They turn my innards to ice.

But exists there such an agent of vice?"

"Sure," Del said. "The world's full of charming rogues, but how could we get one to cooperate or slip him or her into the mix?"

Puck's eyes narrowed and his pointy ears quivered as they were wont to when his mind became fully engaged.

"Diarmid, methinks, is mildly handsome, aye?

He could be a charmer, were he not shy."

"Diarmid?" Del shrugged. "He's not bad looking but we need a man nobody can resist, someone who oozes charm, someone –"

"Like a fairy?" Puck suggested.

"A fairy would be perfect," Del agreed, "but you told me the fey folk aren't allowed to interfere directly. Besides, there'd still be the problem of introducing a stranger into the fold."

Puck's face lit up with wicked merriment.

"But what if there existed one of kin,

If, to a Player, there was a sly twin?"

"A *twin*?" Del scratched his head. "How could a fairy be a human's twin? Are you trying to confuse me?"

Puck tutted, took Del's hand and led him across the glade.

"In truth, that is not this Goodfellow's plan.

Scurry back with Puck you must to Feyland.

There we shall a conspirator engage

And plot the greatest cunning of our age.

Hurry. I shall explain upon the way."

And Del could get nothing more out of him until they were back in the land of the fey, where the mechanisms of the imp's mind were made clear, the *stooge* was tracked down and cajoled into lending his talents, and the Plan (capitalised from this point on whenever they referred to it) was thrashed out, finalised and set into mischievous motion.

1.[I](vi)

The next morning was overcast, so everybody met at Terence's house. Anna greeted the yawning Players at the door, took their coats and directed them to the study, where steaming cups of coffee and warm, home-made biscuits awaited.

Don and Ingmar were first to arrive. The DJ was sulking. He'd set the alarm for half past six, to get an hour of exercise under his belt, but Don had gone to the toilet in the middle of the night and inadvertently (so he claimed) switched off the alarm, as a result of which they'd overslept, leaving Ingmar no time for anything other than a few quick press-ups.

"Morning, boys," Anna greeted them.

"Morning, love," Don replied, kissing her cheek. Ingmar grunted and pushed past, tossing his coat at her.

"You turned off the alarm clock again, didn't you?" Anna guessed.

Don smiled guiltily. "I'm not a terrible person, am I, Anna?"

"I think you're perfectly adorable," she smiled. "A strong cup of coffee and all will be forgiven."

Diarmid and Del were next to arrive. Del had gone for another walk that morning (having returned from Feyland late the night before) and *bumped into* Diarmid on his way back. Del was avidly chatting to the shy banker, drawing him into a conversation about computer systems.

Felix and Nuala arrived shortly after, giggling and rosy-cheeked. It had been a long, active night, a birthday bout Felix wouldn't soon forget.

"Top of the morning to you," Nuala boomed.

"Salutations, fair maid," Felix called.

"Somebody had fun last night," Anna smiled. "Did you play snakes-and-ladders or tiddly-winks?"

"I didn't see any ladders," Felix laughed, "but there was a godawful huge snake involved."

"There's coffee in the study," Anna told them, "and a bucket of cold water in the kitchen if you need to cool off."

Kate was last to arrive. The rain was falling heavily by the time she ran up to the house, coat draped over her head. Anna held the door ajar and welcomed her quietly. "Kate."

"Anna," the younger woman responded with a nervous smile. "Sorry I'm late. I snagged my tights and had to hunt for a new pair."

"No need to apologise," Anna said coolly. "I'm sure the director won't mind. He's always most understanding where his star actresses are concerned."

Kate gulped, handed over her coat and hurried into the study. Anna followed leisurely, having tossed the coat haphazardly into the airing cupboard. Terence had taken centre stage in the study, propped against the fireplace like a Scottish laird. Anna closed the door and took a seat behind the rest of the Players.

"OK," Terence started. "I know everyone's familiar with the story but it's good to start with a brief summary." Picking up a copy of the play, he displayed the cover as if nobody had seen it before. "*A Midsummer Night's Dream* is a romantic comedy. At its heart are four young lovers, Demetrius, Lysander, Hermia and Helena. Hermia, who's extraordinarily beautiful" – his gaze flicked quickly to Kate – "is in love with Lysander but her father wants her to marry Demetrius. Lysander and Demetrius are both in love with Hermia."

"They're not the only ones," Anna muttered beneath her breath.

"Helena loves Demetrius but he won't look at her."

"I don't know why, because she's *gorgeous*!" Nuala (who'd be playing Helena) piped up. The Players laughed dutifully — Nuala made a similar quip every year.

"Theseus," Terence went on, "the Duke of Athens, is due to marry Hippolyta, the Queen of the Amazons. A group of amateur actors drawn from local tradesmen retreat to a nearby wood to prepare a play which they hope to perform at the royal wedding. One of the actors is Bottom, a vain, egotistical know-it-all."

"Diarmid!" Nuala yelled and everybody applauded. Diarmid grinned sickly.

"While all this is going on," Terence continued, "Oberon, King of the Fairies, is fighting with his wife, Titania. Oberon decides to play a trick on her and sends Puck – a scallywag – off to find a magic flower which will make her fall in love with the first person she sees. When Puck returns, Oberon gives him part of the flower and sends him to use it on Demetrius, since he's taken pity on Helena and wishes to see her united with the man of her dreams. Puck makes a mess of his mission and applies the flower to the sleeping Lysander's eyes. He then changes Bottom's head into that of an ass."

"The good thing about Diarmid playing the role," Don interrupted, "is we won't have to use much make-up for the transformation." Everyone laughed, even Diarmid. Don winked at the banker. "Only joking."

"When Titania wakes," Terence resumed, "she falls in love with the ass-headed Bottom. Lysander wakes and falls for Helena. Adding to the complications, Oberon has since applied the same spell to Demetrius, who also falls in love with Helena. So now both men claim to love her. She thinks they're trying to make a fool of her and gets very upset. Hermia, meanwhile, is stunned.

"Lysander and Demetrius almost come to blows but Puck separates them. They fall asleep and more magic is used on them, as well as on Titania after she's made an idiot of herself with Bottom. It ends with Lysander and Hermia back together. Helena snags Demetrius. Oberon and Titania reconcile. There's a funny final act, where the amateur actors perform their play for the royals. And that's it."

Terence stopped and beamed as if he'd just explained away *Finnegan's Wake.*

"Excuse me?" Del raised a hand.

"Yes?" Terence asked, surprised to be confronted with a question so early.

"I counted ten different names," Del said, "and I'm sure there are others you didn't mention. How are the nine of us supposed to cover so many roles?"

"Doubling," Terence said.

Del shook his head.

"Most of us will play two or three different roles," Anna explained.

"You're allowed to do that?" Del asked.

"Of course." Terence was examining Del suspiciously. "I can't believe an actor of your calibre doesn't know about doubling."

Felix sprang to the anarchist's defence. "He's having us on," he laughed, then clipped the back of Del's head. "You shouldn't tease us."

"Sorry," Del said, smiling shakily. "I won't do it again." That had been a near one. He'd have to keep a closer guard on his mouth.

"Now that the point's been raised," Don said, "how *are* we going to cover all the parts? Are we going to trim down the play?"

"No," Terence said. "We've made significant cuts in the past when we haven't had a full complement of actors, but not this time. We're lacking in numbers but we have the benefit of a visionary director." He preened his imaginary feathers while the others booed theatrically.

"It's really possible to keep everything in with just nine of us?" Kate asked.

"Pretty much," Terence said. "We'll cut a few small roles and redistribute some lines but otherwise..." He glanced around. "I wasn't going to get into the roles today, but I can if you want."

"I think we should have a quick run-through," Nuala said.

"Very well." Terence thumbed through his notes, producing the cast list. "Del's the only one going solo. He plays Puck. I figured, with it being so big a part, that would be sufficient."

"Hear, hear," Del said with relief.

"Diarmid has the task of handling Bottom and Demetrius. It will test him to his limits, but I'm sure he's up to the challenge."

Diarmid smiled uneasily — *he* wasn't so sure.

"Anna plays Titania and Hippolyta," Terence went on. "Don partners her in both roles, as Oberon and Theseus. Kate will play the beautiful Hermia."

"Who else *could* she be?" Anna murmured.

Terence coughed uncomfortably, while Kate squirmed. "She'll also play the fairy who discourses with Puck in Act Two, Scene One."

"He never lets *us* play fairies," Don sniffed to Ingmar.

"Felix will have his hands full with Demetrius and Flute," Terence said, raising his voice. "Flute is the leader of the amateur actors." He cast a mock-indignant eye at Felix. "I hope it doesn't give you ideas above your station."

"I'll remain as humble as ever," Felix declared grandly.

"Nuala plays Helena. She'll also be Starveling *and* Peaseblossom, so no rest for *her* this year. Ingmar has it relatively easy, with just Quince and Mustardseed to worry about. I'll bring up the rearguard with a variety of supporting parts, Snug, Cobweb, Egeus, Philostrate and so on. Many characters but precious few lines. It's a dirty job but somebody's got to do it."

"And there's nobody better for a bit of dirt than you," Anna said quietly from the back of the room but Terence pretended not to hear.

"There are also the parts some of us will be playing as the amateur actors in the final act – Pyramus, Thisbe and the rest of the gang – but we'll leave that added complication for another day.

"So," Terence said, placing the cast list carefully back in its proper place, "if there are no further questions…" The Players all shook their heads. "In that case, let's launch into Act One, Scene One. The court of Theseus, Duke of Athens. Don and Anna, step forward please."

And so it began.

1. [II] (i)

Del had nothing to do in the first act, so was free to sit back and observe. He thought the actors would just recite the lines until they'd learnt them but it proved to be a lot more complicated than that.

First came a basic run-through of the opening scene. The actors read from the script unemotionally, then Terence explained the scene in simple terms. Theseus and Hippolyta are due to marry. Egeus (Hermia's father) enters with his daughter and the two men who love her. Hermia is told she must obey her father's wishes and marry Demetrius or face execution or life imprisonment as a nun. Lysander and Hermia decide to elope and tell Helena of their decision. She chooses to rat them out to Demetrius. And so ends the first scene.

Next there was an in-depth discussion, focusing on how the characters should be portrayed. Don, as Theseus, had to appear regal. The bald drama teacher would wear a wig of short, dark hair for his role as the Duke. He'd brought five wigs down from Dublin and spent twenty minutes debating which to go with. It seemed irrelevant to Del but the others took it seriously.

"I want to appear regal," Don explained, "but not *too* regal in case it takes away from my impact as Oberon. Oberon must be more impressive than Theseus, yet Theseus must stand out from his fellow humans."

"It's difficult," Terence agreed. He was holding a pair of wigs. Don held two more. The fifth was on his head.

"I want him to do it bald," Ingmar said. "I could paint his

head so it would look like it had been tattooed. But he won't have it."

"I don't think a Duke would be bald," Don said stiffly.

"We could pass it off as a genetic condition," Ingmar suggested.

Don withered him with a glare. "How do you intend to work that nugget into the text? 'Now, fair Hippolyta, our nuptial hour Draws on apace; what a pity it is That I am naturally bald?'"

Ingmar sniffed. "I was only trying to help."

"Don's right," Kate intervened, playing peacemaker. "Besides, if it rains, the paint might run."

"That's a fair point," Ingmar conceded. It had rained during eight of the group's previous nineteen outings, on three occasions so heavily that they'd had to perform beneath umbrellas.

As Hippolyta, Anna would wear her hair up in a bun and dress in a gown. For Titania, she'd loosen the hair and slip into a long, white robe. Don would also wear a robe, though his would be open around the chest so that he could exude masculinity.

Kate would appear more or less as herself as Hermia, merely switching to a white robe for her small part as a fairy in Act Two, while Felix would appear bare-faced as Demetrius, donning a beard for his later part as Flute. Easy.

Diarmid, however, was awkward. His flesh reacted furiously to beards or make-up — his face puffed up, his eyes wept, his nose ran. Each year they had to find ways around his allergies.

"We'll dab some mud on your cheeks when you go on as Bottom," Terence told him, "but the mud and change of costume alone won't do the trick. You'll have to deliver performances so varied that people will hardly notice it's the same actor. As Lysander you must be noble and courteous, walk erect, nose in the air. As Bottom you'll be vulgar, coarse, scratch your bum and speak with a burr."

"I don't think he should scratch his bum," Anna said. "This is a family show."

"How about picking his nose?" Felix suggested, with only a hint of a smile.

"It's a possibility," Terence nodded seriously.

"He could fart when he comes out," Ingmar said, his cheeks quivering.

"I'm not sure he could fart on cue," Terence said, "Diarmid, do you...?" He stopped as the actors split their sides. "Why are you laughing? What did I say?"

Once they'd calmed down, they decided on Nuala's look. She'd wear a blonde wig as Helena. As Starveling (the amateur actor) she'd fix a moustache in place. As Peaseblossom (a fairy) she'd don an orange wig and frilly dress.

As Philostrate, a servant of Theseus with no lines in the first act, Terence would appear as himself. He'd be in the act as Philostrate for a mere fifteen lines. When he re-emerged four lines later as Egeus, the only difference would be his cloak, the way he held himself and how he puffed out his cheeks.

With their look decided upon (though Don still hadn't settled on a wig) they finally got around to the acting.

The first three quarters of the scene belonged to Theseus, Lysander and Hermia. Anna had a few early lines as Hippolyta, Terence had an important role as Egeus, while Felix had two simple lines as Demetrius, but the majority of the work rested on the shoulders of Don, Diarmid and Kate, who happily were the most capable of the actors. They slipped into character almost immediately, only stumbling slightly on the Bard's dreaded iambic pentameter.

"Remember," Terence told them, "ten syllables per line. Da-dum, da-dum, da-dum, da-dum, da-dum. 'Four days/ will quick-/ ly steep/ them-selves/ in night.' 'This man/ hath my/ con-sent/ to mar-/ ry her.'"

Ingmar and Don chuckled lustily when Felix as Demetrius, trying to persuade Lysander to grant him Hermia's hand, delivered his lines, and Diarmid as Lysander responded.

"'Relent, sweet Hermia; and, Lysander, yield

Thy crazed title to my certain right.'"

"'You have her father's love, Demetrius;

Let me have Hermia's — do you marry him.'"

"It's true love," Don sighed.

"Ride that Greek cowboy," Ingmar yelled.

"Stop that," Terence barked, though he'd been expecting the interruption. They started this every year. "And don't bother with the rest of your spiel. I know what you're going to say and I'm having none of it."

"Why, Terence," Don grinned, "what on Earth do you mean?"

"You're going to argue that Shakespeare was implying some untoward attraction between Egeus and Demetrius, and you want the parts played for kinky laughs."

"Terence!" Don gasped, his eyes round. "I wasn't going to suggest anything of the sort. Were you, Ingmar?"

"I vouldn't even tink of it," Ingmar said, deliberately exaggerating his accent.

"Methinks the boys protest too much," Kate giggled.

"But seeing as you've raised the subject," Don said innocently, "why *not* give them a sexual spin? If we make Demetrius a lad's lad, it adds a layer of meaning to his relationship with Hermia. We can set it up so it seems he's besotted with Lysander and proposes marriage in the hope that Hermia will become a nun, leaving him free to woo his beloved boy."

"No," Terence roared.

"It *would* be interesting," Anna commented devilishly.

"Look," Terence began, but Felix interrupted.

"I'm not playing a shirt-lifter," he snapped.

"But Felix," Ingmar smiled, "ve are actors. It's our job to pretend. Nobody vill tink any the vorse of you for –"

"Forget it," Felix shouted. "I'm not doing it, and that's that."

"Of course you're not," Nuala said. "Don and Ingmar are only having a bit of fun. Don't get excited, Felix."

"If you really wanted to be daring," Kate said as Felix seethed, "you'd stick Ingmar in as Hermia."

Everybody stared at her.

"Now there's a thought," Don said with delight.

"And a thought is what it's going to stay," Terence said. "If you want to put on your own version of the play, feel free to include as many real life fairies as you like. Out here, this is *my* play, and I'm playing it straight. If you have a problem with that, tough. I'm in charge and my vision stands."

"I disagree," Anna said quietly. "You're the director, but this is *our* play. The group's. I think we should vote."

"*Vote?*" Terence almost gagged. "What the hell is there to vote about? Nobody wants to do this as a gay cabaret."

"That's not the point," Anna demurred. "You're setting yourself up as a dictator and that isn't on. The Players have always operated democratically."

"I..." Terence spluttered indignantly. A dictator? How could she say that? How could his own wife betray him?

"Anna has a point," Nuala said. "I'm not knocking your vision, Terence, but there must be equality."

"Very well," Terence sighed, shaking his head in disgust. "A show of hands. All those who think we should turn the play into a camp shindig?" Nobody's arm went up. "All those who think we should play it straight?" Eight arms shot into the air.

"You see?" Nuala told him. "The same ends are achieved but by consent."

"Fine," Terence snorted. "And please," he said bitterly, to the group in general but more specifically to Anna, "if you see me getting too big for my boots again, yell quickly and yank me back to size. Right. Back to the rehearsal. Felix, start with, 'Relent, sweet Hermia.' And if we *could* get through without any heckling..."

"I won't say a word," Don promised.

"My lips are sealed," Ingmar agreed.

"Let's hope so," Terence sniffed.

Felix studied his lines, fixing them in his mind, then laid the script aside.

"'Relent, sweet Hermia; and, Lysander, yield

Thy crazed title to my certain right.'"

Diarmid answered immediately.

"'You have her father's love, Demetrius;

Let me have Hermia's – do you marry him.'"

There was a barely noticeable pause, while Terence waited for even a hint of a snigger. When none was forthcoming, he launched into his reply as Egeus.

"'Scornful Lysander, true, he hath my love,

And what is mine my love shall render him;

And she is mine, and ...'"

Things flowed smoothly after that and there were no further interruptions until lunch.

*

Kate was tucking into a sandwich when Terence caught her eye and nodded at the ceiling. She glanced around the room. Del and Diarmid were chatting in one corner, Don and Ingmar were out walking, Nuala was on the phone in the hallway, Felix was flicking through a newspaper and – most importantly – Anna was in the kitchen. Kate nodded back at Terence, then trotted upstairs to the bathroom.

Less than a minute later, Terence was knocking lightly on the door. She pulled it open and tugged him in. Their mouths met and his hands roamed. She shut the door with her left foot, then they were falling to the floor. They landed clumsily. Kate giggled and plucked Terence's hand away from her knee. "Not now," she said softly. "We haven't time."

"I can rush when I have to," he mumbled, clasping her knee again.

"No," she said, removing his fingers more forcibly. "We'd be heard."

"OK," he agreed, rolling off. This time his hand alighted on a breast, which was acceptable to Kate. She let him squeeze gently while he kissed her. She was about to run her hands through his hair, then remembered the last time she'd done that — the dye had smeared on her fingers and beneath her nails.

"You were magnificent this morning," he told her.

"Are you still angling for a quickie?" she asked suspiciously.

"No," he laughed. "Seriously. I had my doubts about casting you as Hermia."

"And now?" she asked.

"No more. You're going to be a star."

She gave Terence a bear hug, happiness flooding her system.

"I hope you remember me when you're rich and famous," Terence smiled. His smile, however, was tinged with sadness, because he doubted she *would* remember. His feelings for Kate ran deep but he didn't think she felt the same way.

"Diarmid seems comfortable," Kate said, tickling Terence's hairy belly.

"Lysander's no problem for him," Terence agreed, "but I'm not sure how he'll fare as Bottom, or Pyramus in the final act — he's not so hot at drawing laughs."

"I wonder what Del will be like?" Kate mused.

"Yes," Terence grunted. "I wonder."

Downstairs, Nuala was off the phone and back in the kitchen, lending Anna a hand. She was telling her friend about her newly completed novel. "This could be the big one."

"Are you going to release it under your own name?" Anna asked.

"No," Nuala said. "It's a sequel. If I change the name of the author, it might confuse the public. If it's a success, I can have the entire series rebranded under my own moniker."

Out of the corner of her eye, Nuala spotted Terence and Kate coming down the stairs. She positioned her body in the doorframe to block the sight. "Will I take that tray of sandwiches in?"

"Thanks," Anna smiled.

"No problem," Nuala said, taking the tray and gliding into the study. By the time it reached the first of the Players, half the sandwiches had disappeared, the only traces being two faint lines of crumbs around Nuala's lips.

Don and Ingmar had returned after their short walk and were seated on the couch. Don reached for a sandwich, only to have Ingmar slap his hand away.

"Wait a minute," the German growled and checked between the slices of bread. "As I thought — ham."

"Well, *I* didn't know," Don grumbled.

"Hmm," Ingmar grunted. "We'll wait for the next plate, thank you very much."

"Spoilsport," Don snarled.

"Carnivore," Ingmar snapped in reply.

Nuala moved on, trying not to laugh.

Del and Diarmid were still chatting, only now Diarmid was doing most of the talking. They shook their heads when Nuala offered them sandwiches. She would have loved to know what they were discussing – she'd never seen Diarmid this animated – but Felix was beckoning her, so there was no time to eavesdrop.

"What's up?" she asked, stopping by the side of his chair.

"You are," he replied, "but not for much longer." He grabbed her waist and hauled her onto his lap. She squealed and dropped the tray, sending the last few sandwiches spilling to the floor.

"Let go," she roared, batting him playfully round the back of the head.

"Never," he shouted. "I'm holding you here forever."

"Moron," she smiled, kissing his nose.

"You're up after the break," Felix said, returning her kiss.

"I know," Nuala sighed.

"Nervous?"

"A bit. You know how it is."

He gave her a hug. "Don't forget I'm in your corner if you need me."

"You're a dote," she said. "What are you doing tonight?"

He grinned. "I dunno. Got any ideas?"

"Well, I thought… Oh, hello, Kate." She wriggled free and got to her feet. The younger woman had wandered across and was searching among the sandwiches on the floor for one which might be edible.

Kate smiled. "Sorry to disturb you but I'm famished. Normally I pack my own lunch but today I forgot."

"Wait a second," Nuala said, going down on her knees. "I think one or two are alright." She picked up a couple of sandwiches, examined them and tossed them away. Finally, under the chair, she found one with hardly any fluff or dirt.

"Here," she said, handing it to the embarrassed actress. "This one's fine."

"Thanks," Kate said weakly. "You needn't have gone to so much trouble."

"No trouble at all," Nuala declared.

"Well, thanks again," Kate laughed, then strolled back to her own corner.

Nuala watched her leave, a smile plastered across her face. When she returned her attention to Felix, he had his head buried in another paper. "Is there room on that lap for me?" she asked coyly.

"No," he answered gruffly.

"What's wrong?" she asked, surprised at the change of tone.

"Just leave it," he snapped.

She pouted and stormed off to the kitchen to help Anna with the next plate of sandwiches. Silly little man with his silly little mood swings. Well, two could play at that game. Just wait until he next came flirting. Nuala could be momentously frigid when she wanted.

A few minutes later, Terence stuck his head into the kitchen, where Anna and Nuala were loading up plates. "Managing, ladies?"

"Fine," Nuala said.

"Grand," Anna grunted.

"Make them thick," he said. "I like my troops well fed."

"If you want to make them, make them," Anna said quietly. "Otherwise shut up and get the hell out."

Terence stared at his wife. Nuala coughed into a fist and felt her ears turn red. She would have fled but Terence was in her way.

"What's got into you?" Terence whined.

"Have fun upstairs?" Anna asked.

"What are you talking about?" Terence acted dumb. "I was on the bog. Is that against the law? Do I have to receive written permission before passing a stool?"

"Were you alone?" Anna asked.

"Of course," he said. "I was on the toilet. Who else would be with me? I can wipe my arse myself. I'm not a —"

"I saw Kate coming down with you," Anna said. She glanced at Nuala, who was blushing fiercely. "I spotted them over your shoulder."

"So what?" Terence asked, less sharply. "She used the toilet in the hall. I used the one in our bedroom."

"You used the toilet in our bedroom?" Anna asked.

"Yes," Terence lied.

Anna cocked her ears and listened to the gurgling of the pipes above her head. "Sounds like just the toilet in the hall to me."

"This is crazy," Terence growled. "I'm going back to the others. Feel free to join us once you've regained your sanity." He marched back to the study, furiously feeding his sense of indignation to drown out the inner cries of guilt.

In the kitchen, Anna calmly finished filling the sandwiches, wiped her hands on her apron and picked up one of the laden trays. "Ready?"

"Are you alright?" Nuala asked uncertainly.

"Dandy," Anna replied, though inside she felt far from it. "I'm not the one who sloped off with his tail between his legs."

"If you want to talk... or anything..."

"Nothing to talk about," Anna said. "Now" – she clapped her hands to shake off the crumbs – "let's take this lot in. I can hear the rumbling stomachs from here."

The women passed around the trays in the study, said nothing about their encounter with Terence, and before long rehearsals were back underway.

*

Terence was in a foul mood after the break and poor Nuala bore the brunt of his tyrannical petulance. As Helena, she had two long speeches to make near the close of the first scene. They would have been hard enough to get through at the best of times, but with Terence glaring at her and snapping at the slightest fault, they became intricate tongue-twisters which she found impossible to master.

"'Call you me fair? That 'fair' unsay again.

Demetrius loves –'"

"'Again unsay,'" Terence roared. "'That 'fair' again unsay.' It has to rhyme with 'Whither away.'"

"Sorry," Nuala said. "I'll get it right this time."

"Only if you feel like it," Terence replied bitingly.

He said nothing more while she stammered her way to the end of the scene, only sat brooding, head bowed, listening with icy impatience. Kate and Diarmid, as Hermia and Lysander, made a few mistakes but nothing major. They flipped back the pages when they were finished and started again.

"'God speed, fair Helena!'" Kate began. "'Whither –'"

"Hold it," Terence snapped. Kate looked at him. "That was fine. You two take a break. I want to focus on Nuala's part."

"It's only the first day," Kate interjected, sticking up for the glum-looking Nuala. "Why don't –"

"If I want your opinion," Terence said, "I'll solicit it."

Kate blanched. Terence had never addressed her this rudely before.

"Now," Terence said to Nuala. "We'll take it a line at a time."

Nuala gulped, then nervously launched into her opening line.

"'Call you me fair? That 'fair' again unsay.

Demetrius loves your fair: O happy fair!

Your eyes are lodestars, and your tongue's sweet air

More tuneable than lark to –'"

"Stop!" Terence roared. He jammed his hands over his ears.

"What's wrong?" Nuala asked. "I got the lines right."

"There's more to Shakespeare than getting the lines right," Terence growled. "The words have to flow. The rhyme has to be brought through subtly, not hammered out like something a school kid has learnt to recite."

"I thought this was just a run-through," Nuala said unhappily. "We normally don't bother with delivery until –"

"Don't tell me what we normally do," Terence shouted. I want to try something different. I want to do it *right*. That concept's not alien, is it? You've never done it right before, but there's a first..." He stopped and composed himself. "From the top, with a little life this time, if possible."

Nuala managed – after much effort – to deliver the opening to his satisfaction, but it wasn't long before she was in trouble again, caught on what should have been a simple couplet.

"'Were the world mine, Demetrius being bated,

The rest I'd give to be to you translated.'"

That was how it should have gone but Nuala couldn't get it right. "'Were the world mine, Lysander being...' Sorry. 'Were the world's mines...' No. Give me a minute. Alright. I've got it. 'Were the world mine, Demetrius being bated, The rest I'd give to you to be trans–' Damn, I nearly had it. I'll get it right this time."

But she didn't. For fifteen torturous minutes she failed to shape the two lines correctly. When an actor was struggling in this fashion, Terence would normally leave the scene and try again another day, but this time there was no reprieve. He stood over Nuala like a dog, snarling at her every mistake, never correcting her or offering advice.

Felix would usually have leapt to his wife's rescue but his nose was still out of joint over the incident with Kate during the break, so he sat back, enjoying the humiliation of the woman he loved.

Diarmid and Ingmar were too frightened of Terence to complain. Don wasn't afraid but he was in a mild state of shock — he'd never seen Terence lay into someone so aggressively and wasn't sure how to react. Kate was still smarting from the sting of his rebuke and wasn't about to jeopardise her position with the director by opening her mouth again, while Anna had other worries on her mind. Del, meanwhile, was anxiously thinking only about himself — if this was how Terence treated old, trusted friends, what would he be like with a newcomer?

Finally Nuala could take no more and collapsed into a weeping bundle. The breakdown took the irate Terence by surprise and drained him of his anger.

"Nuala?" he asked, laying a hand on her broad, trembling back. "Are you OK?"

"It's not my fault," she sobbed. "I know the words, I *do*, but they won't come. They're in here" – she slammed the side of her head with a furious fist – "but they won't..." Her tears drowned out the last word.

Terence stepped back, aghast. Nuala was his oldest friend, his closest confidant. How could he have treated her so brutally? "Oh, no," he moaned, dropping to the floor beside her. "I'm sorry." He was crying as well. "It was my fault. I pushed too hard. I was cruel."

"No," Nuala wept. "I'm a stupid old biddy who doesn't know her lines after twenty years of –"

"No!" Terence insisted. "Nobody could perform with a bastard like me on their back. I'm sorry," he sobbed again. "Can you forgive me?"

"I'm the one who should be forgiven," Nuala cried, hugging Terence, burying her face in his shoulder.

Del gawped at the pair on the ground. Was every actor supposed to bond with the director this way? Del was happy to do almost anything in the name of a prank, but breaking down into a weeping wreck and throwing himself into the arms of Terence Devlin... He'd have to think about that one.

"That's..." Terence sniffed between sobs. "That's enough for today. It'll put us behind schedule but we'll leave it there. We'll put in extra hours tomorrow to get through the rest of the first act. You can go now."

Everybody filed out, silent as a train of ghosts, leaving Terence and Nuala to their tears. Anna fetched the coats and handed them over with whispers. "See you tomorrow." "Thanks for coming." "Things will be better in the morning."

When the others had left, Del popped upstairs, stuck on a jacket and hurried down. "I'm going for a walk," he told Anna.

"Thanks," she replied with a smile.

"Is... I don't mean to..." He glanced towards the closed study door. "Do we *all* have to go through that?"

"No," she said. "That was a once-off."

Del was unable to hide his relief. "Thank heavens for that," he grinned. "I'll be back later. Don't bother doing a dinner. I'll have a snack."

"See you later," Anna said and closed the door behind him. "A once-off," she murmured again. God, she hoped so.

1.[II](ii)

Diarmid was sitting at his laptop. It wasn't turned on but his fingers were roaming the keyboard, his gaze blankly fixed on the comatose screen. He jumped when the doorbell rang, rose and walked slowly to the front door, where Del Chapman was waiting, coat held over his head to shield him from the rain.

"Can I come in?" Del asked and Diarmid stood aside. Del took off his coat and dumped it on the floor. Diarmid retrieved the coat and hung it on a hook, then led the way through to the living room.

Del sunk back in a chair and crossed his legs. "This is more like it," he smiled. "Terence and Anna's furniture is a nightmare. You couldn't –"

"I didn't invite you here to talk about chairs," Diarmid interrupted.

"You didn't invite me at all," Del retorted. "I invited myself. Got anything to drink?"

"If you mean alcohol, no."

Del glowered at the actor, then clicked his fingers. "Sit down."

Diarmid sat as ordered and gulped. "You said you'd tell me more about my twin," he whispered.

"Your parents told you about him?" Del asked.

"They said I wasn't alone in the womb," Diarmid answered cagily.

"Did they tell you what happened?"

"He was stillborn." Diarmid's voice was barely audible. This was something he hadn't spoken about before. His mother and father had never discussed Diarmid's twin in front of him. He'd learnt of his sibling only by eavesdropping, and on her deathbed, his mother, delirious from painkillers, had called pitifully for her long lost son.

"What did they do with the body?" Del asked.

Diarmid shrugged uneasily. "Does it matter?"

"What if I told you there *was* no body?" Del said softly. "What if I said your twin was born healthy?"

"You'd be a liar," Diarmid gasped.

"Would I?" Del countered.

"I don't understand what you're getting at," Diarmid said. "Is this part of a sick joke? How did you find out about my twin?"

Del ignored the banker's questions and came back with some of his own. "What if I were to tell you that your twin didn't die? What if I said he was kidnapped from the ward shortly after birth and that your mother and father, far from being devastated, took the abduction in their stride? Would you be shocked to know that, while the police scoured the country for the baby, your parents never spared him a second thought?"

"What kind of a monster are you?" Diarmid asked, visibly shaken.

"The kind who isn't a monster at all," Del replied.

"If you claim to be my long-lost twin, I won't buy it," Diarmid said quickly.

"I'm not your twin," Del laughed.

"But you know where he is?" Diarmid pressed sceptically. "You can put me in touch with him?"

"Maybe," Del answered guardedly.

"I knew it," Diarmid snapped. "This is a sting. You must think I'm the greatest eejit ever to crawl out of a bog. I don't know where you come from or what your game is, but if you think I'm going to be suckered by the likes of you, you're –"

"Fairies took him," Del said quietly, stopping Diarmid mid-breath.

"*What?*"

"They spirited him away to Feyland, to rear him as one of their own."

"You're mad," Diarmid sighed, smiling with relief.

"Your parents were sterile," Del continued.

Diarmid chuckled. "They didn't do too badly for a couple shooting blanks. Two children, one human, one fairy. Pretty good going."

"They struck a deal with the fey folk," Del said.

"This gets better and better," Diarmid grinned ghoulishly.

"Your father was a pagan in his youth," Del went on. "This forest lies close to the borders of Feyland. He sensed their presence and made contact."

"A hotline to Feyland," Diarmid howled. "They have one of those in the White House, next to the phone for Martians."

"He cut a deal with Oberon," Del pressed ahead. "In exchange for fertility, your mother would bear two children, one of whom they could keep, one who'd be given to the fairies. Your mother agreed, because –"

"– a bun in the oven's worth two in the bush," Diarmid said, cackling wildly.

Del sighed. "Your parents considered fleeing when your

mother conceived, but feared the curse of the fairies. In the end they stayed and raised no fuss when one of the fey folk slipped into the delivery room and pinched the obligated child."

"I've heard enough," Diarmid said stonily. "It's time for you to leave."

"Don't you want to know why I'm telling you this?" Del asked.

"No," Diarmid said. "Please leave."

"Your left armpit is hairless," Del said softly.

Diarmid blinked. "Excuse me?"

"Sweat doesn't gather there. It never itches. You used to shave your right pit, so both sides matched, but you've grown out of the habit."

"You're good," Diarmid admitted. "I don't know where you got your info from, and I'm certain you're crazy, but you're good. So go on. Tell me the significance of the bare patch. Is it the mark of the fairies?"

"Kind of." Del cleared his throat. "Would you mind taking off your top?"

Diarmid's eyebrows shot up.

"Please," Del said. "Humour me."

"If you try anything funny..." Diarmid warned.

"I won't budge from this chair," Del promised.

Diarmid decided he might as well play along. The sooner he complied with this fool's wishes, the sooner he'd be rid of him. He was going straight to Terence after this, to tell him about the impostor in their midst. This was what came of doing a stranger a favour.

Diarmid stood and tugged off his shirt. He was wearing a vest underneath. He left that on. There were some protective coverings he would never abandon, not even to comfort a crank.

"What now?" he asked.

"Rub spit on the three middle fingers of your right hand."

Diarmid stared at him.

"I know," Del winced. "I'd have chosen another way, but..." He shrugged.

Diarmid wet the middle fingers. He was starting to enjoy this. It wasn't every day you got the chance to witness magnificent madness up close.

"Rub the fingers into your left armpit," Del said and Diarmid did as instructed. "Now lick them and do it again."

Diarmid followed the ludicrous orders. "A third time for luck?" he asked.

"No need," Del replied. "Look behind you."

Diarmid glanced over his shoulder, giggling fitfully.

The giggles stopped when he saw the shimmering gate of jewels where his fireplace should have been. He took several involuntary steps backwards. When the gate swung open, he yelped and collapsed into a ball, wrapping his hands over his head.

When, after a few seconds, he found himself still alive, he peered through his fingers and saw a small, man-like figure emerging through the gate.

"You got him to do it," the little man laughed.

"Of course," Del replied smugly.

"Friend Chapman, you are a true rogue indeed,

You could have simply brought him to the glade."

"More fun this way," Del grinned.

"Will the shock prove too much for the poor dolt?" the pointy-eared, half-man asked. "He appears as stunned by a lightning bolt."

"He'll recover," Del said, then crouched by Diarmid's side. "Get up."

"This isn't happening," Diarmid whined. "It isn't real. It can't be."

"It's real," Del said.

"What... what is it?" Diarmid asked, pointing to the gate.

"A portal to Feyland."

"And *that*?" He pointed towards the thin, poorly dressed figure examining the television set with much interest.

"That's Puck," Del said. "The original."

"The original and undoubted best," Puck added immodestly. "Wastrel imitators are all the rest."

"I hope you're not including me in that," Del said.

"If the cap chafes not the wearer's stout head,
  Then like a snail's shell, it befits its bed."

"This isn't happening," Diarmid moaned again. "It's a bad dream. I fell asleep at the keyboard and I'm imagining the whole thing."

Puck tapped the human on the shoulder and grinned. His small, sharp teeth put Diarmid in mind of a cat's.

"There is only one true nightmare in life:
  That is to wake hand in hand with a wife."

"Make him go away," Diarmid pleaded. "I don't know how you summoned him, just... please... make him go away."

"I'll banish him if you want," Del promised. "I'm not doing this to scare you. But aren't you forgetting why I came?"

Diarmid rubbed the balls of his palms into his ears. "I can't think!" he wailed. "I can't think! I can't —"

"Your twin."

The shaking and whining stopped. Diarmid lowered his hands and raised his head. "You mean that wasn't a... there's really...?"

"Take my hand," Del said.

Diarmid clasped the limb, relieved to be touching something substantial in a world gone mad.

"Get to your feet," Del commanded and Diarmid rose. The fairy — *Puck?* — looked much less threatening from this height. "Feel better?"

"Slightly," Diarmid wheezed. He studied the portal. He could see trees and meadows on the other side, and the freshest air he'd ever experienced was wafting into his room on a soft breeze.

"Listen closely," Del said. "Everything I told you is true. You have a twin in Feyland who's your mirror image. If your curiosity's been piqued and you want to get to know him..."

"I can *meet* him?" Diarmid's face was a mask of wonder. "He's through *there?*"

"Yes," Del said. "A few short steps. But only if you want to. We won't force you into anything you might —"

"Shut up and lead the way," Diarmid snapped, truly authoritative for the first time in his life. A twin. He wasn't alone. He had a brother. A *twin*!

"After you," Del smiled and guided the young banker past

the pulsing walls of the portal. "I thought I handled that rather well," he remarked to Puck as they left the world of the mortals and the gate dissolved behind them.

"Not bad," Puck agreed in the way of the humans, "but that was the easy bit. It is the next stage I am worried about. It is fine reuniting them after all these years apart but how will you convince them to separate again?"

"Trust me," Del smirked. "I know what I'm about."

And they were gone.

1.[II](iii)

As humans measure time, mere minutes passed before the portal to Feyland reappeared in Diarmid Garrigan's television room. In fairy time, however, the equivalent of three days had come and gone. When Del Chapman returned to the world of mortals, his cheeks were covered with stubble and his voice was strained from arguing with the twins. They'd agreed to participate in his Plan, but only following a personal plea from Oberon and Titania.

Del made sure the coast was clear, then beckoned to the cuckoo child. Finn – as his mother had named him – emerged hesitantly, nose wrinkling at the foreign smells, eyes watering. "This is my twin's home?" he asked uncertainly.

"We told you it was no palace," Del said.

Finn looked distraught.

"I had never dreamt of such poverty.

Is this the lot of all humanity?"

"Some have it a lot worse," Del told the fairy.

"How can there be worse than this grim hovel?

'Twas built by a shade, to make souls grovel."

"Believe me," Del said, "in many places this would be considered luxury. We're on Earth now. Things are different."

Finn wandered the room, fingers brushing over the furniture and bric-a-brac. He was the spitting image of Diarmid and wearing his brother's clothes, which – though they'd seemed stiff and stuffy on Diarmid – clung to him sensuously, as if tailor-made.

"What is this?" he asked, tapping the top of the TV set.

"A television," Del said.

Finn's eyes filled with wonder. He crouched down and stared deeply into the blank screen.

"Even in Feyland we have heard of these,

The greatest of Mankind's many follies.

Is it true that some misfortunes stayed glued

To this wicked demon their whole lives through?"

"It's claimed its fair share of couch potatoes," Del admitted.

Finn tapped the screen, then examined the back of the set and its sides. He was clearly puzzled.

"I fail to see the charming attraction;

What in this beast saps humans of action?"

Del flicked a button on the remote control and a music channel burst onto the screen, a maelstrom of noise and colour. Finn screamed and would have fled back to Feyland, except the portal had closed. Del switched the TV off before the shock proved too traumatic for the ethereal visitor.

"It is a world!" Finn gasped. "Inside the box — a world!"

"As many worlds as you could count," Del agreed. "Do you want to see a few more?" He pointed the remote in jest.

"Nay!" Finn shouted.

"This may be how humans choose to exist,

But Finn shall not be lost in murky mist.

Let the tempting monster rest as it may

And let you and I focus on the play."

"Exactly what I wanted to hear," Del smiled. "Take a seat."

Finn studied the chairs suspiciously.

"They don't bite." Del sat to prove it was safe.

Finn eased his behind onto the edge of the sofa but remained alert. In a world where boxes could spring to monstrous life, nothing was to be trusted.

"Now, Diarmid," Del began.

"Finn," Finn corrected him.

"It's *Diarmid* here, remember?" Del growled.

"Aye," the fairy laughed. "It slipped my mind."

"It mustn't again," Del said. "The others are bound to notice a difference – you look the same as your brother, but your eyes are livelier and you smile more easily – but as long as it's not too alarming, they'll pay it little heed. If, on the other hand, you get your own name wrong..."

"Fear not. 'Twas but a momentary slip.

'Twill be the last to 'scape this clumsy lip."

"The rhymes have to go too," Del warned him. "We don't speak like that here. Remember what I told you in Feyland?"

Finn pulled a face. "Talk as if you mean to bore. Speak with your head, not your heart. Say what you see, not what you dream. Be dull, not poetic."

"That's the way," Del agreed.

"It will be difficult but I will try. Stranger clouds have been known to stretch the..." He spotted Del glaring. "...heavens," he ended weakly.

"We've a long night ahead of us," Del sighed. "Luckily we don't have to mingle with the others until morning, so let's squeeze in more practise. What do we say instead of, 'The morning rests like love's soup on the land; May this day flow like the grains of Time's sands?'"

Finn mentally scoured his lexicon of new phrases. "Good morning?" he tried.

"Excellent," Del beamed. "And when we want to accuse someone of engaging in unnatural relations with his female parent, we call him a mother what?"

And so the lessons continued.

ACT TWO

2. [I] (i)

Del and Finn met the others in the glade at ten the next morning. The merchant of chaos was sticking close to the cuckoo. He'd rung the Devlins the night before to say that he'd decided to stay with Diarmid. Terence thought his fierce display had frightened Del off, so he raised no objections.

"We're going to split up for the first session," Terence said once his troops had gathered. "Don, I want you to take Del and Kate aside and run them through the first part of Act Two, Scene One. It's when Del makes his entrance as Puck. Kate's the fairy who helps introduce him."

"I'll work them hard," Don grinned.

"Diarmid and Ingmar." The changeling was glancing around at the humans – with the exception of his twin and Del, he'd never been this close to their kind before – and Del had to give him a dig in the ribs. "Pair off and concentrate on Act One, Scene Two, where you play Bottom and Quince. Also, I want you to have a quick run through the latter half of the first scene of that act, where Lysander and Hermia make their plans to elope."

"Surely we need Kate for that?" Ingmar interrupted.

"Kate will be OK," Terence said. "Right now I want to make sure Diarmid's up to scratch. You can play the part of Hermia, Ingmar. Don't spend much time on it — just check that Diarmid's fluent."

"Diarmid knows every line of the play," Anna said, smiling at her old friend. Finn smiled back uncertainly.

"I want to be *sure*," Terence said testily. "The rest of us will practise our lines as the tradesmen in the second scene. We'll also go back and practise the first act. I particularly want to focus on Nuala's role as Helena, but I'll be gentle this time." He smiled reassuringly at the huge woman. "Does everybody know what they have to do?" he asked to a chorus of grunts and groans. "Then chop-chop, people."

*

"I'm glad he split us up," Del said, opening his copy of the play in the shade of the trees — they had taken themselves off to one side of the glade. "I was dreading making my first stab at things in front of the group."

"Terence took that into consideration," Kate smiled. "He's a great director."

"He's not bad," Don grunted. "Occasionally brutal and heavy-handed, but he has his moments."

"He's wonderful," Kate insisted, "and I've worked with loads of directors, so I should know."

Don and Del smiled knowingly at each other.

"Methinks the lady's tongue is rooted in her heart," Don said.

"What does that mean?" Kate snapped.

"Nothing," Don said innocently.

"There's nothing between Terence and me," she declared.

"Of course there isn't," Don murmured.

"Listen," Kate huffed, "I don't want you spreading idle –"

"'How now, spirit; whither wander you?'" Del interrupted. Kate stopped and stared at the rough-visaged rogue. He tapped his copy of the play.

"Oh," she said. "Give me a moment." Her finger quickly searched for her place and she took a deep breath.

"'Over hill, over dale,

Thorough bush, thorough briar,

Over park, over pale,

Thorough flood, thorough fire.'"

She continued with her opening speech. Del followed the words on the page, readying himself for his first burst of rhyme, pleased that he'd averted a row. There would be much arguing between the Players over the next two weeks but it was best not to let life get *too* complicated *too* swiftly — he didn't want things spiralling completely out of control. Not yet.

*

Diarmid was in a strange frame of mind, Ingmar mused. The banker, normally so serious, kept fondling flowers and staring round the glade, giggling fitfully. He didn't seem interested in the play. They'd started off rehearsing the Quince and Bottom roles, but after twenty minutes Ingmar realised he was wasting his time – they'd get nowhere with the more challenging material today – and suggested they return to the first scene and practise Diarmid's dialogue as Lysander.

"'Or, if there were a sympathy in choice,

War, death, or sickness did lay siege to it,

Making it momentary as a sound,

Swift as a –' *Look!*" Finn shouted, breaking off from the text. He pointed at the sky, where a plane was passing overhead.

"It's a plane," Ingmar said sourly. "What about it?"

"It soars so high, at a whirlwind's mad speed,

Like a god on wings in time of great need."

Ingmar blinked. "It's a plane," he said again. "You act like it's the first time you've seen one."

"I have seen many, in the lands of dreams,

But never..."

Finn stopped. When he locked gazes with Ingmar again, he was smiling shyly — he'd remembered who he was supposed to be. "Sorry. I was up all night and I am giddy. I will try to concentrate. Where were we?"

"You're acting peculiar," Ingmar laughed. "Was it only the play you were up with?"

"What do you mean?" Finn asked and Ingmar mimed smoking a joint. "Ah, the magic weed. Nay, of that I had no need. I sat naked, in the night, immersed in the play, bound to it tight."

"Naked?" Ingmar smiled. "I must come over to rehearse with you sometime."

"That would be nice," Finn said innocently.

Ingmar's eyes narrowed. Was it possible...?

"I hear Del's staying with you," the German remarked casually.

"Aye," Finn replied.

"Did he stay up with you last night?"

"Aye."

"Was he naked too?" Ingmar asked slyly.

A puzzled smile lifted Finn's lips at the edges. "In soul he was as bare as I, naked as a blind eagle's eye."

For a moment Ingmar's expression was blank. Then he cleared his throat and launched into his lines as Hermia, but although he had only to feed the words to Finn, the DJ found it hard to focus and spent the following hours fluffing his speeches and stuttering to distracted stops, losing his way whenever he gazed into Finn's twinkling – *inviting*? – eyes.

*

Terence spent more than half the morning session going over the first scene of Act One, allowing Nuala all the time she needed to come to terms with her pivotal role as Helena. It was slow work but she was improving. She fudged a lot of lines but she did that every year. By the night of the play she'd be capable of delivering most of the dialogue. Those lines she was still having problems with would be dropped or altered.

Anna had little to do. Her main task was to observe the other actors and pass comment if they erred. She wasn't bothered. Later, as Titania, she'd have seventy-odd lines in the second act. That would be her chance to shine.

When Terence felt it was time to move on, he fast-forwarded to the second scene, where the tradesmen divided up the parts of their play. There was little of the scene left, with Ingmar and Diarmid out of the equation, but that meant they were able to get through it quickly.

Terence was playing Snug, who in the play-within-the-play would perform the parts of a wall and lion. Nuala was Robin Starveling, a tailor by trade, who'd be Moonshine in the sub-play. Felix was Flute, who'd cross-dress come the finale, to play the lady Thisbe.

"We're dropping the character of Snout," Terence told them. "I'll take his lines in Act Three, Scene One, and as Wall in the final act."

"Why not give the role to Anna?" Nuala asked. "She's free in those scenes."

"That's OK," Anna said. "I don't –"

"She's *not* free," Terence interrupted. "In Act Three, Scene One she has to be onstage, asleep, as Titania."

"But surely we could –" Nuala began.

"Please," Terence said. "I know where I want my actors and when. We proved our democracy yesterday. Do we have to go through that rigmarole again?"

"Sorry," Nuala simpered. "I just felt sorry for Anna. She has nothing to do and I didn't want her feeling excluded."

"Really," Anna smiled, "I'm –"

"Anna will have plenty to do," Terence said, silencing his wife again. "Now, if you're through challenging my authority, shall we proceed?"

"Sorry," Nuala giggled. "I'll raise my hand if I want to ask a question in future."

"You'd better," Terence winked. "Now." He shook his sheets. "The play –"

*

"– is obviously about latent homosexuality," Don said. Del and Kate exchanged wry smiles. "Well, it is!"

"We discussed this yesterday," Kate said.

"You call that a discussion?" Don snorted. "I don't want to camp things up or load the play down with sexual references, but the truth deserves an airing."

"What truth?" Del asked. "I've been through the whole thing and I didn't find anything remotely homosexual in it."

"It's there for those who choose to see," Don grunted. He

flicked through his copy of the play. "Act Two, Scene One. The twentieth Line.

'...Oberon is passing fell and wrath,

Because that she as her attendant hath

A lovely boy stol'n from an Indian king;

She never had so sweet a changeling,

And jealous Oberon would have the child

Knight of his train, to trace the forests wild.'

You see? Oberon's *wrathful* because his wife stole a *lovely boy*. He's *jealous* — he would *have* the child. Do I need to draw a picture?"

Del scratched his chin. "You think there's anything to that?" he asked Kate.

"Of course not," she replied. "Oberon just wants the boy to be his henchman."

"With all the fairies of his kingdom to choose from, he's going to raise a fuss over a human?" Don laughed aloud.

"There's something to what he says," Del murmured.

"Nonsense," Kate huffed. "Besides, Terence vetoed it and would kick up a stink if you raised the subject again."

"Terence isn't all-seeing," Don said. "We could devise our own interpretation."

"Uh-uh," Kate said quickly. "I'm no saboteur."

"What are you proposing?" Del asked Don.

"The words are set in stone," Don said, "but the gestures are ours. We could work in a few suggestive routines. Like, 'jealous Oberon would have the child.'" The bald six-footer gyrated his hips in a lewd manner. "And, 'I do but beg a little changeling boy To be my henchman.'" He rubbed his hands on the air in front of his crotch, as though brushing his fingers through a thick head of hair.

"That's disgusting," Kate shouted, but she laughed too.

"We could do it," Don said to Del. "With you as Puck and me as Oberon, we could work in enough small gestures to develop the characters as they were meant to be portrayed. We keep them secret until the night of the show, slip them in live, and there's sod all Terence can do about it."

"A wicked plan," Kate giggled.

"But you won't inform on us if we decide to forge ahead?" Don asked.

"I'm not sure," Kate purred. "It'll depend."

"On what?"

"What sort of a gift you were planning to buy me this Christmas."

Don laughed. "A most overwhelming bauble, to be sure. And you, Del?"

Del's gaze was focused on Finn and Ingmar across the glade. They were seated beneath a large oak and, from this distance, might have been a couple of lovebirds. "A man falls in love with a handsome boy and breaks with his long-term partner," Del muttered. "That has wonderful possibilities. I say we go with it."

Neither of the actors could have guessed that he wasn't referring to the characters in the play.

*

Felix only had a few lines as Flute and should have mastered them swiftly, but he was deliberately fluffing them, mixing up the order of the words and cutting in on Terence's lines as

Quince. Nuala knew what lay at the root of his antics but the rest of the Players were bewildered.

"'What is Frisbee? A wan–'" Felix began.

"Stop," Terence roared, tossing his notes into the air. "What are you doing? We don't have time for this crap."

"Sorry if I'm not good enough," Felix sulked. "Give the part to somebody else if you don't think I'm up to it."

Nuala snorted.

"What's the problem?" Terence asked. "It's a simple scene. A fool could do it. Anna, take his place." His wife's eyebrows arched at the (accidental?) insult but she said nothing. "I'm Quince, you're Flute. Got it?"

"I think so," she answered drily.

Terence cleared his throat.

"'Francis Flute, the bellow's-mender?'"

"'Here, Peter Quince'," answered Anna.

"'Flute, you must take Thisbe on you.'"

"'What is Thisbe? A wandering knight?'"

"'It is the lady that Pyramus must love.'"

"'Nay, faith, let not me play a woman: I have a beard coming.'"

"There," Terence grunted. "Three short and simple lines."

"If they're that simple, *you* handle them," Felix sniffed.

"I'm playing Snug."

"Let's swap," Felix said.

"We can't," Terence growled. "It would screw things up later in the play."

"Then let Ingmar play Flute. He played him the last couple of years. Besides, it's more fun having a heterosexually challenged person in the part. Ingmar knows how to wear a dress. He can –"

"Wait a minute," Terence said, eyes widening. "This isn't because you have to wear a dress in the final act, is it?"

Felix gulped guiltily.

"I don't believe it," Terence groaned.

"I don't like wearing dresses," Felix said quietly.

"I've seen you in one or two in my time," Nuala chuckled, recalling an evening a few weeks earlier when she'd come home to find Felix draped across the stairs in one of her sexiest dresses. Though she didn't mind his harmless fetish – he dressed up regularly and they usually had lots of fun – it was a very personal matter for Felix and he never discussed it with her when he wasn't in drag.

"Shut up," Felix snapped, reddening.

"Come on," she cooed. "You don't have to wear lacy knickers or anything." She paused mischievously. "Unless you want to."

"What's that supposed to mean?" Felix thundered.

"I've noticed certain lingerie items mysteriously disappearing recently," Nuala said. "I thought the washing machine was chewing them up, but maybe –"

"Woman!" Felix yelled. "Shut your mouth."

"Nobody's implying anything about your sexual preferences," Terence sighed.

"There's nothing to imply," Felix shouted.

"Of course not," Terence agreed. "If it will make things easier, you can simply drape a shawl around your shoulders and speak in a squeaky voice."

That placated Felix. "It's not that I wouldn't do it if it was necessary," he said. "I just don't feel I need to cross-dress for so small a part."

"No need in the world," Terence lied. There was no way he'd let Felix get away with only a shawl, but they could debate that later. Right now he just wanted to make sure the Northerner knew his lines.

Felix smiled at Anna and Terence, frowned at Nuala – they'd have words about this later – then cleared his throat and trotted out his lines.

"'What is Thisbe? A wandering knight?'"

"'It is the lady that Pyramus must love,'" Terence replied.

"'Nay, faith,'" Felix said, emitting a mock-hysterical shriek, "'let me not play a woman: I have –'"

*

"'– a widow aunt, a dowager,

Of great revenue, and she hath no child.

From Athens is her house –' Another!" Finn shouted as a second plane passed overhead.

Ingmar smiled. This new, unexpected side of the normally reserved Diarmid was a refreshing surprise. Ingmar didn't know what had brought about the change but he approved of it wholeheartedly.

"Have you ever been in a plane?" Ingmar asked.

"Never," Finn said sadly.

"I could take you up one day," Ingmar said. "I have a friend who's a pilot. I could wangle a couple of seats for us if you –"

Finn gasped, grabbed Ingmar's hands and kissed the

knuckles as fairies in his world were wont to do. "If you could truly take me there, Ingmar of the Dorslaer, you would have my love from now until the cessation of time."

Ingmar stared at the thrill-struck banker, then at his saliva-shined knuckles. "I'll see to it as soon as I can," he gurgled.

"Morning boys," came a voice. Ingmar spun on his heels, heart leaping, afraid that Don had read his mind and stormed across the glade. He relaxed when he saw it was only Del. "Having fun?" Del asked.

"It's proving to be a... fruitful session," Ingmar smiled.

Finn's assessment was more colourful.

"Ingmar has promised to treat me most fair:

He's vowed to guide me soaring through the air,

Propelled across the skies on most strange vanes

Of wondrous, magic, dream-like aeroplanes."

"*Has* he now?" Del murmured, eyeing the German as he blushed and averted his gaze. "Do you mind if I borrow Diarmid for a couple of minutes?"

"Please," Ingmar said quickly, his accent becoming all too evident, "take all the time you like. Ve could do vith a break. Ve veren't getting very far in any case."

"Splendid," Del beamed, leading Finn into the forest. When they were out of sight he asked Finn how things were progressing.

"Progressing?" the fairy replied.

"With Ingmar," Del said. "Are you getting on well?"

"Methinks he is at heart a noble knight;

In his company I take great delight."

"More a queen than a knight," Del snickered. "I saw you kissing his knuckles. What was that about?"

"His offer to fly set my mind a-burn;

Some of the joy I felt due to return."

"I know better parts of him to kiss if you want to spread joy," Del grinned.

"Tell me them quick, and in the twist

Of my lips I will those parts kiss."

Del's grin deepened into a frown. "I know you've been celibate your entire life, like the rest of the minor fairies – Puck explained all that – but you know what sex is, don't you?"

"Of sex and its ways, I am well aware;

One plays the stallion, the other the mare."

"As good a definition as any," Del laughed. "But are you aware that sometimes two *stallions* or *mares* frolic together?"

Finn looked perplexed.

"Two of the same in a sexual act?

You jest with poor Finn — it cannot be fact."

"Fact is sometimes stranger than fiction, my friend," Del said. "You know the story of the birds and the bees, but let me tell you what happens when the boys choose to play while the girls are away..."

*

When Finn returned, Ingmar noted the young man was in an even stranger mood than before. He kept examining the German and seemed continually on the verge of asking a question, but never did.

"Vot is it?" Ingmar finally snapped.

"Nothing," Finn said quickly.

"Yes it is," Ingmar disagreed. "You've been eyeballing me suspiciously since returning from the vood. Vot's up?"

Finn chewed his lip a moment before replying. "Del told me... is it true...?"

"Is *vot* true?"

Finn cleared his throat. "You and Don."

"Vot about us?" Ingmar asked, perplexed.

Finn leaned forward and whispered, "What is it like?"

"Vot's *vot* like?" Ingmar was growing more confused by the second.

"At night, when all the lights are dim,

And you climb into bed with him

And nature unleashes its rucking flood:

How rage the waves when both are of male blood?"

Ingmar stared, stunned. "You vant to know vot it's like in bed vith Don?" he asked incredulously.

"I cannot imagine the sensations

Which accompany such gay relations.

Would you take the time to broaden my mind

And explain the full passions of your kind?"

"Vot's brought dis on?" Ingmar asked. "And vhy are you speaking in rhyme?"

Finn blinked. "Sorry. I did not realise. Will you tell me what it is like?"

Ingmar glanced across the glade at Don. "It's not something one can easily describe. I vould have to *show* you." He arched his eyebrows.

"You mean when Don's long worm you next time hook,

You would have me there to sneak a quick look?"

"Vorm? Sneak a...? *Nein!*" Ingmar yelped. "Mein Gott, if he even heard us joking! Vot I mean is, if you're *truly* interested, I could arrange a private preview, as it vere."

Finn looked confused. "I must confess ignorance."

Ingmar reached across and gently stroked the skin of Finn's exposed right forearm. "Ve could meet early one morning, give it a try, see how it goes."

"That is a most generous offer," Finn said with delight. "In the meantime..." He reached behind his back and produced a flower. He'd picked it in the forest at Del's command and smothered it with love dust. "This is a wondrous bud with a most strange scent. See what you can make of it."

Ingmar leaned forward and the hairs in his nostrils curled. His pupils dilated as the molecules of magic dust wafted up his nose. His legs went weak and he'd have toppled to the floor had Finn not been there to support him. The changeling held the flower up to the human's nose for a good thirty seconds before discarding it, then laid his acting partner down on the grass.

It took five minutes for Ingmar to surface. When he recovered his senses, he remembered little of the preceding few hours. His mind was awash with images of magical fields stretching towards the horizon, untouched by the hand of man.

"Vhere am I?" he asked, his voice peculiarly hollow.

"The glade," Finn answered.

Ingmar smiled. "Yah. Grass. Blades. Pollen."

"We were practising the play," Finn reminded him.

"Yah," Ingmar grinned. "All the vorld's a stage." He tried getting to his feet but his limbs wouldn't obey. He fell back and laughed. His gaze wandered to the heavens and his face filled with awe. "Look!" he gasped. "A plane!"

2.[I](ii)

During the break at the end of the morning session, Anna rested beneath the trees, hiding from the sun. She could feel her skin reddening, a problem whenever they had a rare spell of fine weather in Limerick. She wasn't built for sunshine.

Anna rubbed the back of her neck. There was a long afternoon still to come — another few hours and she'd be stinging. Perhaps she should nip to the village for sun cream. It would mean delaying the start of the session, which would annoy Terence, but...

A hand alighted on her shoulder. "You look like you need some of this."

Anna glanced up. The sun was behind the standing figure, and for a moment she felt like Jack staring at the Giant. Then she squinted and smiled. "Hi, Nuala. Need what?"

"This," Nuala said, producing a bottle of sun cream.

"You're an angel," Anna beamed. "Where'd you get it?"

"Brought it," Nuala said, sitting down beside Anna. She was smiling giddily. "I got caught out once on a holiday to Scotland. You go up there, sun's the last thing on your mind, but I happened to arrive during an oddly hot summer. Went skinny-dipping and spent most of the day bare-arsed. The rest of the holiday, I popped blisters and picked at my peeling skin. I've never left home unprotected since."

"I hate sunburn," Anna said.

"Me too," Nuala nodded. "The nipples were the worst."

"Don't," Anna winced.

Nuala laughed. "Turn round and let me at you."

"It's alright," Anna said. "I can do it myself."

"Nonsense," Nuala snorted. "It's a small bottle. I don't want to waste any."

Anna shrugged and turned. She was wearing a loose cardigan, which the older woman tugged down, baring the shoulders. Nuala shook the bottle, then squeezed some of the cream onto the exposed skin. Anna shivered.

"You're getting goose pimples," Nuala observed, lightly brushing the thin hairs of Anna's upper arms.

"It's cold," Anna said.

"It'll be lovely once I smear it in."

"You'll blow on your hands first, won't you?" Anna asked. "To warm them up?"

"Little miss fussy," Nuala laughed. "I wish I had a bucket of ice to dip them in — that'd teach you to complain."

"I'm not complaining. I'm just — Ooohhh!" Anna bleated as Nuala slapped both hands on her shoulders. They were freezing! She tried pulling away but Nuala held her tight. "They're cold," Anna squealed.

"Don't worry," Nuala said. "They'll be fine in a moment."

Anna fidgeted, but as the seconds passed, Nuala's palms warmed and she began to relax.

"Better?" Nuala asked and Anna nodded in response. "Ready for the smearing?"

"You'll take it gently?" Anna asked.

"You'll think a family of spiders are spinning webs across your back," Nuala promised, then began kneading softly.

Anna was tense at first but soon melted beneath Nuala's assured touch — the older woman was an accomplished masseuse.

"Del showed me the most amazing flower earlier," Nuala said as she toiled, her gaze fixed to Anna's neck, glistening and beautiful. "It was nothing special to look at but it had an extraordinary scent, how I imagine opium smells. That's something I've always wanted to try. Wouldn't it be wonderful to slip into a world of dreams whenever you wished, where everything was possible and every desire was sated?"

Anna grunted, barely registering the words. She could feel herself sliding into a daze, her cares and worries vanishing. "That's heavenly," she murmured, letting her head tilt back, eyes shut so she could focus on nothing but the pleasure.

Nuala's fingers slid round to massage Anna's throat and the top of her chest. Anna gurgled happily, her head falling even further back until it was nestled in Nuala's lap.

Nuala's mouth dried. Anna rarely wore a bra while they were rehearsing and from this position Nuala had a clear view of her friend's cleavage. She could see the nipples, hardening beneath the fabric of the cardigan. If she focused on the breasts, she could imagine it was somebody else she was massaging, an even younger and more attractive Player...

Nuala's hands made large, slow circles, each revolution bringing the tips of her fingers closer to the breasts. She studied Anna's face. From its dreamy look, Nuala knew her friend must be oblivious to all but the most immediate sensations. Taking a deep breath, preparing an apology in case Anna became aware of what was going on, she slipped the tips of her fingers beneath the material of the cardigan.

She paused to check Anna's expression — no change. She rubbed the bones of the chest, taking her time, working downwards as slowly as she dared. Her head was a sea of white noise, and though she was conscious of what she was doing, she didn't really understand what she was up to. It was as if something had taken hold of her senses. Something otherworldly. Something *fey*.

She spread her fingers and moved to the sides of Anna's breasts. She spent a minute idly caressing the buffer regions, then brought the hands up with all the delicate skill she could muster, until each was cupping a thick, fleshy nipple.

The world seemed to stop for Nuala. Until that crazy moment, the only breasts her hands had been near were her own. Although strange feelings had been stirring inside her since she'd met Kate Pummel, she'd never seriously considered making a move on any member of her own sex, certainly not an old and trusted friend like Anna. She didn't know why this was happening. A few minutes ago she'd been idly chit-chatting with Del. One sniff of a strange flower later and here she was, her hands leading her to pastures new.

Those hands now moved a little to either side of the nipples, making room for the thumbs, which sensuously circled and pressed on the hardening flesh. In her dazed state, Anna believed she was merely fantasizing. She thought Nuala was still massaging her shoulders, that the delicious quivers she was experiencing were the product of her drifting mind.

After a while, Nuala's right hand reluctantly relinquished its hold. The fingers lifted and ever so slowly unbuttoned the cardigan, exposing the right breast in all its glory. Nuala's mouth was a desert and she had to moisten the back of her lips several times before they'd part. When they did finally separate – and before she could allow herself time to think – she lowered her head and fastened on the stiff, inviting nipple.

Nuala sucked slightly harder than she'd meant to, and Anna groaned and stirred uneasily, but her eyes remained shut and she failed to emerge from her daydream. Nuala waited for six agonised heartbeats before resuming her explorations, this time slower and tenderly. She extended her tongue and flicked it over the head of the nipple, then ran it over the stretch of lovely brown aureole, pressing deeper into the soft flesh each time.

When her mouth finally left the breast, it was to kiss the nape of Anna's neck. Her left hand also came up, to run through the prone woman's hair. Nuala's lips and tongue traced the outline of Anna's neck up to her chin, which she kissed. Her head drew back as she moved up to meet the lips and she gazed lovingly down at the woman in her lap. Nuala wished she could hold her here forever. "Kate," she murmured, leaning forward. She came within a breath's width of latching onto those promising ripples of red, then…

…stopped.

"*Kate*?" she muttered. The clouds of eroticism parted. "This isn't Kate." She ran a thumb – which had moments before been busily engaged with a nipple – over the motionless woman's lips. "Nice, but not Kate. This is…" Her eyes widened. "Merciful heavens," she gasped, returning to her senses. She glanced over her shoulder but nobody seemed to have seen.

The right breast was still showing, but not for long. Nuala yanked the cardigan over it and buttoned it up quickly. She ruffled Anna's hair, waited a few moments to get her breath back, then slowly shook her half-slumbering friend.

"I'm finished. Anna? Are you awake?"

Anna's head shifted. Her face scrunched up, then relaxed. Her eyes opened. She blinked uncertainly, then smiled at Nuala.

"I didn't fall asleep, did I?"

"Nearly," Nuala said nervously.

"I guess standing about all morning in the heat exhausted me." She sat up. "Are you finished with the cream? Am I safe now?"

"Yes," Nuala sighed. "You're safe."

Anna giggled. "I never knew you were so skilled with your fingers. Did you study professionally?"

"Just naturally talented," Nuala replied.

"Well, come on," Anna said, taking the bottle of cream. "Turn around."

"Turn...?" Nuala wheezed.

"You need this as much as I do," Anna said. "Let me repay your kindness."

"You mean... you'll do for me what I did for you?"

"Sure," Anna said, smearing the cream onto her fingers.

"I doubt it," Nuala whispered wryly as she turned and bared her shoulders, "but I suppose one can always live in hope."

*

Del was relieved when Nuala stopped short of delivering the kiss. He hadn't meant for that to happen. Nuala was supposed to target Kate, not chase Anna. He didn't want the Players fracturing after just a couple of days — while that would please the fey folk, it would ruin his merriment.

Thankfully, Nuala had stalled at the final hurdle and the moment of danger had passed. Puck had warned him of the initial disorientation sometimes caused by the dust. Hopefully her head was clear now and there'd be no more unexpected forays. He'd take more care in future.

As Anna began rubbing sun cream into Nuala's back, Del slipped out from behind the tree which had hidden him from the sight of the women and turned for the glade. He crashed into Kate – who'd popped up out of nowhere – and almost sent her sprawling.

"Ow!" she winced, twisting an ankle.

"Sorry," Del said, bending to offer his assistance. "Are you OK?"

"I came to see what you were up to," Kate said, rubbing her ankle. She stared past him, to where Anna and Nuala were perched. Her eyebrows lifted when she spotted Nuala's bare back. "Ogling the ladies, Mr Chapman?"

"Certainly not," Del replied breezily. "I'm no Peeping Tom."

"Then what were you doing?"

"Thinking," he said and she smiled sceptically. "It's true. I was thinking about Anna's role and I automatically wandered over to observe her."

"Anna's role?" Kate frowned.

Del smiled to himself. The magic dust would create plenty of friction over the coming days but he didn't want to rely on it too heavily. There were other ways to rock the boat.

"What do *you* think of Anna's lines as Titania?" he asked, sitting beside Kate. "She's got loads in the second act, hasn't she?"

"A fair few," Kate agreed.

"A lot of that scene is padding," Del said slyly.

"Not all of it," Kate disagreed. "It establishes her character, lets the audience know about her conflict with Oberon and explains why he uses the magic potion on her, to make her fall in love with Bottom."

"Sure," Del said, "but it drags. A few cuts and it'd play more effectively."

"You think Shakespeare got it wrong?" Kate asked witheringly.

"I'm just saying, a lot of that scene seems redundant. Am I wrong?"

Kate chewed her lip. Finally, in the thinnest of whispers, she said, "I've always found it a little draggy. There's too much there. The scene starts with me, as a Fairy, and Puck, and we both have long, colourful speeches. Then Titania warbles on and on. Last year, that was the point where I felt the audience turn. It's hard to maintain interest in one extended speech after another."

"My thoughts exactly," Del said. He lowered his voice. "I know you have Terence's ear, and I thought –"

"What do you mean?" Kate asked sharply.

"He listens to what you say because he respects you as an actress."

"Oh," she smiled. "Does he? I hadn't noticed."

"If you suggested cuts, he'd be inclined to pay attention."

"I don't know," Kate said. "It's not fair for one actress to pass comment on another behind her back."

"I guess you're right," Del sighed. "I didn't dare approach him myself. You have to be really self-confident to argue those kinds of points. I'd melt as soon as he raised a counterargument."

"Maybe he wouldn't," Kate said. "Maybe he feels the same way we do."

"Maybe," Del said. "But Anna might think we were criticising *her* rather than highlighting a problem with the role. She's married to Terence — one word in his ear and we'd both be on our way back to Nowheresville."

Kate's nostrils flared. "I'd like to see her try to drive *me* out."

"Wives have ways of influencing their husbands," Del murmured.

"Nobody drives Kate Pummel out of a play," Kate hissed.

"Still," Del said, "it might be best to leave it. Terence wouldn't stick up for us if we got on the wrong side of Anna."

"He would if we were right," Kate huffed. "There's no way I'd let that old battleaxe..." She caught herself, coughed and forced a pale smile. "I'll mention it when the time is right."

"You're sure?" Del asked. "I'll back you up if you give me the nod."

"I can handle it," Kate assured him, getting up.

"That's great. Thanks." Del rose also and glanced at her shapely legs. "How's your ankle?"

"Fine," she told him as she hobbled purposefully away.

"Mighty fine," he sighed. He'd have liked to make a play for Kate, but as the conductor of chaos, he had to stay concentrated on each instrument. No favourites. It was one of the drawbacks of responsibility, one of the many reasons he normally avoided it as widely as the plague.

"To every dog its day," he consoled himself, then set off after the departing Kate. Not long after that, Nuala and Anna emerged, oiled up and ready to go, and once they'd returned to the fold, the afternoon session commenced.

2.[I](iii)

The afternoon kicked off with Del and Kate practising in front of the others. Del was nervous – this was the first time he'd performed to an audience – but he flew through the scene as if born with the lines in his mouth. It helped that the character he was playing was so close in spirit to his own.

"'Thou speakest aright;

I am that merry wanderer of the night.

I jest to Oberon, and make him smile

When I a fat and bean-fed horse beguile,

Neighing in likeness of a filly foal.

The wisest aunt, telling the saddest tale,

Sometime for threefoot stool mistaketh me;

Then slip I from her bum, down topples –'"

"Hold it a second," Terence interrupted.

"Did I get it wrong?" Del asked, glancing up.

"Not at all," Terence said. "I just want you to slip in some exaggerated moves. For instance, when you're talking about being a stool and say, 'Then slip I from her bum,' crouch low, then leap to one side and chortle gleefully."

Del scratched his head. "You don't think that's a bit obvious?"

"You're playing an imp," Terence reminded him. "The king of jesters. Subtlety isn't something Puck was renowned for."

Del recalled his meetings with the devious fairy. Puck cut an animated figure by all means but there was also a dignity in the way he carried himself. "I'd rather not play it too broadly," he told Terence. "Puck's a stylish rogue, not a crass buffoon. He should –"

"Del," Terence smiled benignly. "This is the twentieth time I've had dealings with our sharp-tongued friend. I think we'd both agree that I know more about the character and his ways, yes?"

"I suppose so," Del muttered.

"This is the way we always do it," Don said, weighing in on his friend's side. "Puck's baseness marks a nice contrast with the regal airs of Oberon and Titania."

"I see," Del said, understanding what Don really meant was that the dumber Del appeared as Puck, the better Don would look as Oberon. Del cleared his throat and began again.

"'Thou speakest aright;

I am that merry wanderer of the night.

I jest to Oberon, and make...'"

This time he pulled every animated trick he could muster. He screwed up his face, blew out his cheeks, hopped around like a horse, crawled on the grass like a crab, and made a hue and cry about the word 'bum.' It was ludicrous, but when he finished, Don and Terence clapped and said, "That's the stuff. Well done."

Del took the compliments as though he believed they were genuine but inside he was seething. Though he'd previously sought to undermine the Midsummer Players purely for sport, that was the case no longer. His nose had been put out of joint. Now it was personal.

*

Once Del and Kate had finished, Terence launched into the next section of the second act. It belonged to Anna and Don as Titania and Oberon, and he planned to get it out of the way by the end of the day. In the play the royals entered with their personal retinues, but as the Players were short on numbers, Terence had decided to dispense with the 'trains' and instead the two actors emerged alone.

Don had left his wig at home — it was too hot to be in full attire. His bald head glistened in the sun and occasionally the watching Players had to shield their eyes from an especially intense glare.

Anna was oblivious to the shiny head. She was focused on her role and nothing could distract her. To take her mind off her marital woes, she'd thrown herself into the play this year and was determined to give a hell of a performance.

"'Then I must be thy lady. But I know

When thou hast stol'n away from Fairyland,

And in the shape of Corin sat all day

Playing on pipes of corn, and versing love

To amorous Phillida. Why art...'"

She was on sparkling form and barely had to glance at the script. She had the words memorised, delivered every line perfectly, and glided round the glade, circling Don as if she was a dancing harpy and he the object of her deepest desires and darkest fears.

Don hadn't expected such a performance and he struggled to keep up. He spoke too quickly, fudged a couple of his lines and even dropped his copy of the play at one point. He was growing more flustered with every passing line. He started to think that Anna was doing this to belittle him and his face began to redden.

Anna noticed nothing of her partner's ire. She was in a world of poetry and magic. She'd never before been so struck by the wonder of the words, the beauty inherent in each carefully constructed phrase. *This* was why the plays had lived on, why audiences turned out, year after year, even for amateurish productions such as theirs. At last she was in tune with the Bard and she was finding it glorious.

The glory wasn't to last. As she drew to the end of her final speech – in which she elaborated on her friendship with the mother of the human boy whom Oberon coveted – Don lost his place on the page.

"'But she, being mortal, of that boy did die,

And for her sake do I rear up her boy;

And for her sake I will not part with him.'"

When Anna stopped, Don realised it was his turn to speak. He half-remembered his line and lurched into it. "'How long... how long...'"

Anna wasn't listening to Don and failed to note his difficulties. She heard him mumble something and then lapse into silence, so assumed he'd delivered his line. Without a second thought, she continued.

"'Perchance till after Theseus' wedding day.

If you will patiently –'"

"Hold it," Don roared, jolting her out of her fugue. She looked up, bewildered, to be faced with a glowering, red-faced Don. "I didn't finish my line."

"Didn't you?" Anna blinked nervously.

"You weren't listening, were you?" he snapped.

"Not really," she admitted with a sheepish grin. "I was

looking ahead to the next line. I –"

"You didn't stop to think," he shouted. "You were so wrapped up in your own *grande dame* performance, you never paused to see how I was doing. This is meant to be a line reading, not the final rehearsal."

"I know," Anna said.

"So what are you up to?" he stormed. "Why the big performance?"

"I wasn't aware it *was* that big," Anna said coolly. "I was merely delivering the lines in what seemed a fit fashion. I'm sorry if that offended you. Next time I'll do them without any passion or art. That way we should be on level terms."

"What's that supposed to mean?" Don croaked.

"Let it drop," Ingmar said, tugging at his lover's sleeve, but he was brushed aside roughly.

"Are you saying you're better than me?" Don screeched. "Are you calling my professionalism into question?"

"I'm sure that's not what she's –" Terence began but got no further.

"If the cap fits," Anna sniffed. "I know I'm meant to be the quiet, anonymous one, and you're supposed to hog all the glory, but this year I'm giving it my all. If you can't match me, you'll have to settle for second best."

"Is this your doing?" Finn whispered in Del's ear.

"No," the mischief-maker grinned happily.

"Perhaps we are not needed here," the changeling murmured. "They are poised to come apart by themselves."

"It looks that way," Del agreed. "Tell me, is there an antidote to the lust dust?"

Finn nodded.

"Then I want you to return to Feyland when practise is over, find a pouch of the other dust and bring it back."

"Why?" Finn asked.

"I want to lift the charm from Nuala. This is moving too fast for my liking. If Nuala makes a move now, things could blow up on us."

"Is that not the plan?" Finn asked.

"The plan's to put an end to all future performances," Del said. "If they break too soon, it might wreck this year's show, but that's no long-term guarantee. Humans have a nasty habit of reconciling their petty differences."

Anna was still ranting. Though Don had started the argument, her fury had sapped him of his, and now he cowered before her.

"– what you do in Dublin," she shouted. "I don't care how important you are up there. This is my patch. I'm sick of you making me look like an idiot. I know as much about this play as any of you. Why shouldn't I shine? Just once, why can't it be me taking the bows?"

"I'm sorry," Don replied miserably. "I was wrong to have a go at you. I won't do it again."

"I hope not," Anna said, calming down.

Del glanced at Kate. This would be the perfect time for her to chip in with her criticism. Del didn't think she would – timing of that order seemed too much to wish for – but he tried nudging her hand mentally. "Speak up," he pleaded inside his head, gaze fixed on the actress. "Now. Now! *Now!*'

Kate shifted uneasily and then – because of his urgings or

by coincidence? – stepped forward and cleared her throat.

"Kate?" Terence asked with a smile, assuming she'd stepped in to defuse the situation.

"The problem might be the amount of lines," she said.

"*Problem*?" Anna snarled, firing up again.

Kate said, "I think the reason Don's having trouble matching Anna –"

"Hold on," Don barked. "I can match her. I was only –"

Kate ignored him and ploughed ahead. "– is that it's hard to concentrate when there's such a morass of unnecessary lines."

"*Morass*?" Anna stared at Kate incredulously.

"If we trimmed the lines," Kate said, "it would make it easier for Don to raise his performance, which I'm sure he can," she added, acknowledging the spluttering Dubliner with a condescending nod.

"I don't need a handicap," he snarled. "It wouldn't matter to me if she had double the number of lines. I was only caught out by the unexpected –"

"Kate has a point," Del chipped in. "The scene *is* ponderous."

"You think so?" Terence asked, scratching an ear.

"Some of those lines are my favourites of the entire play," Nuala said, coming to Anna's aid, hoping to make amends for her earlier, unfathomable violation. "'Therefore the winds, piping to us in vain, As in revenge have sucked up from the sea Contagious fogs.' Great stuff."

"Some of it's super," Kate agreed, "but a little goes a long way. I think people would be more inclined to like her if we shortened her early speeches and –"

"Nobody's touching a word of my speeches," Anna said firmly.

"It's not a criticism of *you*," Kate said, grinning boldly. "You handle the lines wonderfully. It's the –"

"Shut up, you little bitch."

Kate's jaw dropped, and hers wasn't the only one.

Anna smiled wolfishly at the startled Players. "I'll cut the balls off the man who tries taking my lines away. The tits, if it's a woman," she added.

"Now, Anna," Terence began, "that's not –"

"This isn't a debate," she screamed. "If you want to shorten lines, cut somebody else's. I'm keeping mine." She eyeballed Kate. "I've had too much taken from me already. The lines remain. If you've a problem with that" – she took a step forward – "step into the ring. Best woman wins."

Kate's lips quivered. "I was only passing a comment," she whimpered.

Anna smiled and ran a fingernail across the trembling actress' cheek. "Little girls should stick to what they know," she murmured. "Some things are sacred to a woman. Some things, she won't allow anyone to mess with. You'll find that out... when you grow up."

Anna tapped Kate's cheek, then turned and, still smiling, said, "I'm going home. I know my lines. I've proved I can deliver them effectively. There's no need for me to tarry. I'll see you all tomorrow. Good evening."

She strolled away, pausing only to pick a flower, which she swung by her side as she strode. Her regal departure would have put even the real Titania to shame.

The Players watched Anna depart, then all eyes settled on Terence. The director coughed. "I, ah, think we should... The lines stand, yes?" Seven heads – including Kate's – quickly nodded. "Then, ah, I think we..." He looked down at his copy of the play, then at his colleagues, seeking inspiration. When none was forthcoming, he shook his head despairingly. "We'll call it a day and meet here again in the morning, or at my house if it's raining. Nuala, perhaps you and Felix could practise your roles as Helena and Demetrius at home?"

"Of course," Nuala said.

"No problem," Felix agreed.

"Thanks. I might pop across to see how you're getting on, assuming Anna's not..." He coughed again, then shrugged and set off for home, meaning that for an unprecedented second successive day, the efforts of the Players came to an abrupt, premature conclusion.

2.[II](i)

Terence cracked his knuckles, settled back in his ornate leather chair in the study and listened to the soft creakings of the house. This was the first chance he'd had in more than a week to relax. He had the house to himself and, though he had much to do before the end of the day, he could do it in solitary silence. After seven gruelling days with his troops, it was a much-relished treat.

Terence tried to work a midway break into the proceedings every year. It was good to give the actors a day off. Morale dropped if they were worked too hard. Some years it wasn't possible — if they were behind schedule, a break was out of the question — but this year they'd zoomed along nicely. Apart from the early bumps, it had been a smooth run. Nobody had trouble with their lines — even Nuala was more adept than usual — and the performances were peaking perfectly. Things were going so well, he almost hadn't called the break, as he was half afraid the interruption might knock them out of shape.

That said, some things were going a little *too* well for his liking. Take the rapport between Kate and Diarmid. They portrayed lovers in the play, so there had to be a romantic *frisson* between the pair, but they seemed to be taking matters further than necessary. The two had spent a lot of time together and Kate always appeared to be holding onto the shy — though not so shy recently — banker's arm. Was it possible her and Diarmid...?

He frowned, then smiled. No, the thought of celibate

Diarmid making a move on one as worldly as Kate was ridiculous.

Cracking his knuckles again, he swept all thoughts of Kate and Diarmid from his mind. Midsummer's Eve was a mere six days distant. It was time to generate public interest. Many of their patrons were old friends and acquaintances who came every year (whether they liked it or not), but Terence was always looking to attract new custom. Limerick wasn't the Mecca of the Irish tourist industry and those few stragglers who found themselves stranded in the county usually wound up with little to do. A spot of outdoor theatre could pass for a big attraction when there was nothing else on offer and Terence meant to capitalise on that.

He'd had flyers printed up the previous month and these were now in boxes beneath his desk, waiting to be distributed. They'd leave most of the flyers for another few days – it didn't pay to hang leaflets on posts too far in advance, since they could be washed away with one good downpour – but Del, Diarmid, Kate and Anna were spending the day in town, and he'd sent some flyers with them, to be placed in restaurants and shop windows.

There were guest invitations to be issued, for sponsors and relatives. Terence kept these to a minimum – the Players couldn't afford many freeloading guests – and spent the better part of an hour fiddling with his list of names, eliminating and adding on after much deliberation.

And the media had to be alerted. He had a few associates on the local papers, whom he phoned, and sent emails to the rest. He also informed the local radio stations and sent a few hopeful emails to the national press. From past experience he knew not to expect many replies, but there was always a chance. Even after nineteen years of obscurity, he believed that fame and fortune were just a roll of the dice away. One nugget of luck... the right review from the right reporter... a travelling news crew with an afternoon to fill...

In every dispatch, Terence made prominent mention of the fact that this was their twentieth anniversary. Reporters loved anniversaries, so maybe this would stir up interest. Was this to be their year? After two decades, would they finally arrive on the national scene in a blaze of media glory?

Terence smiled as he daydreamed. A personal assistant. Money for decent costumes, an overhead canopy (no more performing under umbrellas in the rain). They might knock down some trees to create more space. Perhaps hire a couple of professional actors. Maybe film it and stream it online. The options were endless.

Having sent his final email, Terence spent the rest of the day on social media sites, spreading the word that the Midsummer Players were back in town — anyone interested?

*

Don and Ingmar were out walking. Don hadn't been eating much at the table since they'd arrived, but hadn't lost any weight. Ingmar had a notion that his partner was being secretly supplied by Kate with snacks, but had yet to catch them in the act. A day of strolling would do wonders for his pudgy lover — no chance for a naughty nibble.

Ingmar started humming, then began to sing out loud.

"'You spotted snakes with double tongue,

Thorny hedgehogs, be not seen.

Newts and blindworms, do no wrong,

Come not near our Fairy Queen.'"

They were lines from his song in the play, sung near the start of the second act to a sleepy Titania, and they'd been the cause of some resentment in the camp. Normally the fairies with Titania shared the singing duties. This year there were three of them, played by Ingmar, Nuala and Terence. Terence wasn't much of a singer but Nuala had been looking forward to the crooning.

On the first few run-throughs they'd divided the lines as usual, but during a midday break, Ingmar had disappeared into the forest with Finn and Del, and when he returned he was soon monopolising the act. Whereas before he had been softly crooning, now he sung out loud, each note pitch perfect. The actors listened, dumbfounded – except for the changeling and the rogue – then burst into applause as he drew to a close.

"That was superb," Terence congratulated him.

"Thank you," Ingmar blushed.

"I never realised you had such a voice," Anna commented.

"You know me, never one to boast."

"That solves our singing dilemma," Terence beamed. "The song is yours. You can take the whole thing, even the chorus."

"That's not fair," Nuala objected. "I want to sing too."

Terence shrugged. "You'd sound like a frog next to Ingmar. My advice is to keep your trap shut."

Nuala had been in a foul mood ever since.

"'Weaving spiders, come not here;

Hence, you long-legged spinner, hence!

Beetles black approach not near;

Worm nor snail, do no offence.'"

Ingmar trailed off into silence and bent to pick a flower.

"That was beautiful," Don complimented him.

"Thanks," Ingmar said, sticking the flower behind an ear. "I think I'll become a gypsy. Would you still love me if I lived in a caravan?"

"I'd love you if you lived on a tip," Don laughed, pulling the trim vegetarian in for a kiss. "You've certainly got the voice of the gypsies. Where did you pick it up? You never sang this sweetly before."

"I'm a man of many talents," Ingmar said, fluttering his eyelids.

"I know a woman who'd love to string you up by your *talents*," Don chuckled.

Ingmar's look darkened. "I didn't mean to edge Nuala out. That was Terence's idea, not mine."

"I know," Don said.

"Nuala thinks I went behind her back," Ingmar fretted.

"She'll get over it."

"I hope so. I'd hate to make an enemy of her."

"You'll make an enemy of *me* if you don't answer my question," Don joked.

"What question?"

"Where'd you learn to sing so magnificently?"

Ingmar blushed. "Nowhere special."

Don would have let it drop but the blush sparked his curiosity. "Why are you blushing?" he asked.

"I'm not," Ingmar laughed.

"You are," Don said sternly. "I want to know why."

"It's nothing," Ingmar insisted.

"If it was nothing, you'd tell me."

"I know how you are," Ingmar said. "You get upset about little things."

"I'm getting upset right now," Don growled.

Ingmar pouted. "Diarmid taught me."

"*Diarmid?*" Don frowned. "What does he know about singing?"

"You'd be amazed," Ingmar said. "His voice makes mine seem like Tom Waits. He approached me the other day and offered to give me some lessons. We've been meeting since then, when I go jogging. He –"

"You've been meeting with Diarmid behind my back?" Don roared.

Ingmar winced and pushed himself away. "Not *meeting*," he said. "Just meeting. To work on my vocal chords."

"I bet that's not all you've been working on," Don sniffed.

"I'll pretend I didn't hear that," Ingmar said.

"Then I'll say it louder," Don shouted.

"I knew you'd act like this," Ingmar sulked. "It's why I didn't tell you."

"How am I supposed to act? You've been having secret rendezvous behind my back, getting up to God alone knows what, and you want me to –"

"I've been rendezvousing vith nobody," Ingmar snapped. "Diarmid's been kind enough to teach me how to sing in his spare time. That's all there is to it."

"Then why not tell me before?" Don asked.

"There was nothing to tell," Ingmar replied. "Diarmid doesn't vant people to know how sweet his voice is – you know he hates the spotlight – and he made me promise not to mention it. I'm only telling you now because I know the filthy things your mind vill conjure up if you don't hear the truth."

"That's not a nice thing to say," Don moaned, stung by the accusation.

"Don," Ingmar said, laying his hands on his lover's shoulders. "You know it's you I love. I could never be unfaithful." Not true. Though he did love the teacher, monogamy wasn't his strong suit and there had been many flings in the past. But not this time. (Not yet anyway.)

"You've really only been singing?" Don asked.

"Of course," Ingmar laughed. "This is *Diarmid* we're talking about. Remember when he came to Dublin? We took him to a gay bar and he nearly ran."

"That's true," Don muttered.

"I thought he was going to faint when the drag queen blew him a kiss," Ingmar giggled.

Don gave Ingmar a quick peck. "Sorry. It's all the veg. My mind's turning to mush. I need a good, thick steak."

"You need a good, thick something," Ingmar agreed with a wink.

"Come on," Don laughed, linking arms. "Let's go hit the sack. Work off the pounds in bed."

"The forest floor's as sweet a bed as any," Ingmar murmured.

"And get my arse all scratched and mossy?" Don grunted. "No fear."

*

Things were tense in the Hill-Shay household. Neither Nuala nor Felix appeared capable of saying anything without infuriating the other. That morning they'd almost come to blows over whether Weetabix tasted better with cold or hot milk.

When Terence announced a rest day, Felix made up his mind to take Nuala to town. Hit the shops, a few drinks over lunch, a trip to the cinema, end the day in a pub with live music. Make love upon their return. All marital problems dissolved.

Nuala had ideas of her own.

"I think we should stay and rehearse," she said.

"*Rehearse?*" he groaned.

"I want to make sure I know all my lines," Nuala said.

"We can do that another night," Felix said.

"I hate leaving things until the last moment." Nuala smiled sweetly at her husband. "Of course, *you* can go if you want."

He was tempted to storm off, but something was going on inside Nuala that he couldn't understand, and he wasn't sure how she'd react if he left now.

Felix wasn't the only one perturbed by the situation. Nuala was in the dark too. She wanted to go to town – had been on the verge of broaching the subject when Felix spoke – and couldn't believe it when she heard herself announcing her intention to stay home.

Examining her motives later that morning, in the bathroom, she reasoned that she'd cried off in the hope that Felix *would* go by himself. Being brutally honest, she admitted it had been designed to force him to abandon her and thus provide her with the fuel to storm out and seek asylum with…

Kate. In a moment of clarity, she realised it all boiled down to her feelings for her fellow actress. That was why she'd been baiting Felix and rowing with him at every opportunity. She was looking for an excuse to leave him for Kate.

"What am I doing?" she moaned. "This is lunacy. Destroy a marriage in the hope of a roll in the hay with a woman who probably thinks nothing of me, who's already involved with Mr Big Time Director? I must be mad!"

Madness or not, she couldn't stop. In here she could be calm and logical, but as soon as she was faced with the tiny man in his platform shoes, she knew that logic would crumble and the nit-picking would start again.

When she returned to the living room, Felix was waiting with a glass of lemonade and a plate of biscuits. They'd rehearsed the early scenes that morning but there was still a long way to go and Nuala was glad he'd thought to break out the refreshments. She started to thank him, then stopped and pulled a face. "I'm tired of this."

Felix frowned. "Tired of lemonade and biscuits?"

"Tired of the play." She yawned theatrically. "I won't bother with the rest."

"But we stayed home to rehearse," Felix spluttered. "We could have gone to town with the others but you said you wanted —"

"I've changed my mind," Nuala interrupted. "I'm going to read a book instead. You don't mind, do you?"

Felix glared at her, then hurled the plate and glass against the wall, where they shattered. "*Mind?*" he snarled. "Why should I *mind?*"

He marched to the front door and kicked it open. The last she saw of him, he was goose-stepping away into the forest, face as dark as a goblin's, leaving Nuala alone in the house, caught in a state somewhere between elation and guilt.

*

Del, Finn, Kate and Anna cruised the shops in Limerick. The two men were happy to trail after the women, waiting patiently while they tried on different outfits. Finn's gaze was glued to the passing humans. He was fascinated by their various shapes, colours and sounds.

Kate emerged from a cubicle in a hideous red dress, which made her look like a bruised strawberry. "What's it like?" she asked.

"It's... singular," Del said carefully.

Finn was less tactful. He burst out laughing. "She looks like a fox with its insides turned out," he howled.

Del grimaced and prepared for the fireworks.

Kate glared at Finn, then glanced down at the costume and laughed. "He's right," she shrieked. "Thank you, Diarmid." She snorted at Del. "*Singular!*"

"I didn't want to hurt your feelings," he protested.

"I'd have hurt *you* if you'd let me buy this monstrosity," she grunted, before disappearing back into the cubicle.

Del eyed Finn sourly. "It's not always a good idea to tell the truth," he said.

"What do you mean?" Finn asked.

"Women are strange creatures," Del explained. "Sometimes it's better to spin a lie. You were lucky this time but you won't always be."

"I do not understand," Finn said.

"When a woman asks for an opinion," Del said, "she's normally not interested in what we think. Usually she has her mind made up and it's our job to second guess her and deliver a verdict that matches her own."

"You mean," Finn said, brow furrowing, "we should ignore our own judgement and speak not as our hearts dictate?"

"If that's what the situation calls for," Del agreed.

A few minutes later, Anna emerged in a beautiful peach dress which made her look years younger. She twirled for the men and giggled girlishly. "What do you think?" she asked. "Is it a little round about the hips?"

"You look like a pig dressed up for slaughter," Finn beamed.

Anna's face dropped. "I... a... *what*?"

"Your butt, your breasts and stomach do extrude;

All flair and fashion those foul togs exclude."

Anna was crestfallen. "Excuse me," she sobbed and dashed back into the safety of the cubicle.

Finn turned to Del and grinned. "Is that the way?"

Del tugged at his collar. "You have much to learn, young one," he groaned.

Kate and Anna didn't say much to each other over the course of the day. Anna was certain that Terence was having an affair with Kate – he'd spent every spare moment of the past week with her – and Kate knew that Anna was onto them. The younger woman was expecting an attack, but Anna just felt weary.

The city began to disorient Finn as they moved from shop

to shop. It was fun to gawk at the human world, but as a reared creature of magic he needed to be in touch with nature. The lack of grass and trees stabbed at his soul, and after a couple of hours he felt as if he was suffocating. Grabbing hold of Del's arms, he gasped, "Need... air."

Del studied the fairy-raised's ashen face with concern. "What's wrong? Are you asthmatic?"

"Can't... breathe. City closing in... on me. Feel... like I'm dying."

Del got his bearings. "Ladies," he said to Kate and Anna, "we've had enough of the shops. Do you mind if we head off by ourselves?"

"No," Anna replied.

"Of course not," Kate said.

"We'll meet you in the People's Park... when?" Del asked.

"We won't be much longer," Anna said. "An hour?" She checked with Kate, who nodded.

"Great," Del smiled. "See you soon."

He ushered Finn away before the women noticed his aggrieved state and started asking questions. Finn's symptoms alarmed Del. His face was grey, his lips were blue, his eyelids fluttered like a bird's wings, and his chest and stomach heaved. He thought about taking Finn to a hospital, but decided to try the park first.

When he spotted grass, Finn gave a croaky shout of joy and rushed forward. He stumbled through the gate and threw himself face down on the carefully kept lawn. By the time Del caught up, he had his lips spread and was breathing in the green. People were staring at him oddly.

"How do you feel?" Del asked when Finn finally sat up.

"The fit has passed. I now feel almost grand;
 Praise the heavens for this small plot of land."

"I thought you were going to drop dead," Del said.

Finn nodded seriously.

"I too was thinking my last hour had come;
 This barren city is wretchedly rum."

"What happened exactly?" Del enquired.

The changeling frowned.

"The air turned thick; my legs went weak;
 Ev'ry breath I inhaled did reek
 Of empty lives and cold steel dreams;
 In ev'ry brick I sensed trapped screams."

"But you're OK now?" Del asked and Finn nodded. "How about the rest of the day? Will we call off the trip and head back to the forest?"

Finn thought about it. "I would like to continue," he said.

"Will you be able?"

"I think so. If I proceed with caution,
 I believe I can take this cold world on.
 What affected me most was the grim shock;
 That way I shall not again be so caught.
 Besides, in part, it still appeals to me:
 There's much yet of it which I wish to see."

"What if you have another attack?" Del asked.

"Then to this green we must make haste
 And not one precious second waste."

"And if we can't make it in time?"

Finn smiled.

"Then strip me, my friend, and bury me deep

And trust the dark lord of the dead to keep

Me safe and sound these long and lonely years.

Think of me sometimes, and shed a few tears."

"You're not taking this seriously," Del growled. "I thought you were going to die."

The fairy shrugged. "And if I had?"

Del blinked. "Dying doesn't bother you?"

"My life I've lived to the glorious hilt;

What matter if the world should tilt

And send me spilling through the ancient dark?

I can say, 'Alive, I'd a lark.'"

Del sighed. "OK, but don't blame me if you go toes-up."

"In the land beyond, I would lay no blame,

In your heart you need feel no crushing shame.

Finn makes his own calls. So be it."

"Fairies!" Del sniffed and dropped back on the grass, where he lay until the ladies arrived, absorbing the rays of the transcendent summer sun.

2. [II] (ii)

The rest of the day passed unremarkably. They had lunch in a cosy café then returned to the park to walk off the meal. They spent a few more hours touring the shops then struck for home.

"What will we do tonight?" Anna asked as she drove, taking it slowly, enjoying the golden tinge of the evening.

"I was thinking of having an early night," Kate said.

"Pooh!" Anna snorted. "This is our last chance to cut loose until the end of the show. We're not going to waste it sitting in."

"How about an expedition to a local public house?" Finn suggested. "I have heard much about those places. We do not have any in –"

"Forget the pubs," Del interjected, elbowing the fairy in the ribs. "How about a campfire?"

Anna frowned. "We're in the middle of a forest, Del. Open fires aren't a good idea."

"We'll be careful," Del said.

"What about a barbecue?" she replied.

"Everybody has barbecues," Del laughed. "When was the last time you sat by an open fire and cooked sausages on sticks and leapt through the flames with your skirt bunched above your knees?"

"He makes it sound attractive," Kate smiled.

"Of course," Del said craftily, "Terence might not approve. Perhaps we should check with him before we finalise any plans."

Anna snorted. "Like *he* knows anything about setting fires. Last time I trusted him with a box of matches, he set his eyebrows ablaze." She considered it, but only briefly, mention of Terence having already decided her. "We'll do it."

"Hurrah!" the others cheered.

"But we keep it small," she warned, "and we take care, and if I don't get the pick of the sausages, there'll be hell to pay."

They passed Felix on their way back. He was sitting atop a gate, staring down between his knees. They stopped and told him about their plans for the night. He promised to tell Nuala.

"He looked out of sorts," Anna remarked as they pulled away.

"The party will cheer him up," Del assured her.

"So it's a party now," she smiled. "A few minutes ago it was just a fire."

"You can't have a fire without a party," Del grinned. "We'll stick on Beach Boys songs and pretend we're by the sea. The men will wear sarongs and the women will go topless."

"Like hell," Kate cut in. "*We'll* wear sarongs and you lot can go bottomless."

"Couldn't do that," Del grinned. "Not around an open fire. A stray spark might hit the *little man* and send him up in flames."

"Wouldn't be much of a loss, I'd guess," Kate sniffed.

"Maybe not me," Del agreed, "but Diarmid's allegedly a ten-incher."

"Ten inches?" Kate asked, studying the supposed banker in a fresh light.

"Ten inches of what?" Finn asked innocently and couldn't understand why everyone burst out laughing.

They dropped by Don and Ingmar's cottage to invite them to the festivities. The pair were sitting in deckchairs out front, butt naked. Ingmar draped a towel across his lap when he spotted the car approaching but Don let his tackle dangle freely, unperturbed by the inquisitive gazes of the Players.

"Having fun?" Anna asked, rolling down the window.

"Relaxing," Don said. "We had a busy afternoon."

"Doing what, I wonder?" Anna smirked, ogling the tall man's exposed organs.

"Have you no shame?" Kate called from the back seat.

"Nothing to be ashamed of," Don replied.

"You see what I have to put up with?" Ingmar sighed.

Anna told the lounging couple about the campfire and party.

"I might come in a toga," Don mused.

"Why not come as you are?" Anna suggested.

"And risk roasting my nuts? No thank you."

Anna glanced at Kate and the women shared a rare laugh. "Must be an inbred fear of every member of the species," Kate giggled.

"Do you have speakers for our phones?" Anna asked Ingmar.

"I never leave home without them," Ingmar said. "I'll be happy to play DJ too."

"Until tonight then," Anna said, driving on.

"You can be a repulsive beast sometimes," Ingmar smiled, leaning across to deliver a playful sock to Don's jaw. "Poor Diarmid didn't know where to look."

"If you can't stand the heat..." Don winked.

"What say we head indoors?" Ingmar asked.

"*Again*?" Don rolled his eyes. "I'm nothing but a sex machine to you."

"True," Ingmar laughed. "And you'd better hope your gears don't wear down or it'll be goodnight Vienna and onto pastures new."

"So cruel." Don pretended to sob.

"Come on," Ingmar said, dragging the taller man to his feet. "We won't have much time if we're going to this party."

"We'll have time," Don assured him, removing Ingmar's towel and admiring his naked form. "I can work quickly when I have to."

*

They built the fire in the middle of a copse near Anna and Terence's home. The branches of the trees hung well back from the centre and there was no wind to carry live sparks.

The fire was lit at eight but the party didn't swing into gear until after nine, as the sky began to darken.

Terence hadn't come – he was glued to his computer and rudely waved away Anna when she interrupted him to ask – and Felix turned up without Nuala, saying she wasn't feeling well (in truth he hadn't returned home to invite her), but several people from neighbouring houses wandered in and were welcomed, and by ten the tiny glade was packed with life, laughter and song.

Ingmar only played a few tracks in the end, as the revellers supplied their own songs. Ingmar would have been annoyed any other time but tonight he sang more than any of them, showing off his new, bewitching voice.

"Can you grant anyone the gift of song?" Del asked Finn as the German led the way through a rousing version of Leonard Cohen's *Hallelujah*.

"Only if they have the potential," Finn said.

"Do you think *I* have potential?" Del asked. "I fancy myself as a singer."

Finn shook his head. "When the gods of music passed you as a child, somebody had their fingers in your ears."

"Oh well," Del shrugged. "I'll settle for the sweet music of chaos. Now," he said, lowering his voice, "are we clear on the agenda?"

Finn nodded. "I will set pulses racing with my charm and otherworldly allures, yes?"

"Yes," Del agreed, "but play it cool. Save the actual sex for later."

"I am looking forward to my first carnal bout," Finn said. "Celibacy never suited me, perhaps because I am not Fey born."

"Look forward to it all you want," Del said, "but don't rush it. Your time will come. A couple more days and you can rut away to your heart's content."

"And you want me to target Ingmar first?" Finn asked.

"Yes," Del said. "The dust has worked its magic and he's ready to fall into your arms. It's time to let him know you wouldn't be averse to such an encounter. Plant the seed of a liaison in his mind, but don't let him plant *his* seed."

"It shall be as you say. And after Ingmar, Kate?"

"Yes," Del said, "but wait for the signal. Mingle with the others when you're done with Ingmar, and I'll give you the nod when it's time to make the move."

"You are sure Kate is attracted to me?" Finn asked.

"She's got a soft spot for you," Del assured him, "and I'm going to feed her a few lies that'll have her chasing you from here to Donegal. Now, all set?"

"Ready and willing," Finn replied.

"Very well." Del breathed in smoke from the fire and smiled sultrily. "Let's hunt!"

*

"Your voice is still improving," Finn noted, tapping Ingmar's shoulder.

"It's magnificent," the German agreed, turning to welcome his mentor. Those around him were pleading for another song but he waved them away and led Finn aside, where they squatted to chat. "I recorded myself yesterday. When I played it back, it took my breath away. How can I have had this voice all these years and never uncovered it?"

"There is no magic involved," Finn lied. "You could have been singing like a lark long before this if the right person had taken an interest in you."

"But how do I do it?" Ingmar asked. "I've been practising the exercises you set, and gargling that oil of yours, but surely there's more to it?"

Finn smiled. "The mastery of song is no great mystery. Some people chance upon the techniques themselves. Others need guidance."

"Were you guided?" Ingmar asked.

"Yes," Finn said, pulling a sad face as Del had taught him. "I met a wonderful man one day, walking by the banks of the Shannon. He looked lonely, so I sat and tried striking up a conversation with him. He replied to none of my overtures, but when I rose to leave, he produced a tin flute and played a haunting melody, then told me to sing. He began playing again and, to my joy, I found myself singing along. When the tune ended, I asked if it was magic. He shook his head and told me music was like air — what one person breathed out, another breathed in. He said he had merely breathed his music into me."

Finn stopped and gazed at the fire, trying to look moody and mysterious.

"What..." Ingmar stopped and cleared his throat. "What happened to the man?"

"I do not know," Finn said. "I left in a daze and did not look back. I never saw him again." Finn allowed a sob-like sound to escape. "I think of him often. Many times I have wondered what would have happened if I had stayed."

Ingmar stared at the banker's long face. The story had touched him (as Del guessed it might) and in his mind it had nothing to do with music — it was a tale of unrequited, unrecognised love.

"There, there," he said, draping an arm around the banker. Finn clutched the limb. As Ingmar looked at him, Finn shyly ran a finger from Ingmar's elbow down to the wrist, and smiled like a vixen.

*

Don noticed the lingering embrace – he'd been watching Finn and Ingmar closely from the opposite side of the fire – and his nostrils flared.

"Reckon there's something going on there?" Del asked. He

had been hovering behind the bald drama teacher, waiting for the right moment to step in.

"What do you mean?" Don asked.

"Diarmid and Ingmar," Del leered.

"I beg your pardon," Don said icily, "but Ingmar and I are a couple."

"It's hardly a monogamous relationship," Del purred. "From what Ingmar's said, I thought the two of you were free to wander as you pleased."

"When did he say that?" Don barked.

"He's said it a few times," Del replied. "He's been over our place a lot recently and he happened to remark one night that –"

"It's a lie," Don hissed. "Ingmar and I are true to each other."

Del appeared crestfallen. "Maybe he said it as a joke and I took it the wrong way. I'm always making silly slips like that."

"Spreading vicious rumours of that kind will win you no friends," Don growled.

"Sorry," Del said. "I wouldn't have said anything, only, seeing them together like that, I thought..."

"*What?*"

Del shrugged. "I'd better not say."

"*Say.*"

"They look cute together."

"They're not *together*," Don steamed. "They just happen to be sitting side by side." He hesitated and glanced at the canoodling pair. "With their arms around each other," he reluctantly added.

"It's probably entirely innocent," Del said.

"I'm sure it is."

"Nothing to it at all."

"Of course not."

"Still," Del said, "I've felt uncomfortable around Diarmid this last week. I never know quite how to act around your kind."

"My kind?" Don blinked.

"You know..." Del lowered his voice. "Gays."

"Diarmid isn't gay," Don snorted.

Del stared at Don as if the taller man was batty. "You didn't know?"

"Know what?"

"I thought it was common knowledge."

"*What* is common knowledge?"

"Of course I could be wrong," Del muttered. "He hasn't actually said..."

"Are you trying to tell me," Don said slowly, "that Diarmid is homosexual?"

"That's the impression I got," Del said. "He's wandered into the bathroom more than once while I've been in the tub. And he's *very* touchy-feely. Then there's his browsing history."

"*Browsing*...?" Don couldn't believe he was hearing this, yet at the same time it never occurred to him that Del might be making it up.

"I needed to get online," Del said. "Diarmid's laptop was on the table. I didn't mean to pry but the history box was open and I couldn't help but notice all the gay porn links."

Don's face blanched.

"So when Ingmar started dropping in," Del went on, "and I saw how close they were getting and heard what he said about being free to play the field, I assumed... Hey, where are you going?" Don had stopped listening and was storming away.

"To break up a courtship," the big man snarled.

"I hope it wasn't something *I* said," Del smirked, then dodged around the fire to find a position which afforded a clearer view.

*

Ingmar was explaining his theory of interstellar propagation – it was his belief that mankind's ancestors had been dropped on this planet by a passing spaceship – when he felt a large paw grab his arm. Turning, he found himself staring up into two red bowls of fire. "Don," the DJ grinned shakily. "Vot is –"

"We're going home," Don snapped. "Now!"

"But I vas talking vith –"

"I know what you're up to," Don shouted, "and *talk* has nothing to do with it."

"Wait," Finn murmured. "You have caught the wrong end of the stick."

"It's more than *you'll* catch," Don growled.

"Don!" Ingmar gasped. "Vot has got into you? You're acting like a madman. Calm down dis instant or I'll –"

"You'll do nothing," Don swore, tugging Ingmar to his feet, and without another word he dragged Ingmar away. The German screamed and kicked at his captor but he was powerless in the larger man's grip.

"I'm sorry," Ingmar called to the startled onlookers. "I don't know vot's come over him. Please don't let it spoil the party..."

The two disappeared into the trees, arguing loudly. While everyone else was staring after them, Finn sought out Del and they exchanged congratulatory grins.

"Two down," Finn whispered out of the corner of his mouth.

"Five to go," Del concluded with a wink.

*

While Del set about ensnaring Kate, Finn passed the time talking with Anna. He liked the older woman. She was his twin's best friend and he could see why. She was a plain, uncomplicated, honest person, and there was a lot to be said for that.

Anna was wearing an old-fashioned summer dress and keeping a close watch on the flames when Finn sat down beside her.

"It is a grand fire," Finn said, warming his hands.

"A little too grand," Anna said. "I was letting it burn out but some idiot tossed a fresh load of logs on when I wasn't looking."

"That was me," Finn said, then laughed at her sharp look. "I kid you. I do not know who fed the flames. Do you want me to make enquiries?"

"No," Anna said. "It's fine." She lay back and smiled. "You're in high spirits these days."

"The sun has affected me."

"You've never been this giddy before."

Finn shrugged. "It was time for a change. Do you agree?"

"I liked you the way you were," Anna said.

"More than you like me now?" he asked.

"I wouldn't say that." Her smile widened. "It's nice to see this new side of you, but I don't think you *needed* to change."

"Change is good," Finn declared.

"No arguments there," Anna sighed. "I could do with a change or two myself."

Finn studied the woman in the glare of the fire. "Your marriage is not fulfilling you," he noted.

Anna glanced at him, surprised. "Not like you to pass such an open comment."

"But it is true, aye?" he persisted.

She nodded. "It's true."

"You are thinking of breaking your vows?"

"Maybe. I don't know. There are the children to consider."

"Children need love to flourish," Finn said.

Anna blinked. "You're saying I should leave Terence?"

"I am saying you should not make excuses not to," Finn corrected her. "I am no expert and have no wish to interfere, but I believe you should follow your heart, no matter how hard the path. Your children may find it easier to love you if they sense love *in* you."

"You're very wise tonight," Anna remarked.

"To every fool, a moment of pure insight," Finn chuckled.

One of the revellers stepped too close to the fire and his foot sent a shower of sparks shooting up into the air. Finn and Anna watched silently as the tiny flickers quenched and vanished into the night.

"It's not just the children," Anna said as darkness returned. "Where would I go? How would I start over? I'd be lonely. I've never lived as an adult by myself. I wouldn't know how to survive as a solo act."

"You could find another partner," Finn said.

"Too old," Anna sighed. "Too ugly."

"You are not old," Finn said earnestly. "Nor ugly. The world is full of men who would love a woman like you."

Anna laughed. "A greying frump with one foot in the grave?"

"You are not old," Finn said again, firmly this time.

"But I feel old," Anna sighed.

Finn's eyes narrowed. "How old?"

"Like a woman of sixty," Anna groaned.

"That is easily cured," he told her.

"Sure, a face-lift and liposuction and I'd be good as new," she smirked.

"I am serious," he said. "Feeling old is an ill which may be simply rectified."

Anna sniffed. "In that case, go ahead and rectify me. What's your prescription? Funny movies? Dirty jokes?"

"Burn your knickers," Finn said.

Anna coughed. "Excuse me?"

"Burn your knickers," Finn beamed.

"Are you kidding?" she squealed.

"You are wearing knickers?"

"Of course."

"Then slip them off. Nobody will see. Your dress is long and will cover your modesty. Ball them up and toss them on the fire. Watch them burn. Tell me then how old you feel."

"You're crazy," Anna gasped.

"Only old people are crazy," Finn said. "The young are eccentric." He leaned close to her. "Be eccentric, Anna."

She stared at him and then, before she had time to analyse it, her hands rode up beneath her dress, snagged the elastic rim of her knickers and yanked them down more fiercely than she'd intended. The knickers caught on her heels but one good kick and they were free. She held them up wonderingly.

"Feel the grass," Finn said. As she lowered her hands, he corrected her. "Not with your fingers — with your bare cheeks."

She shook her head wordlessly but gave her backside an exploratory wiggle. A look of delight crossed her face and she shifted her bum about with more fervour, flattening the grass around her in a wide, uneven circle.

"Well?" Finn smiled.

"It feels entirely different," she gushed.

"Remember that feeling the next time your years weigh heavily on you," he urged her. "Only a young woman reacts to so basic a delight. Now, the *coup de grace*." He nodded towards the flames.

Anna licked her lips hesitantly, glanced around the copse to ensure no one was watching, then tossed the garment high above the tongues of the fire. The hot air forced the material to billow outwards, and for a horrified instant she was sure the knickers would float into the sky for all to see, but then they collapsed, landed on a log and singed at the edges. The middle turned yellow, then red, and within seconds they were a ball of burning flame.

Anna watched the knickers burn down to ash, feeling a heat between her legs which was a match for that of the fire. When she faced Finn, it was with an awed expression.

"You see?" he said smugly.

"Yes," she breathed, touching his hands with one of her own, staring into his eyes but not really seeing him, imagining instead a brave knight who had ridden to her rescue and rid her of the awful knot of worry in her gut. "Yes," she said again. "I see." And this time her hand closed over his, her sentiments plain to read. Those sentiments were lost on the innocent Finn, but not on Del, whose mischievous gaze missed nothing.

*

Del was with Felix, Kate and a handful of the neighbours. At some point, several deckchairs had materialised, and Kate was reclining in one, waited upon by a number of excited young men — Kate Pummel was a girl who knew how to play to a crowd.

Del had mingled with those on their feet for a while, before working his way through to Kate's side, where he'd stubbornly remained, despite some digs in the back and kicks from would-be love rivals.

Felix was getting drunk and creating a scene. Kate had offered him her chair but he refused to sit. At first he'd rambled on about nothing, boring all within earshot, but as the night progressed, he'd started weaving amusing tales and was now the centre of attention, bleary-eyed but silver-tongued.

He was acting out scenes from Nuala's books, and his hilarious renditions – he recited her clumsy lines with a straight expression – had reduced several of his audience members to tears of laughter.

"If Nuala hears about this, she'll string him up," Kate giggled to Del.

"And not by the neck," Del agreed.

"Then," Felix roared behind them, "Lady Petrella knocked the soup bowl to the floor." He made a sweeping motion with an unsteady arm. "'That too-sweet soup is poisoned!'" he squeaked, adopting a shrill voice. "'And there sits the man who poisoned it!' she yelled, pointing at Prince Gorvial, the King's half-brother — a dwarf." Felix squatted and narrowed his eyes. "'It couldn't have been me,'" he said in a gruff voice. "'I'm too short to reach the table.'"

"Are the books really that awful?" Del asked Kate.

"From what I've read of them, yes," Kate winced. "He's being cruel but true to the source. Actually," she added in a lower voice, "from what Terence told me, I believe they had a humongous spat following the publication of that book — *The Dwarf Prince*. You know how sensitive Felix is about his height. He thought she was having a dig at him. It's the only one of her novels that they don't have in their library at home — it's tucked away in her wardrobe."

"'You tall people don't understand us short people,'" Felix yelled. "'We have feelings too, just in smaller measures.'"

Del, who'd been watching Finn and Anna out of the corner of his eye, decided it was time to press the changeling's case. He affected a heavy sigh, tapped Kate's arm and directed her attention towards the distant pair.

"There's the man *I* envy," he said.

"Diarmid?" Kate asked, squinting.

"He's going places," Del said wistfully, sipping at the glass of wine that he'd hardly touched all night.

"Going where?" Kate asked.

"Nowhere," Del said, trying to blush. "I didn't... I mean, I shouldn't... Oh, what the hell, I have to tell someone." He whispered in the actress' ear. "He's in the middle of negotiating a movie deal."

Kate laughed uncertainly. "*Diarmid*?"

"I heard him on the phone a few days ago," Del lied. "He's about to sign with a renowned British studio. They want to make films over here because of some tax incentive. It's a three-film deal. They've promised him a decent support role in each feature."

"Diarmid. In the movies." Kate looked flummoxed. "How? He doesn't act in anything other than *A Midsummer Night's Dream*. Are you sure of this?"

"Positive," Del said. "He's not just been hired as an actor. He's also a financial partner — a producer. That's how he got involved in the first place. One of the studio bigwigs was over here. He met Diarmid through the bank and recognised him from when he was here on holiday and saw the Players perform. A few days later he rang Diarmid for financial advice. They arranged a meeting and things progressed when Diarmid learnt that they were looking for an investor to help out on the producing side. He offered to put his own money in and –"

"What money?" Kate interrupted.

"Diarmid's rich," Del said. "Didn't you know?"

She shook her head, eyes wide.

"Anyway," Del continued, "the studio guy took Diarmid up on his offer but he also flew over their director, who screen-tested Diarmid and said he was just what they'd been looking for, and the upshot is that Diarmid's going to be a producer *and* an actor."

"I can't believe it." Kate didn't know whether to laugh or cry. "Why hasn't he said anything to us?"

"You know what Diarmid's like," Del replied. "Plays things close to his chest. I've been tempted to bend his ear since finding out, but I don't think I'm —"

"Bend his ear for what?" Kate asked sharply.

Del hid his smile. "A part in the movie."

Kate's eyes grew round. "Diarmid's involved in casting?"

"He's a producer," Del said. "Producers can hire whoever they want."

"Diarmid... movie... casting..."

Del saw dreams blossom to life inside Kate. Part of him felt guilty for the crash that lay in wait at the end (that small part of him always stung when his actions threatened to cause people hurt, as it had when he'd turned Don against Ingmar earlier in the night — it was why he would never make a true villain), but acting was a hard life. You had to be tough to make a go of it. If Kate couldn't bounce back from this, she really didn't deserve to be in the game.

"That's probably another reason he's keeping the news to himself," Del said. "If word spread among the Players, we'd all be pestering him for a role. You won't tell the others, will you? I'd hate for him to know that I'd eavesdropped."

"I won't breathe a word," Kate promised, gaze fixed on the nondescript banker as if he was Cecil B. DeMille.

"I bet you won't," Del muttered softly, then left her to her dreams and turned to find out what happened to the dwarf prince at the end of Felix's story.

*

Anna told Finn she'd be back in a couple of minutes, then retreated discreetly into the forest, where she found a bush and watered the lilies. She smiled when her hands automatically searched for her knickers, then stood and smoothed out the creases in her skirt.

Her conversation with Finn had provided her with the brightest moments of the entire week... the month... the year! In fact she couldn't recall when she'd last felt so alive. Finn had given no indication that he was attracted to her but a churning in her gut insisted the young banker fancied her. After so many years of feeling unwanted, it was marvellous to be desired.

"I am sixteen, going on seventeen," she half sang. "Oh, Master Garrigan, sir, we shouldn't!" She almost skipped back to the party, light of spirit and free of heart. Nothing could take this joy away from her. She was on cloud nine, everything was dandy, and...

Entering the copse, she froze as her universe shattered. There, on the other side of the fire, Kate Pummel had an arm snaked round Diarmid, a lewd smile plastered to her face. She was leading him away from those nearest them, to the edge of the copse, where they lay beneath a huge tree, immersing themselves in shadows.

"Diarmid's made a conquest," Del chuckled, popping up at the frozen woman's side. "Must be a weight off your mind."

"I... what... huh?" Anna was finding words hard to come by.

Del coughed. "Most of us are aware of the tension between yourself, Terence and Kate. We think a lot of you and Terence, and we'd hate to see anything upset your marriage. If Kate's interest has shifted to Diarmid, that's a good thing."

"The bitch," Anna said softly. "She's out to destroy me. First she seduces my husband. Now she steals Diarmid from me."

"Diarmid?" Del acted surprised. "I thought you were just good friends."

Anna shook her head bitterly and didn't reply.

"That really grates with me," Del said. "I despise women who can't keep their hands off taken men. Aren't there enough free guys in the world? It would be great to bring her down a peg or two."

"There's nothing you can do to a woman like that," Anna said glumly.

"I'm not so sure," Del said. "Every woman has a weak point — pride. No one likes being bested by another. If you hit her where it hurts, she'd feel it."

"What are you talking about?" Anna asked.

"Diarmid's a windsock," Del said. "He'll blow with the breeze. Kate can't be around him all the time. If an enterprising lady were to play up to him..."

Anna's lips pursed thoughtfully. "Could I...?" she whispered.

"Of course," Del egged her on. "If you turn on your charms and —"

"He made me burn my knickers," Anna said.

Del blinked, momentarily knocked off course. "Pardon?"

"He made me take them off and toss them on the fire."

Del whistled. "Well, there you go. That's a sure sign of interest. Let Kate fool about with him tonight. Let her think she's won. Tomorrow, you start. Take your time. Tease him. Make him want you like he's never wanted anyone before. Then, when the time is ripe and Kate's seething with jealousy..."

"...tear into him," Anna concluded, licking her lips with relish.

"I don't think you need be quite so savage," Del said.

"I'll rip him to pieces," she growled lustily.

"I'm not sure —" Del began but was quickly silenced.

"I'll make him my love-slave," Anna purred. "I'll torture him with delight and leave him begging for more. By the time I'm finished, he'll be crawling to me on all fours, wailing for mercy. When I've destroyed him completely, I'll parade him before Terence and Kate." She turned her back on the pair, the fire and the copse, and glided off into the night like a deadly bird of prey, leaving a slack-jawed Del to wonder how much of her intent he should convey to his innocent friend.

*

As the embers of the fire glowed dully in the early hours of the morning, and those who'd partied the night away slipped back to their beds, Del decided there was one more flame to be fanned before calling an end to the night's work. He told Finn to take Kate home but to do it quietly and not let anyone see.

"And if she asks me in?" Finn enquired.

"Gently refuse," Del told him.

"What if she insists?"

Del went eyeball to eyeball with the changeling. "Re. Fuse."

"Spoilsport," Finn sulked.

Del waited until the pair had departed, then homed in on the intoxicated Felix. The insurance agent had run out of wind a couple of hours earlier and sunk into a vacant deckchair, where he now sat muttering to himself about virulent wives, hen-pecked husbands, cross-dressing and height restrictions.

"Enjoy the party?" Del asked, pulling up a chair for himself.

Felix glared at his fellow Player and snorted something unintelligible.

"What was that?" Del asked.

"Too tall," Felix barked. "All of you. Giants. Serve you right if gravity... bloody big..." He trailed off into a series of bitter noises which even Henry Higgins would have had trouble deciphering.

"Did you enjoy the party?" Del tried again when Felix had rumbled to a halt.

"Party?" A faint smile lifted the corners of Felix's mouth. "Yes, that was fun. I danced a polka."

"Did you?" Del asked, wondering which party the soused Felix was recalling.

"I danced a polka in a polka-dot dress," Felix giggled. "Nuala's. Too big." He started guiltily. "She's not here, is she?"

"No," Del assured him. "Nuala isn't here."

"She doesn't like me talking about her dresses," Felix said. "Says it's unmanly. Doesn't understand." He burped. "Just getting in touch with my feminine side."

"Of course," Del agreed, inwardly wondering what the hell the short man was babbling about. "Have you seen Kate recently?"

"Kate?" Felix echoed. "What does she look like? Is...? Oh, *Kate*. No, I haven't seen her."

"I've been looking for her for ages," Del said.

"Have you?" Felix smiled stupidly.

"Last time I saw her," Del said slowly, "she told me she was going to check on Nuala."

"Girls' night out," Felix said, nodding absentmindedly.

"She wanted to go and *comfort* her," Del said.

"Everybody needs a little comforting now and then," Felix agreed.

"They're very friendly," Del said. This was proving harder than he'd thought. Would he have to draw a picture to get his unsubtle message across?

"Friends should be friends, right to the end," Felix sang.

"I think Kate has the hots for Nuala," Del said, opting for the blunt approach.

"Hots?" Felix frowned.

"Kate fancies her. I've seen the way she looks at her when you're not about."

"Kate fancies...? That's not right," Felix grunted, twisting in his chair. "It's the other way round. Nuala's the one with eyes for..." He sat up and looked around the copse with renewed interest. "Where's Kate?"

"That's what *I* was asking," Del reminded him. "Last time I saw her, she said she might head over to *your* house. Said Nuala might need some –"

"– *comforting*!" Felix gasped, stumbling out of his chair. "I have to get home. Can't have that sort of thing... my own roof." He clapped Del's back and Del noticed tears in the small man's eyes before he lurched away drunkenly.

Del watched Felix leave and remained in his chair until the glade had cleared. The small man's tears had caused Del to inwardly wince, but as he always did when his conscience interjected, he jutted his chin out stubbornly and waited for the voice of compassion to fall silent. When it did, and he was free to objectively assess the last few hours' activities, he was pleased to note that it had been a productive night. There was still no telling which way the seeds he'd planted would grow, but all in all he felt he was on top of the game.

Finally, in response to the morning breeze and the smouldering campfire, the agent of the fairies wended his way home to bed. When dawn rolled round, the ashes, empty bottles, discarded items of clothes and scraps of rubbish were to be found littered around the copse, but, as with parties the world over, not a single deckchair remained.

ACT THREE

3. [I] (i)

The first scene of the third act involved every Player bar Kate and Don. In the play, Titania is asleep on stage. Oberon has applied his secret potion to her eyes while she was sleeping, so she'll fall in love with the first person she sees when she wakes. Puck, meanwhile, has used his portion of the love juice on Lysander, mistaking him for Demetrius. When Lysander wakes near the end of the second act, he falls head over heels for Helena, who believes he's mocking her and runs away. Lysander deserts his true love, Hermia, to follow his new object of fixation.

The act would begin with the play's amateur performers entering the glade where Titania sleeps, to practise their lines. Finn was lined up as Bottom, Ingmar as Quince, Nuala as Starveling, Terence as Snug, Felix as Flute. The part of Snout had been written out and Terence had added the character's lines to his own.

It was meant to be a quick-moving scene in which Puck substitutes Bottom's head for that of an ass, the rest of the actors run off in fear, and Titania falls for the pompous, disfigured Bottom. Normally the Players raced through it, but most were out of sorts after the party and stuttered through unsteadily.

Felix's head was ringing. He couldn't remember how much he'd had to drink, or what he'd been up to – the entire evening was a blank – but he guessed it hadn't been pretty. His fellow Players had been slapping his back all morning, grinning wickedly, while Nuala hadn't said a word to him.

Nuala had sat up in bed for hours, prepared to forgive and forget. When Felix hadn't materialised by midnight, she'd switched off the light and sunk into a furious sleep. That would have been bad enough, but then Felix rolled in in the early hours, roaring Kate's name, demanding to know where his wife was hiding her. He searched the entire house, flicking on all the lights, screaming something about not allowing Kate to whisk his wife away from him.

Anna was distant, planning her conquest of Diarmid. She was confident of winning him over, but she also wanted to hurt Terence while wooing his friend — this was revenge time. Would it be best to be discreet and let word of her affair slip over breakfast? Or should she go for the jugular and allow Terrence to find herself and Diarmid in the glade one morning, naked, panting, covered in sweat? It was a tough call and it was distracting her.

Kate was also preoccupied with Diarmid Garrigan. She'd never studied him at length before, but now that she did, she had to admit he was by no means repulsive. But even if he'd been hideously deformed, she would have found him to her liking. *Movies*. The word had echoed through her head all night. A real-life movie producer, and she had the chance to seduce him.

But could she be so mercenary? Though she'd initiated relationships with men who could help her career in the past, she'd never set out to bed a man purely for a break. She had always been attracted to them. If she went after Diarmid, it would only be to star in a movie. Was she ready to go to that extreme?

The answer, she'd concluded after a night of soul-searching, was yes. When she was rich and famous, she could go on a chat show, sob about it and clear her conscience, as was the fashion for celebrities these days.

Finn's distracted state was a result of Del's telling him he had to seduce Anna as well as Kate and Ingmar. He felt too much was being asked of him. Besides, he liked Anna and didn't want to harm her. "It is unnecessary," he'd pouted. "She was not part of the original Plan."

"The Plan's evolving all the time," Del said. "Don't blame me — you're the one who ordered her to whisk off her knickers."

"I was only being kind," Finn protested.

"This world wasn't meant for kindness," Del told him brutally. "As of today, whenever Anna smiles at you, reply with a wink. That's an order."

Finn was considering fleeing back to the land of the fey. He wasn't enjoying the fiasco. He'd grown attached to these silly, bickering humans and no longer wished to see them flounder. He'd give it a few more days, but if things didn't shape up to his liking, he'd flit to Feyland and cower beneath a bush until this was over.

Ingmar and Don had passed a tight-lipped night together. Don was convinced something was brewing between Ingmar and Diarmid, and would hear nothing of Ingmar's protests.

"I wouldn't cheat on you," Ingmar told him. "Not here, with the play coming up, and certainly not with one of your friends."

"Meaning you *would* cheat in Dublin, with a stranger?" Don snapped.

"That's not what I meant," Ingmar whined.

"Tell it to your fancy boy," Don sniffed.

The row had upset Ingmar. He wouldn't have minded if he'd been guilty, but they hadn't got up to anything. (*Yet.*) He was being punished for something he hadn't done and that was an unusual experience — normally Don's suspicions were justly grounded.

Terence, meanwhile, was fretting over the attention that Kate was lavishing on Diarmid. Yesterday he'd convinced himself that he was imagining the connection between them. Today it was impossible to ignore the way her gaze followed the nondescript banker around the glade. (He hadn't noticed Anna's similar obsession with their old friend.) He was sorry he hadn't attended the party. Something must have passed between them. But *what*?

Del was the only Player in high spirits. From his perspective this was a glorious day and he delighted in every sour look and mutter. He was careful to adopt a dour expression to match the other sullen faces, and spoke his lines with as little enthusiasm as the rest, but inside his heart was singing.

*

Things livened up in the afternoon, when they moved onto the second half of the scene, where Titania wakes and falls in love with Bottom. They didn't bother with the cumbersome ass' head in rehearsal. It was safely stashed away in Terence's attic and would be brought down only on the day of the performance.

Anna got as close to Finn as she could, and uttered her

lines with a deep throb in her throat and a minxish gleam in her eye.

"'What angel wakes me from my flowery bed?'" she cooed as she stretched her arms and yawned. (She was wearing a tight shirt, to highlight her cleavage.)

Finn sang a little song – disguising his usually magnificent voice in order not to take away from Ingmar – and muttered a couple of lines in a disinterested fashion. He got a shock when Anna wrapped her arms around him and stroked him in places where his own hands would have paused.

"'I pray thee, gentle mortal, sing again;

Mine ear is much enamoured of thy note.

So is mine eye enthralled to thy shape,

And thy fair virtue's force perforce doth move me

On the first view to say, to swear, I love thee.'"

Finn gawped at the actress, not sure how to respond.

"Go on, Diarmid," Terence chuckled. "Put some heart into it."

Finn cleared his throat and continued with his lines. When Anna came to her next sizeable chunk of text, she smothered him in caressing, quivering flesh.

"'Out of this wood do not desire to go:

Thou shalt remain here, whether thou wilt or no.

I am a spirit of no common rate;

The summer still doth tend upon my state,

And I do love thee. Therefore...'"

Terence's brow furrowed as he realised how turned-on Anna was. She appeared on the verge of ripping off Diarmid's clothes and ravaging him. Was it the play she was so enamoured with, or the Player?

The director chewed a fingernail while considering this fresh twist. To the best of his knowledge, Anna had never been unfaithful. Regardless of how much he'd fooled around, Anna had always been waiting for him at home, and he'd assumed she always would be. He should have been excited by the idea of his wife's possible infidelity — it would be the excuse he needed to break with her and head off into the sunset with Kate. But Terence wasn't at all excited. Instead he found himself surprisingly wrathful.

Ingmar's gaze was glued to Anna's hands as they roamed Finn's body. He was imagining his own hands in those positions. When a couple of her fingers brushed the actor's groin, the DJ had to fan his face with his copy of the play to hide his lecherous blush. And when it came time for Ingmar to play one of the fairies assigned to tend to Bottom by Titania, he tucked his hands into his armpits to stop them straying to join Anna's.

"'Be kind and courteous to this gentleman,'" Anna ordered the fairies. "'Hop in his walks and gambol in his eyes.'"

"I wouldn't mind a *gambol* or two," Ingmar sighed to himself.

"'Feed him with apricocks'" – Ingmar made a strange choking noise at that point and had to turn aside to muffle the sound – "'and dewberries.'"

"It's too much," Ingmar groaned.

"Are you alright?" Terence enquired, glad to interrupt.

"Stomach pains," the German gasped.

"Can you continue," Terence asked, "or do you want to take five?"

"I'll be fine," Ingmar promised. "Just a passing pain."

"It had better be *passing*," Don sniffed, having guessed from the bulge in his lover's trousers the real cause of Ingmar's discomfort.

"OK," Terence said. "Anna, you're on."

"'Peaseblossom, Cobweb and dear Mustardseed!'" Anna trilled, never releasing her vice-like grip on the trapped Finn. (The 'dear' was Terence's addition. Having dropped Moth – one of the fairies – he had affected the iambic pentameter and felt the inclusion of an extra syllable would merit the approval of the author.)

"'Ready,'" Nuala boomed as Peaseblossom.

"'And I,'" trilled Terence as Cobweb.

Ingmar took a final breath, then turned. "'And I,'" he sighed as Mustardseed.

Anna gave the trio their orders, then bid them make themselves known to the ass-headed Bottom.

"'Hail, mortal!'" Nuala cried, bowing to Finn.

"'Hail!'" Terence tittered, waving a hand.

Ingmar hesitated, then dropped to one knee, snatched Finn's left hand away from the grasping Anna and touched it to his lips. "'Hail,'" he said softly.

"That's not in the play," Don shrieked.

"I'm improvising," Ingmar said, pecking Finn's fingers one by one. "'Hail!'" he called out cheekily each time his mouth puckered.

"Terence," Don roared. "Are you going to let him get away with that?"

"I think it adds to the mirth," Terence purred.

"I like it too," Del said quickly.

"It's a good idea," Felix said. "Especially since you've altered the text to refer to him as *dear* Mustardseed."

"Hark at Mr Critic," Nuala snorted, jealous that all the attention was now focused on Ingmar.

"It's a wonderful idea," Kate chipped in.

"There we have it," Terence decided.

"But it's homosexual," Don protested. "One man kissing another's hand... If *I'd* suggested that, you'd have shouted me down."

Terence frowned. "Ingmar's playing a fairy who's been told to fuss over Bottom. Nobody will read anything into a humorous knuckle kiss."

"But..." Don shook his head. "Forget it," he growled, then sat down in a huff.

The actors returned to the play. Finn asked the three fairies for their names, then made antique jokes about their derivations. As Titania launched into the final speech of the scene, Ingmar locked gazes with Finn.

"'Come, wait upon him. Lead him to my bower.

The moon methinks looks with a watery eye,

And when she weeps, weeps every little flower,

Lamenting some enforced chastity.

Tie up my lover's tongue; bring him silently.'"

The fairies were supposed to clamp their hands over Finn's mouth at that point and lead him off, but before Nuala and Terence could act, Ingmar pushed a startled Anna aside, threw his arms around Finn and dove in for a passionate kiss.

"No!" Don roared, coming to his feet in a rage. "I'm not having that!"

"It *is* a little strong," Terence agreed, ogling the kissing pair.

"Well, he *was* ordered to 'tie up' Bottom's tongue," Felix chortled.

"Pull him off," Anna screeched, battering Ingmar's shoulders with her fists.

"I think Diarmid would love to be *pulled off*," Del murmured in her ear, unable to hide his impish grin.

"This isn't right," Kate shouted, seeing a threat to her dreams of fame in the unexpected clinch.

"Go, Ingmar," Nuala cheered, believing the kiss to be a joke.

"He'll smother that boy if he's not careful," Felix noted.

"No!" Don was roaring. "No! No! No!"

Finally, slowly, the embracing actors drew apart. Finn was smiling oddly, while Ingmar's radiant glow verged on the radioactive.

"Um... Ingmar?" Terence said. Ingmar turned giddily, as if in a dream. "I don't think we can allow that. Kissing the fingers is one thing, but –"

"– sucking face is a disgrace," Kate hissed.

Del came to Ingmar's defence. "He was only being literal."

"I don't know about literal," Felix laughed. "He was certainly being *liberal*."

"Did he hurt you?" Anna squealed, rushing to Finn's side.

Finn laughed. "He opened up new windows of delight. Sun now shines where my soul knew only night. How could there be hurt in so joyous a kiss?"

"*Joyous?*" Anna gasped. "Oh, Diarmid," she sobbed and lurched away, wailing, "Betrayed!"

"Ingmar, I'm sorry," Terence said, "but there's no way we can –"

"It's alright," Ingmar said, emerging from his daze. "I was only testing a theory. We don't have to use it in the play."

Terence relaxed. "That's OK then."

"No it's not," Don bellowed and dug a finger into Ingmar's chest. "What the hell are you up to?"

"Exploring the parameters of the role," Ingmar grinned.

"Exploring the parameters of Diarmid's arse, more like," Don replied.

"What can I say?" Ingmar smirked. "I lost myself in the play."

"You'll say more later, trust me," Don barked, giving Ingmar's chest another dig, then turned his back on his lover and took off. He paused at the edge of the glade and pointed an angry finger at Finn. "As for *you*..." His finger shook and his jaw worked itself up and down. He tried issuing a threat but his mouth wouldn't form the words, and in the end he just stuck the finger up rudely and left it at that.

Ingmar knew there'd be hell to pay for this but he didn't care. If nothing else came of his pursuit of Diarmid, at least he'd had one moment of bliss. Those supple lips had been like nothing he'd ever experienced — he thought it might be what it would feel like if he could kiss a cloud.

"Well," Del said, moving up close to Finn, "what was your first real kiss like?"

The changeling licked his lips and frowned. "Interesting," he said. "Though as Ingmar stuck his tongue down my throat, I feared I might faint from lack of oxygen. Next time I will take a deep breath before I lock lips."

3.[I](ii)

Rather than abandon rehearsals in the wake of Don and Anna's departure, Terence kept the remaining Players together and spent the afternoon flicking through the last couple of acts. They didn't do much more than read the lines out loud – taking turns to fill in for the missing pair – but it kept them busy.

They wrapped about an hour earlier than usual. It had been an exasperating day. The only positive aspect was that things had to improve from here. Tomorrow, Terence believed, the Players would be back to normal, ready to forge ahead at full speed.

Kate lingered after her fellow actors had departed, then cuddled up to Terence, burrowed her head in his chest and sighed moodily. "I'm glad to see the back of that one," she said.

"Um," Terence grunted. His arms hung loosely around her, not clutching her tight as they usually did.

"Think we'll be ready on time?" she asked.

"Probably."

She dug a finger into his navel and twirled it the way he liked. "Coming over to my place tonight for a little extra *practise*?"

"Maybe," Terence said, not sounding overly eager.

Kate stepped back and stared up at the brooding director. "What's wrong?"

"I'm tired," he said.

"It's not just that. There's something more."

Terence looked worried. "Did you see the way Anna was clawing at Diarmid?"

"Yes," Kate laughed. "Poor Diarmid didn't know where to look."

"Do you think...?" Terence paused.

"What?" Kate prompted him.

"Are Anna and Diarmid getting... *close*?"

"Absolutely not," Kate gasped. "Diarmid could never be attracted to a frumpy old biddy like that. Besides, you told me Anna doesn't fool around."

"People change," Terence said. "She used to be predictable, but now... I don't know. She might be interested in him."

"What if she is?" Kate sniffed. "She'll end up looking like a fool."

"I don't want her to look foolish," Terence snapped.

"Why do you care how she looks?" Kate wondered.

"She's my wife," Terence said stiffly.

"In name only, you told me."

He coughed. "Well, yes, I mean, we haven't been enjoying the best of... but we share the same house and bed. How does it look if she throws herself at every Tom, Dick and Harry?"

"Is that all that's bothering you?" Kate asked quietly. "How it reflects on you?"

"Of course."

"It couldn't be that you still love her and are jealous?"

"Don't be ridiculous." Terence forced a laugh. "I wouldn't be with you if I had any love left for her."

"People don't always recognise love until it's under threat," Kate said wisely.

"You don't know what you're talking about," Terence barked. "You're a stupid little girl who... Where are you going?" he asked as she turned her back on him.

"Home," she replied curtly.

"By yourself?"

"Yes," she said. "*A stupid little girl?* Maybe, but if I am, I'm growing up fast and starting to see you for what you really are."

"Meaning?" Terence growled.

"Work it out yourself," she said, slipping away beneath the trees.

"Bloody women," Terence grumbled. He stubbed the ground with his toes and glared around the glade, then hefted his bag of notes up onto his back. Anna and Diarmid. Diarmid and Kate. Was there anything to either equation? It didn't seem likely. And yet...

"Always a bloody, 'And yet,'" he snarled, then struck for home.

As he strolled, he played with the notion of Kate or Anna running off with Diarmid (*Diarmid!*), and to his unease he couldn't tell which betrayal would hurt the most. A few days ago, the thought of losing Kate would have left him a nail-biting wreck, while seeing Anna trot off into the sunset with a toy boy would have filled him with cheer. Now that he considered the possibilities in greater depth, he honestly couldn't say.

The one thing he did know was that his old friend Diarmid had better watch out. Terence had brought the shy youngster into the ranks of the Midsummer Players and, by God, he could just as easily boot him out.

*

Ingmar's fingers trembled as he unlatched the garden gate. There was no sign of Don. He wished he hadn't been so empty-headed in the glade. Finn's kiss had been the highlight of his day, but there was a long night ahead and a seething lover to placate. Why couldn't he have waited until they were alone? What had possessed him to do it in front of the Players?

He crept across the lawn. Lights were on in the living room and kitchen, which was a good sign. He'd been afraid the house would be couched in darkness, Don lurking in the shadows, a long, curved knife in one hand.

The door was open and Ingmar let himself in. He stood in the hallway, waiting for Don to confront him. When there was no sign of his irate lover, Ingmar called out the bald man's name.

"In here," came the response from the living room.

Ingmar entered (leaving the door ajar in case he had to make a quick escape) to find Don lounging on the couch, reading a magazine, munching a ham sandwich. He smiled at Ingmar and saluted him with the sandwich. "Popped into the village," he mumbled. "Stocked up. Ham, roast chicken, steak." He took another bite of the sandwich and peered at Ingmar over the crust. "You don't mind, do you?"

"Of course not," Ingmar replied swiftly.

"I'm sick of eating like a rabbit," Don informed him.

"It's fine," Ingmar said.

"Glad to hear that." Don belched and wolfed down the rest of the sandwich. "*So* good. That was my fourth." A pause. "It won't be my last." Another pause. "Any objections?"

"None," Ingmar squeaked.

"It won't do my weight any favours," Don mused.

"You're in good shape," Ingmar lied. "You can carry a couple of extra pounds."

Don beamed and patted his stomach. "Come here," he said, tapping the foot of the couch with his heel. Ingmar approached slowly. "Sit," Don said, and stuck his feet on Ingmar's lap. "I'm dying for a foot massage."

Even though Ingmar detested giving foot massages, he meekly rolled Don's socks off and began squeezing and rubbing the sweaty feet. If this was to be his punishment, Ingmar considered it a let-off.

Don smiled as the DJ tickled his insteps and worked at his heels. Letting his head hang back, he wiggled the big toe on his left foot. "Be a dear and give that little monster a suck, will you? It's been itching all day."

Ingmar gulped, but to refuse would have been to risk Don's wrath. Screwing up his courage, he lowered his head and wrapped his lips around the ugly big toe. He kept his eyes shut.

"That's fantastic," Don gurgled. "Now the other one."

The right toe was home to a nasty verruca. Don lanced it with a pin two or three times a month, and had tried every sort of an ointment he could find, to no effect. (Don didn't like doctors and only went if it was a real emergency.)

Ingmar regarded the rough-shaped, brownish wart with repugnance. Don had been at it with the pin earlier, so it was an open sore and the area was littered with tiny pieces of dead skin. Ingmar could feel his stomach rumbling in revolt.

"I can't," the German wheezed.

Don studied his partner's pasty face and smiled sadistically.

"Suck that toe," he said menacingly, "or my glorious good temper won't hold."

Ingmar closed his eyes and clamped his lips around the grotesque toe.

"That's the ticket," Don purred.

Ingmar cried as he sucked but he didn't let up. He kept at it for five minutes, five of the worst minutes of his entire life, taking his punishment like a man.

"You can stop now," Don said. When he saw his lover's tear-rimmed eyes, his heart melted a little and he held out his arms. Ingmar collapsed into them and sobbed as the drama teacher's broad fingers combed and tousled his red hair.

"I'm sorry," Ingmar cried.

"So you should be," Don reprimanded him softly.

"I don't know what came over me."

"*I* know," Don grunted, but let the matter drop. "We'll say no more about it, put today's events behind us and pretend they never happened. A good night's sleep and all will be forgotten. Yes?"

"Yes," Ingmar agreed, inwardly smirking as he once again re-lived the delicious stolen kiss.

Don tilted Ingmar's head back, studied the DJ's lips, then gently closed them with his right thumb. "Go rinse your mouth out."

"Right away." Hurrying to the bathroom, he filled his mouth with Listerine, ran cold water and splashed some over the back of his neck while he gargled.

Back in the living room, Don reached beneath the couch and extracted a doll that he'd bought in the village. It was a stubby-haired soldier with piercing eyes and moveable plastic hands. Don had stripped it bare and scratched a name across its chest — *Diarmid.*

"Little Diarmid," he murmured, smiling icily as he held the doll up to the light. Lowering it again, he took a firm hold of the flexible head and began rotating it. He twisted it around, eight times in all, eventually allowing the face to settle in a backwards position.

"Diarmid, Diarmid, short and gay," he crooned, "wilt thou steal Ingmar away?" He put his teeth around the doll's left hand and savagely bit off the appendage, then spat it on the floor. "Not if I have any say in it!"

*

Nuala and Felix returned home after rehearsal and changed clothes. Nuala fixed a sandwich for herself, then told Felix she was going to pay Anna a call. "Don't know how long I'll be," she said.

"Take all the time you want," he replied.

"I will."

It was their longest conversation of the day.

While Nuala traipsed off to play the Good Samaritan, Felix cooked a meal and washed it down with a bottle of wine. He lit a candle and set it in the middle of the table. As he chewed his food, barely tasting it, he stared at the flickering light and reflected on the sad state of his marriage.

In the midst of Felix's musings, there was a knock at the door — Del. "Mind if I come in?"

"Make yourself at home," Felix told him, glad of the company. Leaving the remains of his meal, Felix uncorked another bottle of wine and they retired to the living room. He stuck on some classical music, turned the volume down, and they spent a pleasant few hours chatting. They discussed their jobs, the situation in the North, differences between the two cultures. Del spun tales from his misbegotten youth, Felix fed him gossip about the Players, they talked about books, music and future plans. Finally the topic of marriage raised its head. They were on the third bottle of wine by this time.

"I love her," he sighed. "I've never cheated. There have been opportunities — I do a bit of travelling in my line of work — but I've never given in to temptation. 'Thou shalt not commit adultery' is law as far as I'm concerned."

"Does Nuala believe that too?" Del asked.

"Absolutely," Felix said. "I wouldn't have stuck by her if she didn't. I'm not a man to be cuckolded. If I ever found out she'd been unfaithful..." He drew a finger across his throat.

"You'd kill her?" Del asked, alarmed.

Felix tutted. "I'd *divorce* her. I'd come out of it quite well. Nuala's made a nice bit of money from her books, even if they haven't been bestsellers."

Del forced a fake smile. "I'm glad Nuala's never been unfaithful."

"Why should you be *glad*?" Felix frowned.

"No reason," Del said quickly. "So, if she's not giving you the run-around, why are you considering divorce?"

"I never said I was considering it."

"You sound like you are."

Felix ran the fingers of his right hand across his chin, where his beard would have been if he hadn't shaved it off for the play. "I'm not sure where I stand with Nuala any longer," he said. "I can't ask for the salt at breakfast without being drawn into an argument."

"Maybe you need a marriage counsellor," Del suggested.

Felix sighed. "Or a marriage *exterminator*."

A long silence followed. Del wanted to offer words of encouragement but he was here on a mission. When he eventually spoke, it was with a heavy heart but determination. "I probably shouldn't be saying this, but..."

"What?" Felix asked when he didn't proceed.

"Has Diarmid come over here recently?"

Felix shook his head.

"You haven't seen him?" Del pressed.

"Apart from at rehearsals, no. What's this about?"

Del cast his gaze at the floor. "He sneaked out of the house at least three times in the past week, late at night when he thought I was asleep."

"You think he's been coming here? But why...?" Felix's eyes narrowed. "Surely you're not suggesting...?"

"At first I thought maybe he was an insomniac or an amateur astronomer," Del said. "I asked him about it but he brushed my questions aside. Then, last night, I was out walking after the party and I saw him letting himself out of *your* house."

Felix stared suspiciously at his guest. "I don't believe you."

"I'm just telling you what I saw," Del said.

"You think, if they were having an affair, they'd do it beneath the roof where I was sleeping?"

"I didn't say they were having an affair," Del said. "I'm just telling you what I saw. There was no sign of Nuala. Maybe he was here for another reason. I just... Hell, I shouldn't have said anything. I'll leave before I say more."

Del got to his feet but Felix pushed him back down. "*More?*" he growled.

Del made a show of clearing his throat. "Don't force me to do this," he begged. "I like Diarmid and Nuala. I'm probably making a mountain out of a molehill."

"What is it?" Felix snapped. "Tell me whatever lie you've concocted and quit sitting on it like a brooding hen."

"I'm not lying," Del gasped. "I'm just trying to help."

"Like you helped last night?" Felix smiled bitterly. "I'm a little – make that a *lot* – hazy on the details, but I recall you bending my ear before I stormed home and made an ass of myself. Is this what we were talking about?"

"No," Del said. "This is different. It's..." He reached into his pocket, produced a pair of panties and tossed them to the stunned Felix, on whose head they neatly landed. "I found them in my bathroom. If they're not Nuala's, I'll say nothing more, but if they are..."

Del trailed off into silence and waited for Felix to speak. He'd fetched the panties from the house earlier that day. He'd crept in through an open window and found the sexy knickers in a small bag full of lingerie at the foot of a wardrobe in the bedroom. He had no guarantee that Felix would recognise the undergarments, but Del guessed he would. Husbands might struggle to identify a wife's dress or blouse at an identity parade, but he figured there were precious few who wouldn't be able to spot a familiar pair of lacy knickers.

Felix removed the panties from his head with trembling fingers and studied them wonderingly. They were bright blue, with pink hearts stitched into the rear cheeks and a red rose tattooed to the fabric of the crotch.

Del could tell by Felix's reaction that he knew the knickers intimately and gave himself an invisible pat on the back. Believing his wife to be an adulteress, Felix would explode and either a) have a raging row with Nuala which would result in one or both of them upping stakes, b) launch an attack on Finn, which would lead to the Northerner's ejection from the ranks of the Midsummer Players, or c) simply storm off in a huff and never be heard from again.

Felix was turning the panties around in his hands.

"I'm really sorry," Del said, "but you stuck up for me when you agreed to keep my identity secret. I had to repay the debt. Believe me, I wish I hadn't –"

"They're not Nuala's," Felix said quietly.

Del smiled supportively. "You don't have to lie."

"You don't understand," Felix said. "These aren't Nuala's. I don't know what Diarmid's doing with them, but..." He trailed off into silence, then pocketed the panties. "Can you keep a secret?"

"Of course," Del said, puzzled by Felix's reaction.

"These panties aren't Nuala's," Felix said again. "She doesn't know they exist."

"Felix –" Del began, but before he could continue, Felix said something which stopped him dead in his tracks.

"They're not Nuala's," Felix barked. Staring Del straight

in the eye, struggling desperately to present a dignified front, he said, "They're *mine*."

*

Anna wasn't at home. "She went out walking, said something about heading for Poet's Rock," Terence told Nuala, who thanked him and turned to leave. "If you find her," he said, "will you ask her not to stay out late? It's supposed to get quite chilly tonight. I wouldn't like her catching a cold." He flushed. "What with us being this close to Midsummer's and all."

Poet's Rock was a chair which had been carved out of a large rock. Many years ago, a local poet was rumoured to have relaxed there every day to compose his thoughts. It wasn't much of a monument, but the poet still had a small following, so it drew a handful of curious tourists most years.

Nuala found Anna perched upon the stony chair, head buried beneath her arms. Nobody else was in sight. Birds were chirping in nearby trees, settling down for the night. It was dark and cool, the chair shaded from the setting sun by a curved stone wall that partly encircled it, which had been added recently to lend more gravitas to the otherwise isolated, sorry-looking chair.

Nuala coughed and Anna's head bobbed up. She smiled when she saw who it was. "Come to cheer me up?" she sniffed, her face stained with dried tears.

"I came for a spot of inspiration," Nuala grinned. "I'll be starting a new book when the play finishes. Thought I'd fish for fresh ideas." Nuala crouched down and leant against the stone wall, so she was level with the sitting Anna.

"I made an ass of myself, didn't I?" Anna asked.

"Yup," Nuala agreed.

"You don't have to sound so happy about it," Anna said, taken aback.

Nuala shrugged. "I gave up worrying about looking foolish years ago." She laid a hand on her friend's arm and gave it a squeeze. "Mind telling me what it was about? Fawning over Diarmid? Wailing about his 'betrayal'?"

Anna hiccupped bashfully. "A silly, middle-aged woman's flight of fancy," she sighed. "I thought he had the hots for me. Guess I was wrong, huh?"

"Why do you say that?" Nuala asked.

"You saw the way he acted with Ingmar," Anna said.

"I saw the way *Ingmar* acted with Diarmid," Nuala corrected her. "Just because the German hit on your toy boy doesn't mean –"

"He's not my toy boy," Anna squealed. "We've never done anything. It's not like... Why are we even having this conversation? I read his signals the wrong way and overreacted when I realised I wasn't the only one with designs on him. I knew Kate was after him, but Ingmar's advance and Diarmid's reaction caught me on the hop. No big deal."

"Kate's after Diarmid?" Nuala asked, surprised.

"Seems to be," Anna nodded.

"What about Ter–" Nuala bit her tongue.

Anna smiled. "Poor Terence is about to be squeezed out."

"That's good, isn't it?" Nuala asked. The wall was cold, so she leant forward. "Leaves the way clear for a reconciliation."

"Assuming I want it," Anna said softly.

"Don't you?"

"I don't know," Anna answered honestly. "Last night, when Diarmid appeared to be chatting me up, it felt good to feel wanted. Terence will come back to me, even if Kate doesn't dump him. I'm his safety net, the boring wife he can always fall back on." She shook her head and shivered — she was only wearing a light top. "Maybe I've been there to catch him once too often. Maybe this time I'll let him fall."

"It's a big decision," Nuala said.

"It hasn't been easy," Anna agreed. "And it's not something I've rushed. This has been building for ages. I'm sick of being treated like a dog. Whether we patch things up and continue, or separate and go our own ways, something must change. I can't live like this any more."

"Tell me about it," Nuala sighed.

"What?"

"Oh, nothing. We'll get to my problems later." She stood and stretched. "Will you leave him?"

"I want to," Anna said, "but I'm afraid my world will crumble and I'll never recover."

"Nonsense," Nuala scoffed.

"Is it?" Anna asked sadly. "I'm not far off my fortieth, and I look and feel older than I am. What prospects do I have?" She began to sob. "Where would I go? Who'd waste their time on a pudgy old drudge like me?"

"Don't," Nuala said, weeping a little herself, and hugged Anna tight. "You're not old. You're beautiful. You've let yourself go, there's no denying that, but buy some new dresses, change your hairstyle..." She used a thumb to wipe away tears from Anna's cheeks. "Clean your mush."

Anna managed a choked laugh.

"You could stay with me," Nuala said suddenly.

"What about Felix?" Anna asked.

"He won't have any say in it. If he's still around," she added softly.

"Are you serious?" Anna asked.

"Absolutely," Nuala said, amiably pinching the tubby woman's arm.

"That's kind of you," Anna said, "but it wouldn't really solve anything. I'd have a roof over my head but what about a partner? What about love?"

Nuala's eyes met Anna's and something passed between them which caused both to pause. Nuala was remembering that day in the glade. Anna was recalling it also, the warmth she'd felt as Nuala massaged her.

"There *could* be... *love*," Nuala croaked, her voice barely more than a whisper. She thought about Kate and the silly crush she'd had on the young actress, then put all thoughts of her from her mind once and for all and focused on the present. On the real.

Nuala's lips sought Anna's. Anna was concentrating on Nuala's eyes – so deep, so mysterious – and barely noticed her own lips parting to seal a breathless kiss. They remained locked for no more than a couple of seconds before Nuala withdrew, giving Anna space to think and breathe.

Anna didn't do much thinking. Instead she pressed forward, initiating a second kiss herself. This one was longer and more passionate.

Nuala tugged Anna to her feet and the women operated in

silence. Anna's hands raced the length of the larger woman's back, scuttling up and down like a pair of nervous spiders. Nuala acted with more purpose. Her right hand descended until it located the hem of Anna's knee-length dress. Her broad fingers lingered on Anna's knee, before sliding upwards to explore her soft inner thigh.

Anna's legs parted and her mouth moved. She sank her teeth into Nuala's neck and nibbled, moaning lightly as the fingers crept higher.

Nuala's hand slipped to the outside of the thigh and rode up to the hip. She was searching for Anna's panties, unaware that she was wearing none. (She'd left her underwear at home following the previous night's encounter with Finn). After some confused fiddling, the fingers crept down and across until they were centred on the soft, thick hair which decorated the divide between the legs.

Anna gasped as she felt fingers where previously only Terence's had been. Nuala made no move to penetrate, but softly rubbed the outer walls of the sensitive flesh, making gentle circles with her large, shaking fingers. She started to pick up speed, but then Anna winced and stepped back.

"What are we doing?" Anna asked, more confused than alarmed.

"I don't know," Nuala said. Both women's hearts were beating rapidly and their faces were red. "I don't know," Nuala said again, and they stared at each other, their gazes locked questioningly as the world around them darkened into twilight.

*

Kate was heading home after her row with Terence, when she changed her mind and altered course. If she retired, she'd spend the rest of the night brooding, and she didn't want to grant Terence that satisfaction. Without really considering it, she made a beeline for Diarmid's house.

Del opened the door just before she knocked. "Mind if I come in?" she asked.

"Make yourself at home," he said, slipping out. "Diarmid's in the kitchen."

"Where are you off to?" she asked.

"Going for a walk," he said, furtively fingering a hidden pair of knickers ahead of his showdown with Felix, unaware of the twist of ownership he was soon to run into. "I may be some time."

He took off, leaving Kate alone with Finn, who was in the kitchen, nervously heating up a frozen dinner in the microwave. He didn't like this world's strange technology and would have preferred to leave the cooking to Del.

"It won't bite you," Kate trilled, noting his apprehension.

Finn jumped and turned, raising his fork defensively. When he saw who it was, he blushed and lowered the utensil. "Kate," he greeted her.

"Who were you expecting — masked hordes of Ninja warriors?"

"I have not got the hang of this infernal machine yet," Finn told her, keeping a wary eye on the bright lights of the microwave.

"What's to get the hang of?" Kate chuckled. "Stick the food in, set the timer — that's that."

"The time bit catches me out," Finn replied. "I am not used to human measures. In Feyland, minutes are nothing. We take no notice of them. We –"

"What are you blabbering about?" Kate interrupted.

Finn's blush deepened. "My thoughts are still with the play. It takes me a while to drag myself back to normal after –"

A bell sounded and the light of the microwave quenched. Finn gave a shout of pleasure and turned to the oven. He extracted the steaming meal and peeled a layer of plastic from the top. He sniffed the fumes and wrinkled his nose. "How people live on such mush is beyond me," he muttered. Then, "Hungry?" he asked aloud.

"I am, actually," Kate said. "Mind if I root through the freezer?"

"Go ahead," Finn said, tipping his dinner onto a plate. "If you discover anything resembling proper food, I will swap with you."

Kate chose a pasta dish, heated it up, and joined Finn at the kitchen table. He was halfway through his humble meal, holding a knife and fork in one hand, using them as a single instrument to shovel food into his mouth.

"Why not use a spoon?" Kate asked after a minute of in-credulous observation.

"Del said I had to get accustomed to knives and forks," Finn mumbled.

Kate frowned. "You must know how to use a knife and fork."

Finn grew wary. "I forgot," he said quietly.

"You *forgot*?"

Finn grinned, quickly switched the knife to his right hand, and used the tools as Del had taught him. "Fooled you."

Kate shook her head wearily. "Big boys and their little games."

They finished the meal in silence. Kate was ruminating on her bust-up with Terence, wondering whether she should ring him later.

"You look sad," Finn remarked as he scraped his dish clean. He didn't like the food but he'd been in a state of constant hunger since stepping over from Feyland — this world took its toll on the stomach.

"Not sad," Kate said. "Thoughtful." She made an effort to smile. "You were the centre of attention today. I thought Anna and Ingmar were going to come to blows over you."

"Can I help it if I am so popular?" Finn grinned.

"I couldn't believe how they acted."

"*I* could not believe that you did not step in to fight for me," Finn said slyly. "I was waiting for you to come to my aid and claim me as your own."

"Silly." She flicked a leftover pea at him, then remembered that he was a producer who could provide her with a career break. Should she be firing peas at such a man? She decided she should — her best chance of impressing Diarmid would be if he wasn't aware that she was trying to impress.

"*Is* there anything between you and Anna?" she asked.

"Air, trees and walls at the moment," Finn replied.

"Seriously," she said.

"No," he answered after a teasing moment of hesitation.

"And Ingmar? That looked like a steamy kiss from where I was standing."

"You should have been where I was," Finn laughed. "No, I am flattered by their interest, but both are attached and I do not wish to interfere where Cupid's arrows have already pierced and joined."

"A man of principles," Kate cooed. "What if..." She paused. "What if someone was interested in you but was seeing another man? A married man?"

Finn leant forward mischievously. His right hand sneaked into his back trouser pocket and undid the pouch of fairy dust which he'd been carrying around in case of emergencies. He knew Del didn't want him making inroads yet, but he'd grown tired of taking orders from the dictatorial Mr Chapman.

"You know what I would do?" he asked in a low, playful voice.

"What?" Kate asked, leaning forward merrily to meet him, thinking this nothing but a cheerful tease.

"I would" – Finn brought the pouch forward and jammed it between his chin and Kate's – "blow on them!" he yelled, giving the sides of the bag a sharp squeeze, shooting a cloud of fairy dust up into the air. A lot of the dust was sucked in by Kate, who inhaled with shock, and Finn puffed at the rest, directing it towards her mouth and nose.

Kate nearly choked. She stumbled backwards, hands flapping wildly. Her chair tipped over and she fell heavily to the floor.

"Are you alright?" Finn rushed around to help her.

Kate struggled to her hands and knees. She was still coughing and her eyes were watering, but more and more air was finding its way to her lungs, and the worst of the panic attack had passed.

"Kate?" Finn asked, gingerly patting her back. "Should I run and fetch help?"

"I..." Kate gasped.

"Yes?"

"I..." She took a long breath and a small smile split her dust-caked lips.

"Do you want a drink of water?" Finn asked.

She shook her head. "I..."

"What is it?" Finn groaned helplessly. "What are you trying to say?"

Kate fixed her gaze on the trembling changeling. Her smile spread and her tongue darted out to lick the dust from her lips. "I'm horny as the devil," she growled, then grabbed Finn by the arms and leapt to her feet, spinning him around. His legs struck the table and he fell, yelping, landing face down on the table.

Finn rolled round, groaning, onto his back. He was staring up at the kitchen light, which blinded him momentarily. When he raised a hand to shield his eyes, he spotted the advancing Kate. She looked like a tigress, an effect heightened by the low, throaty growl she was emitting.

"Kate..." Finn began nervously but got no further. At the speed of sound, she fell upon him. After a brief struggle, she was kneeling over his spreadeagled form, triumphantly twirling his trousers — which she'd wrestled off with her hands and teeth — above her head.

"Now we're ready for business," she chortled.

"Kate..." Finn bleated but again got no further. Tearing her shirt open and ripping off her bra, Kate yodelled raucously.

Then, taking hold of the fairy's never before exercised manhood, she swooped in, scattering plates, knives, forks and glasses in every direction. Finn whimpered softly, then grabbed onto the edges of the table and braced himself for the onslaught.

*

Three hours later, a cold, stiff, bewildered Finn prised himself free of the table and stumbled to the bathroom on legs of jelly. Kate remained in the kitchen, curled into a kittenish ball on the floor, smiling satedly.

Finn's back felt as if it would never bend again. He ran a basin full of warm water, then dunked his head and held it there until he ran out of breath. When he finally came up for air, he met his reflection in the mirror and stopped to stare. He barely recognised the face, which had been stripped bare of innocence.

"It was like being caught in a hurricane," he whispered. Great gods, if every encounter between the sexes was this highly charged, no wonder humans spent so much time sleeping!

"Diarmid," Kate sung from the kitchen. "I'm ready for round five. You're not ducking out on me, are you?"

Finn doubted there was anywhere he could duck to, even if he'd wanted.

"Coming," he called, gaze still fixed on his reflection. Slowly, impishly, his face flowered into a smile of sheer wonder. "If my brother could see me now," he laughed, then trotted back to the kitchen for the fifth kinetic bout. And this time, despite Kate's protestations, Finn took the bit between his teeth and tried the ride from on top.

3.[II](i)

A glade in Feyland. Enter OBERON, king of the Fairies, and Titania, his queen.

OBERON: The sun dawns on the land of the mortals.

TITANIA: Shall we hence and view it from our portal?

OBERON: Nay. The sight 'plexes me. Know you the time?

This day and two more: Mid Eve shall be nigh.

TITANIA: This bothers you, my loved and noble lord?

OBERON: Faith, my queen, it bites like a sharp-edged sword!

Three more days, and on the fourth: the Players!

TITANIA: But what of our chaotic human knight?

OBERON: That fool shall never set matters aright.

Ten days he's had to bob and duck and weave,

Yet I spy no respite this looming Eve.

TITANIA: He vowed to take things down to the wire.

OBERON: Of such suspense, I have no desire.

By now all should be blood and salty tears.

Chapman knows not the torment of our years.

If only I could have deployed cruel Puck:

By now he would have set their plans amuck.

TITANIA: Your words are born of exasperation;

Such panic suits not thy lofty station.

OBERON: My lady, of course, is perfectly right;

Yet I had such high hopes for this year's night.

I planned to host a party of such size

It would have startled ev'ry pair of eyes.

Pigs I planned to hoist aloft, engulf in

Flame and then shoot off into the sky to

Squeal and burn: the moon, her blushes to hide

Would have turned. Now all that waits is the play.

'Tis no wonder my face seems long as day.

TITANIA: No wonder, my lord, and yet my heart thinks

You do the poison of defeat swift drink.

Our human's odd ways are twisting and sly;

Perhaps he flounders and has gone awry;

Yet maybe you do write him off too soon:

Does not the sun toy strangely with the moon?

OBERON: Moon? Sun? Lady, these globes are not the same!

TITANIA: I never claimed they were. And yet the game

Is not so far removed. Heed me now and

My words will be proved. Does not the hot sun

Control the night by the cool reflection

Of that world's satellite? And yet the moon's

Face is not always aglow; it lights in

Quarters; it comes, it grows, and then it goes.

OBERON: Moons! Suns! Quarters! The point, madam, the point!

TITANIA: The point, my sullen lord, is plain, 'tis this:

The heavens play games with their astral twists.

The brash sun seeks; the coy moon hides; and this

Has been the pattern since the start of time.

Engaged though they are in heavenly sport,

This world does not suffer; it wants for nought.

These strange forces we cannot understand;

So it is with the minds of mortal man.

This human's plot to us seems doomed to ruin;

But were we two babes, gazing on the moon

When only one quarter showed of its ring,

Would we not think it a flawed, fragile thing?

The ways of gods and men are strange;

We should not wish them rearranged.

OBERON: Words, my good lady, on which I must dwell,

But for now: silence. Who visits our dell?

Enter Diarmid Garrigan, a human.

Ah — Diarmid. Let's converse with him awhile,

Adopt his crude manner and ape his style.

Hello, Diarmid, my old friend. Please, no need to kneel.

Arise, old boy, arise. It is a lovely day, is it not? How have

you been since last our paths crossed? It has been so long

since we met, I feared you might be lost.

TITANIA: You slipped, my lord.

OBERON: Say?

TITANIA: A rhyme did work its way into the middle of your

blunt and simple words.

OBERON: Did it in truth? The news does not surprise me.

These humans speak with devilishly tricky tongues. To string

words together randomly is no little feat, to reel out sounds

whose shapes do not meet. It is... I did it again, did I not?

TITANIA: I fear so, my lord.

OBERON: Never mind. I shall practise. You are well, Diarmid?

DIARMID: In most fine fettle, good king Oberon.

OBERON: Please, Diarmid, let us dispense with the

formalities. I get enough of that in the ordinary business of

the day. You are not of this domain. You owe me no fealty.

DIARMID: 'Tis true, my lord, and yet I would entreat:

Please fashion not for me a special seat.

I have worked hard in order to fit in;

I'd beg to be treated the same as kin.

OBERON: Very well. In front of your peers there shall be no special favours or treatment. You may bow and scrape like all the rest. But in return, I would beg a favour of you.

DIARMID: Anything to please my good, noble lord.

OBERON: When we're by ourselves, can we dispense with the charade? I will be Oberon, a fine, handsome cut of a figure, but no more than that. This gorgeous creature on my arm is Titania, a woman of many virtues and graces, but in no other way remarkable. And you shall be plain and simple Diarmid, an honest young man, straight-talking and unimpressed by royalty. Agreed?

DIARMID: If that is what my good... I mean, if that's what you want, friend Oberon, that's how it shall be.

OBERON: Splendid! I think some wine is called for. Titania, will you pour?

TITANIA: My pleasure, husband. Tell me, Diarmid, before you sip and lose your wits to the grape, how have your days been amongst our fair and fickle people?

DIARMID: In all truth, good Titania, I must admit I've known no better times than those spent here. These have been the most glorious days of my entire life. I've raced butterflies through fields of golden corn. I've challenged giants to rock-throwing contests: he who hits the sun with his stone and shatters it is the winner. I've swum naked through rivers with nymphs of the water, then climbed the highest trees with their cousins of the woods.

OBERON: You have overcome your fear of the body, then? When first you arrived, you refused blankly to strip unless cloistered from all prying eyes. It caused much merriment among our good people.

DIARMID: I blush at the memory of such days. And yet I know, were I to return to the world of the mortals in the morning, I would once again seek to hide from nature what nature saw fit to endow me with. It's hard to explain, but here it feels right to run bare-bottomed across the plains; I have learnt to take no notice of nudity. But in the human sphere, bodies have different meanings. There is sex in that land, and one is always aware of it. Here, the display of flesh is a parade of innocence. One spies a naked baby, a naked teenager, a naked adult, and there is no difference. In my land, the state of the body is forever linked to that of the mind: it is not possible to admire a figure without that person reading into one's lingering gaze. Here, if one is caught gazing, the object of your interest will pose and titter; in that other world, the person will take offence or interpret it as a come-on.

TITANIA: Yours is such a complicated world. Yet do you not miss it?

DIARMID: Never.

TITANIA: Not even slightly?

DIARMID: I will be truthful: at first, there *was* one thing I did miss awfully, the memory of which still brings a wry, regretful smile to my lips from time to time.

TITANIA: Was it a loved one you left behind?

DIARMID: Nay. I loved none as much as I love thee and thy kind.

OBERON: A brand of drink? A delicately flavoured sweet?

DIARMID: The food and drink of my world are as chalk and sawdust compared to Feyland's simplest meals.

TITANIA: Could it be the weather? Each day here is glorious, I know, but some of the humans who have visited us over the years have been bored by the atmospheric monotony.

DIARMID: After nearly thirty years of life in soggy Ireland, no amount of sun could be deemed excessive. The weather is the least thing I miss.

OBERON: I have it! You pine for technology. Televisions, cars, ovens which have never seen a real flame, games of lights and odd buzzes that require a keen eye and a quick hand.

DIARMID: You grow closer, friend Oberon. But, to get to the bottom of the matter, I'll put an end to your guessing and reveal the one thing of my world which I would wish to have here. It is simple and it is this: indoor plumbing.

TITANIA: You mean toilets!

DIARMID: Indeed I do, good lady. Toilets, washrooms, outhouses, lavvies, loos, bogs, crappers. By any name, they're most wondrous. I took them for granted before crossing the portal to Feyland, but now, having crouched more times than I can count over a hole in the ground, having searched for a thick fern and all too often laid hold of one which crumbles in the hand at the most inconvenient of moments, I realise that the most magnificent of all mankind's many inventions is the simple, functionary W.C.

OBERON: Well, fear not, young Diarmid. Four days more, as humans measure time, and you will once again be washing your hands to the music of a gurgling cistern.

DIARMID: Four days, my lord? Say it is not so!

OBERON: Midsummer draws near. Time moves slower here than in the realm of the mortals, but move it does. We cannot avoid the dreaded mechanisms of that universe entirely. No magic is that strong.

DIARMID: But... four days! So short a time. I seem barely to have arrived. There is so much still to do.

OBERON: You have my sympathy, Diarmid, but facts are facts. It will appear longer, if that is any comfort. To you, those four days will seem like months.

DIARMID: Days, months, years: what of them? My lord, I *never* want to go back. Can't I stay? Accept me as one of your own, Lord Oberon, and I'll be loyal until my dying day. I'll serve you well, as well as any human ever did, and stall at no order.

OBERON: Your wish may not be granted, my friend.

DIARMID: But why? Have I given offence to my lord and lady?

TITANIA: You know you have not. And I would give much to have you here indefinitely: your presence brings a light to my lord's eye that I have not seen since Master Shakespeare himself walked among us. Yet the words of my husband must also be mine. It is not in our power to retain your services. When your brother returns at the conclusion of Midsummer's Eve, you must hence to your place among the mortals.

OBERON: We would keep you if we could, Diarmid, but there are rules even the king and queen of the fairies must abide by. We made a pact with your parents before the day of your conception: in return for blessing them with children, we would have the right to take one of the twins and raise it as our own; that we have done. But the other half of our deal was to leave the second child where it was. Were we to grant sanctuary to both of you, even if it was of your own free will and desire, we would be in breach of our oath to your parents.

DIARMID: I see. The word of the lord of the fey must never be tarnished. It would be wrong of me to ask that which would place you in so difficult a position. May I withdraw my request, my liege?

OBERON: Request withdrawn. Come, Diarmid, weep not. Feyland is not the place for tears. There is plenty of time left. Enjoy yourself. Make use of your days. Fill your mind with memories so wonderful and plenty that they will never be depleted.

TITANIA: If it is any consolation, Diarmid, you may come visit us from time to time. Once every full moon, if you wish.

DIARMID: Your majesties are kind, but I do not think I will take up your generous offer. Leaving this beautiful land once will be hard enough. I could not face repeated exiles.

TITANIA: If there was any way...

DIARMID: Fret not, madam. Your generosity is bountiful and I curse myself if, by pleading, I seem to have cast it into doubt. Rules are rules. I accept that. Please: let us say no more about it. When my time comes, I shall leave with a smile, tinged with sadness though it may be, and bear nothing but love and thanks for the lord and master of Feyland. Have I your permission to take myself hence? I was on my way to a wrestling match with an ogre when I chanced upon your graces.

OBERON: Permission granted. Go with our blessings.

TITANIA: And our love.

Exit Diarmid.

OBERON: There goes the cream of all the human crop.

TITANIA: It made my heart heavy to see his drop.

You are sure there's no clause in our contract

Which would permit us his pain to detract?

OBERON: None. His parents are dead. The deal is sealed.

We can't interfere with fate's turning wheel.

Come, good lady, let us put this behind;

Sorrow's sad rags suit not us or our kind.

Let us go forth and lose ourselves in joy

And weep no more for the lonely young boy.

TITANIA: I shall try, my lord. But his pleas touched me.

OBERON: Me also. But the die are cast. Your arm,

My lady, that we might forthwith depart?

TITANIA: 'Tis yours, my lover and my lord.

Exeunt.

3.[II](ii)

Felix was keeping a close watch on Finn (thinking, of course, that he was keeping a close watch on Diarmid). In the hours following Del's production of the knickers, the small Northerner's state of shock had slowly turned to confusion. Why had the banker raided his stash of female garments? Was he trying to blackmail Felix? That made no sense — Felix wasn't rich. Was it part of some warped game? Had he meant to expose the panties at a later date, to shame Felix in front of the others? Possibly. But what was his motive? There was no history of bad blood between the two men.

Del had been unable to provide answers. Stunned by Felix's revelation, he had withdrawn to rethink his strategy, leaving Felix to his own troubled deliberations.

Late in the night, Felix saw the light. He recalled the way Ingmar had kissed the banker, the glow on Diarmid's face when they'd parted, the significant glance (this was an invention of Felix's) he'd shared with the Northerner in the wake of the kiss. It all fell into place with sickening clarity — Diarmid fancied him!

It was crazy. It was without precedent. It was disgusting. But it was *true*. It had to be. Diarmid had a crush on Felix, which was why he'd been spending so much time around him (again, this detail was imagined). That was why he'd crept into the house while Felix was asleep and stolen a pair of his knickers. (He never stopped to wonder how Diarmid could have known the panties were his and not Nuala's). Which begged the question — what else had he done while Felix was sleeping?

A torrid stream of images sprang to life, and soon Felix was terrifying himself with nightmarish visions of a lewd Diarmid performing all kinds of unspeakable acts on the slumbering insurance salesman.

Relations had been cool between them since. In the play they spent much of the third act verbally sparring as Demetrius and Lysander, arguing over Helena. Under normal circumstances they'd have paired off to practise in private, but Felix wasn't prepared to risk a one-on-one encounter with the closet homosexual, and he insisted on having at least one other Player in attendance at all times.

Tension built as the scene progressed. The play called for friction between the men and Felix happily provided it. Kate, as Hermia, believing Finn's (Lysander's) pledges of love for Nuala (Helena), begged him to stop treating her with scorn.

"'If she cannot entreat, I can compel,'" Felix growled.

"Excellent, Felix," Terence commended him. "I can see the fires of jealousy dancing in your eyes."

Del had told Finn nothing of the previous night's encounter with Felix, and the changeling was ignorant of his acting partner's feelings. He smiled as Terence complimented Felix, then pulled a stern face.

"'Thou canst compel no more than she entreat;
Thy threats have no more strength than her weak prayers.
Helen, I love thee, by my life, I do:
I swear by that which I will lose for thee
To prove him false that says I love thee not.'"

Felix snarled and yanked a startled Kate aside, stepping forward to confront Finn. "'*I* say I love thee more than he can do,'" he muttered over his shoulder, his indignant eyes fixed on Finn's.

"Oh, this is marvellous," Terence sighed happily.

"'If thou say so, withdraw, and prove it too,'" Finn shouted, drawing an imaginary sword from an imaginary scabbard.

"'Quick, come,'" Felix yelled in reply, scrabbling for a sword which didn't exist. When he remembered he was weaponless, he paused, then gave Finn a shove which sent him toppling.

"Hey!" Terence called, alarmed. "There's no need to be so rough."

"Sorry," Felix said, though he wasn't. "Let me help you up." He reached down and offered the fallen man his hand. As he pulled him to his feet, he put his lips to Finn's ear and hissed, "Keep your filthy paws to yourself, *fairy*!"

Finn blanched. Terence had to call twice and click his fingers in front of the actor's eyes to bring him back to his senses. It wasn't Felix's threat which worried Finn — it was that last word. Felix had called him a *fairy*. Finn knew little of slang and had taken the insult literally. He believed Felix knew what he really was and feared it was only a matter of time before he was outed as a cunning impostor.

*

Anna was adjusting the laces on her boots – it had rained during the night and the grass was damp – when Nuala approached. "How are you feeling?" she asked.

Anna looked up and smiled uncertainly. "Strange," she said.

Nuala bent and ran her fingers through the wet blades of grass. "What happened last night?" she murmured.

"You've forgotten?" Anna asked incredulously.

"Of course not," Nuala said. "I mean *how* did it happen? I didn't set out to seduce you."

"It was hardly a seduction," Anna said. "We kissed. You felt me up a little. That was all."

"Even so..." Nuala grinned ruefully.

"I don't know what came over me," Anna moaned.

"Are you sorry?" Nuala asked.

Anna hesitated. "I don't know what I feel. Shame. Guilt." She shrugged. "But excitement too. I woke this morning almost wishing we'd gone further."

"In for a penny, in for a pound," Nuala chuckled. She glanced about the glade and located Felix. "Would our husbands mind? Would doing it with another woman constitute a betrayal in their eyes?"

"Not in Terence's," Anna giggled. "He'd probably want to join in."

"I'm not so sure about Felix," Nuala sighed.

"Anyway," Anna said, "we didn't do anything."

"We came close," Nuala said.

Anna shook her head. "For a moment it seemed like we might, but we didn't and we won't."

"What about this morning's wish?" Nuala prodded her.

Anna winced. "I often think strange things in the morning, but we're not" – she lowered her voice – "lesbians. Best to put the crazy thoughts behind us."

"That's what you really want?" Nuala asked.

"It's..." Anna paused. "It's for the best," she finished ambiguously and flashed Nuala a nervous little smile.

*

Finn pulled Del aside at the first opportunity, to pass on his ominous news. Del was studying Anna and Nuala, who were deep in conversation.

"Notice anything odd about those two?" he asked the changeling. "Nuala hasn't glanced at Kate this morning, and Anna's been acting –"

"Never mind the women," Finn hissed. "We have been rumbled."

"What are you talking about?"

"Felix *knows*."

"Knows what?"

"Who I am... Feyland... the Plan."

"How could he?" Del frowned.

"I do not know, but he does. He called me a *fairy*."

Del pondered that. "What did he say exactly?"

"He knocked me down — you saw?"

Del nodded.

"When he bent to pick me up, he whispered in my ear, 'Keep your filthy hands off me, *fairy*!'"

"Holy hounds of Knocknagown," Del crowed. "He must reckon you knew the knickers were his and took them for a keepsake."

"What knickers?" Finn asked.

"Quiet," Del snapped. "Let me think." His eyes closed as his brain whizzed. When they opened thirty seconds later, he was calm and self-satisfied. "You know the great thing about this world? As soon as one door shuts, another opens. Come," he said, taking Finn by the elbow. "We must act quickly. Here's what you're going to do…"

*

Terence Devlin was a troubled man. He'd rung Kate several times the previous night, without reply. To make matters worse, when Anna returned from her walk, she'd been distracted and spent the tail end of the night avoiding him. Terence's dreams had been awash with visions of the two women running off into the sunset with a smug, smiling Diarmid.

The positive aspect of the morning was that Anna had abandoned her apparent desire for Diarmid. She no longer clung to him or fawned over his every word. The negative was that Kate's interest in the banker had deepened. The two had been exchanging meaningful looks all morning, alternately steamy and simpering.

In the second scene of the third act, Kate as Hermia had to suffer the slings and arrows of outrageous fortune (as the Bard himself once put it), as Lysander, under the influence of the magic potion, spurned her for Helena. It was normally an easy scene to play – few ladies had trouble working up tears as their opposite number laid into them – but things weren't going according to plan.

"'Ay, by my life;

And never did desire to see thee more.

Therefore be out of hope, of question, of doubt;

Be certain, nothing truer — 'tis no jest

That I do hate thee and love Helena.'"

Finn's lines should have been delivered with a mocking sneer, but his face was full of light and love, and the words flowed from his mouth as though coated in honey.

Kate, on the other hand, was going overboard on the despair. It was supposed to be an amusing scene, and though she had to cry, the audience weren't meant to believe she was truly unhappy. Hermia was no Ophelia, and her sorrows would be put right in the fourth act. Yet Kate wailed her eyes out as Finn turned a (warm) cold shoulder on her, and by the time of her final speech, she was sobbing so hard, the Players could barely make out her words.

"'Never so... weary, never so... in woe,

Bedabbled with the... the dew, and torn with briars –

I can no further crawl, no further... further... further...'"

"Cut!" Terence roared, springing forward like a lion. "What is this crap?"

Kate wiped her cheeks and stared at him wonderingly. "I'm... a-acting the p-part," she stuttered.

"You're acting the *maggot*," he retaliated. "If you do that on the night of the play, the audience will have left to drown their sorrows by the end of the act."

"You want me to hold back?" she asked.

He turned to his troops for encouragement.

"You *were* laying it on a bit thick," Nuala said as gently as she could.

"You would say that," Kate sniffed. "We all know you can't work up tears to save your life."

"Hey," Nuala growled, "if you can't take a little constructive criticism, maybe it's time you –"

"Please," Terence interrupted. "Let's not –"

"Keep out of it," Kate snapped. She faced Nuala, her eyes cool and fierce. "You were saying?"

Nuala gritted her teeth. "I was simply pointing out that an actress who can't take advice is an actress who doesn't belong on the stage."

"Is that so?" Kate smiled thinly.

"It's a well-known fact."

"*You* can take advice?"

"I like to think so."

"Then take this." Kate leant forward until they were nose to nose. "Get a facelift, you ugly old hag!"

"You bitch!" Nuala howled, grabbing Kate's hair.

"Ladies!" Terence shouted, rushing forward to separate them. "There's no need to –" One of Nuala's elbows connected with the side of his head and knocked him out of the way.

"You're a ham," Nuala yelled.

"At least I'm not half-baked," Kate shrieked.

"You wouldn't be in this play if you weren't screwing the director," Nuala screamed.

"*You* wouldn't be in it if you *were*," Kate retorted.

An open-mouthed Finn sidled up to Del. "They are crazy," he muttered.

"Just excited," Del smirked. "I spiked their drinks earlier — a concoction Puck brewed up for me. It'll wear off in a couple of hours but until then their hackles will rise at the merest critical suggestion."

Felix, Don and Ingmar had managed to separate the warring women and were holding them apart.

"Let me at the cow," Kate screeched.

"I'll rip her eyes out," Nuala bellowed.

"They might do damage in this state," Finn noted.

"They'll calm down soon," Del assured him. "A few minutes and they'll be best buddies, until somebody says something to set them off again."

In perfect timing, Nuala and Kate stopped struggling and looked sheepish.

"I'm sorry," Nuala said. "I shouldn't have been so quick to pass judgement."

"*I* was wrong," Kate responded meekly. "You were only trying to help."

The men relaxed their holds and warily moved out of the way.

"Put it there," Nuala said, offering her hand.

"Oh, come here," Kate laughed, delivering a bear hug. She expected Nuala to take advantage of the opportunity to cop a feel but to her surprise the older woman quickly broke the embrace.

"Are you OK, Terence?" Don asked the stricken director.

"Fine," Terence grunted, tenderly probing his face. He spotted Finn walking towards Kate and watched intently as the banker whispered something in her ear which made her giggle. He'd definitely have words with her later and stop this budding romance before it went any further. He wasn't about to lose his mistress to another man, certainly not *Diarmid*.

"Let's take it from the start," he barked. "And Diarmid?" he said, as the actor took his place. "Try it with a little more venom this time."

*

While Terence was still in two minds as to whether or not the fake Diarmid posed a real sexual threat, Don was convinced that the banker was a modern day Casanova, stalking the land and snatching loved ones away from the arms of their partners. All that morning he'd been *accidentally* bumping into Finn, jostling him whenever they passed. As the day progressed, he took to coughing when Finn was reciting his lines, causing Finn to lose his place, never allowing his performance to flow. It was childish and petty but Don relished each minor triumph and could barely constrain himself while waiting for the next.

Ingmar and Del noted Don's behaviour – the rest were too wrapped up in their own problems – but neither made any move to stop him. Del was delighted to see the bald actor's temper mounting, while Ingmar didn't want to interfere in case it enraged Don.

"Oops! *So* sorry," Don chuckled as he sent Finn sprawling for the third time in an hour. It was early afternoon and the changeling was on his way to the woods for a call of nature. "I keep tripping you today," Don smiled, picking Finn up.

"Think nothing of it," Finn said. "These things happen."

"They certainly do," Don murmured. "Going for a leak?"

"Aye," Finn said. "The bladder bulges. I must ease the pressure or burst."

"We wouldn't want *that* to happen. Come," Don said, taking the smaller man's elbow. "I too need to drain the python."

They walked a short way into the woods, Don taking slow, leisurely steps, Finn hopping anxiously along beside him, wishing he'd hurry.

"I never thanked you," Don said after a while.

"For what?" Finn asked.

"Ingmar's voice."

"You need hardly thank me for that," Finn smiled. "It was my pleasure to teach him. It is always a joy to bring out the hidden potential in others. Shall we stop at this bush?"

"Let's walk some more," Don grunted, ploughing ahead. "I'm enjoying our chat. We should talk more often. I've hardly seen you this year."

Finn took a deep breath and tried sucking back the liquid which was starting to drip. "Can we talk after we relieve ourselves? I really need to go."

"Soon," Don smiled. "There's a patch up ahead that I've always been fond of."

"*Far* up ahead?" Finn asked.

"Not far," Don promised. "Tell me, how's life?"

"Life is fine," Finn said, "but my bladder –"

"Any girlfriends on the scene?"

"No." Finn was dancing from foot to foot.

"*Boy*friends?"

"No," Finn answered, biting his lip.

"But there have been?" Don pressed.

"No. I... I have to..." Finn darted off to one side and unzipped his flies.

Don grinned, then joined the banker. He glanced sideways as he was urinating and drew in his breath sharply. The man beside him was *huge*. Where the hell had that snake come from? Don had seen all that Mrs Garrigan's son had to offer the last time he'd stayed with them in Dublin, when he'd glimpsed him coming out of the shower, and it had been nothing to crow about. But this was a different proposition. He must have been for an operation. No wonder Ingmar was sniffing around him like a dog around a bitch in heat.

"What's *in* that?" Don asked, nodding at Finn's flopping tackle.

Finn stared at Don oddly. "Flesh. Blood. The usual."

"How come it's so big?" Don snapped. "It wasn't that size before."

Finn shrugged, finished his business and began doing up his flies. "Fresh air and plenty of cabbage," he joked.

"Are you taking the piss?" Don snarled.

"Taking it? I have just gotten rid of it," Finn replied.

Don reddened, then gave his manhood a shake and sent a stream of urine flying over Finn's lower trouser legs and shoes.

"Sorry," Don gurgled as Finn leapt backwards, "but accidents happen, yes?"

"I guess," Finn answered despondently. He wasn't naturally inclined to see the worst in people but in this instance a tiny inner voice was howling indignantly, 'That was no damn accident!'

*

Back in the clearing, trouble was brewing again. Nuala had been struggling to remember her lines in rehearsals, so Terence had been working with her to eliminate the most troublesome ones, but today her tongue was flying (a result of yet another potion, administered by Del via a cucumber sandwich during lunch) and soon she was trotting out lines that they'd agreed to dispense with.

"'Injurious Hermia, most ungrateful maid,

Have you conspired, have you with these contrived

To bait me with this foul derision?

Is all the counsel that we two have shared,

The sisters' vows, the hours that we have spent

When we have chid the hasty-footed time

For parting us — O, is all forgot?'"

Nuala was supposed to skip thirteen lines at this point and come in with, 'And will you rent our ancient love asunder.' But she forgot to omit them and continued with the unedited text.

"'All schooldays' friendship, childhood innocence?

We, Hermia, like two artificial gods

Have with our needles created —'"

"Hold it," Kate shrieked.

Nuala paused and regarded Kate suspiciously.

Kate turned pleadingly to Terence. "We'd agreed to cut those lines."

"That was when I was having trouble with them," Nuala said. "I can recall them now."

"But we agreed," Kate huffed. "We can't say one thing one day and something different the next."

"We did agree to drop the lines, Nuala," Terence noted.

"I know," Nuala snarled, "but they're not a problem any longer. I want to reinstate them."

"What if you forget again?" Kate asked.

"That won't happen," Nuala insisted.

"But what if it does?" Kate persisted. "I have to know going into a performance what my acting partner is going to say, so I can come in at the right time with my response. We aren't doing improv."

"You do know," Nuala shouted. "I'll deliver every line, as written. You doubt me? Go ahead. Ask me for any speech from any part of the play. Go on, test me."

"Nobody wants to test you," Terence said. "If you think you can master all your lines, fine, but forgetting them one day and recalling them the next..."

"What he's trying to say," Kate cut in, "is can we depend on you? Can we trust you to go out on Midsummer's Eve and not make a total cock-up of –"

"*Cock-up?*" Nuala bellowed. "I've been doing this play for twenty years, and the only cock-up I ever made was allowing Terence to give one of the main roles to an amateur who'll never amount to a hill of beans."

Kate's eyelids dropped. "I assume you're referring to Del," she hissed.

"Assume what you like," Nuala smiled. "Everybody knows who I mean." She turned her gaze on her colleagues, but they all averted their eyes, not wishing to get involved. Finally she set her sights on Anna, who would surely back her up. "Anna," she boomed. "Tell her."

"Tell her what?" Anna asked, wishing she could sink into the forest floor.

"That they can depend on me."

Anna's cheeks reddened.

"Go on, *tell* them."

"Well," Anna said hesitantly, "there *was* that time you forgot nearly all your lines in the final act."

Nuala's mouth shot open to issue a denial, but then she recalled that horrible night. "OK, that isn't a glittering jewel in my crown of past performances, but that was one of our first productions. We were all prone to slips in those days."

"Yes," Anna said, "but then there was the time – five years ago? – when you were playing Bottom and forgot the names of Titania's fairies."

"Granted," Nuala snapped, "but I wasn't supposed to be Bottom. The actor who was playing him had to pull out a week ahead of the play, so I only had a handful of days to get to grips with the character."

"I know," Anna said. "It's just, you challenged me to tell them that they could depend on you, and..." She shook her head miserably.

"I didn't realise it was a *challenge*," Nuala said icily. "I thought I was asking a friend for help. Silly me. I won't make the same mistake twice."

Terence cleared his throat — the time had come to play the peaceful arbitrator. "Nuala, you're a valued member of the troupe and always will be, but all of us have our weak spots. I can't handle a major role *and* direct. Felix doesn't have the build to play Theseus." Felix started angrily at that. "Anna's grown too long in the tooth to ever be a convincing Helena or Hermia." Anna glared at her husband. "And *you* have trouble memorising chunks of verse. It's no big deal as long as we acknowledge our limits and work within them."

"OK," Nuala sighed. "I hear what you're saying."

"You shouldn't feel in any way belittled," Terence assured her.

"Don't treat me like a child," Nuala barked. "I'm not one of your pupils."

"I never said –"

"'Is all the counsel that we two have shared,'" Nuala shouted, returning with a vengeance to the play, silencing all further speeches of Terence's.

"'The sisters' vows, the hours that we have spent

When we have chid the hasty-footed time

For parting us — O, is all forgot?'"

She paused, sneered at a defiant Kate, glared reproachfully at a disconsolate Anna, then jumped ahead to her designated lines and delivered them bitterly, keeping her gaze fixed meaningfully on Anna.

"'And will you rent our ancient love asunder,

To join with men in scorning your poor friend?'"

3.[II](iii)

Kate stepped down off a bar stool, having stuck a poster to the window, and received a standing ovation from the assembled drinkers, delighted by the flash of leg that she'd revealed. Kate smiled and took a bow. "Don't forget," she reminded them, "a night of mirth and merriment is guaranteed. And," she added, "I'll be wearing a dress that makes this one look like a nun's."

A round of cheers raised the rafters and she had to dodge a multitude of advances and offers on the way to the door.

"Stay for one drink," a mangy farmer cried, blocking the door. "Just one, for poor old Danjo."

"Sorry," Kate smiled, "but if I made an exception for you" – she dropped to the floor and slid between the farmer's legs – "I'd have to do it for all. Come to the play," she called over her shoulder as Danjo cursed. "We can have a drink then."

Ingmar was outside, smirking. "What do you think the reaction would be if *I* tried that?" he asked. "I've lovely legs."

"I don't think they'd be impressed," Kate said.

"Maybe I should do it at the next bar we visit."

"You can if you want," Kate smiled, linking an arm through his, "but don't expect me to help wash off the tar and feathers."

They were close to the river and wandered along the banks awhile, watching gulls swoop and caw overhead. They'd been pounding the streets for an hour. The actors had all set out at six that evening to put up posters and pass out the last of their fliers. They'd split into four groups. Nuala, Anna and

Del took bicycles and set off for the local villages. Terence and Don were focusing on the larger rural towns and covering a lot of ground — it would be two or three in the morning before they returned. The final four were targeting Limerick city. Finn and Felix had taken one half, Kate and Ingmar the other.

"How many posters do we have left?" Kate asked.

"A dozen," Ingmar replied.

"That's not much."

"And about a hundred fliers each."

She grimaced. "If we'd come during business hours, we could have handed them out in no time. Trying to palm them off on people at this time of night..."

"We could dump them in the river," Ingmar suggested.

She sighed. "And when nobody turns up to see the play, who do you think will cop the blame?"

"After your performances in the last couple of pubs, a low turnout is the least of our worries," Ingmar said. "We'll probably have to turn people away."

"I'd make a great salesgirl," Kate smirked.

"You'd make an even better stripper," Ingmar joked.

"That's an idea," she mused. "A few striptease numbers would do wonders for the show."

"Terence would certainly enjoy it," Ingmar said.

"Yes," Kate sniffed. "He would, wouldn't he?"

Ingmar's ears pricked up. "Things not rosy in the husband-stealing garden?"

"I didn't steal him," Kate hit back.

"You didn't spurn him either," Ingmar reminded her.

She grimaced and stooped to study her reflection in the water. She leant so far over the edge of the bank, Ingmar was half afraid she was considering throwing herself in, and positioned himself to catch her if she tried.

"What do you think of Diarmid?" Kate asked without turning.

"A charming young man," Ingmar said. His eyes narrowed. "Surely you haven't been sniffing around him too?"

Kate turned and smiled. "I've done more than sniff."

"You haven't!" Ingmar's jaw dropped with dismay.

"Last night," she boasted. "His house. On the kitchen table."

Ingmar looked for a bench. Finding none, he sank to his haunches. "I don't believe it," he groaned.

"It's not the sort of story I'd make up."

"What was it like?" Ingmar asked.

Kate blinked. "Nice."

"Just nice?"

Her cheeks dimpled as she smiled. "It was wild," she admitted. "Diarmid's an animal."

"What kind of animal?" Ingmar pressed.

"The wild, mad, insatiable kind. The long, round, hard and able kind."

Ingmar's eyes widened. "*Diarmid*?"

"Hung like a stallion," Kate giggled.

"Incredible," Ingmar muttered. Then he frowned. "But yesterday, Anna and he seemed awful friendly."

Kate shrugged. "I didn't see any sign of her last night."

"You're a vixen," Ingmar laughed. "First Terence, then Diarmid. Are any of us safe?"

"You and Don," Kate smirked.

"Oh well," Ingmar sighed. "There goes another dream up in smoke."

Kate frowned. "You had plans for *me*?"

"Certainly not," Ingmar spluttered. "I meant he-who-walks-like-a-stallion."

"You had the hots for Diarmid?" Kate squealed.

"Didn't you guess after yesterday's pass?"

"I thought you were joking, trying to make Don jealous. Diarmid's not gay."

Ingmar's eyebrows raised mischievously. "Isn't he?"

"No. Before last night, I might have said... but now... definitely no."

"A bowl of carrot soup does not a vegetarian make," Ingmar noted.

"I made love to him," Kate said stiffly. "There's not a gay bone in his body."

"I kissed him," Ingmar countered. "I believe he could be swayed."

"And you reckon you're the one to sway him?" Kate huffed.

"I might be," Ingmar said smugly.

"Even though you know he and I are an item now?" Kate growled.

"All's fair in love and war," Ingmar smiled.

Kate considered the DJ's words. She didn't think he stood a snowball's chance in hell with Diarmid, but Ingmar had a sharp tongue when bitter. Even in losing, he could sour things between them. Diarmid was a simple soul. A few cruel words from the cunning German and everything could be off.

"Tell you what," Kate said. "If you think you're so hot, let's bet."

"What sort of bet?" Ingmar asked.

"Forget the chase. I'll set it up. You and Diarmid, alone. If you can seduce him, I'll abandon all claims. If you fail, he's mine."

"A one-shot deal," Ingmar mused.

"Winner takes all," Kate agreed.

"You're on." He offered his hand and they shook. "I hope you've kept Terence on standby," he chuckled.

"*I* hope Don doesn't learn of your fiendish plan," Kate retorted.

"We're dicing with death, aren't we?" Ingmar noted.

"Absolutely," Kate said.

"It's thrilling, isn't it?" he beamed.

"Simply scintillating," she trilled.

*

Del was having a tough time figuring the state of play between Nuala and Anna. Neither woman was in a talkative mood. They worked like drones, mechanically sticking up posters and handing out fliers.

"I haven't been on a bike in years," Del said as they crested the top of a hill. "I bet you two do a lot of cycling."

"Um," Anna replied.

"Eh," Nuala grunted.

Del hadn't expected trouble between Anna and Nuala, and while he was keen to exploit their strained relationship, he didn't want to forge ahead blindly. He had to find out what the matter was.

They pulled into their sixth small village of the evening and began plastering the lamp posts. Anna bent to pick up her pile of posters, grimaced and rubbed her back. Del spotted this and a glimmer of a plan formed.

"Are you OK?" he asked.

"Fine," she said.

"Honestly?"

Anna sighed and straightened. "A twinge. It'll pass."

"You have to be careful with backs," Del said.

"It's fine," Anna said again. "I'm just not used to bending so much."

"You should head home," Del said. "A hot bath, an early night."

"She can't," Nuala squawked. "We've work to do. I'm not carrying her load."

"I never asked you to," Anna said.

"Just as well you didn't," Nuala snapped.

"Actually," Del said, "you could head home early as well, Nuala."

Nuala snorted. "Nothing wrong with *my* back. I could go till dawn."

"I'm sure you could," Del agreed, "but I wouldn't like to send Anna home by herself in case her back started to spasm along the way."

"*Spasm?*" Anna sounded alarmed.

"It almost certainly won't," Del said, "but if it does, and you fall from your bike, and you're alone..."

Anna and Nuala exchanged uncertain glances.

"What about the posters?" Nuala asked.

"And the fliers?" Anna added.

"I'll take care of them," Del promised.

"But you don't know the countryside," Anna said. "You might get lost."

Del smiled. "I have satnav now that my mobile is working – the reception is way better here – and I can ask for directions if that fails me. Go home."

"If you're sure…" Anna said.

"I'm positive."

"It *would* be best if I went with her," Nuala said.

They shared glances again – what was going on between them? – then mounted their bikes.

"When will you be back?" Nuala asked, trying to sound casual.

"Not for ages," Del said. "I'll find a pub when I'm done and have a few drinks."

He watched the ladies cycle away, waited until they were out of sight, then dumped the posters and fliers behind a bush. "So much for publicity," he grinned. He waited five minutes, then hopped on his bike and took an alternate route home.

*

It was ten o'clock and Don and Terence were propped beside a broken jukebox in a deathly quiet pub. They'd covered a vast amount of territory over the last four hours. This would be their one break of the night.

Two unfinished pints and a couple of half-eaten sandwiches adorned their table. Terence was leaning on the jukebox, pushing buttons, while Don tried picking a splinter out of a thumb with his teeth.

"Why's it so quiet?" Don asked, wiping spit from his thumb, grunting as he realised the splinter hadn't come out.

"No idea," Terence said. "I haven't been here before. Maybe the building's infested with rats." Don had been reaching for his sandwich but blanched when he heard that. "Only joking," Terence smiled.

"I wish you wouldn't," Don said, pushing the sandwich aside.

Don glanced around the dimly lit pub. A barmaid who couldn't be a day under seventy was reading a magazine behind the counter. A middle-aged man slumped nursing his pint in one corner, while a younger man sat at the far end of the bar studying the racing results in a crumpled newspaper.

"Are you going to finish that?" Terence asked, nodding at Don's sandwich.

"No," Don said. "You want it?"

"No, but we've a long night ahead. You might want to bring it for later." He paused. "I can pick out the rat hairs if you like."

"That's not funny," Don said stiffly.

Terence sipped his pint. "It's probably because the jukebox is out of order," he said, referring to the funereal atmosphere. "I could ask the barmaid to turn on the radio — she surely has one stashed away somewhere."

"I like the quiet," Don said. "I just wish there were more people about."

Terence took one more bite of his sandwich, wrapped the remains and checked his watch. "Five minutes and we'll be off."

"What's the rush?" Don asked.

"I want to hit as many pubs as I can before last call," Terence said.

"There's plenty of time," Don laughed. "Pubs here don't close till one or two in the morning."

"Most don't," Terence agreed, "but they only remain open to regulars after the official closing time."

"So we miss a couple of pubs." Don shrugged. "So what?"

"*So*, maybe there's a tour operator in one of them," Terence said. "He's got a load of Japanese visitors on his hands and is wondering what to do with them. He sees our poster, clicks his fingers and decides to bring them our way."

"Unlikely," Don muttered.

"Probably," Terence said, "but we live in hope."

Don rolled his eyes, but there was no point arguing with the director. "How about this place? We gonna ask them to put one up?"

"I'm not sure," Terence said. "If tonight's turnout is anything to go by, it hardly seems worthwhile." He yawned. "At times like this, my spirits dip. Twenty years, and we're still scrounging for an audience."

"The theatre's a hard life," Don said comfortingly.

"Even so," Terence sighed, "after twenty years you'd think we'd be getting a good number of returning customers." He lowered his voice and asked a question which he'd been silently sounding to himself the last three or four years. "Are we any good, Don?"

Don frowned. "What do you mean?"

"The Midsummer Players," Terence hissed. "Are we any good? Honestly."

Don studied his old friend's anxious face and couldn't bring himself to break the cold hard facts of life to him. "The Players are decent," he lied.

"Thank God." Terence leant against the jukebox and smiled weakly. "It's hard to be objective when you're on the inside. It'd be awful to have worked so hard all these years, only to find out I'd been wasting my time."

"I can assure you," Don said diplomatically, "I wouldn't be coming year after year if you were no good."

"You're a true friend," Terence said, a lump in his throat.

"Works both ways," Don replied, smiling fondly.

They returned to staring at the deserted pub. A huge artificial fish hung over the bar, its glassy stare seemingly fixed on the actors.

"How do you think things are going this year?" Terence asked.

"It's shaping up nicely," Don answered truthfully. "I was worried about the minimal cast, but you've prepared well and I don't think our low numbers will count against us. Nuala and Anna are sharper than they've been in years. Kate's quality, raw, but we're lucky to have her."

"I'm not sure about Felix," Terence mused. "He's looked rocky."

"Felix is uneven," Don agreed. "And Ingmar will never set the stage alight, but they'll both get by. You and I will be flawless of course."

"Of course," Terence grinned.

"Del..." Don frowned. "What do *you* make of him?"

Terence hedged his bet. "He's unpolished but energetic,

and he's captured that elusive Puckish air. Sometimes I could swear he has pointy ears."

Don laughed. "He can memorise the lines, his expression's fine, his movements are spot on, but he's unpredictable and I don't like unpredictable actors. There's no telling how they'll perform on the night."

"Well, nothing we can do about it now," Terence said. "It's too late to find a new Puck." He paused. "We've left one out, haven't we?"

"Diarmid," Don said grimly.

"Diarmid," Terence sniffed.

They looked at each other darkly, Don thinking about Ingmar's eyes lighting up whenever the banker was in close proximity, Terence wondering how involved his once-shy young friend might be with Anna and Kate.

"What's happened to him?" Don asked. "He's always been shy, anonymous, but this year..."

"He's been acting strangely," Terence said, "but not from the start. The first couple of days he was his normal self."

"That's right," Don agreed, casting his thoughts back.

"Do you recall when he changed?" Terence asked.

Don frowned, then nodded slowly. "When Del moved in with him."

Terence picked up his glass and shook it at the barmaid. "Another, please." Without looking at him, she laid her magazine down and poured.

"I thought you wanted to move on," Don said.

"In a while." Terence chewed his lip. "What's different about Diarmid?"

"He's more confident," Don replied. "He moves gracefully, where before he shuffled. He never looked a person straight in the eye, but now he glides from spot to spot like Lord Muck, studying people openly."

"Women used to scare the wits out of him," Terence said. "Not any more."

Terence's drink arrived. Don downed the last of his and gave the glass to the barmaid. "Another, please, m'dear."

"Rush hour," she grumbled, trundling away with the empties.

"You know what he's like?" Terence said. "A man who just lost his virginity. He's got that, 'Look at me! I've been laid!' bounce to his step."

"You make a fair point," Don grunted.

"Raises an interesting question, doesn't it?" Terence said. Don stared at the director. "*Who* laid him?"

Don studied the splinter in his thumb with great interest. "Do you have any suspects in mind?"

"A couple. How about you?"

Don shrugged. "It could have been somebody from work."

Terence shook his head. "He hasn't seen anyone apart from us since rehearsals commenced."

"Well, it wasn't me," Don laughed.

"Nor me," Terence smiled.

"Shall we include Felix out?"

"I think we should."

The barmaid returned with Don's drink but he didn't glance at it. "Nuala?"

"I doubt it," Terence said. "What about Ingmar?"

Don stiffened but answered calmly, "I wouldn't rule it out but it would surprise me." He waited a beat. "Anna?"

Terence winced. "I don't want to think so, but Diarmid's been acting oddly, and so has Anna. Put two and two together..."

"Might it have been Kate?" Don asked.

"No," Terence said with certainty, even though he wasn't by any means sure.

"That leaves Del," Don noted.

Terence leant forward. "Is Del...? If it's true that one gay can spot another..."

Don laughed drily. "That's a myth. I hadn't pegged him for one of us but you never can tell."

"The thing is," Terence said, "if it *was* Del, and that's why Diarmid's floating on cloud nine, you'd think Diarmid would be hanging off Del as if he was the saviour Himself, but I haven't noticed anything untoward between them."

"Me neither," Don said. "They're close – sometimes I get the absurd feeling that they're a pair of conspirators – but I haven't clocked any sexual attraction."

Terence shook his head, bemused, then raised his glass. Don took a sip from his own, before lifting it in response. "A toast," Terence said sarcastically. "To Diarmid."

They clinked their glass.

"Diarmid," Don agreed bitterly. "Long may he prosper."

"In hell," Terence added.

"Amen," Don concluded.

Beaming tensely, they sank the beers, settled their bill and departed.

*

"You have pretty hands."

Felix had been sticking up a poster on the boarded-over window of a dilapidated house, but froze at Finn's coy remark. His head swivelled and he fixed the doppelganger with his iciest stare. "*What*?"

"Your hands are beautiful," Finn said. "If you were a woman, you —"

"If I was a *what*?" Felix shouted, letting the poster drop.

"A woman with those hands could model them and —"

"Listen, *fairy*," Felix snarled (using the word again because he'd seen how it had shaken his nemesis the first time), jabbing Finn's chest with a couple of fingers. "Keep your eyes the hell away from my hands, and every other bit of me as well."

"What is the matter?" Finn asked. "I was passing a compliment."

"Men don't pass compliments about other men," Felix declared.

"That is sexist," Finn sniffed.

"I don't care." Felix bent to pick up the fallen poster.

"Nice bottom, too," Finn giggled.

"You son of a —" Felix started to roar, but Finn quickly raised his hands.

"I am only teasing you," he said. "You should not be so sensitive."

"I'm not half as *sensitive* as some I could mention," Felix grumbled, but let the subject drop and stuck up the poster, before hastily moving on.

"Your nails could do with a manicure," Finn commented.

"I told you," Felix snarled. "Keep. Your. Eyes. Off."

"Just trying to help," Finn twittered.

"Don't."

"And if you do not tend to those cuticles –"

"I won't warn you again."

"– you will need an operation."

Felix paused. "Operation?" he asked reluctantly, taking the bait.

"You have small hands," Finn said, "but the flesh around the base of the nails is thicker than it should be. Do you get a tingling in your fingertips sometimes?"

Felix nodded slowly.

"That will get worse if you do not act. All you have to do is push the cuticles back with your nails after washing, every time. End of problem."

Felix examined his fingers. "How do you know so much about it?"

"I have read up on the subject," Finn said. Of course he hadn't — the advice was Del's, who had dated a beauty therapist once and knew about these things.

"They really operate for something like that?" Felix asked.

"It is a minor operation," Finn told him. "No risk or pain. But why put yourself through it?"

Felix grunted and dropped his hands. "Thanks."

"My pleasure." A pause. "You should use a moisturiser too. Your skin is dry. If you like, I could recommend –"

"Don't push it," Felix growled.

"Push what?" Finn asked.

"Your luck. I'm grateful for the advice about the cuticles,

but I still don't want you studying me up-close. I don't mind what you lot get up to by yourselves, but if you're thinking of including me in your warped games, forget it."

Finn blinked slowly. "'You lot?'" he asked, mock-perplexed. "'Warped games?' What are you talking about?"

"Don't act the innocent with me," Felix hissed. "I *know*."

"Know what?"

Felix hesitated, then whipped out the pair of knickers which Del had given him. He shook them in front of Finn's eyes, then thrust them back in his pocket.

"Oh," Finn said, acting crestfallen. "How did you...?"

"Never mind," Felix snapped.

"So my secret is out," Finn sighed, kicking a discarded can out of his way. He waited a moment, then smiled slyly. "But so is *yours*."

Felix grew defensive. "What are you talking about?"

"Come on," Finn said. "Why deny it? You would not have the gear if you were not playing queer."

"Not true!" Felix screeched.

"Then why the fancy knickers?"

"They're Nuala's."

"They were not in Nuala's drawer."

"A present. I was going to give them to her."

Finn smiled. "They are not Nuala's size."

"I... they..."

"Look," Finn said kindly, laying a hand on the small man's shoulder, "there is no need to fear it. We can explore together. You can dress up for me. I will not tell anyone. I can be your special friend and you can be mine."

Felix started to shake. "Get your hands off of me!" he screamed. "I'm not gay!" A necking couple across the road looked over, startled, then hurried on their way.

"Then why the knickers?" Finn asked again.

"I don't have to explain myself to you."

"No," Finn agreed, "but perhaps you owe *yourself* the benefit of the truth?"

"There is no 'truth,'" Felix shrieked. "I just like dressing up. I like the feel of a woman's clothes and seeing myself in them. I'm a transvestite, OK?" He saw a woman at a nearby set of traffic lights, staring at him, her eyes wide. "I'm a transvestite!" he roared, spreading his arms Christ-like. She yelped and raced across the road, even though the lights hadn't changed. An angry driver blew his horn but she ignored the threat of death and ploughed ahead.

"A transvestite," Felix said quietly to Finn. "That's all. I'm not gay."

"You are certain?" Finn asked.

"Positive."

"You have not gone out dressed as a woman, hoping to turn men on?"

"No!" Felix exclaimed. "A bit of role play in the bedroom is one thing, but to take it out on the streets..." He shuddered.

Finn nodded slowly. "I may have misjudged you."

"You certainly did."

"I am sorry."

"You should be." Felix was beginning to relax. He even managed a shaky smile. "I misjudged you too. How come you've hidden it all this time?"

"Hidden what?" Finn asked.

"Your" – Felix lowered his voice – "gayness."

"There was nothing to hide," Finn sighed. "I was not interested in men, but since we started rehearsing this year, I have had the hots for you. You turn me on, Felix."

Felix didn't know whether to feel flattered or horrified. "That's strange," he grinned sickly, "but I can't return your feelings. I could never... with a man."

"That is what I used to think," Finn said. He smiled sadly, then brightened up. "Still, there are a few days before rehearsals wrap and we go our separate ways. Time still for the worm to turn."

"Now, look, there's no way –"

"Come on," Finn said, snatching Felix's posters and fliers from him, planting a quick kiss on his cheek. "Race you." He ran ahead, laughing, leaving a bewildered Felix to follow slowly, rubbing his cheek, worrying about the days – and nights! – to come.

*

Anna carefully stashed her bike away in the shed, then walked around front to where a bemused Nuala was waiting, arms crossed. Saying nothing, Anna produced a set of keys and led the way into the house. In the kitchen, she switched on the kettle and rooted through biscuit tins, avoiding Nuala's gaze. Nuala watched her silently for a time, before deciding she'd had enough of this nonsense.

"What's the problem?" she asked coolly.

"Problem?" Anna tipped four chocolate digestives onto a plate.

"Why didn't you stick up for me in the glade?"

Anna shrugged. "I thought you were in the wrong."

"Bull," Nuala snorted. "Even if I was, you should have stuck up for me to spite Terence and Kate. What's going on?"

Anna sighed and sat down. "I don't know. I wanted to side with you but thought the others might realise..."

"Jesus, Anna, all we did was kiss," Nuala barked.

"Not quite all," Anna reminded her.

"We did a lot less than Terence and Kate have been doing."

"We're not talking about them. We're talking about us. And I don't want people knowing there *is* an *us*."

Nuala smiled. "I didn't realise we'd become a fully fledged item."

"We haven't. That's what's confusing." Anna gave the table a thump. "If we'd done something to feel guilty about, I might not feel so bad, but to be on the edge, lingering but not committing..."

The kettle boiled. Since Anna made no move towards it, Nuala took it upon herself to make the tea. She stuck three bags into the pot and poured in the water, stirred and left it to brew.

"I'm confused too," she said softly. "I barely slept last night. I spent the time composing speeches to define my feelings and clear things up between us."

"Come up with anything good?" Anna asked hopefully.

"Nope."

Nuala tested the tea, then poured two cups, adding sugar and milk to Anna's. She laid Anna's cup down on the table. The steam rose and dampened the chubby woman's fringe.

"If we ignored our feelings," Anna said slowly, "and agreed never to speak of them again, do you think we could put this behind us?"

"I don't know," Nuala said. "I'm not good at lying to myself."

"It's only a few more days," Anna said. "Then we can keep out of each other's way. The next time we meet, maybe we'll be able to look back on this and laugh."

Nuala cocked a spurious eyebrow. "You reckon?"

Anna stared into her tea. "No," she said miserably.

"There's another option," Nuala said and Anna looked up. "We go for broke and see how it works out."

"That's a big step," Anna said quietly. "Are you prepared to take it?"

"It's not mine to take," Nuala replied. "I did the early running. I'm not going to campaign for a serious fling, only to have you come back later and say I seduced you. If you want to take this further, *you'll* have to push the boat out."

"But you'd let me push?"

Nuala smiled weakly. "I think so."

They sipped their tea. The kitchen was deadly quiet, except for the beatings of their aggravated hearts.

"What if Terence caught us?" Anna said. "Or Felix?"

Nuala pulled a face. "This is between you and me. When you choose, one way or the other, it has to be for the right reasons. If you don't want to betray Terence, fine, but don't deny yourself if it's only because you're afraid of him."

Anna lowered her cup and closed her eyes. "This is what I'd like you to do. Go up to my bedroom, undress, then stand in the middle of the room with your eyes shut. Don't open them until I tell you. If I catch you looking, it's over, OK?"

"A magical mystery tour," Nuala grinned.

"*OK?*" Anna spoke sharply this time.

"OK," Nuala agreed. "Only don't leave it too long — I might get frightened and run." One more sip, then she went up.

The setting sun had warmed the bedroom and coloured it with a rosy glow. Nuala took off her clothes and carefully folded them over the arm of a chair. She paused when it came to her underwear, but not for long. When she was completely naked, she stood at ease and allowed her eyelids to lower.

For what seemed an age, she stood alone, naked, exposed. As a gentle breeze wafted in through the window, which was open a crack, she worried about Peeping Toms and was on the verge of crossing the room to close the curtains. But then she heard footsteps on the landing and all was forgotten save for the soft, approaching tread.

Anna said nothing when she entered. She stood by the foot of the bed and Nuala could feel her friend eyeing her. She wanted to cover herself with her hands, or look to see what Anna was up to, but didn't dare. Finally she heard Anna undressing – the unmistakable sound of cloth rasping over flesh – and she relaxed.

A minute later, a soft pair of hands alighted on her shoulders. Her head lifted at the touch but her eyes remained closed.

"Turn a little this way," Anna directed her. "Now walk forward until I tell you to stop." Nuala stumbled ahead, wondering what Anna had in mind. "Stop." Anna stepped into

Nuala's back and pressed close against her. "Put your hands behind your back," she said and Nuala obeyed. "Open your eyes."

Nuala's lids lifted and she found herself gazing at her reflection in Anna's full-length mirror. Anna was tucked behind her, so only her arms and hands were visible, sticking out in place of Nuala's.

"Don't move," Anna said. Her head was pressed between Nuala's shoulder blades and the warm breath on her back caused her knees to buckle. "Don't say anything. Just listen. I've often stood before this mirror, naked as you are now. I do it when Terence is out, if I'm feeling low and need cheering up. I call it my magic mirror, because no matter how wrinkled I get or how much weight I put on, in this mirror I always see myself as I was twenty years ago."

Anna's arms folded across Nuala's stomach and her hands came to rest on the larger woman's belly.

"I love this mirror," Anna said. "I love to watch myself. I love to play with myself. I love to watch myself play."

Her fingers spread and traced circles on Nuala's flesh. After a while they crept up to explore the lower curves of Nuala's breasts, then homed in on the nipples. Nuala gave a small groan of pleasure, but was otherwise silent.

"This is the only way I can do it," Anna croaked. "I can't face you, not the first time, but this way it seems like there's only one of us in the room, like *I'm* the one I'm touching."

Anna's right hand slid down Nuala's stomach until it found hair and softness. Nuala groaned again. Her fingers twitched behind her back and she realised how close to

Anna's thighs her hands were. Slowly, she rotated them, massaged the thighs with her palms, then let them gravitate upwards.

Anna tensed when she felt Nuala's fingers stroking the same areas that she herself was exploring, then sighed happily and moved closer into the hands. They remained locked like that for a long time. Then Anna's left hand finally moved. It came up, found Nuala's jaw and gently turned the big woman's head so they were face-to-face.

They exchanged lustful stares for a second, then kissed. Nuala's body spun as if on skates and now they were breast-to-breast as well as face-to-face. They kissed passionately, stumbled backwards and collapsed on the bed.

Their loving was slow and heady, and lasted longer than either had intended, far into the night. They said little. Felix and Terence were forgotten, along with their earlier hesitation. All that existed, all that they knew, was the bed and each other. For them, at that time, there was nothing else in the world.

They completely failed to notice a body climbing the tree outside the window. They didn't hear the twigs snapping or the leaves rustling. They didn't even hear Del's gasp. Nor did they hear his ensuing chuckle. And they certainly didn't see the delighted smile that split his face in two, like a meteor streaking from left to right across the face of the moon.

ACT FOUR

4. [I] (i)

It was the day before Midsummer, and to Del Chapman, all was sweet chaos.

It had been raining steadily since early morning, which ruled out a trip to the glade, meaning they had to hold the dress rehearsal in Terence and Anna's house. This was a tense affair at the best of times — having to undertake it in cramped conditions turned it into a living nightmare.

Because there were so few Players this year, most of the actors had a number of costume changes, which added to the confusion. The first scene of the fourth act was the trickiest. It started with Anna, Finn, Terence, Ingmar, Nuala and Don on stage, all except Finn in their fairy guises. Ingmar, Nuala and Terence would pamper the ass-headed Finn, then exit, Nuala and Terence to change into their Helena and Egeus costumes. Del, as Puck, would enter in their absence, as Oberon lifted the spell from Titania, while Puck removed Bottom's fake head.

In the play, Bottom should stay on stage, asleep, but since Finn was also playing Lysander, Terence had created a scene where Oberon sends him off sleep-walking. While the lord and lady of the fairies celebrated their reunion, Finn would have to switch into his Lysander gear and sneak back to another part of the glade with Felix, Nuala and Kate. The four would lie down to play the sleeping lovers (Puck lulled them to sleep during the preceding act) and wait to be woken.

When Don, Anna and Del exited, Don and Anna had to quickly slip out of their fairy gear and re-enter moments later as Theseus and Hippolyta, accompanied by Terence as Egeus. While they were changing, the spotlights – they had two weak outdoor lights, to supplement the lanterns and torches which they'd set up to ring the glade – would pick out the sleeping quartet, buying time for those off-stage.

The lovers would wake up cured, Lysander back in love with Hermia, Demetrius in love with Helena. They'd head for Athens to prepare for Theseus' wedding to Hippolyta. Moments later, following another quick change of costume, Finn would return as the sleep-walking Bottom, come to his senses, and go off looking for his acting buddies, who bumbled on at the start of the next scene.

It was the most complicated scene of the play and it relied entirely on timing. If they got it right, they'd earn the respect and applause of the audience. A foot out of place and they'd look like a bunch of talentless hams.

Ingmar, in charge of costumes and make-up, was feeling the pressure. He needed to know exactly which costume every Player required, and had to work out the quickest way of slipping them into each new outfit. He'd spent much of the past couple of weeks discussing the problem with Terence, but now that the day of reckoning had arrived, he found himself flustered and lost.

Don was no help. Normally he assisted and made corny jokes to lighten the mood, but this year he left Ingmar to his own devices and stood aloof, laughing whenever Ingmar made a mistake, yawning ignorantly when asked for advice.

The situation worsened as the day progressed. As always, there were rips and tears to be stitched, some of the costumes needed adjusting, make-up went missing or got mixed up. By lunchtime the DJ was a nervous wreck and didn't dare stop for a break in case he collapsed and never recovered.

Terence was almost as stressed as Ingmar. Nothing was working. The Players knew their lines but only Del and Finn appeared to have mastered their roles. Anna and Nuala giggled their way through the play. Kate seemed lost in a world of her own. Don and Felix were sore-headed bears, and Ingmar was a stuttering mess.

A sage director would have called a conference and calmly thrashed things out, but Terence's answer was to scream abuse at everyone and threaten to walk if they didn't cop themselves on.

"You're supposed to be a nobleman," he shrieked at Don, "not James Dean! Get rid of the pout. Straighten up. Lose the drawl.

"Concentrate, Kate! You take your bows at the end of the play, not the middle, so stop preening.

"Nuala! Anna! Quit yapping and deliver the damn lines.

"Ingmar, please, one line without a stammer, just one.

"Smile, Felix, smile. You look like a man whose piles have burst.

"Are Del and Diarmid the only two who realise that if we don't get things right today, we never will? Maybe I should get rid of the rest of you and leave them to do the whole play by themselves."

Most years, Terence wouldn't have called a lunch break the day before the big performance, but he was so disgusted with the way things were going, he got to a point where he could no longer stomach it. "Take half an hour," he told his sullen Players. "Maybe, when we come back, we can have a bit of *acting*, or is that too much to ask?"

Tossing his notes across the room, Terence stormed upstairs to brood in the sanctuary of the bathroom. Silent and downcast, the rest of the Players split up and circulated around the gloomy, rain-shrouded house.

*

"Do you need a hand?" Finn asked.

Ingmar glanced up from the dress he was mending – one of Kate's – and smiled shakily. "It's OK," he said, laying the material aside. "I'm almost finished."

"You look worried," Finn noted, and his concern wasn't entirely faked. "You should rest."

Ingmar laughed desperately. "I'm afraid to stop. If I do, I might never start again." The German sat back and rubbed the base of his neck.

"Stiff?" Finn asked.

"A little," Ingmar admitted.

"Would you like a massage?"

Ingmar looked around to see where Don was.

Finn chuckled. "Surely Don cannot object to *that*." He slid behind the costume designer and began massaging his shoulders and neck.

"Mein Gott," Ingmar breathed. "That's wonderful."

"These muscles are bunched up," Finn tutted. "You need to unwind. Here, have a sniff of this." He handed Ingmar a pouch of fairy dust.

"What is it?" Ingmar asked.

"A little pick-me-up. Perfectly harmless."

"You're sure?"

"Trust me." Finn stuck a finger in the pouch and it came up glittering. He held it to Ingmar's nostrils and smiled. It would have been impolite to refuse, so Ingmar inhaled. He immediately felt ten times lighter. His cares disappeared and the weight of the world lifted. He gazed into Finn's sparkling brown eyes and saw love and promise in them.

"Thank you," he said softly.

"My pleasure," Finn smiled. "Let me get –" He was dipping his finger into the pouch for a second snort, when Don clattered into his back and knocked him sideways. The pouch fell to the floor and the remainder of the dust was lost.

"Terribly sorry," Don snarled.

"No –"

Don turned his back on the toppled changeling and strode away.

"– problem."

"Are you OK?" Ingmar said, picking Finn up and brushing him down.

"He is a brute," Finn grunted, checking for broken bones.

"Sit down," Ingmar said, making space on his workbench. "Tell me what was in that bag."

"A little of this," Finn said, sitting. His hand brushed against Ingmar's left leg, then clasped the knee. "A little of that."

"Tell me more," Ingmar purred, crossing his legs so the hand was sandwiched between two inviting calves.

*

Don saw Ingmar trapping Finn's hand and almost flipped. He started across the room again, eyes misting with rage, but before he could fall upon the men, Del stepped into his path.

"Don," he said. "Can I have a word?"

"Not now," Don grunted, trying to push past.

"It's important," Del said, taking a side-step so he was once again in the drama teacher's way. "It's about Diarmid."

Don hesitated, his fingers clenching and unclenching alarmingly. Then, after a quick check to make sure Finn's hand hadn't made any further progress, he focused on Del. "What?"

"Come outside," Del said and led Don onto the porch, where they could feel the chill of the pelting rain. "Have you noticed anything strange about Diarmid?"

Don laughed brutally. "You could say that."

"He's been hanging around your place, shadowing you and Ingmar?"

"Shadowing one of us, yes."

Del pretended to sigh. "I hope you don't think I'm snooping, but what time did you get home the night before last?"

Don frowned. "The night I was out with Terence?"

"That's the one."

Don shrugged. "Half three or so. Why?"

"I got home about one," Del lied. "I was passing your house when I noticed a figure coming out. I thought it might be a burglar, so I snuck up and prepared to pounce, but it was Diarmid."

"Diarmid was alone in the house with Ingmar?" Don roared. "I'll kill them!" He turned to rush back inside but Del stalled him.

"Ingmar didn't get home till almost two," he said.

Don paused. "You mean Diarmid was there by himself?"

Del nodded.

Don rubbed his bare crown, confused. "Why?"

Del removed a pair of boxer shorts and passed them to a startled Don. "He was carrying a bag," Del said, spinning much the same story that he'd spun the cross-dressing Felix. "I found it under his bed this morning. This was there as well." He showed Don a photograph of himself and Ingmar.

"He snuck into the house to steal Ingmar's boxers and a photo?" Don roared. "The sick son of a bitch."

"That's what I thought," Del agreed. "I've seen the way he's been cuddling up to Ingmar."

"You've noticed it too?" Don hissed.

"But there was another picture in the bag," Del said, "and this one left me flummoxed." He drew out the second photo – he'd pinched both the night after putting up the posters – and handed it across. The photo showed Don, clad only in a tartan kilt, hanging from a caber being held up by two strapping Scotsmen.

"I remember when this was taken," Don said. "Two years ago. The Highlands. But..." He frowned. "Why steal a photo of *me*?"

"Are you sure those shorts are Ingmar's?" Del asked slyly. It hadn't been easy figuring out whose were whose – the lovers didn't have separate drawers – but he felt relatively sure that this pair belonged to the larger of the duo.

Don studied the boxers again. "I can't be positive – we swap underwear a lot – but I *think* these are mine."

Del waited for the penny to drop.

"He's after me, not Ingmar," Don gasped.

"It looks that way," Del said soberly.

"But..." It was too much for Don. "Why the show with Ingmar?"

"Two possible reasons," Del said. "One, he wants both of you. Or two, he's been after you from the start and has been using Ingmar to drive the pair of you apart, so he can move in when you split and stake his own claim."

It was absurd but Del knew it would work. That was the beauty of jealousy — it made a mockery of reason.

"Then he's not really interested in Ingmar?" Don asked.

"Doesn't look like it," Del said.

Don smiled. "I was afraid I was losing him. I thought –"

"I wouldn't get too relieved," Del interrupted.

"What do you mean?" Don snapped. "You said he's using Ingmar to get to me."

"I said it looks that way," Del corrected him. "Even if I'm right, it still leaves the question of how far will he go?"

Don's lips pursed thoughtfully.

"You were going to thump them a minute ago, weren't you?" Del said.

Don smiled sheepishly.

"If we're right," Del continued, "that's what Diarmid wants. It'd drive a wedge between you and Ingmar, then in he'd slip."

"The fiend," Don growled. "What should I do?"

"Tomorrow's your last day here," Del said. "I'd suggest you sit back, stay calm, do the show, then high-tail it out of here as fast as possible."

Don nodded. "Good advice. Thanks, Del. I owe you one."

"Think nothing of it," Del said, hiding his smirk until the bald man had gone back inside. Don trying to bottle-up his rage — ridiculous! He'd never be able to manage it. But a short delay was all Del required. If Don had gone for the two of them now, there'd have been time for him and Ingmar to make up. But following Del's pep talk, he was going to sit back and let them fool around. Watching them flirt would drive the drama teacher crazy. By this time tomorrow, he'd be fit to burst, which was when Del planned to apply the fatal pin.

"You're a nasty young man, Del Chapman," he giggled to himself as he turned his back on the rain and headed in. "That's why I love you."

*

Kate turned the handle of the bathroom door, only to find it locked. "Sorry," she called and turned to head back downstairs.

"Wait," came a reply. There was a soft scuffling sound and then a cautious Terence opened the door a crack. He looked left and right, then swung the door open and gestured her in.

"It's alright," Kate said. "I can wait."

"Get in here," Terence growled, grabbing her. He slammed the door shut and locked it again. "I've been waiting for you. What took you so long?"

"I had no idea where you were," Kate replied, rubbing her arm where he'd grabbed it. "I only came up to use the loo."

"We have to talk," Terence said, sitting on the edge of the bath. "What's gone wrong between us? A few days ago we were red-hot. Now we're nothing."

Kate sighed. "I'm not sure I can explain," she began. "I enjoyed our fling, but that's all it was. It's for the best that we quit before things get too complicated."

"That's not how I saw it," Terence snapped. "I wanted to leave Anna for you."

"For God's sake, don't," Kate gasped. "I don't love you. Our affair was a brief flame that burned brightly, but now the flame's been quenched."

"Don't feed me sappy Mills & Boon lines," Terence snarled. "I'm no fool. I know what's going on. It's Diarmid, isn't it?"

Kate hesitated. "I don't know what you mean."

"You've dumped me for him, haven't you?"

"Of course not. Diarmid has nothing to do with this. We just —"

"I'll leave her," Terence moaned. "Give me your word that you'll stick by me and I'm all yours." He fell to his knees and clasped her hands. "Will you take me, Kate?"

Kate stared into the director's eyes and gulped. "You love Anna," she croaked. "Your children too."

"I love you more," Terence swore.

"Where would we go? How would we live?"

"I don't care. All I want is to be with you. I'd die if I lost you."

Kate removed her hands from Terence's. "You won't die," she said.

"Kate!" Tears welled in Terence's eyes but she steeled her heart against them.

"I'm not sorry for what we had — it was lovely while it

lasted – but it's over and we have to go our own ways. You're upset. You don't know what you're saying. You'll –"

"I know exactly what I'm saying," Terence cried. "I love you. I want you. I must have you."

Kate took a deep breath. "Then you're a fool," she said bluntly.

Terence's face crumbled. "Wh-wh-wh-what?"

"Look at you," Kate said cruelly, hating herself for having to hurt him, but knowing it was the only way to break his fixation. "You're almost fifty, wrinkly, starting to bald. I'm a young, attractive woman, my entire life ahead of me. What makes you think I'd ruin myself for a run-down old fart like you?"

Terence reacted as if kicked in the gut. "You don't mean that," he wheezed.

"It couldn't work," Kate said. "We belong to different eras."

Tears rolled down Terence's cheeks. "We could have something beautiful," he sobbed. "We could be happy. We –"

"Why do you cheat on Anna?" Kate asked quietly.

"What's that got to do with it?" he moaned.

"You cheat because you're dissatisfied," Kate answered for him. "She's not the looker she was. You feel you deserve better. Five or six years, Terence, and that's how *I'd* feel about *you*."

"If you loved me," Terence croaked, "looks wouldn't matter."

"That's the problem," she sighed. "I never loved you. I only fancied you."

"You said... you loved... me." Terence's voice was breaking. "You... said..."

"Never," Kate interrupted. "And you don't love me. You love Anna. No matter how badly you've treated her or how many times you've cheated, Anna's the one your heart belongs to."

"No," Terence sniffed. "She's fat, ugly, dowdy."

Kate rolled her eyes. "Remember what you said a moment ago, about looks not mattering if you love someone?" She tore off some toilet paper and wiped his cheeks. "You need to stop fooling around. Acknowledge your love for Anna and stick by her, or make a clean break and start over." She kissed his forehead platonically. "Either way, you and I are finished."

A stunned Terence nodded, pulled a handkerchief out of a pocket and blew his nose. That seemed to clear his head and he laughed ruefully. "I've been a silly old ass, haven't I?"

"You bared your soul," Kate told him. "I don't see anything silly in that."

Terence smiled weakly. "What happens now? Do we pretend nothing happened between us?"

"We don't have to pretend anything," Kate said, "and I hope we can still be friends, but it's best we keep out of each other's way for a while." She cleared her throat. "It might sound odd after all the dramatics, but would you mind leaving me alone now? I've got to pee awful bad."

Terence laughed again. He checked his face in the mirror, splashed water over it, then headed for the door. He paused with his hand on the knob and glanced over his shoulder. "Can I ask one question?"

"Sure," she said, squeezing her legs together. "As long as it's a short one."

"You and Diarmid...?"

She blushed and nodded.

"Mind if I ask why? I don't mean to sound like a sour loser, but you can do way better than him."

"You've underestimated Diarmid," Kate sniffed. "There's a lot more to him than meets the eye."

"Such as?" Terence challenged her.

She considered telling him about Diarmid's superior chopper but decided not to rub salt in the wounds. "He's very talented," she said. "He's going places."

"What are you talking about?"

"If I tell you something, do you swear to keep it secret?"

"What is it?"

"You have to swear."

Terence sighed melodramatically. "I swear."

"Diarmid's getting into movies," Kate said proudly.

"What?"

"He's going to become a producer."

Terence gawped at her. "Where did you pick up that nonsense?"

"It's not nonsense," she said.

"Diarmid told you this?"

"No — Del."

"Del?" Terence echoed.

"He overheard Diarmid talking on the phone."

Terence stared at her for a couple more seconds, then burst out laughing.

"What's so amusing?" Kate said coolly.

"Come on," Terence guffawed. "Diarmid, a movie producer? He hates movies. He doesn't even watch them."

"You don't have to watch movies to work in them," Kate said.

"True," Terence said, "but a producer has to deal with loads of people, and we all know how much Diarmid loathes social interaction."

"You're just jealous," Kate huffed.

Terence shook his head and unlocked the door. "Think what you like of me, but I've known Diarmid a lot longer than you have, and this movie story is bollocks." His smile spread. "Know what it sounds like?"

"I'm sure you'll tell me no matter what I say," Kate sneered.

"It sounds like a shy man fancied a girl and sent a pal to tell her he's someone special, to spark her interest in him."

"That's..." Kate stopped, her eyes widening.

"And it worked," Terence crowed. "You didn't look at him twice before he was a fledgling producer. Now he's got you wrapped around his little finger."

"You don't know what you're talking about," Kate gasped, her face white.

Terence's smile grew wistful. "I made a fool of myself, but my feelings for you were genuine. I slept with you because I wanted you. In all honesty, do you really want Diarmid?" When there was no answer, he slipped out and closed the door on a silent, gobsmacked Kate Pummel.

*

Anna and Nuala fell giggling into the closet beneath the stairs. "Howdy, lover," Nuala chuckled, kissing Anna's chin.

"Big howdy right back atcha," Anna replied, squeezing the breasts she'd recently got to know so well.

"Last night was wild, wasn't it?" Nuala sighed happily, finding Anna's lips.

"Even better than the first time," Anna mumbled through the kiss.

The door to the closet creaked open a notch, frightening the embracing ladies. When they realised they hadn't been discovered, their heartbeats slowed to normal.

"You look good today," Nuala remarked, studying Anna's face in the thin beams of penetrating light.

"Meaning I looked awful yesterday?" Anna smirked.

"No, but today you're... It's hard to put into words."

"You don't have to," Anna said. "I can see what you mean by looking at *you* — your face has it as well."

"What's *it*?" Nuala asked.

"Freedom," Anna answered, sliding a hand down the inside of Nuala's trousers.

"I like the taste of freedom," Nuala sighed, nibbling at Anna's neck while five wriggling fingers set her insides on fire. "Not too much," she gasped. "We've got to go back and face the others."

"I wish we didn't," Anna groaned. "I wish we could run away and never see any of them again."

"Why don't we?" Nuala asked.

Anna paused. "You mean it?"

"Sure. Pack a bag. I'll get mine. We'll ride off into the sunset."

Anna smiled. "You make it sound simple."

"Isn't it?"

"What about our husbands?"

"Stuff 'em!"

"And my children?"

"We'll send for them later. We'll move some place cheap but beautiful, Mexico or South Africa, buy a huge house and make love every day."

"How would we live?" Anna said.

"I've got savings," Nuala said. "I can go on writing. You can get a job. It'll be paradise."

Anna smiled dreamily. "You've convinced me. Let's go."

"Really?"

"No," Anna laughed. "The last couple of days have been wonderful, and maybe we *will* ride off into the sunset together, but I'm confused. I don't know what I'm doing or why. For the time being, let's stick with the sex, OK?"

"Fine by me," Nuala smirked. "I like the sex." She kissed Anna again. "You on for tonight?"

"Name the time and place."

"The glade, if it stops raining, as soon as we can get away from the morons we call husbands."

"The glade," Anna murmured. "It's been years since I had sex outdoors. What if the rain doesn't stop?"

Nuala pulled a face. "Then I'll provoke a row with Felix, he'll storm out in a huff, and we can get down and dirty in my place."

"You've such a way with words," Anna giggled.

"That's not all I have a way with," Nuala said, tweaking her lover's nipples.

They shared one final kiss and a grope, then let themselves out and returned to the study, and their act of innocence was far more convincing than anything they'd ever performed in the play.

4.[I](ii)

The dress rehearsal continued after the break. Though the Players were no better than before, Terence didn't ride them so hard — he was too morose to care about the faltering actors. They stumbled through the final act, and it was awful. Lines were forgotten and costumes confused, actors forgot the names of their characters, where they were supposed to stand, how they were to speak.

Terence barely said a word to his bumbling troops. When they got to the end he mumbled, "Fine," then returned to the start of the play for another run-through.

The first scene of the second act was the only one which didn't require Finn's presence. He was heading out for some fresh air when he noticed Felix standing near the door, practising his lines. The changeling grinned. "Hi, sexy," he said softly.

Felix almost dropped his copy of the play. "Buzz off!" he snapped.

"That's no way to speak to one who loves you," Finn cooed.

"I'm warning you..."

"Calm down," Finn laughed. "I won't bite."

"Damn right you won't."

"You still haven't admitted your true feelings," Finn noted.

"Don't start with that rubbish again," Felix growled. Finn had spent most of the previous day badgering the Northerner, who was beginning to feel the strain.

"Why won't you accept that it's meant to be?" Finn asked. "Give me one night and see if you –"

"I won't give you one minute, never mind a whole night," Felix said.

"A minute might be enough," Finn said. "I'm so hot for you, I don't think it'd take me long to –"

"Stop!" Felix shouted, startling the rest of the Players. "Leave me alone. I don't want to hear any more." Throwing his copy of the play at Finn, he shoved past to the others. "My turn," he grunted and launched into his lines as Demetrius, even though it was too early in the scene. Nuala thought about chastising her diminutive husband, then saw the look on his face and played along.

Ingmar, meanwhile, had fetched the fake ass' head. It was the worse for wear and he wasn't sure how many more years they could squeeze out of it. He'd have to pester Terence into buying a new one. As Ingmar combed knots out of the hair, he caught Don studying him. The drama teacher had been acting strangely since the break. His furious gaze of the morning had been replaced with a pitying stare, which flummoxed the DJ — why should Don *pity* him?

One of the ass' ears was hanging crooked, so Ingmar began twisting. He was still thinking about Don, not paying attention to what his hands were doing. All of a sudden there was a snapping sound and the ear came off in his hand.

"Oops," Ingmar laughed.

"Must be a Van Gogh model," Del joked.

"A bit of glue and it'll be right as rain," Ingmar vowed, rising to fetch his tub of trusty adhesive.

"For Christ's sake," Terence shouted, stopping the German dead in his tracks. "We need that head tomorrow."

"I know," Ingmar said nervously.

"We can't parade it in front of the public with one ear missing."

"It von't be missing," Ingmar said, his accent surfacing thickly. "I told you — I glue it back on, yah? It vill be goot as new."

"It won't be good as new," Terence yelled, finding his inner rage again and welcoming it back — fury helped block out sadness. "How can it be good as new when one of its ears is dangling loose?"

"It... it... it..." Ingmar began to shake.

"What will people say?" Terence stormed. "They'll think we're a stingy pack of bastards who won't shell out for a decent ass' head."

"And they'd be right," Anna murmured but Terence pretended not to hear.

"I can't believe you're so bloody clumsy," Terence continued.

"I didn't mean to break the stupit ear," Ingmar wailed, tears rolling down his cheeks. "It's your fault. I told you ve needed a new head but vould you listen? Nein! You vere too mean, too —"

"You said nothing to me about a new head," Terence interrupted.

"I did," Ingmar howled. "Last year, after the show, I said ve'd be lucky to get another performance out of it. You laughed unt said it vould be fine."

"Last year?" Terence snorted. "Why didn't you say anything a week ago? That would have given us time to —"

"Last veek?" Ingmar shrieked. "How could I tell you last veek vhen you don't let me get it down until today? Hah! I spit on your *last veek*." He coughed up a wad of phlegm and spat on the floor to prove his disgust.

"Calm down, Ingmar," Kate said, alarmed. "It's no big deal. We can sort it out, I'm sure, if we only –"

"It *is* a big deal," Terence shouted. "I'm the director, so I'm the one who'll get crucified by the critics."

"I vish you *vere* bloody crucified," Ingmar roared. "I vish someone vould stick you on a cross unt... unt..." He could say no more. Knocking the ass' head to the floor, he stomped on it, burst into a flood of tears and collapsed. "I can't go on. All day, people shouting unt harassing me. I can't continue. I can't!"

All eyes turned to Don as Ingmar buried his face in his hands and sobbed. The bald man hesitated, then stepped forward and laid an arm across his lover's back. "Come on," he said gently. "Let's go for a walk." There was no answer. "Ingmar?" He gave him a soft squeeze.

Ingmar lumbered to his feet. "But vot about...?" Ingmar kicked the ass' head.

"Somebody else will fix it. You need a break. You've been pushing yourself too hard. A couple of..." His voice faded as they left the room.

The Players stared at one another, then at the battered head, then at Terence, who pulled a face. "I hate these temperamental Europeans. Alright." He pointed at Del and Finn. "Get the glue. Anna, brush away the worst of the dirt. Kate..." He looked for the ear but couldn't locate it. "Find the ear. Let's go, people. We don't have time for hysterics. Now, Nuala," he said as the others got busy, "let's get it clear once and for all exactly which speeches you wish to keep..."

*

A subdued Ingmar was eventually led back to the study by Don, who was being nicer to the German than he'd been in ages. The ear had been glued onto the head and would be fine as soon as it dried. Nothing further was said about it and Ingmar got back to sorting out the costumes and make-up.

Finn edged up to Kate during a quiet moment and pinched her bottom. "You are quiet today," he observed.

"Thinking," she told him. Her gaze was serious. Was Terence right about the banker? Had it all been a ruse to get her into the sack? She hadn't thought Finn capable of such deception, but...

"Fancy some shared *thinking* when the sun goes down?" he asked.

"Maybe."

Finn frowned. "You do not sound enthusiastic."

"We'll discuss it later," Kate said.

The changeling shrugged, ambled past the busy Ingmar and winked. Ingmar made sure Don wasn't watching, then winked back. He felt guilty immediately – Don had been so kind during their little walk – and signalled Kate over.

"Listen," he said, "I've been thinking about our bet. I'm not sure –"

"I'll set it up tonight," she said. He'd wanted her to arrange the rendezvous last night but things hadn't worked out. "The glade. As soon as we're done here."

Ingmar hesitated. He'd been on the verge of calling it off,

but now that she was offering him a clear-cut chance...

"Won't it be wet?" he asked.

She glanced out the window. The rain was easing at last and she could see some breaks in the clouds. "It'll have stopped raining by then," she said confidently.

"But the grass won't have dried," he objected.

Kate sniffed. "That's your problem. You didn't stipulate conditions when we made the bet. Do you want to withdraw your challenge?"

Ingmar grinned. "Not likely. The glade it is. You can get him there?"

"I can get him there," Kate smiled. The smile faded as she turned away. "And if Terence is right," she whispered to herself, "you can have him for all that I care."

Finn was on his way over to Del when Don took him by the arm and led him aside. The fairy tensed – he thought he might be in for a thrashing – but Don only smirked and tapped his nose. "I'm on to you, Master Garrigan."

"Oh?" It was the only safe answer Finn could think of.

"You've been sly but I can be slyer."

"Can you?"

"Make all the moves you want — they won't get you anywhere. Not with *me*." He waved Finn on his way.

"These people get odder and odder," Finn muttered.

As Finn drew up beside Del, Anna was asking Terence if she could pop upstairs for a break.

"Another? It's only been a couple of hours since the last." Terence tutted but consented. "Don't be long. We've still much to cover."

"Call if you need me."

Del saw the look she exchanged with Nuala and wasn't surprised when, a minute later, Nuala also asked to be excused. "I want to phone my agent," she told Terence. "I meant to do it before I left home but I forgot. I'll pay for the call."

"Don't be silly," he chuckled. "Go ahead."

"You don't mind?"

"As long as you're not on the phone all night."

She slid out.

Del waited a minute before whispering in Finn's ear. Finn nodded and cleared his throat. "Is it alright if I go home briefly?" he asked.

Terence rolled his eyes but gave Finn a curt nod.

"I will be quick about it."

"Take all the time you like," Terence said drily.

Finn let himself out the front door and closed it lightly, then stood to one side, sheltering from the rain.

Del counted to fifty before making his move on Felix. "Did you hear the door shut?" he asked quietly.

Felix frowned. "No. So what?"

"I wonder if Diarmid actually left."

Felix stared at Del. "Why wouldn't he?"

Del coughed into a fist. "When he opened the door to this room, I glimpsed the telephone stand in the hallway and I didn't see Nuala anywhere near it."

Felix looked blank.

"I've been thinking," Del said. "I know we concluded that Diarmid had his sights set on you –"

"Too bloody true," Felix snorted.

"– but maybe we were wrong."

Felix shook his head. "The way he's been sniffing about me recently…"

"That's what bothers me," Del said. "Until a few days ago, if Diarmid had feelings for you, he did a fine job of keeping them hidden. Now he's covering you like a rash. It doesn't seem right."

"What are you saying?" Felix asked.

"Maybe his advances are a smoke screen. Maybe I was meant to find that pair of undies. Maybe he wants you thinking he's gay as a lark."

"Why…?" Felix trailed off into silence. "Nuala exits," he whispered. "Says it's to make a call but doesn't call. Diarmid says he's leaving but we don't hear him leave." His gaze slowly rose to the ceiling. "They couldn't…"

"Where Diarmid's concerned, anything's possible," Del remarked.

Felix's jaw set firmly. "I'm going up there," he growled.

"I think you should," Del concurred.

"But if I don't find them wrapped in each other's arms" – he gave Del a dig in the ribs – "I'm coming back to kick your arse from here to Timbuktu."

"Me?" Del squeaked. "What have I done?"

"You've been stirring the pot ever since you arrived," Felix said.

"I'm only looking out for you," Del moped. "I consider myself your friend."

"Maybe you are," Felix said. "And if what you're saying proves true, I'll accept you as such. But if I find you've been raising a stink for no good reason..." He left the threat hanging and headed for the door.

"Where are you off to?" Terence asked, surprised.

"Upstairs," Felix answered without slowing.

"But it's your turn," Terence protested.

"Let somebody else take it."

"We can't. This isn't..." But Felix was already gone. "What the hell is wrong with people today?" the director snorted.

"Nerves," Del said, stepping forward. "I'll take Felix's lines until he returns. Where are we?"

Terence cursed the day he'd become involved with such an undedicated crowd. Then he told Del, "It's Flute's first line as Thisbe. 'O wall, full often hast thou heard my moans.'"

Upstairs, the walls were hearing plenty of moans. Felix heard them too as he mounted the steps and traced them to the bedroom door. He stood there a moment, listening to the sighs, grunts and muted cries. They were going at it like a pair of cats. Had they no shame?

Felix looked for something to brandish as a weapon but the landing was free of blunt instruments. "Never mind," he thought. "My fists and feet will do."

He considered kicking the door open but opted for the soft approach — better if he could sneak up on them unobserved. Besides, he might damage himself if he attacked the door.

He turned the handle slowly, praying it wasn't locked from the inside.

It wasn't.

Sliding in, he smiled. It would be good to lay into that wife-stealing banker. He didn't care if he went to jail — it would be worth it, just to see the sonofabitch pleading and bleeding.

He made out a pair of figures on the bed – they'd half-closed the curtains – and moved in on them like a panther closing in for the kill. At first they appeared to be a single entity, two heads, four arms and a flurry of legs, but as he got closer he was able to separate the two shapes. That was important. He didn't want to hurt Nuala. Despite what she'd done, she was still a woman, and Felix didn't believe in hitting women. So he paused at the foot of the bed, searching for the female form. Only... there appeared to be... two of them...

Felix's smile vanished. He bent over for a closer look, to be absolutely certain – it was a minor miracle that the lovers didn't spot him – then stumbled out of the bedroom in a daze. He leant against the wall and numbly dwelt on what he'd witnessed, then wound his way downstairs, back to the study.

Terence was in deep conversation with Ingmar and Don, while Del was chatting with Kate. Del spotted the stunned Felix and excused himself. Kate wandered over to see what the other three were talking about.

"Well?" Del asked quietly but Felix couldn't answer. "Did you find them?"

"I... I need to sit down," Felix wheezed.

Del led the befuddled insurance agent to a chair. Once he was seated, Del asked if he wanted a drink.

"No." Felix's eyes were wide.

"You found them, didn't you?" Del tried to sound morose. "Believe me, Felix, I'm not glad I was right. I wish –"

"Diarmid wasn't there," Felix said.

Del beamed. "That's wonderful. You had me worried for a second. I thought –"

"It was Anna."

Del feigned confusion. "Anna? What do you mean?"

"It was Anna. In the bedroom. Anna."

Del let his eyes narrow. "Diarmid and Anna? The fiend! What will Terence say when he finds out?"

"Not Diarmid and Anna," Felix snapped. "Nuala and Anna."

"You've lost me," Del said.

"Upstairs," Felix whimpered. "Nuala and Anna. On the bed. Making love."

Del's eyes widened and he gasped. He was overdoing the theatrics but Felix was too shocked to notice. "No! It can't be!"

"Nuala and Anna," Felix sobbed again.

"It's hideous," Del moaned. "What are you going to do?"

"I don't know," Felix sighed. "How can I compete with...?" As he struggled to find the words to express himself, the door opened and Nuala breezed in.

"There now," she smirked. "That wasn't so long, was it?"

Felix started to shake. Del thought he was about to leap across the room to confront her. He shifted aside, so he wouldn't be in the way, and waited for the sparks to fly. But before Felix could act, Anna sauntered into the room.

"Hope I didn't keep you waiting too long," she smiled.

The fight drained from Felix and he groaned softly. Del was disappointed and wondered if he should give the Northerner a verbal dig, but figured it would be best to let things lie for a while. Give him a chance to stew.

Del patted Felix on the back, told Terence he was going to the toilet, then went and fetched Finn.

"How did it go?" Finn asked.

"Like a dream," Del said. Then, thinking of Felix, he amended his opinion. "Like a *nightmare*."

Back in the room, Terence was still involved with Don and Ingmar. He reached a decision just as Del and Finn were coming in, asked Ingmar for something, then cautiously made his way across to where a dejected Felix sat slumped in a chair.

"Ahem," Terence said jovially. When there was no reaction, he tried again. "Ahem!" At the fourth attempt, Felix lifted his head and stared at Terence with devastated eyes.

"You're on," Terence said, handing Felix a balled-up piece of material.

Felix turned the cloth around in his hands without unfolding it. "Can't you go and pester somebody else?" he croaked.

Terence frowned. "I'm not pestering you. It's time we finalised your costume for the final act, where you play Thisbe."

"Play, play, play," Felix sighed. "Is that all you think about?"

"We have to do this," Terence insisted. "Everybody else has been sorted. Yours is the last costume. It'll only take a few minutes. You can slip it on over your own clothes — in the play you'll be wearing it over your Flute costume."

Felix realised the only way to get rid of the annoying director was to try on the blasted outfit. Getting to his feet, he gave the costume a shake and it unrolled. He raised it high and spent a couple of confused seconds trying to locate the legs. When it dawned on him that there weren't any, an awful calm washed over him. "This is a dress," he said softly.

Terence smiled. "Yes, but not a real dress. You slip it on over your clothes. It's not –"

"This is for a *woman*," Felix shouted. "I'm not wearing this." He dropped the dress to the floor and ground his heels on it.

"Hey!" Ingmar yelled. "I spent the last half hour stitching that together."

"If you like it so much," Felix snarled, "*you* wear it." He kicked the dress high into the air and across the room — amazingly, it landed on Ingmar's head.

"Felix," Terence groaned, "it's only a bit of fun. Thisbe *has* to appear in a dress. It's the –"

"We agreed," Felix roared. "I said I wouldn't do it if I had to wear a dress, and you said that was fine."

"There was no point complicating life early on," Terence whined. "I figured, as you grew into the role, you'd see how silly you were being and –"

"You lied to me."

"No, Felix, I –"

"You lied!" He whirled on Del, fire in his eyes. "Did *you* know about this?"

"It's news to me," Del replied honestly.

"I won't do it," Felix said, facing Terence again.

"But you have to," Terence protested. "How else are you going to convince the audience that –"

"To hell with the audience," Felix screeched. "I'm not

going out there dressed as a freak, not for you, not for the Players, not for –"

"I think you would look cute in a dress."

Felix turned slowly. "What?"

"It is a great idea," Finn said, smiling coyly. "You should wear *just* the dress, plus maybe sexy knickers, lacy tights... You would look peachy."

"You... you..." A darkness fell over Felix's face. His pupils contracted until they were pinpricks in two pools of icy hatred. Finn saw what was happening but kept his grin fixed in place.

"I could help you dress, if you liked," Finn murmured.

"You..."

"And *un*dress, when you are finished," Finn added.

"You bastard!" Felix finally snapped. With a yell straight from a war movie, he threw himself on the startled Finn – he hadn't expected *this* vehement a response – and pummelled him with his fists.

"Help!" Finn squeaked, feeling his ears redden from the blows.

"I'll kill you," Felix roared. "I'll rip your guts out and stuff them up your arse, then rip them out again!"

"That would be sore," Ingmar muttered to Don.

"I'll rip off your manhood and force you to eat it!"

"I wouldn't mind seeing that," Don replied.

"When I'm through with you," Felix screamed, "you'll be –"

An arm snaked around his throat and dragged him back. He choked and beat at the arm but it held him firmly. Then a leg kicked his out from beneath him and he was being supported solely by the arm.

"Get him out of here," Nuala bellowed, nodding towards the gasping Finn, never slackening her hold on her husband.

"My ears!" Finn howled.

"Forget your ears," Del said, hoisting him towards the door. "If you stay and he gets loose, your ears will be the least of your worries."

"I did not know he would go crazy," Finn said. "I was only trying to raise his goat."

"Consider it well and truly raised," Del chuckled, leading him towards the door. Felix gave a fiery grunt when he saw his prey escaping but Nuala knew what she was doing and the closest he got to the departing Finn was when one of his wild kicks connected with the fairy-raised's thigh.

"Ow," Finn winced. Then, to Del, he whispered, "Did I do wrong?"

"You did a marvellous job," Del assured him, "but there's a time to provoke and a time to run." He opened the door and hurried Finn outside.

"I'm letting you go now," Nuala told the raging Felix. "If you try to chase them, I'll knock you down and sit on you." Dropping her arm, she gave him a shove that sent him to his knees. "Stand back," she warned the rest of the Players. "If the fight's not out of him, he could be dangerous."

Felix coughed and rubbed his bruised throat. "You nearly choked me to death."

"Pity I didn't," Nuala retorted.

"What was it all about?" a shaken Kate asked from near the back of the room.

"Pride," Nuala answered. "Silly, childish pride. He —"

"I saw you in the bedroom," Felix screamed, pointing an accusing finger at her. Nuala turned white, as did Anna. "I thought you were with Diarmid, so I sneaked in. I *saw*."

"What's he rabbiting on about?" Terence asked.

"Anna too," Felix shrieked, switching his finger to the smaller woman.

"Shut up," Nuala hissed, taking a threatening step forward.

"They were screwing upstairs," Felix yelled, scrambling backwards to avoid the advancing colossus.

"Who were?" Terence still hadn't got it.

"Our wives," Felix howled. "Nuala and Anna, in *your* bed, going at it like a pair of life-long lesbians."

Nuala halted. Anna stopped breathing. Kate gasped. Don and Ingmar raised their eyebrows. Terence...

Terence *gawped*. First at Felix. Then at Nuala. Finally at Anna.

"No," the director sighed.

"Yes," Felix laughed viciously.

"Not my Anna."

"Your Anna, Nuala's Anna, everybody's Anna."

"You're lying."

"Look at them," Felix shouted. "Guilt's steaming out their ears."

Terence took a stumbling step towards his wife. "Anna?" he wheezed. "It's not true. Tell me it isn't." Anna made no reply. "Anna?" he asked again. "Anna?" His voice was the same each time. It neither rose nor fell. "Anna?"

"I hope you're proud of yourself," Nuala sneered at Felix.

"What about you?" Felix retorted. "I'm not the one who

snuck upstairs with my best friend's wife. I'm not the one breaking the law."

"It's not against the law," Nuala said.

"It's against the law of the church," Felix roared. "You've betrayed me and destroyed our marriage, and for what? A quickie with the local frump."

"Hey," Anna objected weakly, automatically.

"Not just a quickie," Nuala said darkly.

Felix stared at her. "That wasn't the first time?"

"Hardly," she laughed.

"Nuala," Anna groaned.

"How long has it been going on?" Felix was trembling.

"Years," Nuala mocked him. "Every time your back's been turned."

"With Anna?"

"Yes."

"Just Anna?"

She paused. "That would be telling."

"Anna?" Terence asked again.

"You're a... You're nothing but a..." Felix could find no words to express his contempt. Nuala, seeing sorrow mingling with disgust in his eyes, began to relent. She made no apologies but said nothing to further inflame the situation.

"You've ruined me," Felix sighed.

"Anna?" Terence said.

"You ruined yourself," Nuala muttered, but without conviction.

"I didn't deserve this," Felix said quietly. "Whatever you feel I've done to hurt you, I didn't deserve *this*."

Nuala stared at the floor, embarrassed beyond response.

"I'll go now," Felix said and calmly took his leave. He brushed past Del on his way but paid no attention to him, or to Finn, who was cowering behind the mischief-maker. He didn't know where he was going. He just had to get away.

"Anna?" Terence was staring at her and she was staring back at him, crying, unable to answer, while Kate, Nuala, Don and Ingmar hovered in the background, stiff as corpses, white as ghosts.

Del stepped into the room, Finn close behind, and beamed at everyone. "Did we miss anything?"

4.[I](iii)

There was no continuing after Felix's bombshell, and the dress rehearsal drew to an early conclusion. Nuala and Anna stood at opposite sides of the room, staring uncertainly at each other and their fellow Players, except for Terence, who had retreated upstairs.

Kate cleared her throat and smiled crookedly. "I'll be off," she gurgled. "Get a good night's sleep. Have a hot bath. Tuck in with the play and…" She trailed off, then voiced the question on all their minds. "There *is* going to be a play, right?"

Anna glanced at the younger woman and shrugged. "I don't know."

"Surely," Kate said, "after all this time and effort, we can't just abandon it."

Anna smiled wanly. "Some things in life are more important than the play," she said without reproach. "I'll call you in the morning." She addressed the rest of the Players. "I'll call you all, once I've talked with Terence."

"Will you talk with Felix, too?" Nuala laughed edgily but Anna didn't reply.

As Kate left, Del tapped Finn. "Go after her. Make sure she sticks around."

Finn nodded and took off. He caught up with her halfway down the garden path. "Kate," he stopped her. She was crying. "Are you alright?"

"Do I look alright?" she sobbed. "Two weeks busting a gut, and now…"

"It is not over," he told her. "The play will proceed.

Terence will not abandon a production because of personal problems. When tomorrow dawns, he will take a long, hard look at things and decide to plough ahead."

"But if Felix doesn't return..."

"We will work around it."

Kate giggled pitifully. "It was some turn-up. Sweet little Anna and big, burly Nuala. Nothing would surprise me after that."

"Listen," Finn said, "maybe this is not the right time, but we have the best part of a night to kill, so why not...?" He left it hanging.

Kate dug out a handkerchief and blew her nose, remembering her promise to Ingmar. There was nothing he could do if she broke it, but she was curious. She wanted to know how Finn would react if tempted. If he *did* swing both ways, it would be best to discover the truth now.

"Meet me in the glade," she told him, "half an hour from now."

"Half an hour it is." He smiled. "You will not do anything silly, will you?"

"Like what?" she asked.

"Run out on us?"

She snorted. "I'm no quitter. I'm going nowhere until this is over."

"And then?" Finn asked.

She paused. This was her chance to commit herself, to let him know they had a future together if he wanted. But how to say it without revealing the fact that she knew about his movie ties (assuming he *had* such ties)?

"Have you ever thought about quitting your job at the bank?" she asked.

Finn – who'd heard nothing from Del of his move into producing – considered the question from his brother's point of view. "No," he said.

"No?" Kate's smile dropped.

"Perfectly happy at the bank."

She laughed uneasily. "What if someone..." She hesitated, then came right out with it. "What if a movie producer asked you to pitch in on a deal?" There. It was out in the open. No more pretending. Now he knew she knew the truth and they could talk freely.

But Finn knew nothing of the so-called truth. "I would turn him down flat," he said, assuming that was what she wanted to hear.

Kate stared at him. There was no hint of deceit in his voice or expression. A dreadful cold weight settled in her stomach.

"*Has* a movie producer ever asked you for backing?" she asked quietly.

Finn ran a hand through her hair. "You are in shock. Maybe we should make it an hour before we meet. You could do with a rest."

"Diarmid," she growled, grabbing his hand. "Tell me truthfully, you aren't a producer? Nobody approached you with a deal to make movies?"

Finn frowned, concerned. "Are you sure that you are alright? Perhaps we should take you to a doctor. You look awfully pale."

Kate's world was crashing down around her but she managed to keep her wits. "Did you ever put Del up to anything?"

"What do you mean?"

"Did you ask him to play a joke on me, feed me a silly story about you to make you look good?"

Finn frowned, beginning to sense that something had taken place behind his back. "Take no notice of what that one says. Del Chapman's a born liar. If he tells you the sun rises in the east, look west in the morning."

"There's no movie deal?"

"I know nothing about movies," he said, "and I had nothing to do with whatever lie he fed you."

She nodded slowly. "Thank you for your honesty. I'll go home now."

"Do you want me to come?"

"No. I'd rather be by myself."

"The glade is still on?" he asked.

"Yes," she said, starting down the path again. "The glade's still on."

He watched her go, then went in search of the silver-tongued Del, determined to wring the full and undoubtedly ugly story out of him.

*

Don and Ingmar were readying themselves to leave when Finn burst in and dragged a startled Del away, to interrogate and berate him all the way home.

Don smiled at Ingmar and the ladies. "Every house is having its share of trouble today. Ready, Ingmar?"

Ingmar nodded and laid the repaired ass' head safely on his vacated chair. He'd been busy packing costumes away, assuring they'd be in good shape for the play if it went ahead. He coughed to attract Anna's attention. "Tell Terence, if you're talking to him later, that everything's ready if he wants it. A lot of the suits are held together with little more than dust and hope, but they'll get us to the end of the play."

Anna smiled faintly. "Thanks, Ingmar. You did a wonderful job. Terence would be heaping praise on you if he was here."

Ingmar blushed happily. "That's kind of you." He faced Don and raised an eyebrow. Don nodded and they departed...

...leaving Anna and Nuala alone.

Nuala let out a long, ragged breath and sank into a chair. "This is the worst day of my life." She frowned, considering the lows of the past. "Well, Martin's dying was a downer, and there have been a couple of other major blows, but otherwise this is the grand stinkeroo."

"You're taking it well," Anna noted.

Nuala shrugged. "It hasn't sunk in. I feel like this is happening to someone else and I'm just watching. I'm waiting for normal service to be resumed."

Anna smiled wretchedly. "I don't think we'll ever see normal service again, not with Terence and Felix."

"Felix surprised me," Nuala said. "I thought he'd explode if he ever found me in bed with somebody else. I hadn't expected the quiet desperation."

"He was in shock," Anna said. "Terence too. To find out we'd been unfaithful with each other..."

"Odd that *that* should make a difference," Nuala said. "I'd have thought finding your wife with another woman would be preferable to discovering her with a man. Most men seem turned on by the idea of lesbianism."

"Fantasy-wise, yes," Anna agreed. "I don't think it's the same when it actually happens. What do you think they'll do when they recover?"

"Felix will probably file for divorce and never speak to me again," Nuala sighed, "but Terence might prove more forgiving."

Anna shook her head. "I wounded him in front of his closest friends. He'll never forgive me for that."

"Well, never mind those two," Nuala said. "What about us? Do we head off into the sunset now, like we discussed?"

"I don't know," Anna said. "This has all happened too fast. The affair was one thing, but this is something else. I don't know what to do."

"You know what I want?" Nuala asked.

"A drink?" Anna guessed.

"Later. First, a walk. I want to get out of this room – it feels like we've been stuck in here forever – stretch my legs and breathe fresh air. Tire myself out and come back with a clear head. Take things from there."

"Sounds good," Anna said.

"Care to join me?"

Anna thought about confronting Terence, which she'd have to do if she stayed. "Let me get my jacket."

"Get mine as well," Nuala said. "I need to pop to the toilet."

"Be careful," Anna warned. "If Terence sees you, he might attack."

"Don't be silly," Nuala laughed. "Terence wouldn't..." She stopped, struck by a recollection of a book she'd once written. Unlike the majority of her books, *Love's Last Gamble* ended on a down note. The hero had fought tooth and nail to win the heart of the one he loved, only to find her at the end in the arms of another. He'd retreated to the cellar of his house, poured a glass of wine, drunk it slowly, then strolled upstairs, pausing on his way to pick up an axe. The book ended with him entering the bedroom but the implied message – that he'd chop the lovers up into tiny pieces – was clear.

"Actually, I'll skip the toilet," Nuala said. "I can duck behind a bush. Come on. Let's get our coats and hurry."

*

When Finn was through lecturing Del about lying and concealing secrets from him, he went looking for a change of clothes.

"Where are you off to?" Del asked grumpily, trailing Finn to his bedroom. He hadn't liked having his wrists slapped, but was wary of upsetting the changeling this close to the final day, so he hadn't bitten back.

"I am meeting Kate in the glade," Finn replied.

"You haven't fallen in love with her, have you?" Del asked.

"I like her," Finn answered. "That is all."

"Then why get so aggressive when you found out I'd lied to her?"

"Because you also lied to *me*," Finn snapped. "I looked like a fool."

"That's all that's bothering you?" Del asked.

Finn hesitated. "No. The dirty tricks are upsetting me. What we are doing here is nasty and cruel. I know this is what I signed up for, so I cannot complain, but I am starting to regret saying yes to your Plan."

"It's too late for regrets," Del grumbled, refusing to admit to himself that he was harbouring misgivings as well. "The lie got you in her pants, didn't it?"

"I did not want to ensnare her this way," Finn shouted. "To charm her would have been delightful, but to trick her in so rotten a fashion…"

"You recall why we're here, don't you?" Del asked softly.

"Of course," Finn said. "To disband the Players and ensure they never perform again. That does not mean we have to wreck their lives."

"That's what Oberon would have done," Del said. "He craved bloodshed."

"I know," Finn sighed. "You have come at this artfully for the most part, but at times you have been vicious. Poor Terence and Felix."

"It wasn't me who put Nuala and Anna together," Del said.

"But you sent Felix up to spy on them."

"I didn't hear you objecting. You were quite amused at the time."

Finn nodded. "I am guilty too. We have both done things we should not have. Only, now that we are close to the end, surely we can show compassion? Why must we continue turning the screws when success is in our grasp?"

"Is it?" Del asked.

"Felix will never perform with the Players again. Nuala and Anna will forsake Terence. We have undermined the core. The rest will crumble too."

"You don't know as much about humans as you think," Del said. "Forgiveness comes easy to us. Trust me, if we leave things as they are, this time next year the Players could be one big happy family again, all the stronger for the trials we put them through. We have to finish the job."

"Then there is more to come?" Finn asked sadly. "You intend to inflict further damage?"

Del smiled oddly. "Who said anything about damage? Chaos isn't all pain and loss. Sometimes a gentle hug can cause more confusion than a savage blow."

"I do not understand," Finn said.

Del winked. "Keep watching. We might redeem ourselves yet." He checked his watch and whistled. "You'd better hurry if you're to keep your date with Kate."

"What are you doing tonight?" Finn asked, slipping into his shoes.

"Not sure yet. Why?"

"Can I bring Kate back later, if the glade proves too damp?"

"Sure. I'll be out of here as soon as I have a wash and a shave. The house is yours and Kate's till ten."

"Why ten?" Finn asked.

"That's when I'll bring over another friend for you to play with." Finn frowned and Del had to remind him, "The smitten Ingmar."

"You are bringing him tonight?" Finn chewed his lip. "I am not sure..."

"Chickening out?"

"After my bout with Kate, I may not have the stamina for another encounter."

Del laughed. "I have faith in you."

"How will you get him here?" Finn asked.

"I'll figure something out." He paused. "You're sure you don't mind? Doing it with a man, I mean."

Finn smiled. "I will tell you when I have tried it."

"Adventurous little sod, aren't you?" Del grinned.

"I was raised to be inquisitive."

"Go on, have a good time. Just be sure you're back by ten."

"I will be here," Finn promised, and took to the woods. Del watched him depart, then struck for the bathroom, plotting furiously.

*

Ingmar had been waiting in the glade for three-quarters of an hour and was on the verge of abandoning the night as a lost cause when he heard snapping twigs. Drawing into the shadows, he held his breath and crossed his fingers. Moments later, Finn strolled into view. "Kate," he sung. "Katie-pie, Katie-pie, wherefore art thou, Katie-pie?"

Ingmar's heart sank. The banker wasn't here for him — it was Kate he desired. He sighed sadly. It had been a pleasant dream while it lasted. He turned to leave.

"Kate?" Finn called, his sharp eyes catching the moving shape in the gloom.

Ingmar paused. Since he'd been spotted, he might as well face the music. He could pretend he was just out walking. "It's only me," he said, stepping back into the glade.

If Finn was surprised to see the German, he didn't show it. "It is a beautiful night, is it not?"

Ingmar glanced up at the bright sky, lit by twinkling stars and a generous slice of moon. "Majestic," he agreed.

"Have you seen Kate?" Finn asked.

"No."

"I was supposed to meet her here. Perhaps she fell asleep — she looked tired when last I saw her. I will tarry a while, then search for her if she does not show. Will you keep me company?"

Ingmar smiled. "I'd be delighted."

The two men shifted to the centre of the glade and spoke softly. They didn't discuss anything important, made no mention of Nuala and Anna or the knife edge on which the fortunes of the Players rested. Half an hour passed pleasantly, but following the hoot of the night's first owl, Finn told Ingmar he must leave.

"Actually," Ingmar said hesitantly, "we had a little bet and I don't think Kate truly intended to meet you tonight."

"Oh?" Finn smiled peculiarly. "Why not?"

Ingmar took a deep breath. "Because she knew *I'd* be here."

"How could she have known that?" Finn asked.

"She told me to come."

A puzzled frown creased the corners of Finn's eyes. "Why would she ask the two of us to come and not show herself?"

Ingmar said nothing. He dared not.

As Finn studied the blushing DJ, the light dawned. "You knew I would be coming," he gasped. "*You* are my date."

"Behind door number three..." Ingmar chuckled.

"Kate agreed to this?" Finn asked disbelievingly.

"We had a bet," Ingmar repeated. "I thought if I could get you by myself, in a romantic setting... Kate agreed to set it up, assuming you'd reject me. I was to have one uninterrupted shot, and if that failed, I'd back off for good."

"I see," Finn said neutrally.

"I can't believe how silly we were," Ingmar giggled nervously. "It seemed like a good idea at the time, but now that I'm here, I realise how ridiculous it was."

"Why is it ridiculous?" Finn asked.

"To think you'd fall into my arms and melt. I was blinded to reality by lust. If you promise not to tell anybody, I'll leave now and –"

Before he could finish, Finn kissed him. It was only a brief peck but it shook Ingmar to his core. When Finn pulled back, he was smiling. "I do not want you to leave," he said.

Ingmar gulped. "You mean...?"

Finn kissed him again. Slower this time. Longer.

"Oh my," Ingmar croaked when they parted. "I have to sit down."

"Allow me," Finn said, whipping off his waterproof coat – he'd been thinking ahead, albeit with Kate in mind – and laying it on the damp grass. He took Ingmar's hand and slowly coaxed him to the ground.

Ingmar's eyes were wide as he stared into Finn's milky blue globes. "You're serious?"

Finn took off his jumper and undid the buttons of Ingmar's shirt. "Does this answer your question?"

"Oh my," Ingmar said again, only this time it was a cry of delight and not a grunt of surprise.

*

A distraught Kate was watching the two men. She had arrived while they were talking, picked her spot with care to ensure maximum cover, and borne witness to the kisses and all that had followed.

She told herself it shouldn't matter – her interest in Diarmid had been wholly career-based – yet she'd enjoyed their time together. He'd been a lively lover and a good friend. Seeing him slip away in this fashion tore at her heartstrings, and for some strange reason she'd never before felt so alone.

Weeping softly, she decided it was time to make a tactful withdrawal. She didn't begrudge Ingmar his conquest — she could take defeat gracefully.

Turning quicker than intended, she bumbled into a low, sharp branch. It jabbed her painfully, causing her to wince and stumble backwards. Her heel caught on a root, her arms flailed, gravity took hold and she toppled out... into the glade.

Ingmar was naked, in the process of sliding Finn's trousers over his ankles, when Kate burst through the bushes behind them. The DJ yelped and spun, jerking the trousers off Finn and covering himself with them, sure it was Don charging forward to rip them apart. Then Kate raised her hands and apologised, and he relaxed.

"I'm sorry," she cried. "I was leaving and ran into a branch. Please don't think I did this on purpose. I'll go now. I won't say another word. I'm sorry."

Finn stared curiously at the hand-wringing actress and noticed her tear-stained cheeks. Leaning over, he whispered in Ingmar's ear. The DJ frowned.

"But I've never... with a..."

"So?" Finn smiled. "I have never done it with a man. Why should we not share equally in the experiment?"

Ingmar hesitated, then grinned and addressed the forlorn Kate, who was beating a hasty retreat. "Stop, madam." She glanced at him. "My partner and I both agree that you can't storm in here, then waltz off as you please. There's no saying where you'd go or who you'd tell."

"I said I was sorry," she groaned. "I won't tell anyone. What more do you –"

"We think you should stay," Ingmar interrupted. "You can't run and sing if you stay and swing."

"Stay and...?" Kate was having trouble figuring out what he meant. When understanding struck, her jaw dropped. "You don't mean...?"

"We most certainly do," Finn laughed.

"Two's company," Ingmar smirked. "Three's a wowzer."

Kate stared at the naked men and began to smile. "You're crazy," she shrieked.

"Maybe," Finn agreed. "Do you want to get crazy too?"

"It's a once-in-a-lifetime offer," Ingmar told her. "Decide quick before I come to my senses and withdraw it."

Kate stopped laughing. "OK, but there's one condition."

She slipped off her coat, loosened the buttons on her blouse and started towards the awaiting men. "If anybody mentions a *sandwich*, I'm out of here."

*

Anna and Nuala heard the sounds of love-making and detoured to investigate. They'd been walking in silence, arms linked, immersed in their private thoughts.

"Who do you think it is?" Anna asked as they crept up on the glade of sultry sighs and merry moans.

"Villagers," Nuala said.

"Maybe it's Terence and Felix," Anna giggled, "paying us back."

Nuala had to stifle an intense bout of laughter. "Don't," she gasped.

When they parted some ferns at the edge of the glade and spotted the trio in the centre, a fairy could have knocked them over with a leaf.

"I wasn't so far off," Anna said in hushed tones after a while.

"I can't believe it," Nuala said. "Diarmid and Ingmar... Kate bossing them about. My God, what's she doing now? She won't! That's too much, I can't watch, I..." Nuala's eyes widened. "Is that legal?"

"I don't know about legal," Anna grinned, "but it looks like fun."

Nuala stared at the younger woman, shocked. "You're not thinking of...?"

"Why shouldn't we?" Anna replied. "Squeeze in as many kicks as we can before we have to face the music."

"But... it would be an orgy."

Anna smiled. "Do you want to die without trying at least one orgy?"

Nuala's lips twitched, and then, to her surprise, she felt herself nodding.

Anna strode forward, more determined than Nuala had ever seen her, and there was nothing the larger woman could do except follow.

They were almost upon the writhing trio before Ingmar noticed them. "Oh," he said, giving the others a dig.

"Is this a private function?" Anna asked brazenly.

"Or can anyone join in?" Nuala quipped.

"Ladies," Finn smiled, shoving somebody's leg out of the way. "Is this not a most marvellous night for love?"

"Marvellous indeed," Anna murmured, eyeing his manhood. "Do you see that?" she muttered to Nuala.

"I see it, I see it," Nuala purred.

"What about me?" Ingmar huffed. "I'm no Mickey Mouse."

"Most commendable," Anna agreed politely.

"Well?" Kate said, bumping the men aside with her hips. "Are you going to stand there gawking, or have you the guts to get down and get with it?"

"That sounds like a challenge," Nuala said.

"I never could resist a challenge," Anna chirped.

"Are there any rules?" Nuala asked, sliding off her dress.

"Only one," Ingmar smiled. "Anything goes."

"That's a good rule," Anna said, dropping to the ground and cuddling up to the inviting Kate, once an enemy, now about to become a most intimate friend.

"Right," Nuala said, setting her sights on the men and taking them (literally) in hand, "let's see what tricks we can get up to with these."

"We're in trouble," Finn chuckled.

"We certainly are," Ingmar agreed as Nuala dropped to her knees. "I suspect things might be coming to a head..."

*

Don didn't know where Ingmar was when Del called round. "He went out as soon as we got back," he grunted. "I haven't seen him since."

Del was nonplussed by Ingmar's absence. "Will you tell him I need him when he returns? It's important. There's a snag with my costume and –"

"I wouldn't worry," Don said. "I doubt there's going to be a show tomorrow."

"Still," Del said, "I'd rather have it sorted, just in case."

Don sighed. "OK, I'll tell him." He paused. "You don't want to stay for dinner, do you? Steak and chips."

"No thanks," Del said. "Places to go, things to do."

Don pulled a face and closed the door.

"Where the hell is that dopey Kraut?" Del muttered as he left. "If he blows my Plan, I'll swing for him. I need that conflict between him and Don."

Still grumbling, he took off through the forest. As had happened with Nuala and Anna, he was wandering aimlessly when strange sounds drifted to his ears. He ignored them at first, immersed in his thoughts, and had almost passed the glade before realising that was where the noises emanated. He stopped and smiled. Finn and Kate were enjoying themselves.

He was tempted to wander over for a peep, except there were more pressing matters to attend to. Right now he had to find...

At a sharp squeal and a round of giggles, Del paused. That wasn't just Finn and Kate. No matter how good a time they were having, they couldn't be making that much noise. What was going on?

It didn't take him long to find out – it was hardly a case for Sherlock Holmes – and when he discovered the five thrashing bodies he stood, mouth agape, not sure what to make of it all. There were limbs everywhere, mouths opening and closing, flesh being fondled and licked and...

He rubbed his eyes to make sure he wasn't dreaming. Could this be a mirage, or Puck playing tricks on him? But when his sight cleared, the scene was the same.

Slowly, he began to smile. "Good man, Finn," he chuckled. "I don't know how you did it, but God bless your innocent little changeling soul."

He felt supremely satisfied as he stood, concealed in the shadows, observing the actors romping away. He'd succeeded. Whatever happened tomorrow, the Midsummer Players could never return to the status quo. Everything had changed and nothing could ever again be the same.

As he watched, he felt part of himself stirring. He glanced down, surprised – sex had been the furthest thing from his mind this past fortnight – then thought, "Why not? I've toiled hard, so why shouldn't I treat myself?"

Stepping forward, he cleared his throat, attracting the attention of the Players. "Room for one more?" he asked with a cheeky smile, and the raucous roars were all the invitation he needed to join in and round out the numbers to a dirty half-dozen.

4. [II] (i)

Joan Casey leant across her desk and studied her calendar's message for the day – *Man creates the evil he endures* – then checked the date and wished for the umpteenth time that it would magically skip a day, but it remained Midsummer's.

She sighed and picked up her Midsummer Players pamphlet. *We, the cast and crew of... pleased to extend our most cordial of invitations... admit one (1) person, free and gratis...* Didn't the fools know those words meant the same thing? *...on this, the twentieth anniversary of...*

Twenty years! Great heavens, when would the madness end?

Joan hadn't been to every performance but had been covering the Players since the start. She'd been a fresh young journalist twenty years ago, eager to land a job with a local newspaper. Working freelance, she'd paid to see the Players' debut.

They were awful. She'd only stayed to the end in order to chronicle the catastrophe to its full extent. She'd hurried home and written the most scathing review of her life, slamming the actors, calling for them to be banned.

She posted the article to several editors but only one replied — Jimmy Meegan, of the Limerick Clarion. He liked her writing style and was prepared to offer her a temporary position. She jumped at the chance. The Clarion was small-time, and the pay was lousy, but she wouldn't be there long and figured it would serve as a stepping stone to better things. (Twenty years later, sitting in her Clarion office, she was able to smile at her foolish, youthful certainty.)

Jimmy Meegan taught her many things during his eight years as her supervisor, but the first lesson was the one she best remembered. He'd talked her through her review of the play and told her that no local paper would print such an article. If she wanted to get ahead in this business, she had to lie.

"Limerick's a small place," he'd explained. "We have to applaud chancers like this. Their relatives and friends buy our paper every week. If we slag them off, we lose customers."

"But what about truth?" Joan cried. "What about honesty and integrity?"

"Stuff 'em," Jimmy growled. "For us, every hurling match that involves a team from Limerick is an epic. If a local writer publishes a book, we treat them like Joyce. If fools band together and stage a version of *A Midsummer Night's Dream*, we clap like seals. Those are the cold, hard facts of local journalism. If you can't stomach them, you've no future here."

She hadn't agreed with him but played along to keep the job. Within three years Joan was employed full-time by the paper, free to write as she desired, but by then she'd come to the realisation that Jimmy was right — you wouldn't get anywhere telling the truth, not if it was nasty. And so, since that first unpublished diatribe, she'd had nothing but public praise for Terence Devlin and his Midsummer Players, but privately she'd grown to hate them. Just once she'd like to reveal them for what they really were.

Perhaps it would be tonight. Joan had avoided the show for four of the last six years, arranging holidays around that time or sending a junior in her place, but the Clarion had fallen on hard times – the internet was killing them – and they'd had to cut back. She was now solely responsible for the cultural articles. She would have to go and suffer.

"*But...*" she muttered, she'd be damned if she massaged their egos like she usually did. She'd had enough. This year she'd lay into them with everything she had, and to hell with the circulation.

Man creates the evil he endures, she read again, smiling grimly. No longer. Tonight, if Terence Devlin and his merry band weaved their usual brand of evil, she was through enduring. Unless they pulled off something truly spectacular, she'd shoot them down with every critical bullet at her disposal.

*

As it turned off the road, Shane Gallagher honked heavily on his horn at the Amazonite grey Peugeot 3008, which had been holding him to sixty kilometres an hour for the past ten minutes. The driver – a pretty woman in a summer dress – shot him a finger and proceeded in her leisurely fashion.

Shane cursed loudly, glanced at his watch, then in the mirror at his busload of passengers. They hadn't complained about the sluggish pace – one of the buggers actually had the nerve to come up and tell him it was nice to be able to admire the scenery for a change – but if they were late back to the hotel and missed the start of their dinner, there'd be hisses and abuse galore, you betcha.

"Bloody Yanks," Shane grumbled. He hated them, despite the fact that his business largely relied on their patronage.

"Shane, my man." A rotund, balding, middle-aged man in an *I kissed the Blarney Stone* T-shirt slapped the disgruntled driver's back and smiled as if they were best buddies. "Any sign of Bunratty castle?"

Shane took a deep breath and reminded himself that he needed the tips that they would hand him at the end of their tour. "No, sir," he said. "Bunratty's in Clare, as I believe I've told you." Only about twenty times since they set out. "We're doing Limerick today. Clare's on tomorrow's agenda."

"Oh." The Yank didn't seem overly disappointed. Why should he be? One castle was much the same as any other. He was only mentioning it as an excuse to squash up next to the driver and impress the missus and his mates. They seemed to think they were the bear's honey if they *interacted* with the *natives*.

"Still," Blarney Stone drawled, "there's only a stone's throw between the two, right? Limerick and Clare are tiny places, not like the states back home. Couldn't we sneak across the border?" He waved a five euro note in front of Shane's nose, blocking his view of the road and almost causing a crash.

"Sorry," Shane snarled. "Clare's tomorrow. Today it's Limerick. Besides, we're running late. If we don't make up time, you'll miss dinner."

"Gee, wouldn't want that. Carry on, my good man." Blarney Stone gave Shane a friendly squeeze and left the fiver sticking in a hole in the driver's shirt. "Have a drink on me, but only one. Don't want you coming out – what is it you guys say? – *langers* tonight." He laughed and strolled back to his seat.

Shane counted to fifty very slowly, and by the time he reached forty most of his fingers had unclenched. "I'll *langer* you, you jumped-up..." He mumbled some choice expletives beneath his breath and pocketed the fiver.

Four more days. Clare and Tipperary tomorrow, Galway the day after, a long, slow ride to Donegal after that. He was supposed to be on holiday. He'd only taken this load because his wife broke her leg and they'd had to cancel a trip abroad. The Yanks were too much for him. Sooner or later he'd crack and slam the bus into a tree, taking them all to hell with him, laughing hysterically the whole way down.

He slowed going through a village and noticed posters for that night's open-air play. The Midsummer Players. The name was familiar but it took him a while to place it. Then he remembered. His daughter had dragged him to that piece of garbage six years earlier. He'd stuck fifty minutes of gobshites spouting gibberish and that had been that. Without a word he'd got to his feet and stormed off. His daughter wasn't far behind. He'd been expecting a lecture but she seemed relieved. "Aren't you mad at me?" he'd asked.

"Are you joking?" she'd snorted. "They were terrible. If you hadn't upped stakes, I'd have been out of there before you."

Retiring to a pub, father and daughter had spent a good night laughing at the idiots in the play and the bigger idiots in the crowd who'd stayed to the end.

Shane's eyes narrowed cunningly. He was supposed to escort his gang around the city tonight, taking them on an alcohol-free pub crawl. (Just his luck to get stuck with teetotallers.) He'd been dreading it but now he saw a way out.

Three hours, that play lasted. He could drop them there an hour beforehand to *interact* with the locals, then spend most of the night doing exactly as he wished.

Shane smiled and picked up speed as he left the village.

There was a dreadful moment when he feared the tickets might all be sold. Then he recalled the dire quality of the show and his smile returned. Sold out? He doubted it!

"Ladies and gentlemen," he said, switching on the intercom, "do I have a treat in store for ye tonight. Listen up..."

*

Christopher Big swung gently to and fro inside his hammock and gazed out at the beautiful Irish countryside. His eyes alighted on green, no matter where he looked. The locals bitched about the rain but he envied them this emerald paradise. Two more days and he'd have to return to London, where the only green he'd see for months would be if he ordered a Crème de Menthe.

It had been a great holiday. He wished he could have stayed another week, but he was a busy man with clients who cared nothing for their agent's well-being. If he dallied too long in this land of the laid back, he'd return to find his business in tatters. Those in the acting profession were notoriously fickle.

"Don't fall asleep." Christopher glanced up to find his friend Jules standing over him. "You'd wake up red to the bone. This sun would roast anyone."

"I'm covered in sun-tan lotion from head to toe, so I'm safe," Christopher said, then tapped the pole behind his head. "Touch wood."

"Will you be out here much longer?" Jules asked. "The better half and I are going for a drive."

"Count me out," Christopher said. "Days like this are too precious to waste in cars. Look me up when you get back. If

I'm not here, try heaven — that's the only place I'd trade this spot for."

Jules laughed, turned to leave, then paused. "I found one of these earlier, when I was putting out the trash. Must have blown over from the village."

Christopher took a crumpled pamphlet from Jules and studied it curiously. "The Midsummer Players."

"They put this on every year," Jules said. "I don't think they're meant to be any good, but if you feel like checking out the local talent..."

"I doubt I'll go but thanks all the same."

"No problem. See you about six. Have fun."

"I will," Christopher told her, flicking a lock of his carefully groomed white hair out of his eyes and twirling his bushy eyebrows up at the edges.

Christopher was pleased when Jules and her husband left. He enjoyed their company but there were times when one wanted to be alone, moments which were too precious to be shared. After a while he heard a bird singing and looked up. The sun was glaring in his eyes so he stuck the pamphlet over his head and focused. Before he could get a fix on the winged wonder, the singing ceased.

"Oh well," he muttered, lowering the pamphlet. He was about to toss the scrap of paper away, then recalled the dim view Jules took of littering. But he was too lazy to get up and dispose of it neatly. Pondering the mild dilemma, he scanned the advertisement again.

He'd dropped in on a couple of local acts the last time he'd been here, and none of the participants had caught his eye. Besides, he was on holiday. Let somebody else worry about talent-hunting. It was his week off.

He folded the paper and slipped it into his back pocket, to bin later. But then he extracted it and smoothed out the creases. He was on holiday, yes, but that didn't mean he couldn't combine business with pleasure. He didn't get to the theatre much – he'd branched out into TV and film – and on the rare occasions he got along, it was usually to spy a particular actor, meaning he paid little attention to the play itself. It might be nice to sit back as part of an ordinary crowd and just be entertained.

"The Midsummer Players," he murmured, stroking his lips with the edge of the paper. And if one of the local actors *did* happen to be exceptionally talented, he'd surely be the only scout in attendance.

He'd have to check with Jules – he wouldn't go out of his way if it meant missing a splendid night that his hosts had cooked up – but if there was nothing else on the agenda, why not give it a crack? After all, if they'd been going strong for twenty years, how bad could they be?

*

Ferdy Frost was nine years old, a genius, and bored. Unlike most children, he had little time for games. His mind could only be diverted when actively engaged. Books, puzzles and chess were his poison. Without them he was lost.

He wandered the house, angrily kicking walls and doors. His parents should have taken him to the library yesterday but the car had broken down, so he was without fresh reading material. (He didn't agree with eBooks. He was old school.)

There was the computer, of course, but the internet had become the domain of chattering monkeys, he could master most video games in a matter of hours, while his parents didn't like him playing chess with strangers in case they groomed him. (Ferdy had wondered why they were scared of someone pampering him like a dog, until he'd done some further research into the term.)

"Ferdy?" It was his mother, Sally Frost. In her early thirties and (to Ferdy's reckoning) washed-up. A mother and housewife, with no grander desires or aims. What a dullard.

"Are you there, love?" Sally mounted the stairs cautiously. She was more than half-afraid of her one and only child. Sometimes, when he was in a foul mood, he'd lie in ambush at the top of the stairs and bombard her with missiles. Not harmless toys either — he favoured shoes, heavy brushes and paperweights. He'd cracked one of her arms once.

"I've good news, sweetheart." Sally knew she and Arturio – her husband's real name was Arthur, but he'd been Arturio since a trip to Italy six years ago – spoiled the child, but they couldn't help themselves. It was so exciting to have given birth to a genius, a boy with the brains to do anything he liked, destined to leave a considerable mark on the world.

They'd known from a very young age that Ferdy was special – he was such an alert and responsive little thing – but they hadn't known *how* special until taking him for an intelligence test and learning he had an I.Q. in excess of one hundred and sixty. An excited counsellor had warned them to handle him carefully, not to have any more children, give him his way in every matter, and – most important of all – never raise a hand against him.

"Ferdy?" Sally paused a couple of steps shy of the landing. "Can I come up?"

"What's the 'good news'?" Ferdy asked, keeping to the shadows.

"I've got tickets to a play tonight," she told him.

"What sort of a play?" he asked, advancing curiously.

"A local production of *A Midsummer Night's Dream*."

"I've read it," he grunted, losing interest.

"But you've never *seen* it, dear." She smiled hopefully. "They say Shakespeare is meant to be seen rather than read, don't they?"

"Illiterates say so," Ferdy replied sarcastically, but she could tell he wasn't as disinterested as he seemed.

"I know you haven't relished our previous theatre visits, but we've never tried Shakespeare. And this is an open-air version."

"Open-air?"

"They do it in the middle of a forest," Sally said. "And today's Midsummer's, the same as in the play, so –"

"I know what day it is," he said witheringly.

"Of course you do, my darling, I was just –"

"We'll go," he decided. "Just you and me. I won't have Arturio there. The last time he accompanied us to the theatre, he couldn't stop fidgeting. It spoilt the evening for me."

"I only bought two tickets," she told him, proud that she'd anticipated this.

Ferdy sniffed. "You may go now. I wish to prepare for the night ahead."

"Very good, my love." Smiling weakly, she backed down

the stairs and made her way to the sanctuary of the kitchen, where she treated herself to a mug of fresh coffee and thanked God for her son's positive reaction.

Upstairs, Ferdy was rooting out critical appraisals of the play online — he had to grudgingly admit that the infernal web could be useful on rare occasions. He'd never paid the play much mind – it had struck him as a piece of nonsense, the Bard at his crowd-pleasing worst – and he was interested in seeing how many critics had the good sense and insight to concur with his opinion.

An hour later, having explored and absorbed, he sat back and grunted. Though there had been some interesting interpretations of the play, Ferdy had read nothing which made it seem any better than he'd initially surmised. *A delightful piece of whimsical nonsense,* ran the general view, which suggested to Ferdy that they could see its flaws but were too in awe of the Bard to admit the brutal, honest truth that it just wasn't any bloody good.

Well, Ferdy wasn't afraid. In his mind he was already composing a withering review for the next time he was on television. (He was often invited on to shows to sneer at the works of his elders.) And there were the Midsummer Players too. Though they could do nothing to raise his low opinion of the play, there was the question of how they adapted it. If they took a challenging, radical approach, he might commend them for a brave effort, but if they chose to deliver a straight, conservative version, or if their talents weren't up to scratch…

Ferdy smiled savagely. In that case he'd exact revenge on the woman responsible for putting him through such torture.

It had been ages since he'd thrown a fit (it must have been all of three weeks). Maybe it was time to remind his parents who they were dealing with. They'd been getting sloppy — the botched trip to the library and this potentially awful waste of a play. Perhaps they'd forgotten the reason they'd been put on this planet, to cater to young Master Frost's every whim. He wouldn't be long putting them back on track.

Viewed from that angle, he was glad they were going to the play. Either way, tragedy or success, he'd come out of it smiling. As usual – as it should and always would be – Ferdy Frost simply couldn't lose.

*

In University Hospital Limerick, an actor was stirring. Michael Finnt had been lying in a coma for two weeks. Limerick's finest doctors had been unable to explain the patient's condition. There were no external injuries and no signs of brain damage. By all medical rights he should have been back on his feet and out from under theirs in no time.

While hardly a household name, Michael Finnt was well-known locally – he had appeared on national television several times – and there would have been a queue of well-wishers and reporters if his condition had been reported. But his agent, Colin, had demanded secrecy. He was in the middle of negotiating a TV soap role for his client and didn't want reports of a near-fatal car crash souring the pitch.

Of course, if Michael failed to recover, the deal couldn't come to anything, but Colin had bought some time by telling the TV people that Michael was filming a low-budget movie somewhere in mainland Europe.

Colin had hovered nervously by his client's bed the first couple of days, but he had other responsibilities and couldn't play nurse indefinitely. He rang the doctors for reports, and popped by every few days, but wasn't there when Michael began groaning for the first time since being admitted.

His recovery, in fact, went completely unmarked. He was in a private room, so nobody was there to gape as his eyes opened, or to gasp when he sat up and shook his head groggily.

"Where am I?" he groaned. "What's going on?"

He stared out the window. It was a glorious summer's day but it should have been night. The last thing he remembered was driving through the dark, trying to find the turn for Terence Devlin's house.

"What happened?" he muttered, thinking back, and the memories began to return. He'd been driving slowly. Suddenly, out of nowhere, a car appeared. He'd glimpsed a flashing streak of metal, screaming towards him. There'd been the terrible sound of a collision, then...

Nothing. He'd blacked out. Hadn't even dreamt while he'd been unconscious.

Looking around, he realised he was in a hospital. Fearing the worst, he quickly examined himself, checking for severed limbs or facial distortions, but he seemed fine. He was beginning to relax when he noticed the calendar on the table by the foot of his bed, and the date it was turned to — Midsummer's.

That couldn't be right. He couldn't have been dead to the world for an entire fortnight... could he?

Leaping to his feet, he prowled the room, looking for verification. He soon found a newspaper which Colin had left behind. So it was true. He'd been knocked out for two whole weeks. Dazed and shaking, he sat on the bed and scratched his legs.

At least it had got him out of his deal with Terence. Now he wouldn't have to stand up there with that group of amateurs and look like an ass. Perhaps the crash was a blessing in...

Michael frowned. No, damn it, this meant he still owed Terence. Clearing two weeks to practise with the Players had proved troublesome. He'd had to fight with his agent, for one thing, who couldn't understand why Michael was committed to honouring his debt.

"He helped you out once," Colin had sneered. "Big deal. Slip him a thank-you note next Christmas."

If he got the TV deal – and what had happened to *that* while he was oblivious? – there'd be no time in the foreseeable future for a lengthy charity stint.

He checked the calendar again, then looked at the sun. Early afternoon. He still had time to make it. He didn't know what sort of an arrangement the Players had come to in his absence, but he was sure they wouldn't have cancelled. He knew the play by heart, and if he could get there before it started, he could walk straight on.

Even if his replacement refused to step down, he could legitimately claim to have honoured their bargain. It wasn't his fault he'd been unable to rehearse. As long as he turned up in time and offered his services, the director would have to acknowledge that they were quits.

Michael smiled. This could work out perfectly. Two weeks of sleep, trimmer than he'd been in years (a fortnight without junk food had worked wonders for his figure), fresh as a daisy, and his debt paid off without having to raise an eyebrow. If he could just get there before they started...

Ignoring the button that would have summoned the nurses, and not stopping to worry about possible internal injuries, Michael Finnt went looking for his clothes, found them in the lower drawer of a cabinet beside the bed, and dressed. He wasn't sure how he'd get to the glade – his wallet wasn't with his clothes, so he'd no money – but he'd make it even if he had to walk.

Slipping on his shoes, he sneaked out of the room, found his way through a maze of corridors, and stepped out into a day that seemed as wonderful and full of potential as any of history's finest.

*

In Feyland, those name-checked in the dreaded play – thus sworn to eternal attendance – were assembling at the portal connecting the land of magic to that of the humans. Moth was first to arrive, fresh from leaping over waterfalls with the fish of the Hairy Mountain river. He'd barely made himself comfortable on a toadstool when Cobweb arrived. The two had fallen out some decades earlier and said little to each other while they waited.

Mustardseed was next on the scene. He was fat for a fairy and especially merry. Unlike the other fey folk, his delight in the play hadn't abated and he loved to keep abreast of the changes in the land of the mortals. Mustardseed waved to his cousins-in-captivity and addressed them in his usual bright fashion.

"Greetings on this eve of magic wonder.

Are you set for the roar of fake thunder

Which echoes through each well-trod actor's stage?

I am eager. It seems to me an age

Since last we –"

Moth interrupted rudely. It was most uncommon in Feyland for one to cut short another's rhyme, but he was in no mood to listen to Mustardseed warble on.

"There's no stage. We are destined for the glade,

Where, as ever, our senses shall be flayed."

"The glade?" Mustardseed's smile faltered. Even *he* had grown tired of the Midsummer Players.

"I see now why your weary shoulders droop.

But perhaps there'll be a twist to the loop

And the curtains of grim dullness shall part:

This year, I've heard, a spy lurks at its heart."

"I have heard that too," Cobweb said.

"I also," Moth agreed, "but I place no faith in the rumours."

"Here comes Peaseblossom," Moth noted. "Perhaps he knows more."

But Peaseblossom, when they questioned him, knew even less than the others. He'd been spending his time between performances of the play counting the flowers in the Valley of Blossom. He'd been engaged in the count – for reasons he could no longer remember – for years and had yet to reach the midway point.

They were busy discussing the rumours when Puck appeared from behind a bean bush and clipped each of them round the back of the head before they could react.

"As slow as ever, my four tardy friends.

 Your beginnings mark a quick fairy's ends."

"It is not fair," Moth complained.

"You did not give us warning," Cobweb grumbled.

"That hurt," Peaseblossom sulked.

"Sharp as usual, friend Puck," Mustardseed grinned.

"Razor sharp, as I have forever been,

 And shall so be till the sun sheds its sheen."

"Have you heard aught of these rumours?" Moth asked.

"Aye! The rumours!" the other fairies chorused.

Puck scratched his nose and smiled.

"Which rumour would that be? I hear many."

"You know well which rumour we mean," Peaseblossom snorted.

"They say mischief is afoot," Cobweb said.

"Amidst the Midsummer Players," Mustardseed added.

"May their name rot on our fair tongues," Moth concluded.

Puck shook his head teasingly.

"On such matters my sly lips must be sealed,

 Except to say: soon all will be revealed.

 Though with patience I have had little truck,

 Tonight that is the advice of good Puck."

"Puck? Advising patience?" Moth laughed cruelly.

"A solemn omen," Peaseblossom observed.

"I never thought to see the day," Mustardseed said.

"Maybe time has blunted his sharp edge," Cobweb mused.

Puck laughed carelessly, unaffected by their jibes.

"'Twould take more than time to blunt such as I.

But enough of this: our nobles come nigh."

The fairies turned swiftly, sighted the trains of Oberon and Titania, fell to their knees and bowed their heads. Puck merely smiled, plucked a stray flower from the locks of Peaseblossom's hair, placed it between his lips and nibbled while leaning against the worlds-separating portal.

Diarmid Garrigan was with Oberon and Titania, and though there were many long faces among the gathering, his was the longest. For the fairies this was just another venture of minor inconvenience, but for Diarmid those tall gates signalled the end of his most fabulous dream.

Oberon bid the fairies rise, then cast a critical eye over the nonchalant Puck.

"The least you could do is drop to one knee,

Or do we deserve no such courtesy?"

"Deserve it, my lord, you do so indeed,

But Puck would be amiss if he paid heed

To such a weary, old-fashioned custom.

I'd rather, in truth, flash my trim bottom."

"My lord?" Mustardseed raised a hand. "May I speak?"

"Have your say, good master Mustardseed," Oberon replied.

"Your attendants are many. Shall they stay

Or do they come with us to the curs'd play?"

"They come," Oberon answered simply.

"May I ask why, my lord?" Moth humbly enquired.

"No," Oberon told him bluntly.

Titania smiled at the crestfallen fairy.

"Fear not, good Moth, my husband merely jests;

His humour, alas, was never the best.

These noble folk come because on this night

They hope to behold a most wondrous sight:

The final run out – drat the naysayers! –

For that sad group: the Midsummer Players."

The four fairies cheered with delight.

"Then the rumours are true!" Mustardseed gasped.

"My heart fills with joy!" Peaseblossom whooped.

"O wondrous night!" Cobweb sighed.

"O marvellous day!" Moth wept.

"On with that dam'ned, that beautiful play!" Puck shouted mockingly.

"If we are *quite* ready," Oberon huffed, moving forward to lead the way through the portal.

"Lord!" a fairy of his retinue yelled, pointing fearfully at the sky. "The clouds! They gather and close in!"

Oberon glanced up, bemused, to see a small misty cloud descending. It came to ground before the portal, close to a curious Puck, who was confused but not alarmed.

"Could it be an omen?" Titania asked quietly.

"I think not," Oberon answered. "It seems more like..." His frown turned to a smile as the smoke congealed and took shape. "A visitor!" Oberon said, striding forward to shake the hand of the materialising ghost.

"Good master Will! It has been many days

Since last your feet graced the land of the fey."

The shade of William Shakespeare blinked and glanced

around, then grimaced. "Damn it all to hell," he muttered. "I meant to form on the other side of the portal and hide at the back of the crowd."

"You never were much good when it came to directions," Puck remarked.

Shakespeare studied the fairy with evident distaste. "You're here too?"

"I have to be — the bargain, remember?"

The spirit chortled. "Best day's bargaining I ever did. How does the play stand up after four hundred years?"

"About as dull and shapeless as it was originally," Puck replied blithely.

The playwright frowned. He'd never had much time for Puck. Too sharp by far.

Oberon cleared his throat before a row developed.

"We are pleased to see you, good Master Will,

But why have you come? Are you here to fill

Your head once more with fey ideas and thoughts,

To write new plays and amuse the stern gods?"

"The gods!" Will snorted. "That lot wouldn't know a decent play from... And why are you still rhyming? I'd have thought, after four hundred years, you'd have put such foolishness behind you. That iambic pentameter got on my tits when I was alive, so it's the last thing I want to hear now that I'm dead."

Oberon smiled uncertainly. "We are set in our ways. You know how things are in Feyland."

"Don't I just." The spirit shook his head and muttered something beneath his breath. "As to why I'm here, it should be obvious — the play. I've been keeping an eye on how my plays have fared. The first few hundred years were rough — they gave *Lear* a happy ending! Then things came full circle and faithfulness was restored, until *cinema* came along." His shoulders sagged.

"I like the movies," Puck said slyly. "They improved upon the originals."

Shakespeare shot him a withering sneer. "Anyway," he said, dismissing further conversation with a wave of an imperious hand, "I'm here to see that my play is being well served. This isn't the first time I've dropped in on a performance, merely the first time I've made the mistake of materialising on the wrong side of the portal."

"But why this version?" Oberon persisted. "Why here, tonight, out of all the thousands of other venues and times?"

The ghost had the good grace to blush. "I'd heard something about a vendetta. I gather you haven't been impressed with these Players' rendition of the play, so I thought I'd pop along and check it out."

"He came to gloat," Titania sniffed.

"Not at all," Shakespeare protested. "I came only to see what you had planned in retaliation. I've always enjoyed a good revenge story. Check out *Hamlet*."

Oberon wasn't happy – if the play didn't end in disaster, he didn't want the spirit sniggering at their plight – but he forced a smile and extended an invitation. "You are welcome to sit with us if you wish, master Will."

"I don't think our puckish friend thinks much of the idea," the ghost noted, nodding at the imp.

Puck grinned. "Quite the contrary. It is a stupendous idea. If we have to suffer this insufferable fool's poorly padded-out play, I see no reason why he should not suffer too."

"You always were the master of the two-handed compliment," Shakespeare snarled. Then, to Oberon, "It would be an honour to sit with the good folk of Feyland." He'd have rather stood alone, but there were rules of protocol which even the dead had to acknowledge.

"Very good," Oberon beamed. "It will be like the old days, Will. You, me, my subjects, actors, and the play."

"The only difference is that some of the actors are actresses now. You do not mind, do you, darling William?" Puck batted his eyelashes provocatively. "You do not still have a thing about boys in dresses, do you?"

Shakespeare pretended not to hear. "If you lead the way, my lord," he bowed courteously, "it will be my honour to follow."

"Thank you, Will." Oberon was pleased with the show of deference. As one of the dead, the ghost owed him no such respect. Perhaps death had mellowed the once haughty wordsmith, Oberon mused. Then, spying the playwright pinch Lady Titania's bottom as she passed to take her husband's arm, the fairy king turned aside to hide his grin. On the other hand, perhaps not...

Straightening, Oberon cast his gaze around those gathered nearby, making sure all were present who were meant to be, then struck the doors of the portal with his fists. They opened promptly. "Onwards, good people of Feyland," Oberon boomed. "The hour is upon us. The play begins. Let us proceed." He glided through, his beloved wife on his arm, followed by the ghost of William Shakespeare, Puck, the four named fairies, a host of other interested spectators, and, bringing up the rear, a lonely, dejected Diarmid Garrigan.

Diarmid paused at the portal. If he ran now, it would be hours – far more, in fey time – before Oberon could send anyone after him. If he hid well, it might be months before he was discovered. But that would insult his hosts' hospitality, and Diarmid didn't want to offend those who had been so good to him. With a heavy heart, he took one last look at the land he'd grown to love, sniffed its air one final time, then walked through the glittering portal. He felt the doors close behind him, and shivered as he saw the first stars of the mortal evening sky and found his bare feet steeped in the freshly mown grass of an overly familiar glade.

ACT FIVE

5. [I] (i)

The Midsummer Players spent much of the day in a nervous state of suspension. Felix hadn't been seen since stumbling away the night before, and Terence was keeping a low profile. Nobody knew if the play would go ahead or not.

There was little said among the Players about the frolics of the previous night. Kate was too stunned to talk about it, Ingmar, Nuala and Anna were afraid word would leak to their partners, while Del and Finn were basking in the glow of their conquests, holding the information back for when they needed it.

Apart from a brief get-together that morning, the Players hardly saw each other all day. It was the most unusual build-up to a show that any of them had ever experienced.

Anna robotically manned the phone and handled ticket sales from the study. Most people would simply turn up and pay at the gate, but there were quite a few advance bookings this year – perhaps because it was their twentieth anniversary – and she was kept busy. Finally, when Nuala relieved her, she steeled herself and traipsed upstairs.

Terence was in their bedroom, sitting beside the window, staring out blankly. Anna cleared her throat. "We have to talk."

His head turned slowly. He studied her for a few seconds, then switched back to his perusal of the countryside.

"I know I've hurt you," she tried again, "and there's much we have to sort out, but can't we do that afterwards? Right now there are seven other people to consider. We owe them an answer — is the play on or off?"

Terence rose, slipped on a pair of shoes and started past her.

"Where are you going?" Anna asked.

"A walk," he grunted.

"But what about...?"

He was down the stairs and out the door before she could finish. Sighing, she returned to the study to debate the situation with Nuala.

*

Terence strolled through the forest in a daze. Anna's betrayal had shaken him. It wasn't just that he was angry – though he certainly was – he was also ashamed. He knew now how she must have felt all these years, and for the first time realised that actions have consequences, and his had been the actions of a fiend.

Could they continue? He wasn't sure.

He cleared a set of trees and came upon Poet's Rock, which was occupied by a similarly troubled soul. "Hi, Felix," Terence said glumly.

The Northerner looked up and sniffed. "Hi."

"They're looking for you back at the house."

Felix didn't seem bothered. "That why you're here?"

"No," Terence said. "I've problems of my own."

Felix blinked. "That's right. Your wife was the other half."

"Mind if I sit down?" Terence asked.

Felix shifted over and the director parked his bum on the edge of the rocky seat. They stared off in separate directions for a long while, saying nothing.

"Had you any idea she might be...?" Terence asked eventually.

"A lesbian, or just fooling around?" Felix replied.

Terence blushed — he wasn't entirely comfortable with the L word, not applied to his Anna. "Both," he muttered.

He felt Felix's shrug. "I'd no idea she was interested in women. I did think she was cheating on me, but with Diarmid."

"I suspected Diarmid too, with Anna," Terence said.

Felix chuckled drily. "Diarmid was the decoy. He diverted our attention while the wives made whoopee behind our backs."

"You think it was planned?" Terence hadn't considered that.

"Seems that way," Felix said.

"But..." Terence frowned. "Diarmid's involvement drew attention to them. If he hadn't been acting suspiciously, we'd never have suspected them of anything. If this was planned, Diarmid increased their risk of being caught. It doesn't add up."

"Unless they wanted to be caught," Felix murmured.

"Why?" Terence asked.

The little man shrugged again. "I've no answer, but I'm sure there is one."

Terence shook his head. "I think you're barking up the wrong tree."

"Whatever," Felix said with disinterest.

Terence picked up a stone and tossed it at a far-off tree. "Anyway, Diarmid's not important any longer. It's the women we have to worry about."

"I'm not worried," Felix said. "They can run off and join a lesbian commune if they like. Doesn't matter to me."

"It matters to *me*," Terence said. "I've children to think about. If they abscond, she'll take the kids, and I'll have to rearrange my whole life to try and work in regular visits to them."

"It's simpler for me," Felix said. "I just dump the cow and get on with things. Divorce, find someone new, start over."

"If it was that easy," Terence said softly, "you wouldn't be sitting here. You'd be in your car, heading north."

Felix nodded glumly. "I've been up all night, walking, sitting on fences or old logs when I get tired. This is the fourth time I've been to Poet's Rock. You should try it at five in the morning — freezes the arse off you."

"Make any decisions?" Terence asked.

"One minute I'm readying myself to leave, the next I'm remembering our years together, the good times, the shared sad times. It's a lot to turn my back on."

"Maybe we don't have to," Terence mused. "Maybe there was nothing more to it than carnal attraction. Now that it's out of their systems, they might –"

"Don't tell me to forgive and forget," Felix snapped.

"I'm not saying we forget," Terence said, "but if it's not serious between them, surely we can find it in our hearts to forgive?"

"Can you?" Felix asked.

"I think so."

"Well, it's different for me. I was true to my wife. I loved her with everything I had and would have done anything for her."

"So would I," Terence defended himself.

Felix laughed bitterly. "Then why were you screwing Kate? And don't say you weren't, because even I could see it, and I'm not the most alert of men."

Terence gulped. "That was just sex. It wasn't love."

"It's impossible to separate the two in a marriage," Felix said. "When you slip that ring on, it's a commitment, giving your partner your all, promising to stick together no matter what."

"So it's over for you?" Terence asked.

"I could never trust her again. And who's to say this was the first time? You heard her last night."

"That was bluster."

"Probably, but I don't want to go through life in doubt, wondering every time she leaves the house if she'll come back, torturing myself with visions of her with other men." He winced. "Or women." He glanced at the director. "You'd have the same doubts about Anna."

"Maybe," Terence sighed.

A long, contemplative silence followed, broken abruptly when Felix burst out laughing. "We're a right pair of mugs, aren't we?"

"You're not wrong," Terence grinned.

"What about the play?" Felix asked, feeling a need to get away from the morbid topic of their wives. "Will it go ahead?"

"I haven't thought about it."

"Honestly?"

"To tell you the truth, I couldn't give a toss about the play."

Felix laughed again. "Another first. I never..." He trailed off into a thoughtful silence. "What are the others saying about it?"

Terence grimaced. "I haven't seen them rehearsing, so I assume they've decided that the show's been cancelled."

"You know," Felix said, "it *should* go ahead."

Terence stared at him, surprised. "I thought the play would be the last thing on your mind."

"It was," Felix said, "but I just realised that's what everybody else thinks too. I can picture them, sitting around, spirits low, full of regret. They'll be saying it's for the best that it doesn't proceed, that even if you and I turned up, we couldn't deliver commanding performances." Felix stood, his eyes alight. "We should go back and gobsmack them."

"But you've always hated the play," Terence said.

"Yes, but can you imagine our wives' faces if we turn up, arm in arm, focused on the play, acting as though nothing's wrong?"

Terence began to smile. "It'd be better than a deliberate snub."

Felix chortled. "They wouldn't know whether to laugh or cry, to be happy for the Players or disappointed that we think more of the play than we do of them."

"Felix Hill," Terence growled, "you're a sly, vindictive little man." He thrust forth a hand. "Put it there, pal."

"It goes ahead?" Felix asked.

"It goes ahead," Terence agreed, "and it'll be the greatest show ever. We'll lift the rest of them, force them to go through with it, even if they don't want to."

"And when it's over?" Felix asked.

"We'll decide that when we get there," Terence said. "One challenge at a time. For the moment, the play's the thing."

"The play," Felix cheered.

"Onwards," Terence roared, leaping to his feet. "Hurry, man, hurry. We don't have much time. We'll have to work like demons to pull this one off."

*

It didn't take long for word to spread among the Players that Terence and Felix were back and had called a conference. Within minutes every one of the actors had gathered in the study.

Felix sat apart from his fellow Players, calmly studying his hands. Nuala sat on the opposite side of the room, Anna and the others caught between. A few tense seconds ticked by before Terence entered, notes in hand, his old, directorial self.

"I'll be brief," he said. "We all know things haven't been rosy lately, and there's no telling what the future may hold." Anna and Nuala looked worried. "But we have a play to deliver. We've toiled and anguished for two weeks, and I'll be damned if we throw all that away. For the next few hours we focus on the play. All differences must be put aside. If anybody doesn't think they can perform, say so now, then get out of my sight."

He met every pair of eyes in the room. Some dropped or turned away, and several mouths twitched nervously, but nobody voiced a desire to leave.

"Very well. It won't be easy, but great drama never is. This year we'll burn as brightly as we can, and however things go afterwards, we'll leave our audience on a high. Now." He flicked through his notes. "Nuala, I told you I wished to cut some of your lines, but I've changed my mind. I think you can handle the full text. How about it — are you up for the challenge?"

Nuala glanced uncertainly at Felix – his calm demeanour unnerved her, and the last thing she wanted to worry about was extra lines – but she'd look like a fool if she backed down after protesting so strongly in favour of a free tongue.

"That's fine by me," she said, managing a weak smile.

"Then do it," Terence huffed. "From the start, every line. Don't worry about delivery, just prove you know the words. Go."

Nuala took a deep breath, cleared her mind, closed her eyes and began to recite.

"'Call you me fair? That 'fair' again unsay.

Demetrius loves your fair: O happy fair!

Your eyes are lodestars, and your –'"

"Faster," Terence barked. "We haven't got all day."

Nuala gathered speed. "'...and your tongue's sweet air More tuneable than lark to shepherd's ear When wheat is green, when hawthorn buds appear. Sickness is catching.'" She continued like that, from Helena to Starveling, Peaseblossom to Moonshine, never pausing except for breath, never once looking up or aside.

It was a remarkable feat, but when she got to the end, Terence only made a tick with his pen on the notepad and turned to the rest of the Players. "Act Four was horrible yesterday. Today it'll be perfect. Anna, start us off."

Anna opened her copy of the play.

"Forget the book," Terence snapped. "If you don't know your lines by now, you never will."

Anna nodded sombrely and cast the play aside. Closing her eyes, she collected her thoughts, muttered the opening words to herself, then launched into the part.

"'Come, sit thee down upon this flowery bed

While I thy amiable cheeks do coy,

And stick musk-roses in thy sleek smooth head,

And kiss thy fair large ears, my gentle joy.'"

There was a pause when she finished. Del gave Finn a dig in the ribs. "You're next," he hissed.

Finn had been thinking back to the previous night, recalling Anna's naked, writhing body, her weight as she'd straddled him and lashed him on to new heights of passion, but at Del's prompt he remembered where he was and cleared his throat. "'Where's Peaseblossom?'" he asked as Bottom.

"'Ready,'" Nuala piped up, and soon everybody was chipping in, and this time they made no mistakes.

*

It was nearly five o'clock when Don slapped the side of his head and howled. Everybody stopped what they were doing and stared. "The chairs," he screamed. "We haven't set out the bloody chairs."

Terence blinked. "Why not?"

"We never thought of it," Don groaned. "We were so busy worrying about whether or not the play was going ahead, we just –"

"Never mind," Terence interrupted and clapped twice. "Everybody to the shed. We can still do it if we work fast."

"What about the phone?" Anna asked.

"Forget it. We need all hands to the pumps."

The nine Players rushed out the door and over to the glade. There was a huge shed nearby, in a smaller clearing, where they stored the chairs, lights and props such as fake bushes and candlestick holders. Terence unlocked the doors and switched on the lights. (He had arranged years ago for an electricity supply to this clearing and the glade.) "Nuala, Don, Del and I will handle the benches and heavier material," Terence said. "The rest of you drag across chairs."

The actors threw themselves into the task and scurried from the shed to the glade like an army of well-trained ants. Normally they'd only carry two or three chairs each at a time, but today even the weaker members like Ingmar and Kate dragged four or five. It usually took four hours to set up the chairs, lights and props. The Players traditionally handled the job in the early hours of the morning – sometimes the night before, if the weather was good – wrapped by lunch and spent the afternoon rehearsing, but they couldn't take anywhere near that long now. The play was due to start at eight, and they still had costumes to bring over, make-up had to be applied, and some of them would have to go on crowd-duty when the audience arrived, to take money, issue tickets, hawk programmes (a folded sheet of A4 paper, with the cast list, a couple of boxes for sponsors, and a short summary of the company's history), and see them safely to their seats.

At two minutes to six a weary set of actors sank to their haunches in the middle of the glade and stared numbly at the orderly sea of seats. Each was in its proper place, bedecked with an advertising card or coaster.

"We did it," Terence sighed, then repeated it, louder this time. "We did it!"

"What about the spotlights and candles?" Don asked.

"A small matter," Terence sniffed, "easily handled."

"We're going to make it," Anna said with wonder. "Even if we dawdle with the costumes and make-up, we'll be ready on time."

"Probably," Terence agreed, "but let's not get cocky. There are always last-minute crises to contend with. We'll clap ourselves when we're taking our bows at eleven. Until then, we're on red alert." He checked his watch. "We'll rest here a few minutes, then I'll set the candles and get the spotlights in place. You lot head back for the costumes. Anna, bring the tickets and cash-box. Ingmar, you're in charge of make-up. Let the others lug the costumes over and pull them aside for makeovers while they're working."

"Aye-aye, cap'n," Ingmar grinned.

"Kate, Diarmid and myself will take care of the spectators when they arrive, so make us up first. The rest of you can chill backstage when everything's across and Ingmar's seen to you. Slip into your costumes at a quarter to eight. Be ready to go on as soon as the last customer's seated." He glanced around. "Am I forgetting anything?"

There was a long pause. Then Del raised a hand.

"Yes?" Terence frowned.

"Isn't it customary to say 'break a leg?'"

Terence grinned. "Indeed it is. People, break a leg or I'll break your heads." It was his annual comment, and normally the actors groaned in response, but this year, led by an excited Finn, they cheered loudly.

"Hip-hip-hooray!" Finn cried, and the others followed suit.

"Three cheers for the director," Del called, and another volley of shouts rocked the sky-high meadow roof.

"Save your breath," Terence grumbled. "You'll need it for the play." But they could see he was tickled pink. "OK," he said, getting to his feet. "Let's crack on. If you run into a minor problem, shout. If you run into a major one, keep it to yourself." Shooing them away like children, Terence returned to the shed, laid out the sacks of candles, then adjusted an imaginary electrician's cap and set about fixing up the spotlights.

*

As Finn and Del hauled their costumes from Terence's house to the glade, Finn nestled up close to his fellow conspirator for a hushed conversation. "You seem curiously content," he remarked.

"Why shouldn't I be?" Del asked.

"Felix and Terence are back with the others. The play is going ahead. Your meddling has only served to strengthen the Players — Ingmar and Nuala are more confident and competent than they were at the start, Terence is on a high, Felix looks as though he is relishing the idea of the play, and I am a much better actor than my brother. As far as chaos goes, you seem to be on a hiding to nothing."

"Looks that way, doesn't it?" Del grinned.

"The prospect of failure bothers you not?"

"I never worry about failure," Del said. "Life has its ups and downs. You win some, you lose some." His smile spread. "But this is one I plan to win."

"I fail to see how," Finn sniffed.

"That," Del chuckled, "is why I'm a key instrument of chaos, while you're just a pretty face and a nice pair of legs in the chorus-line of life. Trust me, this *will* end on a high. I'm not sure how things will pan out over the next few hours but the scent of victory is thick in the air. Hurry," he said, quickening his stride. "I want to see what Felix looks like when he tries on the dress."

*

The first members of the public arrived shortly after seven, a large party from the States, dropped off by a cackling bus driver. The Americans strolled through the forest, checking out the glade, relishing the fresh evening air and birdsong.

Local villagers were next on the scene. Some were old friends, warmly greeted by Terence and Finn (who pretended he knew them). For others, this was their first time. Not all of them could explain why they'd chosen this year to check out the Players — there was just something in the air, a mysterious haze of promise which drew them like moths to a flame.

By half-seven, the trickle of customers had become a steady flow and the trio manning the gates faced a struggle to stay on top of the situation. Kate tore tickets in half as if they were going out of fashion, while Finn and Terence were rushed off their feet, escorting people to their chairs.

"A good crowd," Finn remarked during a rare lull.

"More than we usually get," Terence agreed. "We'll have to turn some away if this keeps up, or..." He fell into a thoughtful silence, then told Finn to fend for himself and hurried off.

He found Kate on her last string of tickets. Doing a quick head-count he figured there were at least twenty or thirty people queueing who'd have to be turned away, with probably more to come. "Do we have spare tickets?" he asked.

"Loads," she told him, "but we're out of chairs."

"Never mind. Get more tickets ready. Mark them with a green biro." Turning to the crowd, he raised his voice. "Ladies and gentlemen, your attention please. Due to unprecedented demand, I regret to say we've sold out." There was a collective groan. "We do, however, have plenty of standing room, though I must warn you that the play runs for three hours."

"How much does it cost to stand?" somebody enquired.

Terence calculated the mood of the crowd before answering. "Half price."

The people in the queue murmured positively.

"But where are we going to stand them?" Kate hissed.

"We've several spare benches in the shed," Terence said. "We'll stick them behind the chairs — there's space between the last row and the trees."

"They'll never stand still for three whole hours," Kate said.

"We'll have breaks." Terence was thinking it through as he spoke. "Five or ten minutes at the end of each act, as well as the usual twenty-minute interval in the middle. That'll give them a chance to walk around and work out the cramps."

"But –" Kate began.

"Not now," Terence growled. "I've got to organise the benches and tell the others about the breaks. Just sell the tickets and let me worry about the rest."

"What about the chairs that are left?" Kate asked.

"Reserve them for the elderly and disabled. Dole them out as complimentaries — with these numbers, we can afford to throw in a few freebies."

Beaming like a baby, Terence kissed the top of her head, but it was an innocent kiss, born of exuberance rather than lust. "We've made the big time," he hooted, and ran off to find the benches and pass on the news.

Kate shook her head, bemused, then got on with marking the tickets. She told those in the queue to wait while standing arrangements were being finalised. When the benches were in place and Terence had given her the all clear, she nodded at the first in line and started issuing the tickets as swiftly as possible.

*

And so they came, and sat or stood. The American tourists were seated at the head of the glade, with the best view. Joan Casey, as a guest of honour, was among them, along with other invited journalists and celebrities, few though they were.

Viewed from that point, Christopher Big was seated in the left-hand row. He'd come on his own and was intrigued — there was excitement in the air.

Ferdy Frost and his mother sat almost directly opposite Christopher Big. Ferdy had grumbled about not being closer, but there was nothing to be done about it now. Sally prayed he enjoyed the show. He'd been cynical the whole way over, and if it failed to exceed his low expectations, she was dreading the ride back.

The fairies and their distinguished, ethereal guest occupied a collection of seats on one side of the glade. Their presence went unnoticed by the humans, although a few of the more sensitive sensed something odd about the area. Heads tended not to turn in that direction, and when they occasionally did, eyes registered vague shapes, ears recorded muffled sounds, and brains conveniently shielded conscious minds from the fey spectacle. Terence would add up the notes and coins the next morning and, as always, rub the back of his head and wonder why they were short for those seats. He would mean to check into it, but never would.

With all these in place and many more besides (but not Michael Finnt, of whom there was as yet no sign), the box-office finally closed and the actors prepared to take to the stage. A robed and hooded Ingmar crept through the glade, lighting the many candles which would serve as their primary source of illumination.

Conversations ceased as Ingmar passed. When the German lit the final candle, he whirled through the glade, robes floating eerily around him, stopped in the middle, put his fingers to his lips – that silenced the last of the talkers – then slipped back between the trees. The spotlights flared, half-blinding everyone, then dimmed and were quenched. The candles flickered and hissed. A hush descended and people's vision returned.

Moments later the glade gave birth to its tormented Players, and the world's most recent rendition of *A Midsummer Night's Dream* took shape.

5.[I](ii)

The first act went like a dream. Don and Anna cut royal, dashing figures as Theseus and Hippolyta. Nuala remembered all her lines as Helena and struck the right balance between pathos and humour, arousing the audience's sympathy while drawing cruel laughs. Felix seemed six inches taller as Demetrius, speaking and moving with an authority he'd never before revealed. Kate was a little cooler than the others but every bit as impressive.

Finn was nervous at first and fluffed a couple of his early lines as Lysander, but grew in confidence as he progressed. By the time he ducked backstage to muddy up his face to play Bottom in the second scene, he was reaching heights – even this early – that his poor twin brother (watching glumly from the fey side of the glade) had never begun to approach.

The first change passed smoothly. As Nuala brought the opening scene to a close, the others who'd been active slipped into their new costumes. Felix stuck on a beard to play Flute and shed his noble clothes for rags, while Terence turned his outfit inside-out to play Snug. Finn had the most to do – new clothes and a muddy face – but he moved swiftly and was back in place in time. Ingmar, as Quince, was making his first entrance, so he was ready to go.

As soon as Nuala finished speaking, she dashed backstage, dumped her blonde wig, slipped off her fancy clothes – her rags were underneath – and stuck on a fake moustache. The other actors wandered out front while she was changing, drawing laughs by pulling faces and scratching themselves, buying time and establishing the lowbrow nature of their characters. When Nuala was ready, she ambled out, and the five actors gathered at the centre of the stage.

"'Is all our company here?'" Ingmar sniffed as Quince.

"'You were best to call them generally,'" Finn as Bottom answered, "'man by man, according to the scrip.'"

Finn was nothing short of magnificent in the second scene — the audience choked with laughter at his absurd voices and gestures. A couple of people standing on the benches laughed so hard that they fell off, and he worked the sounds into his act, reacting as if they were natural noises of the forest.

A huge round of applause sent the actors on their way at the end of the act. A few eyebrows were raised when no new actors emerged but then Terence told them there would be a short interval, which would be repeated at the end of each act. Those in the seats were disappointed, but those standing were glad of the excuse to hop down and stretch.

"That went splendidly," Terence beamed as he re-joined his troupe.

"I almost burst out laughing a few times," Ingmar chuckled, nudging Finn.

"I never realised you could be so funny," Kate agreed, hugging the changeling.

"I am a man of many talents," Finn smiled, loving the attention.

In one corner, Felix was facing Nuala, his expression grim. "Ready for the next act?" he asked.

"Of course," she replied.

He licked his lips nervously. "I..." He stopped. "We..." he

started, but again got no further. "Look," he finally said, "I've *got* to be nasty to you in this."

"That shouldn't be hard," Nuala said softly.

"I'll be speaking as the character," he growled. "It's got nothing to do with how things stand between us. I don't want you thinking I'm using the play to have a dig at you."

"Fair enough." Nuala gulped. "I never meant to hurt you. What happened was just... I didn't intend..." She sighed. "I'm sorry."

"Sorry you hurt me," Felix replied coolly, "or sorry I found out?"

"Both," she answered honestly.

"We'll talk about it later," Felix said. "Right now, you'd be better off worrying about that moustache. I don't think you'll gain much credibility if you wander out as Helena with a 'tache."

"Oh!" She smiled and peeled it off. "I almost forgot. Thanks."

"Don't mention it." He turned his back on her and walked away. "That's what husbands are for."

*

In the glade, the fair folk of Feyland were busy discussing the first act.

"The actors this year play it from the heart," Titania noted.

"It ranks among the best first acts I have seen in some time," Cobweb agreed.

"Not bad," the ghost of Will Shakespeare said, which was high praise indeed. "The changeling overdid it as Bottom, and

I'm not keen on the little man playing Demetrius, but I've rarely seen a more apt Helena." He glanced at a seething Oberon. "*You* don't seem too impressed."

Oberon spluttered indignantly.

"I did not come to admire the damn play!

 But to rejoice the passing of this day,

 To see our human Puck his talents lend

 To the cause of forcing these Players' end."

"That's the first time I've heard someone complaining that a play's too good," the shade laughed.

"It is not meant to be good," Oberon roared. "It is meant to be a stinker. The Players are supposed to come apart at the seams. There should be chaos, disaster, an end to all future performances. The way it is going, it would not surprise me if we are stuck with them for another twenty years." He shook his head grimly. "I sense treachery in the air. If 'tis so, and Chapman has played a trick on us, I warn you now, ghost, you will have one more for company in the heavens tonight."

"Hush, lord," Titania said. "The Players emerge again. Perhaps this act will provide evidence of our agent's tinkering."

"It had better," Oberon fumed, settling back in his seat as Del and Kate entered from opposite sides of the glade as Puck and an unnamed fairy.

*

Del skipped across the glade, trying not to notice the spectators. The humans didn't bother him but the fairies did. Would Oberon and his retinue find favour in the chaotic entertainment Del had (loosely) planned? And how would they reveal their displeasure if he failed to drive the Players apart?

He met Kate in the centre of the glade and the two launched into their lengthy dialogue. Del was operating on auto-pilot, so his performance wasn't as polished as Kate's, but he did an adequate job, especially for someone new to the stage.

At the appointed moment, Don and Anna, as Oberon and Titania, entered the glade from either end and Del and Kate fell to their knees. The lord and lady of Feyland argued about the Indian boy – Don forgot his plan to slip in a few veiled homosexual gestures – then Titania stormed off, her fairy attendant (Kate) in tow.

Once Don and Del were alone, the bare-chested, blonde-wigged lord of the fairies plotted to torment the love of his life. He bid Puck go and find the magic love herb to rub on Titania's eyelids while she slept, to make her fall in love with the first creature that she saw when she awoke.

Then Felix and Nuala, as Demetrius and Helena, took centre stage, observed by the lurking Oberon.

"'I love thee not, therefore pursue me not,'" Felix grunted, pushing the fixated woman away. He tried to glare at her but found it hard. The grief in Nuala's eyes – staged? real? – touched him deeply.

"'You draw me, you hard-hearted adamant!'" Nuala wailed, throwing herself at Felix's feet, dry-sobbing her way through her next three lines.

"'Do I entice you?'" Felix demanded of her. He stared at his wife and his voice faltered. "'Do I speak you fuh-fair? Or rather do I not in plainest truth Tell you I do not, nor I cannot love you?'" The last words were little more than a whisper.

Nuala failed to notice her husband's plight and ploughed ahead.

"'And even for that do I love you the more.

I am your spaniel; and, Demetrius,

The more you beat me I will fawn on you.

Use me but as your spaniel: spurn me, strike me,

Neglect me, lose me; only give...'"

She stopped. A shudder had run the length of Felix's body. Looking up, she realised there were tears in his eyes, and a devoted set to his face which she remembered from their early courting days.

"'...give me leave,'" she finished, then gulped and continued, her own voice beginning to crack.

"'Unworthy as I am, to fuh-follow you.

What worse place can I beg in your love

(And yet a place of high respect with me)

Than to be used as you use your duh-dog?'"

Felix was crying openly now. His hands closed on hers and he raised her to her feet. When he spoke, it was with a weak smile and a short shake of his head.

"'Tempt not too much the hatred of my spirit,'" he croaked. "'For I am sick when I do look on thee.'"

Nuala was crying too, though it was only as she spoke that she realised why. "'And I am sick when I look not on you,'" she wept, then stopped. It was true. She *did* feel sick without Felix.

"'I am sick when I look not on you,'" she said again, eyes filling with wonder as it dawned on her how close she'd come to driving Felix away forever. Felix... the funny little Northerner... the pompous fool... the man she'd thought so little of... the man she... the man she loved!

"Oh, Felix," she wailed, wrapping her arms around him.

"Nuala," he cried, hugging her with all his strength.

The audience stirred and murmured, confused.

"I don't remember this being in the play," Christopher Big muttered.

"She called him 'Felix,'" Ferdy Frost huffed. "And he called her 'Nuala.' The idiots have forgotten their stage names."

"Hush, dear," Sally said, eyes brimming with tears. She hadn't been able to follow much of the play – Shakespeare was an alien world to her – but she could see the bond of love the two actors shared, and her heart rose high in her chest as they wept unashamedly.

"What's going on?" Terence hissed off-stage.

"Quiet," Anna said and took a step forward to better view the embracing pair.

In the glade, Don didn't know what to do. Felix and Nuala were grasping each other, weeping, the play forgotten. He decided anything was better than standing still, looking forlorn, so, clearing his throat, he went on an improvised walk.

"These humans are funny things," he said. "They start to say one thing, then say another. What twists their tongues? As lord of the fairies, when I speak, 'tis with clear intent."

In the wings, Terence quit wringing his hands and trained a spotlight on the moving Don, drawing the attention of the audience away from the couple at the centre of the glade.

"The way these humans act, 'tis almost as though two minds dwell within each form." Don was enjoying himself. "Were this a play," he chuckled, making eye contact with an American, "those looking on would be bewildered. 'Has this one forgot his lines?' they'd ask. 'Has that one lost the plot?'" He winked. "'Twould be most confusing, would it not?"

"It sure would," the American answered loudly, to the delight of his fellow tourists, who clapped and hooted. Soon, almost everyone was smiling, believing themselves the victims of a subtle theatrical trick.

"Interesting," Christopher Big purred.

"They aren't usually this experimental," Joan Casey thought.

"This is rot," Ferdy Frost huffed. "He's making it up as he goes along."

"He's covering for the stricken pair," Shakespeare's ghost remarked, "but he can't continue indefinitely. Something must be done with the central duo."

As if reading the Bard's thoughts, Terence sneaked into the glade, grabbed Felix and Nuala by their necks and dragged them out of sight. "What the hell's going on?" he mouse-roared.

They paid the fuming director no heed.

"I'm sorry," Nuala sobbed. "What I did was terrible. Can you ever forgive me?"

"Of course," Felix snuffled. "I love you." He wiped tears from his cheeks and smiled bravely. Then he grew grave. "Come with me."

"Where?" Nuala asked.

"North," Felix said.

"Leave Limerick? What about your job?"

"The hell with it — I'll get another. I'm not happy here and never have been. You can be content up North, can't you?"

"Yes," Nuala said.

"Then let's go. This is your world, your friends, your life. I've been living in the shadow of your past and that's come between us. It's time I made a stand."

"Yes," Nuala gasped, delighted to see this new side of her meek husband.

"You'll come with me?" he asked.

"As soon as the play's over," she promised.

"No," he said. "Now."

"But the play..."

"Screw it." Felix's eyes were bright. "If you can walk away from this goddamn play, the rest will be a cinch. We've wasted enough time on follies of the past. Are you with me?"

Nuala searched her heart and decided. "I'm with you," she cried, tearing off her wig and tossing it to the ground.

"Now, see here," Terence spluttered.

"I'm sorry," Nuala said, kissing his cheek, "but a gal's gotta do what a gal's gotta do."

"But... but..."

"Give me a ring sometime," she winked, discarding her clothes.

"No hard feelings," Felix grinned, slipping out of his costume. "Hate to leave you in the lurch – didn't plan it this way – but that's life."

"You can't... what about... wait!"

But Terence was wasting his breath, for without another word, the pair turned and fled, like a young, impassioned couple eloping.

Nuala halted as they passed Anna and smiled nervously. "No regrets?"

"No regrets," Anna smiled.

"You understand?"

Anna nodded. "I hope you have a long and happy future together."

Nuala threw her arms around the chubby woman and gave her one final hug. "I'll think of you often," she said happily, then waved to the stunned remainder of the cast, joined hands with Felix and took off into the night.

"This isn't happening," Terence moaned. "It's a bad dream. I'll wake and..."

His head swivelled to stare at the glade. Don was still entertaining the crowd but the shifting of bums and polite coughing made it clear they weren't prepared to put up with this much longer.

"We're finished," Terence whispered, and in the solemn, silent darkness, he got ready to face the audience and break the news that the show was over.

*

As Terence steeled himself to walk out and apologise, Kate took matters into her own hands. She acted on instinct, not pausing to seek the director's approval — there wasn't time for a debate. Stooping, she plucked up Nuala's wig and jammed it on. Looking around, her gaze alighted on Ingmar. Gathering Felix's abandoned clothes, she thrust them at the startled German.

"Vot are dese for?" he squeaked.

"Get into them," she commanded. "We're going on."

"Ve can't," Ingmar gasped.

"You know the lines, don't you?"

"Most of them," Ingmar agreed, "but..."

"Don't think," she told him, adjusting her wig. "Just do it. If we get to the end of this scene we'll call a break, sort ourselves out, decide if we can continue."

"*Continue*?" Ingmar looked incredulous. "How can ve —"

Kate silenced him with a kiss. "You were most obliging last night," she purred. "I never realised you knew how to show a woman a good time."

Ingmar's face reddened. "Please don't mention that. Don might —"

"— find out," Kate concluded. "*Might*. But if you don't get into those clothes and out front with me pronto, he definitely will."

"You're blackmailing me?" Ingmar couldn't believe it.

"You got it, baby," Kate smirked.

Not daring call her bluff, Ingmar pulled on the costume. Thirty seconds later, the pair took a collective deep breath and sauntered forth.

"Where the hell are you going?" Terence asked as they passed.

"Train the light on us," Kate answered.

Before he could reply, they were beyond the cover of the trees and walking to the centre of the glade.

"What's happening?" Del asked the director.

"I think they're taking over the parts," Terence said.

"Can they do that?" Del asked.

"No. But they're doing it anyway."

Out front, Don was running out of steam. He would make one more circuit, he decided, and if there was no sign of Felix and Nuala, he'd slip away to see what was happening. Then the spotlight shifted and costumed shapes emerged. "Ah!" he boomed. "The quarrelling couple are ready to resume their argument. Let us sneak up again and..." He stopped. The blonde wig and costumes had deceived him, but now he realised this wasn't Felix and Nuala. It was Ingmar and Kate.

"Is it just *my* eyes," he wondered aloud, "or do those two look different?"

The audience laughed. They'd been no more fooled by the change than Don, but since he'd commented on it, they were prepared – most, anyway – to accept this as part of some intricate plan.

"Come," Don said, moving in on the edgy-looking newcomers. "Let us see if we can make sense of this. Perhaps their words will reveal more than their forms."

Once Don was in position, Kate fell to her knees and screeched as Helena.

"'What worse place can I beg in your love

(And yet a place of high respect with me)

Than to be used as you use your dog?'"

Ingmar hesitated, then caught Don's eye. He didn't want to contemplate what would happen if his lover learnt of the previous night's indiscretions. A fling with Diarmid would have been bad enough, but if Don learnt he'd been part of an orgy, with *women* present...

"'Tuh-tempt not too much the huh-hatred of my spirit,'" Ingmar stuttered. "'For I am sick ven I do look on thee.'"

"'And I am sick when I look not on you,'" Kate howled, beating his knees comically with her forehead.

"I like this new actress," one American remarked to his neighbour. "She's funnier than the last."

"But why the change?" came the puzzled reply.

"Some kind of comment on the double nature of humanity, I guess."

"Oh." The neighbour dwelt on that a moment. "Clever."

In the thick of the action, Kate and Ingmar were drawing to a close. Backstage, Terence gave Del a quick pat. "You're up," he whispered.

Del blinked. "You want me to go on?"

"It's go on or go down," Terence sighed. "We're almost at the end of the scene, but we'll pretend it's the end of the act when you and Don come off." The director's mind was working along the same lines as Kate's. "That'll give us time to regroup and think this through."

"But –" Del began.

Ingmar made his exit, limbs trembling, and Terence shoved Del forward.

Del stumbled past Kate, who was also exiting, and spun towards Don, who smiled and waved a hand.

"'Hast you the flower there?'" Don asked as Oberon. "'Welcome, wanderer.'"

"'Ay, there it is,'" Del said, then realised he'd forgotten the prop. Covering the palm of his right hand with his left, he pretended he wanted to hide the flower from prying eyes.

Don understood what was happening and was as careful to hide the *flower* when he received it as Del had been. He boasted of how he would find Titania and apply the magic juice to her eyes. Next he bid Puck take some juice and use it on the young man in Athenian garments (he meant Demetrius, but Puck would mistakenly use it on Lysander) so that he would fall in love with the sad Helena.

"'Fear not, my lord,'" Del said, "'your servant shall do so.'" With that, he brought the scene to a close and the two made a quick exit. Moments later, Terence declared another break, and as the members of the audience pondered the strange twists and turns of the play, the actors met backstage and discussed whether they should stay, flee or commit hara-kiri.

5.[I](iii)

"It's impossible," Terence said bluntly.

"Why?" Kate asked. "We got away with it that time. Why shouldn't we –"

"It's impossible, I tell you," he snapped.

They were discussing – what else? – the play. Kate wished to continue. Terence claimed it couldn't be done. The rest of the cast were keeping out of the debate, most of them too numb to contribute.

"Let's go through it step by step," Kate said. "Explain why it's impossible, because I honestly don't think it is."

Terence closed his eyes and massaged his forehead. He could feel the mother of all headaches coming on. "OK," he growled. "Let's take Ingmar. The second scene of the second act — no problem. He appears as Mustardseed but could get off and change for his appearance as Demetrius. But in the third act, he's Quince. If he filled in for Felix, he'd have to play Flute too, at the same time."

That took the air out of Kate's sails. "And I couldn't play Hermia *and* Helena when they're required on stage together."

"Exactly." Terence smiled benignly. "It's hopeless. Best to let everyone know and refund them. It's disappointing but –"

"Wait a minute," Kate said, thinking furiously. "Anna could play Helena."

"Me?" Anna was alarmed to hear her name being mentioned.

"Why not?" Kate pressed. "She looks more like Nuala than I do. And one of the other men could step in for Felix when Ingmar's required elsewhere."

"This is crazy," Terence groaned. "We'd all be playing three or four roles. We'd make fools of ourselves. I'm going out to tell the –"

"Hold on," Don interrupted. "Kate's got a point."

"What?" Terence gawped.

"My improv was no great shakes but it sowed the seed for a free interpretation," Don said. "If we're brazen about it, we might pull it off."

"*Interpretation*?" Terence shook his head. "What are you talking about?"

"We could revolve the roles and claim we adapted the play to be a reflection on concepts of self and duality."

"You're away with the fairies," Terence muttered without any irony.

"It could work," Don insisted, rubbing his hands together as he considered it. "The same costumes but different actors. Make it a game for the audience."

Terence still had doubts. "That sort of arrangement takes weeks – months – to perfect. To make the rules up as we go along…" He grimaced. "We'd risk looking worse than we already are."

"So what?" Del asked, stepping into the argument. "If we make a mess of it and come away looking like fools, big deal. Let's abandon ourselves to the winds of chaos and let them blow us where they may."

"But we'd look moronic," Terence wailed.

"He might be right," Don said, getting cold feet.

"Well, we *are* morons." Del beamed at the dejected cast. It was time to throw the cat among the pigeons. Would they be eaten or would they fly? Del wasn't sure but it would be fun finding out. "If looking stupid is all that's holding us back, let me remove that worry. I've never acted before. Michael Finnt's been in hospital this past fortnight. I'm a chancer who took you in."

He laughed at their shocked expressions and continued. "There's more. Some of you wondered why Diarmid's been acting differently. I'll tell you why — because he *isn't* Diarmid."

Jaws dropped and heads turned. The changeling blushed modestly.

"That's Finn, Diarmid's twin brother." (Del kept the news of Finn's feyness to himself — best not to make matters *too* confusing.) "Diarmid got sick of the play and asked Finn to take his place. Finn has never acted before either."

He grinned at Terence and Don. "You've been taken in by rank pretenders. But wait, there's more." He pointed an accusing finger at Terence. "This man's an impostor too. Do you know what he teaches at school?"

"No!" Terence gasped. "Don't tell them. Don't –"

"Physical Education," Del roared.

All gazes focused on the shamed teacher. "It's not true," Terence cried. "He's lying. You can't trust a word he says. By his own admission he's a…" He ran out of steam and fixed his gaze on Anna. "*You* told him."

She shook her head. "I don't know how he found out but it wasn't through me. I never opened my mouth, even when I had cause."

"Is it true, Terence?" Kate asked quietly.

"Why have you done this to me?" Terence sobbed at Del.

"Not to hurt you," Del swore. "I just want to prove that we've all made fools of ourselves already. I want you to understand that a bit more foolishness can't make any difference. We only fear those out there" – he waved towards the crowd in the glade – "because of the lies we've nurtured back here. If we strip away those lies, we never need fear anything again."

He licked his lips and went for broke. "Terence. Don. Do you know where your partners were last night?"

"No!" The roars from the other Players were deafening.

"Shut up!" Kate screamed.

"You can't tell them that!" Anna yelled.

"No, no, no, no, no," Ingmar whimpered.

Del ignored their protests and pleas. "While you and Felix sat at home, nursing your wounded pride, the rest of us enjoyed a rare old knees-up."

"What sort of *knees-up*?" Don asked suspiciously.

"An orgy," Del said happily.

"Don't listen to him," Kate screeched.

"He's a liar," Anna moaned.

"No, no, no, no, no," Ingmar continued.

"Six bodies, one mind," Del said with relish. "Men with women, women with women, men with men. No boundaries acknowledged, no taboos respected. Little was said but much was shared."

"Ingmar?" Don croaked.

The German smiled crookedly. "It vas only... a bit of... fun," he squeaked.

"Who did you do it with?" Don asked, aghast.

"All of us," Del boomed.

"With Diarmid?" Don asked and Ingmar nodded sadly. "Not with Kate. Not with Anna. Not with Nuala."

"I lost my mind," Ingmar wailed. "I had all dese bodies around me and behind me and in front of me. Vot could I do, only take dem in turn?"

"I don't believe this," Terence gasped. "An adulteress I could have accepted — but a harlot!"

"If I'm a harlot, what are you?" Anna sniffed in reply. "If you added up all your bits on the side, you'd surpass my total by a half-dozen or more."

"But never at the same time," Terence roared.

Anna shrugged. "I structured my affairs more efficiently than you. So what?"

Terence gawped at her, then at Del and the other Players. And then he laughed. "You're loonies," he yelled hysterically. "Fit for the nut-house, every one of you. Me too, for not realising it before."

"That's right," Del said slyly. "We're all mad. But now that you've caught up, don't you see the point I've been trying to make? It's sane for the mad to *act* mad. If we go out and make asses of ourselves, we're behaving according to our nature. We don't have to worry about looking like fools if we accept that we *are* fools."

"He's right," Terence hooted. "Let's celebrate our idiocy, strip naked and give them a treat." He was half-laughing, half-crying.

"Terence is up for it," Del beamed. "So am I and Finn. Kate? Do you want to board this sorry ship of fools?"

Kate glanced at the crumbling director, then nodded numbly. "If craziness is good enough for him," she bleated, "it's good enough for me."

"Anna?" Del asked.

"I'll support my husband's decision," she declared nobly.

"Ingmar?"

The DJ shook his head. "I can't. I vant to curl up in a ball and die."

"You *will* go out," Don grunted, hauling his lover to his feet. "You've made a fool of me, Ingmar Van Dorslaer, and I'm not letting you leave until I've had a chance to return the favour. We're with you, Del, to the bitter, crazy end." He squeezed Ingmar tightly. "Isn't that right, Casanova?"

Ingmar gulped fearfully. "Votever he says is fine by me," he cried.

"Splendid." Del rubbed his hands together and cackled. "Trust me, you need this. I don't know where we'll end up by close of play tonight, but it has to be a better place than you've been for the past twenty years." He clapped firmly. "Act Two, Scene Two. Anna enters as Titania, with fairies. Who'll be Peaseblossom?"

For a moment there was silence. Then, slowly, Kate raised a hand. "I'll do it."

Del gave her a hug of thanks. "Terence!" he snapped, jolting the director out of his daze. "You'll go on as Cobweb. Now get that brain of yours in gear, to figure out how we're going to handle the rest of the play."

Terence stared blankly at Del, then nodded, his eyes beginning to clear. "OK," he said, his voice a shaky replica of that of old. "Gather round." He thought about it as the Players huddled together, glanced at Del for reassurance – Del winked cockily – and started hesitantly. "Here's how we might just swing it..."

5.[I](iv)

The Players appeared shaken when they emerged for the start of the second half of the second act, but to their credit they rose above their shock and delivered solid performances. Anna was noble as Titania, Ingmar sang beautifully as Mustardseed, Terence kept his knees from knocking together, and Kate pranced around in Nuala's orange shock-wig, humming like a bee as Ingmar sang.

When the fairies exited, Don came on as Oberon and applied the love juice to Titania's sleeping eyes. While he was doing this, Kate executed a quick change and wriggled into her Hermia gear. She took Finn's hand – he was in Lysander mode – and, as Don came off, they strolled on, staring mock-lovingly into each other's eyes.

While Finn and Kate went through their paces, Anna sneaked off-stage. She was supposed to have remained in the glade, asleep as Titania, but Nuala's departure had put paid to that plan. Slipping away as quietly as she could, noticed by hardly anyone in the crowd (though alert Ferdy Frost spotted her), she changed clothes and became the third actress that night to don the blonde Helena wig.

Ingmar, meanwhile, had ample time to dress as Demetrius. His problem was that there was little to the costume. As Flute, Felix had worn a beard, but as Demetrius he'd appeared much as he was, except in fancy clothes. There was no wig or make-up to disguise Ingmar's face.

"They'll know it's me," he moaned to Don. "They won't accept me."

"Maybe they will," Don said. "This is the perfect time to make your entrance as him. You've only got two lines, then you exit. Next time you emerge, yours will be the face they remember. Good luck." And he pecked Ingmar's forehead.

There was a murmur of confusion when Ingmar and Anna appeared. Some were taken in by the wig and thought it was the same actress, but no one mistook Ingmar for Felix. Fortunately, as Don had said, he was only on-stage a matter of seconds, and before the audience could ponder what was going on, Kate had launched into a speech to distract them.

When Finn awoke, his character fell in love with the new Helena, declared his feelings, and was taken for a trickster by the upset woman. She fled, he shortly followed, and Kate – as Hermia – soon exited too, drawing the scene to a close.

*

During the short pause between the end of the scene and the start of the third act – there was no official break, since the actors had used it at the end of the first scene – the spectators discussed the personnel changes.

"It's a statement," one American theorised. "They're saying it doesn't matter who plays the parts — the characters are so great, they overshadow the actors."

"That's a brave move," somebody else commented. "You don't get many actors prepared to admit that they don't really matter in the greater scheme of things."

Joan Casey wasn't sure what the Players were up to but she was enjoying it. She was familiar with the plot but tonight she was struggling to keep abreast of the story, thrown by the changing faces and thoughts of what was yet to come. It was a breath of delightfully chaotic fresh air. She couldn't wait to see how it turned out.

Ferdy Frost, on the other hand, wasn't impressed. "The same actress played Helena and Titania," he complained to his mother.

"Who's Helena again?" Sally asked.

"The one in the blonde wig."

"Surely not," Sally laughed. "The actress playing Titania was asleep in the glade, wasn't she?"

"No," Ferdy said. "She sneaked off and put on the wig. You can't do that. It's against the rules."

"I don't know," Sally smiled. "I'm enjoying it. It's funnier than I imagined."

Oberon was enjoying it too. "They are crumbling," he chortled. "I do not know what is happening, but Chapman seems to be doing his job."

"Did I not tell you, my lord?" Puck smirked. "Have I ever put you wrong?"

"More often than I can count," Oberon growled. "But even the king of fools has to get things right once in a while."

Titania was addressing the shade of Will Shakespeare.

"What do you think has happened to the pair

Who originally strutted out there

As Demetrius and Helena fair?"

"I know not, my lady," the spirit replied. "Perhaps the human Puck has lopped off their heads and buried their bodies 'neath a bush."

"Oh!" Titania's face dropped. "Think you so?"

"No," Shakespeare laughed. "More likely he simply chased them off."

Christopher Big knew nothing about missing actors and human Pucks. As far as he was concerned, the changes were part of the director's carefully worked-out plan. The way he saw it, when Lysander woke and fell in love with Helena, he was seeing her as though for the first time, and so a new actress had been introduced. "This guy's smart," the cultured Mr Big thoughtfully mused. "I wonder if he has an agent?"

*

Don filled in for Felix as Flute in the first scene of the third act. There was an anxious moment when he tried on the smaller man's costume and realised it didn't fit, but since the clothes were little better than rags, he just tore a few extra rips and laced a length of string around the trousers to keep them up. He applied the fake beard clumsily and was unhappy with the results, but when he walked out with the others, his strange appearance drew laughs.

This time the audience accepted the new actor without blinking. The majority of onlookers had been expecting at least one red herring, and might even have been disappointed had the proper actor come out. They thought a cunning game was being played and were looking forward to the fiendish twists, amusing themselves by trying to predict the patterns of the Players in advance.

Del entered as Puck and cast his spell on Bottom, replacing his human head with that of an ass. The other actors ran away, Titania woke – Anna had sneaked back onstage while the others had been performing – fell in love with Bottom, sent her fairies to look after him, and off the five of them skipped.

In the second scene of the act, Ingmar again filled in for Felix as Demetrius. As Don had predicted, the audience members had no qualms accepting him, and the nervous DJ relaxed into the role. He looked flummoxed as Kate – back in Hermia mode – accused him of murdering Lysander.

"'I am not guilty of Lysander's blood,

Nor is he dead, for aught that I can tell.'"

Hermia stormed off, Demetrius lay down and slept, and Oberon laid into Puck for using the love spell on the wrong person. He then sent the imp to find Helena, and squeezed juice over the eyes of the sleeping Demetrius.

Finn and Anna were soon back as Lysander and Helena, Finn protesting that he truly loved her. Demetrius woke and fell in love with Helena. The men argued. Kate as Hermia stumbled upon them and grew confused when Lysander rejected her. The men finally stormed off to find a good place to fight, Helena and Hermia exiting not long after them.

Oberon then stepped forward and told Puck they had to fix this mess. He sent him off to separate Lysander and Demetrius, to lull them to sleep and administer a new potion to Lysander's eyes, which would remove the curse of the love juice.

The scene ended with the four lovers sleeping and Puck assuring the audience that all would be fine when they woke. He slipped away, the spotlight snapped off, the remaining actors hurried backstage while the eyes of the audience members were adjusting, and Terence announced a twenty-minute interval before the start of the fourth act.

5.[I](v)

The Players sat quietly backstage during the break, listening to the crowd stretch their legs and chat about the play. Normally a couple of the actors would be out front, selling snacks and drinks, but nobody felt up to the task.

"I think they like it," Del remarked to Finn.

"Aye," the changeling sighed, and glanced around at his despondent colleagues. Terence was staring at his feet, giggling fitfully. Kate was pulling her hair absentmindedly. Anna was keeping a close eye on Terence, nervously chewing her finger-nails, while Ingmar and Don gazed wordlessly at one another. "The Players do not like it though."

"Give them time," Del said. "There are two acts to go. A lot can happen."

"What *will* happen?" Finn asked and Del shrugged. "You do not know?"

"Not exactly," Del said. "I'm sure we aren't through with the explosions, but as to who'll flare up and when... Your guess is as good as mine."

"Terence has taken the news of the orgy badly," Finn noted. "And Don looks as though he could strangle Ingmar."

"They'll be fine," Del said confidently, then cocked an eyebrow at the young man. "The only one I'm really worried about is you."

"Me?" Finn blinked.

"You've been subdued since last night. I expected whoops, sighs, dreamy grins. Instead you look like a man who's had half his teeth pulled. Didn't you enjoy it?"

"It was most wonderful," Finn said happily. "Never had I dared dream of such bliss."

"Then why the long face?"

"Because I will never know another night like it," Finn said glumly. "I return to Feyland soon. There is no sex there for one of my lowly station."

"I'd forgotten that," Del grunted. "Couldn't you stay? I could hide you."

Finn shook his head. "'Tis a gracious offer but I cannot accept. The laws of Feyland forbid it. Besides, I could not bring myself to betray Lord Oberon — it was by his gracious leave that I came here in the first place."

"Oh well." Del clapped him manfully on the back. "Like I said, two acts to go. Who knows what the night has in store? You might live to party again. Stranger things have happened."

"None that I know of," Finn remarked morosely.

*

Out front, a weary actor had arrived. It had been a long trek from the hospital to the glade. First he'd taken the wrong road, then spent the better part of an hour hitching in vain. When a driver finally stopped for him, he fell asleep in the back seat and awoke thirty kilometres the wrong side of the glade. After more thumbing he'd hitched a ride on the back of a motorbike. And now here he was.

He made his way past the benches and chairs, to where people were strolling. He looked for the Players but found none. "What's happening?" he asked a woman who was jotting down notes in a pad. "Is the play over?"

"Interval," came the reply. "Weren't you watching?"

"I just arrived," Michael Finnt replied, his heart sinking. "Has it been good?"

"Fabulous." Joan Casey looked up from her pad and smiled. "Normally this lot are awful but this time they're a pleasure to watch. I haven't had this much fun at a play since..." She frowned. "Do I know you?"

"No," Michael lied. "What about Puck? Who's playing him?"

Joan checked her notes. "Some guy called Del Chapman."

"What's he like?"

"Fine," Joan said. "They're all good, even the ones who are normally terrible." She studied Michael more closely. "I'm sure I know you."

"I have one of those faces," Michael said and sloped away. He was heading for the wings, to make his presence known, when he heard Terence ordering people back to their seats – "Two minutes, ladies and gentlemen." – and decided not to trouble him. Best to keep out of his way until after the finale.

Mingling with the crowd, Michael found a standing spot at the back, and though he was exhausted, he valiantly stood and observed the rest of the play. The woman with the pen – and the positive buzz of the crowd – had aroused his interest. What were the Players doing this year to stir up such excitement?

*

With everyone back in their seats or on the benches, Anna and Finn opened the fourth act. Kate, Terence and Ingmar were in attendance as Peaseblossom, Cobweb and Mustard-seed, while Don secretly followed as Oberon, chuckling as Titania fawned over the ass-headed Bottom.

One man who wasn't chuckling was Terence. He was at last emerging from his daze, fury flooding his system in place of departing shock. "She betrayed me," he whispered, feeling the awful injustice of it. "With my friends, my colleagues, my partners. She made a fool of me."

("And she didn't even invite me along for the orgy!" he added silently.)

He watched her cavort with the grinning Finn – the ass's head was designed to display the greater part of the actor's face – and the rage within him bubbled up as he listened to her coo over the younger man.

"'Come, sit thee down upon this flowery bed

While I thy amiable cheeks do coy.

And stick musk-roses in thy sleek smooth head,

And kiss thy fair large ears, my gentle joy.'"

Terence snorted loudly, wondering what the *amiable* Finn had *stuck* in his wife. Finn glanced at him, distracted, then ordered Peaseblossom to scratch his head. "'Where's Mounsieur Cobweb?'" he asked, smiling at Terence.

Terence glared and didn't answer.

Finn's smile faded. "'Mounsieur Cobweb?'" he tried again.

"That's you," Anna hissed, giving him a kick. Then she turned to the audience and laughed. "The fool forgets his name," she informed them as Titania. "Good servants are hard to come by."

"'Mounsieur Cobweb?'" Finn gazed pleadingly at Terence.

The director sighed and answered tetchily, "'Ready.'"

Finn smiled and told the fairy to kill a bee and bring him its honey. Terence bowed his head but kept his gaze fixed on the actor. Here was the source of his woes, Finn Garrigan, twin brother to Diarmid if that blaggard Del was to be believed. *He* had led Anna astray.

Anna's actions as Titania further fired the hatred boiling in his heart. The way she cuddled up to Finn, toying with his hair, stroking his cheeks with her nails — disgraceful! (The director forgot that she was only doing as he had instructed.) The way she muttered softly to him,

"'What, wilt thou have some music, my sweet love?'"

"'Or say, sweet love, what thou desir'st to eat.'"

"'Sleep thou, and I will wind thee in my arms.

Fairies be gone, and be all ways away.'"

That was the order for the three fairies to exit, but while Kate and Ingmar made for the wings, Terence remained rooted to the spot. Anna's hands were all over Finn as she spoke her next quartet of lines.

"'So doth the woodbine the sweet honeysuckle

Gently entwist; the female ivy so

Enrings the barky fingers of the elm.

O, how I love thee! How I dote on thee!'"

She bent forward and kissed Finn passionately, after which the two were meant to fall asleep. But that kiss proved the breaking point for the jealous Terence, and before their lips separated he was charging across the glade, screaming, "Bastard!"

Finn's head snapped up, but before he could get a fix on the furious director, Terence was upon him and the two went rolling to the floor.

"Oh my," Anna shrieked, toppling backwards.

"Terence?" Don said uncertainly. "I don't think –"

"I'll teach you to seduce my wife," Terence roared, ignoring Anna and Don, flailing wildly at Finn with his fists, missing with most of the blows.

Ingmar didn't see the fists missing. From where he stood, it looked as if Finn was taking the beating of his life, and the DJ couldn't stand the thought of that beautiful face being reduced to a bloody pulp.

"Hold on, my dove," the German yelled, rushing into the glade. "I'll save you." He threw himself on top of the thrashing pair and wrapped his arms around Terence, trying to drag him away.

Don was furious that Ingmar had leapt to Finn's defence. "Traitor!" he bellowed, launching a kick at his lover, miscalculating and connecting with Finn's backside instead.

"Ow!" Finn screeched from beneath the two men.

"Traitor!" Don screamed again, and flung himself forward to tear Ingmar loose and teach him a lesson he'd never forget.

As Don flew through the air, Terence shrugged Ingmar off, pulled back from the writhing Finn and freed his right arm for a vicious, measured blow. As it hovered mid-air, reminiscent of Robert De Niro's arm in *Raging Bull*, Don's chin struck the elbow, almost driving the bald man's jaw up through the roof of his mouth.

"Yowch!" Terence yelled, his arm bending back from the force of the collision, instantly losing all strength and purpose.

"Uhf!" was all Don managed — moments later he was sliding to the floor, dead to the world.

"Don," Ingmar cried, abandoning the fight to tend to his unconscious lover.

"You killed him," Finn shouted, hoping to stun Terence back to his senses.

"No," Terence gasped. "It was an accident. I didn't mean to... How is he?"

"Hurt bad," Ingmar sobbed. "Help me get him backstage. Quickly!"

The shout jolted Terence and Finn into action. Terence took Don's legs and Finn grabbed the arms. Lifting him, they shuffled back to the wings, Ingmar jogging alongside in close attendance, a dazed Anna trailing behind.

The crowd followed the sequence of events uncertainly. Was this part of the game or had they witnessed a real fight? Was the tall, bald actor – Don's wig had slipped off during the struggle – really in trouble or only pretending? Was this the premature end of the play or the signal for another twisting aside?

As they sat or stood, bewildered, a jubilant Del Chapman emerged as a grinning Puck. He picked up the wig of blonde, curly hair, tossed it into the shadows of the trees, then faced the expectant audience.

"Looks bad, doesn't it?" he said, eyes glittering wickedly. "How can we wriggle out of this one?"

Stooping, he broke off a blade of grass and stuck it between his lips. He manipulated the blade with his tongue so that it tickled his nose. Then he winked, turned his back on the crowd and strolled off, relishing the stunned silence.

*

Backstage, Ingmar rolled up Don's eyelids while the others looked on anxiously.

"Is he breathing?" Anna asked, clutching Terence's arm, afraid she was on the verge of losing her husband to a lengthy manslaughter sentence.

"I didn't mean to do it," Terence whimpered. "I don't know my own strength."

"Does he need mouth-to-mouth?" Kate asked. "I know CPR."

"Never mind him," Finn groaned. "I think I have cracked a bone in my bottom."

"It doesn't look like dere's serious damage," Ingmar said. "I tink he'll come to in a couple of minutes."

"Thank God," Terence sighed.

"Everyone OK?" Del asked, returning from his brief jaunt in the glade.

"Ingmar thinks Don will recover," Kate told him.

"Does that mean he'll be fit to carry on?" Del asked.

"What got into you out there?" Anna demanded of her husband. "You were like a wild animal."

"I couldn't stand it any longer," Terence sobbed. "Seeing you with that... that... Lothario! I don't want to lose you, Anna," he bawled, throwing his arms around her. "I love you. Can we put this behind us and start again?"

"No more fooling around?" Anna asked quietly.

"Never," Terence swore. "And will *you* stay faithful?"

Anna smiled. "That can be arranged."

"Then..." His face lit up hopefully. "You'll give me another chance?"

"I'm game if you are," Anna told him.

"Oh, Anna!" he wailed, kissing her deeply.

"Oh, Terence!" she wept, returning the kiss with interest.

"Isn't love grand?" Del remarked to Finn.

"Forget love," Finn complained. "What about my arse?"

"Rub some grass on it," Del said callously, focusing his attention on Kate, to gauge her reaction to Terence and Anna's tearful reunion. The young woman was smiling and Del knew there would be no further problems in that department.

"I hate to be a spoilsport," he said, tapping Terence's shoulder, "but we've run into an impasse out front. Shall I tell the crowd the show's off?"

Terence wiped his cheeks clean and took a few seconds to reflect. "Off?" he grunted. "Who said anything about it being off?"

"Well," Del said, feigning confusion, "how can we continue now that Don's out of the picture? We've left the crowd hanging mid-scene. Perhaps it's for the best if we call it a night and –"

"We're calling nothing," Terence declared. "If we can survive the passing of Felix and Nuala, one more won't make much difference."

"Are you sure?" Del asked.

"Positive," Terence boomed. "Anna, Finn, resume your positions. Del, are you prepared to go back on?"

"Sure am, boss," Del grinned.

"But I am not," Finn piped up. "I can barely walk with my backside stinging the way it does."

"You'll get out there and dance if I demand it," Terence snapped, silencing the whining changeling. "Del, when you're through as Puck, you'll have to come back on as Egeus later in the scene. Can you handle it?"

"I'll bluff my way through," Del vowed.

"Ingmar, be ready to enter as Demetrius," Terence said.

"What about Don?" the DJ asked.

"We'll tend to him during the break at the end of the act."

"But Oberon," Anna chipped in. "And Theseus. Who'll fill Don's shoes?"

Terence grinned and picked up the blonde, curly wig. "Why did you think I told Del to be Egeus? Quick, Ingmar," he said, unbuttoning his shirt, "get those clothes off Don."

Anna almost burst with pride and love. Then, clicking her fingers at the hesitant Ingmar, she barked, "You heard what my husband said — get those clothes off that snoring lunk. Chop-chop!" And all of a sudden, despite the odds, the Midsummer Players were back in business and preparing for their next assault.

*

Anna and Finn emerged, slowly walked to the centre of the glade, hand-in-hand, eyes closed, and lay down. Terence came on moments later as Oberon. There was some muttering when the audience realised it was a different actor but nobody was outraged. Indeed, a few who'd wagered on the director appearing as the lord of the fairies nudged their neighbours tellingly.

"They are all over the place," the real Titania whispered to the shade of Will Shakespeare.

"Yes," the ghost of the great scribe agreed. "Isn't it delightful?"

The rest of the fourth act was a joy. Terence was solid as Oberon, and when Titania woke cured, and the pair patched up their differences and danced regally about the glade, more than a few sets of eyes misted over. They exited to a warm round of applause and stood beneath the trees, revelling in the moment, then slid out of their costumes and into their mortal garments.

Moments later, Terence emerged as Theseus, Del accompanying him as Egeus. Anna was also supposed to be there as Hippolyta, but since she had to appear as Helena, Terence dropped her name from his speeches and took her lines for himself, resulting in a long monologue concerning the baying of hounds. While he spoke, Anna, Finn, Kate and Ingmar got into position as the sleeping lovers. When Terence and Del chanced upon them, Del gasped and bent over, paying special attention to Kate, since in the play he was now her father.

"'But soft, what nymphs are these?'" Terence asked.

Del replied,

"'My lord, this is my daughter here asleep,

And this Lysander; this Demetrius is,

This Helena, old Nedar's Helena.

I wonder of their being here together.'"

The lovers jolted awake in comic unison and told the pair about their strange dreams. Egeus called for Lysander's head but Demetrius told him he no longer loved Hermia, that his heart now belonged to Helena, so Lysander and Hermia were free to marry.

Terence and Del exited, bidding the lovers to follow them to the temple for the marriage ceremonies. (Terence's last line was, 'Come, Hippolyta,' but at the last second he remembered to change it to 'Come, Egeus'.) The four starry-eyed lovers pondered the events of the night, unable to decide what was real and what was but a dream. Eventually they left the riddle and set off to catch up with their elders.

Following a quick costume change, Finn came on as Bottom. His own head had been returned while he slept. He too was puzzled by the fantastic visions of the night, but, practical man that he was, decided to tell his good friend Peter Quince that the dreams might be written down and turned into a ballad.

As soon as Finn exited, Ingmar, Del and Kate came on as Quince, Flute and Starveling. They debated their missing comrade's fate, Terence entered as Snug, then Finn returned as Bottom, which cheered them up, since they couldn't perform their play for the Duke without him. They asked Bottom what had happened but he said there was no time for the story, that they had to prepare for the play, and so the short penultimate scene came to a smooth close and the actors retired for the final break of the long, eventful eve.

5.[I](vi)

Those who'd been standing throughout the play were glad to step down and relax. The only one who didn't move was Michael Finnt, who was paralysed with love. Though the actors had all been good, he'd had eyes for only one, the fair Hermia — the beautiful Kate.

The pair had met previously but he didn't remember her. He thought he was seeing the divine actress for the first time, and it was love at first sight. He couldn't explain why he'd fallen immediately and eternally in love with her. He just knew in his heart that this was the woman for him, the woman he must woo, win and devote his life to.

While the actor fantasized about Kate, a certain theatrical agent had set his sights on a different Player. Christopher Big had been impressed with the flow of the play. Despite all the changes and jolts, the last few hours had zipped by. It was rare to find an experimental director who could be entertaining and intellectually stimulating. Christopher had very few directors on his books, but he'd been talking with a board member of London's Globe Theatre a few weeks ago, who'd told the agent they were in desperate need of challenging new visionaries.

Examining his programme notes, Christopher read that the director was married to the plump, pretty actress. All well and good. Though Anna Devlin hadn't made a huge impression, she'd delivered a dependable performance. As everyone knew, there was no surer way for an actress to find work than to marry a director. If he could place Terence, he was sure it would mean a job for Anna too, which would mean more money for *him* if he was representing them both.

One person not impressed was young Ferdy Frost. He hadn't been fooled. He knew only too damn well that none of these shenanigans had been planned. He had seen through the desperate blusterings of the Players from the start, and it amazed him that he was the only one in the know.

"These people are stupid," he complained to his mother, having spent the last couple of minutes listening to passersby rave about the play. "Can't they see how disjointed it is?"

"Disjointed, dear?"

"It's a mess," Ferdy fumed. "Two of the actors haven't reappeared."

"Well, I –" Sally began.

"Don't you find that rather peculiar?" Ferdy snapped.

"I suppose, if you put it that –"

"It's obvious what's happened," Ferdy continued. "They did a runner and the others have been improvising, filling in, figuring we're too dumb to notice."

"But they've done a good job, if that's the case," Sally said. "Don't you think?"

"No, I don't," Ferdy glowered. "Come on." He pulled on his coat and began buttoning it up. "We're going."

"Where, darling?" Sally asked.

"Home," Ferdy snorted.

"But it isn't over."

"I don't care. I've had enough."

"But… I want to stay," Sally said. "I'd like to see how it finishes."

"I don't care what *you* want," Ferdy huffed. "Get up off your bum, woman, and drive me home."

Sally stared at her genius son and saw he was determined. Sighing, she bent to pick up her bag, then paused and straightened. "Ferdy, love," she said sweetly.

"What?" he grunted.

Swinging back her arm, Sally delivered a slap to his astonished pus that almost sent him flying.

"Sit down, you little monster," Sally said softly. "Shut up, watch the play, then thank me for bringing you. Understand, my darling?"

"You... you..." For the first time in his life, Ferdy was lost for words. "You hit me!" he squealed.

"Yes, dear," Sally agreed. "And if you don't sit down, I'll hit you again."

Staring into her eyes, he saw that she was serious. Rubbing his stinging face, Ferdy pondered the situation, then lowered himself back onto his seat.

"That's good," Sally beamed and held out a bag of sweets. "Bonbon?"

Ferdy stared at the sweets, then at his mother. After a brief pause, he took one. "Thank... you," he muttered.

"You're welcome," Sally replied, popping a sweet into her own mouth.

At first Ferdy thought his mother had cracked up, but as he sat sucking, he realised this was more than an emotional hiccup. Something in her was different. She was calmer and more collected than she'd ever been. He sensed that there could be no going back. Life for Ferdy – for all the Frosts –

had altered forever. The vicious reign of Ferdy the First had come to its end.

Deep down, buried beneath the arrogance of his pampered genius, a normal nine-year-old sighed happily and whispered, "About time, too."

*

While Ferdy Frost was facing up to an uncertain future, Joan Casey was discussing the play with a middle-aged American in an *I Kissed The Blarney Stone* T-shirt. "It's remarkable," she said. "I've been covering this event for twenty years and I've seen nothing like it. It's as if they've been reborn."

"I don't know about that," the American laughed, "but they've cooked up one hell of a play. My mind's been bending backwards trying to keep up with all the changes, yet I've hardly stopped laughing."

"I'm going to write a glowing review," Joan told him. "I'll use every cliché in the book as usual, but for once they'll come from the heart."

"*I* can't wait to tell the folks back home," the American said. "So much depends on your guide when you come on a trip like this. We were lucky — we hooked up with a guy called Shane Gallagher. Know him?"

"I don't think so," Joan laughed.

"He's a coach driver. We were meant to go on a pub crawl – even though we're teetotal – but Shane dragged us out to this forest." The American shook his head admiringly. "The others and I all agree — when we get home, we'll tell everyone we meet about Shane Gallagher. He's gonna be the busiest driver in Ireland."

"He'll like that," Joan smiled.

"You kidding?" the American boomed. "From this day on, every week for the next twenty years, he'll have *Yanks* coming out his ears. He'll love it!"

*

Though Shane Gallagher would weep when he heard how well the play had been received, the fairies would shed no tears. They were having a grand time. None could recall when they'd last enjoyed a performance of the play so much.

"Will there be another fight in the final scene?" Cobweb wondered.

"'Twould not surprise me," Mustardseed commented.

"The Players are wild this year," Peaseblossom agreed.

"Aye," Moth sighed. He was the only one in any way dejected.

"What is wrong?" Mustardseed asked.

"I am sorry that they have left me out.

I would have liked them my good name to shout.

But in the shake-up the name they have lost;

None seems to recall that fine fairy — Moth."

"Fear not," Cobweb told him. "In years to come your name will ring

More oft' than the angels the lord's name sing."

"'Tis true," Peaseblossom said. "The joy of this most wondrous day

Shall pass. Dull repeats will soon wing our way."

Puck, listening in on the fairies' conversation, turned to Oberon and sighed.

"Your subjects speak the truth, good fairy lord.

If Chapman succeeds, 'tis but a brief chord

Struck, then lost, to the music of foul time;

Plenty strings more shall less pleasantly chime."

"I know," Oberon sighed, "but we can do nothing about that. Let us sit back and enjoy this moment. We will face the sad spectacle of the future in the morning."

The ghost of Will Shakespeare smiled. Four hundred years was no time at all to one of the dead, but to the fey folk it must have seemed an eternity. Perhaps it was time to put paid to that old stipulation of his. He'd enjoyed many laughs at the fairies' expense but there was a point beyond which any joke was no longer funny. Yes, he decided, the time had come to free Oberon and his allies. This would be the last performance that they'd be required to attend. Before returning to the heavens, he'd lift the curse and pardon them their obligations to the play.

His smile widened as he imagined the celebrations. He was keen to tell them the good news, but upon viewing the downcast faces on either side, opted to hold his tongue a while longer. When the play ended, and they were turning to head home... *then* he would speak and set their hearts cartwheeling.

"Timing," the ghost chuckled smugly. There were some things one never lost the knack for, alive or dead.

*

Don recovered during the break. His eyes fluttered open, his pupils adjusted, and he found himself staring into the caring face of his beloved.

"Morning, sleepy," Ingmar grinned.

"Morning?" Don bolted upright. "I can't have been out that long!"

"Calm down," Ingmar laughed. "I was joking. It's night and the play's still in progress."

Don spotted the other Players slipping into their costumes. "Where are we in it?" he asked.

"About to launch into the final act," Ingmar told him.

"How did you manage while I was unconscious?"

"It's a long story and we've no time now — I have to get ready. Do you think you can continue?"

"Give me a moment," Don said. He stood and waited for pain to wash over him. When it didn't, he grunted happily. "I can go on."

"He's OK," Ingmar called to the others.

"Good," Terence said and tossed the Theseus costume across. "Get him into that, and be quick about it — they're returning to their seats."

"Why did you attack?" Ingmar asked quietly while they dressed.

Don stiffened. "I saw the way you stepped in to protect Diarmid, or whatever his name is. I didn't like it."

"I'm a big boy," Ingmar said. "I can do what I please."

"But what happens if it doesn't please *me*?" Don pouted. "Am I supposed to let you throw yourself at every Tom, Dick and –"

"I threw myself at no one," Ingmar protested. "I merely wanted to make sure he wasn't hurt."

"You wouldn't have done it if you didn't care for him," Don said.

"True," Ingmar replied, "but you don't have a monopoly on my feelings. I can care for other people — it doesn't mean I care any the less about you."

"He couldn't love you like I do," Don said quietly.

"Really?" Ingmar sniffed. "Shall I put him to the test?"

"Do what you want," Don sighed.

Del, who'd been paying close attention to the lovers, slipped out of earshot and drew Finn aside for one final set of instructions.

"I am not sure," the changeling muttered.

"But you want it to end on a high," Del hissed, "so that they can live happily ever after."

"Do I?" Finn gazed coolly at Del. "Maybe I have fallen in love with Ingmar and want them to break up, so I can take him back to Feyland with me."

Del's face dropped. "You can't," he gasped. "That would spoil everything. Don would be devastated."

"You care what happens to him?" Finn asked.

"Of course," Del snapped. "I care about all those fools. I want to honour my contract with Oberon but I don't..." He stopped, eyes narrowing. Finn was smiling. "You've no intention of stealing back to Feyland with him," Del said accusingly.

"Certainly not," Finn laughed. "I just wanted to hear you admit you cared." He patted the human's cheek. "You put on a tough front, but underneath you are soft as butter on a warm summer's day."

"That was a mean trick," Del sulked.

"You have played meaner ones," Finn reminded him.

Del grimaced. "OK, you got me. Now, will you play along like I asked?"

"It will be as it always has been between us," Finn said.

"You lead, and I will follow. It has worked well so far — why break the formula now?"

"You know," Del mused, "I'll miss you when you're gone."

"And I will miss being here," Finn sighed, then managed a weak smile. "But all good things must end. Besides, it is not like we need never meet again. If the Players split, you will be welcome any time in Feyland with open arms."

"I don't think I'll pop by too often," Del told him. "Not my kind of place."

"Mine neither." Finn laughed uneasily. "Still, it is home." He stared around at the dark forest. "The only home this poor changeling has," he muttered sadly.

A couple of minutes later, the Players were dressed and in position. The last of the stragglers were back in their seats, everybody was settled, and the very trees themselves appeared to be holding their breath, waiting for the final act of what promised to be the final ever outing for the Midsummer Players.

5.[I](vii)

Anna and Don opened the final act, as Hippolyta and Theseus. Terence was close behind as Philostrate, one of the Duke's pompous attendants. The couple sat in a pair of high-backed chairs, while Terence stood slightly to the left and rear. The royals mused on the story the four young lovers had told them, Theseus dismissing it out of hand. The Duke then noticed the quartet entering and addressed them.

"'Here come the lovers, full of joy and mirth.

Joy, gentle friends, joy and fresh days of love

Accompany your hearts.'"

Had there been enough actors, the four would have sat beside the royals for the rest of the play, but that was impossible given the defections, so the two available lovers – Finn and Kate – along with Del and Ingmar (who'd covered himself in Nuala's costume and wig), stepped fleetingly into the glade.

"'More than to us Wait in your royal walks, your board, your bed!'" Finn replied to Don's welcome. They then slipped away and into their other costumes. The few lines they should have exchanged with the royals during the rest of the act – comments on the antics of the amateur players – would now be divided between Anna and Don.

Theseus asked Philostrate for a list of the night's entertainment. Dismissing the early acts, he grew intrigued by the description of the amateur actors' piece.

"'A tedious brief scene of young Pyramus

And his love Thisbe, very tragical mirth.'"

Don paused as Theseus and scratched his chin wonderingly.

"'Merry and tragical? Tedious and brief?

That is hot and wondrous strange snow!

How shall we find the concord of this discord?'"

Philostrate explained that though the play was short, it was so awful it seemed long, and while it was in theory a tragedy, it had reduced him to tears of laughter during the preview. Theseus ordered it be played. Philostrate begged him to spare them all the agony but the Duke insisted and the actors were sent for. As Ingmar stumbled on as Quince, Terence slipped backstage to get into his Snug costume.

Ingmar cleared his throat and bowed to the royals, fumbling with his fingers, acting nervous.

"'If we offend, it is with our good will.

That you should think, we come not to offend,

But with good will. To show our simple skill,

That is the true beginning of our end.'"

He continued in his clumsy manner, Theseus and Hippolyta passed sarcastic comment, then the other Players, as the amateur actors, made their entrance. Finn appeared as Bottom, cast as the noble Pyramus in the play-within-the-play. Del replaced Felix as Flute, clad in the controversial dress to portray Pyramus' lover, Thisbe. Terence was Snug, here playing Wall (the part would have been Snout's had they not dispensed with the character) and Lion. And Kate was Starveling, who would glitter as Moonshine.

Ingmar rattled through the Prologue, detailing the forthcoming story. Pyramus and Thisbe were in love, he told the royals, and given to whispering through a chink in the

Wall. By Moonshine they agreed to meet at a tomb, but a Lion scared Thisbe away. She dropped her mantle, which the Lion stained with his bloody mouth. Pyramus, finding the mantle and fearing his lover dead, killed himself with his sword. Thisbe, returning, drew her lover's dagger and also committed suicide.

When Ingmar mentioned Wall's name, Terence held up a sheet of brick-printed cardboard. When the Lion was named, he jammed a shaggy orange mane on top of his head and growled menacingly.

While the other actors exited, Terence remained on stage, discarded the mane and held up the cardboard wall. He explained who and what he was, and how Pyramus and Thisbe often whispered through one of his chinks.

Finn, as Pyramus, then returned and took his place by the Wall. He bent, peeped through the hole, beat his chest and moaned,

"'O grim-looked night, O night with hue so black,
O night which ever art when day is not!
O night, O night, alack, alack, alack,
I fear my Thisbe's promise is forgot!
And thou, O wall, O sweet, O lovely wall,
Thou stand'st between her...'"

Finn continued, oscillating his O's in an outrageous manner, milking the ridiculous lines for every possible laugh. It was a fun role for an actor, designed to be played in a deliberate hammy fashion.

Del entered as Thisbe, almost tripping over the hem of his dress. He stopped on his side of the Wall and began beating his chest in mimicry of Pyramus. When he spoke, it was in a high-pitched woman's voice.

"'O Wall, full often hast thou heard my moans,

For parting my fair Pyramus and me.

My cherry lips have often kissed thy stones,

Thy stones with lime and hair knit up in thee.'"

Pyramus heard the voice of his love and the two bent, their lips mere centimetres apart, to croon to one another. After a time the hero sighed and beseeched his fair love, "'O, kiss me through the hole of this vile wall!'"

They puckered up and made wet, kissing sounds. Del then turned to the audience, winked, and yelled triumphantly in a deep male voice, "'I kiss the wall's hole, not your lips at all,'" to remind those in the crowd of the character's earlier plea not to be put in a dress.

That was meant to be that as far as the kiss was concerned, but as Del turned back to the wall, Finn – as the two had plotted prior to coming on – leant forward, grabbed Del and kissed him passionately.

There were laughs from all corners of the glade, but Ingmar cried, "No!" and rushed out to separate the embracing pair. "Stop it," he yelled. "He's mine!"

"What is wrong?" Finn snapped.

"You... he... you..."

"Jealous, sweet pea?" Del laughed and pinched Ingmar's bottom. "You'll have to move aside, Romeo. Finn wants a real man, not a fop."

"A... a..." Ingmar's eyes grew round and, before he knew what he was doing, his fingers worked themselves into a fist and he punched Del with surprising force, straight on the nose. Del hadn't expected that and was caught a beaut. His nose popped and blood gushed.

"Oh my," Ingmar gasped, staring at his bloodied knuckles, then dashed to the safety of the wings.

Letting his head tilt back, Del tried to stem the flow of blood with his fingers.

"Are you alright?" Finn hissed.

"Stay on your own side of the wall," Del hissed back, then added, "Your line."

Remembering where he was, Finn slipped back into Pyramus mode and bent again. "'Wilt thou at Ninny's tomb meet me straightaway?'"

"'Tide life, tide death,'" Del moaned above the pain, "'I come without delay.'"

Taking off in separate directions, the two rapidly made their way to the rear to regroup and tend to the injured nose. Terence, as Wall, lowered the piece of cardboard and turned to address the two royals.

"'Thus have I, Wall, my part discharged so;

And being done, thus Wall away doth go.'"

He hurried backstage, glad of the chance to see what the hell Ingmar was up to, how bad Del's damage was, and if either was fit to continue.

Del was reclining on the grass, holding a handkerchief to his bloody nose. Finn was beside him, studying him anxiously. Ingmar was standing to one side, gazing miserably at the pair.

"Is he OK?" Terence snapped at Finn.

"I think it is broken," Finn replied.

"Can he continue?"

"Yes," Del groaned. "I'm not pulling out this late in the game."

"Good man," Terence beamed, then glared at Ingmar. "I'll deal with you later," he growled, slipping on his lion's mane. "Kate — ready?"

"Ready," Kate answered, appearing beside him in her Moonshine costume. The pair returned to the edge of the glade and awaited their cue.

"Fuss over me," Del whispered to Finn.

Finn glanced over his shoulder at Ingmar, nodded and smiled. "Del, darling," he purred. "My stomach dropped when nasty Ingmar struck you. Your poor nose. Let me kiss it better. I will die if it cannot be fixed."

"Don't lay it on so thickly," Del giggled, but he needn't have worried. Ingmar was too contrite to notice the absurdity of the act.

"I've been a fool," he whimpered. "Is dis what I've put everyting on the line for? A man in love with another, who can never return my feelings? Oh, Ingmar!" He beat his head (softly) and cursed himself in German.

"Has the Plan worked?" Finn asked Del quietly.

"I'd say so," Del smiled. "We've cured him of his infatuation with you. He'll fly back to Don and maybe stay true to him in future."

"I love a happy ending," Finn sighed, removing the hankie from Del's nose. A few drops of blood came with it but the worst of the flow had passed. "Are you sure you can continue?"

"Try and stop me," Del replied, sitting up.

Out front, Terence had introduced himself as Lion, then bid the ladies in the audience not to be afraid, and told them he was really only Snug the joiner. When Kate, as Moonshine, began to explain who she was, Theseus and Hippolyta kept interrupting with wry remarks, until Moonshine burst into tears and sobbed,

"'All that I have to say is to tell you that the lanthorn is the moon, I the man i'th'moon, this thorn bush my thorn bush, and this dog my dog.'"

"'Why, all these should be in the lanthorn,'" Theseus remarked, "'for all these are in the moon. But silence: here comes Thisbe.'"

A brief wave of applause rippled through the crowd when the red-nosed Del hobbled on. He acknowledged the claps with a brief wave, then concentrated on the action. "'This is old Ninny's tomb,'" he squeaked. "'Where is my love?'"

At that moment Terence leapt up as Lion and roared, "'O!'" Del yelped and ran, dropping his mantle. His hands were sticky with blood, so he had to shake them hard to lose the cloth, adding more humour to the scene.

Lion chewed the dropped mantle, then ran off. Finn strolled on moments later as Pyramus, found the mantle, decided it meant Thisbe was dead, realised he could not live without her, and drew his sword.

"'Thus die I, thus, thus, thus!'" He stabbed himself with the sword in time with each 'thus,' then knelt over and lay still.

A couple of seconds passed quietly — then he sprang up.

"'Now am I dead,

Now am I fled;

My soul is in the sky.

Tongue, lose thy light;

Moon, take thy flight.'"

Kate exited as Moonshine. Finn flopped forward and moaned into the earth.

"'Now die, die, die, die, die.'"

And, finally, he was dead. Theseus and Hippolyta passed some snide comments, then Del returned – cowering in fear of another Lion attack – as Thisbe.

"'Asleep, my love?

What, dead, my dove?'"

Del recited a mournful eulogy, then drew the dead man's dagger and studied it (as Theseus wryly remarked) by starlight.

"'Come, trusty sword,

Come blade, my breast imbrue!'"

He stabbed himself theatrically.

"'And farewell, friends.

Thus Thisbe ends –

Adieu, adieu, adieu!'"

Toppling forward in imitation of Finn – careful not to hurt his nose – Del spread himself and breathed his last as the doomed Thisbe.

"'Moonshine and Lion are left to bury the dead,'" Don as Theseus noted.

"'Ay, and Wall too,'" Anna as Hippolyta replied, at which point Finn sprang up as Bottom to correct her.

"'No, I assure you, the wall is down that parted their fathers. Will it please you to see the epilogue, or to hear a Bergomask dance between two of our company?'"

Theseus refused the offer of an epilogue but invited the actors back to do their dance. So Del arose, while Kate and Terence returned, dragging Ingmar along with them. The German caught Don's eye and smiled sheepishly — Don knew nothing of what had happened offstage, took it for a look of love, and winked back.

Kate and Ingmar performed a comical dance while the others surrounded them, clapping and humming. Once the dance came to an end, they bowed to the royals, then to those in the seats and on the benches – except for Del, this was their final appearance of the night – and ran off to tumultuous applause.

With the amateur actors disbanded, Don stood and clapped authoritatively.

"'The iron tongue of midnight hath told twelve.

Lovers, to bed; 'tis almost fairy time.'"

When he was finished, he took Anna's arm and the characters left the glade for their nuptial bed. Following a brief pause, Del emerged as Puck, carrying a broom. He propped himself up with the broom and gazed mysteriously around the dark, silent glade, eventually speaking in a low, hushed voice.

"'Now the hungry lion roars,

And the wolf behowls the moon,

Whilst the...'"

As he delivered his penultimate speech, the others were hugging and quietly celebrating their success.

"Don't get too carried away," Terence said. "Anna and Don have one final turn. Are you ready?"

"Almost," Anna answered, swiftly changing costumes.

Don didn't reply.

"Don?" It was dark back here and Terence had to take a few steps forward to locate his bald friend. He found him in Ingmar's arms, the two entwined, kissing, all wrongs put right between them. Terence smiled softly. He hated to disturb them but there was the play to consider. "Don." He tugged at the drama teacher's elbow.

"Go 'way," Don grunted.

"But what about –"

Don turned and there were happy tears in his eyes. "Terence," he smiled, "be a good chap and piss off." There was no venom in his voice, merely a desire to be left alone with the one he loved.

"But the final scene," Terence gasped. "What –"

A soft hand touched his shoulder. Anna was holding out a wig of blonde curls. "Shall we, my lord?"

Terence checked with Don one last time – he didn't want to deprive his friend of his final bow – but when the actor showed no interest, the director smiled and accepted the wig. "Thank you, my lady. Now where are the robes?"

While Terence was dressing, Kate sat silently in the darkness, brooding on the events of the night. It had been one of the most satisfying of her short career, but now, with the end in sight, she felt empty, as though this was as good as it would ever get. The play had gone well, but who'd been present to bear witness and whisk her away to stardom? Tomorrow it would be back to bit parts, waiting for that elusive break. Waiting. Waiting. Wait–

"Excuse me?" Looking up, she saw a stranger standing over her.

"Can I help you?" she asked.

"I hope so," the stranger said, then dropped to a knee and took her hands in his. "With all my heart I pray you can."

She frowned as his features came into focus. "Michael Finnt?"

"Aye," he said softly.

"I thought you... How did..." She remembered her manners and smiled. "Glad to see you, Michael. Have you been here long?"

"Long enough to spy the most exquisite of creatures lighting up the crevices of this dark forest," he said.

She blinked. "Pardon me?"

"Pardon *me*, madam," Michael replied, "for not chancing upon you sooner, for neglecting you this long. 'Tis an injustice I intend to correct most shortly."

"I'm not sure I..." Kate's head was spinning.

"Will you walk with me, Kate of the Pummels?" Michael asked, rising. "Will you let me tell you of my love for thee and the future I envisage for us both?"

"Love? Future? But..."

"Nay," Michael said, pressing a pair of fingers to her lips. "Think and speak not. Just walk and listen to my words. Will you, my beautiful Kate?"

Kate wasn't sure what was happening, but as she gazed into the actor's eyes, she couldn't turn down his request. Feeling her spirits lift, she nodded eagerly and let him tug her to her feet. Michael turned and led her on a walk along the forest paths, and though the night was dark as death and it was unfamiliar ground, their feet never stumbled nor missed a step.

Behind the departing pair, Terence and Anna had joined Del in the glade. They ambled, arms lovingly linked, blessing the house of the slumbering lovers, promising beauty and good fortune for the children of the mortals. As Terence launched into what should have been Don's final speech, a pair of brothers were facing each other backstage, one as miserable as the other.

"Fair greetings, good brother," Diarmid said sadly.

"Hi," Finn replied glumly.

"How passed your stay in this mortal land?" Diarmid enquired.

"I had a laugh," Finn sniffed. "How did you fare in Feyland?"

Diarmid sighed. "I too was moved to laughter."

"It is a pity we cannot do this more often," Finn said.

"Yes," Diarmid sighed, "but we're bound by the word of our parents. One must to Feyland and one must remain."

"Aye," Finn agreed. "Well, I guess there is no point putting off the moment any longer. I do not want to stay to the end — I hate goodbyes. Shall we exchange places, brother?"

"We'd better," Diarmid said. "I'll return and take your bows, while you slip back to the world of dreams and continue with your joyous life."

"Joyous!" Finn sneered. "Years of picking daisies with a neutered pack of... *Joyous*. Hah!"

Diarmid frowned. "You sound reluctant to return."

"Of course," Finn snapped. "Who would not want to dwell in this marvellous land of sex and cunning creatures, where each day brings trials and pleasures new and unexpected?

Feyland is for fairies. *I* belong here." He groaned. "But I shall away. I shall obey." He took a step towards the fairies in the glade.

"Hold, brother," Diarmid stopped him. The banker was gawping. "You prefer this mortal realm to that of the fey?"

"Of course," Finn retorted. "Do you not love it too?"

"Nay. I despise it with a vengeance."

The twins stared at one another, stunned.

"Looks like the fey folk took the wrong baby," Finn chuckled.

"And left the wrong one behind," Diarmid agreed.

"If only we could..." Finn stopped.

"Couldn't we?" Diarmid whispered.

"Oberon would object," Finn said uncertainly. "The pact..."

"...states that one must go and one must stay," Diarmid mused. "Names were never mentioned. With identical twins, it was thought that one would prove as good or bad as the other."

"Then it is in our hands to trade places?"

"It seems so."

They pondered the situation some more.

Then, slowly, they began to smile.

Terence and Anna were also smiling as they left the glade for what would prove to be the final time. Their heads were touching and they spoke in soft voices. Terence didn't even turn to watch Del deliver the closing speech. He had eyes only for his wife, the most alluring woman in the world.

The director frowned when a man stepped forward to

block their path. He glared at the stranger, determined to shoo him away, but before he could speak, the man babbled, "I know I shouldn't be back here, especially with the close of the play yet to come, but I couldn't wait. My name's Christopher Big. I'm an agent. I know you're not going to be able to give me an immediate answer, but have the pair of you ever thought of turning professional?"

"Professional?" Terence asked uncertainly.

"Do this full time? For a living?" Anna blinked.

"Trust me," Christopher said, "I've been in this game a long time and I'm not given to rash judgements. If you throw in your lot with me, this time next year you could be directing and starring at the Globe."

Terence trembled. "*Shakespeare's* Globe?"

"None other," Christopher beamed.

Terence stared at the agent, then at Anna. "What do you think?"

She shrugged. "I'm through acting – tonight's it for me – but I like the idea of being married to a famous director." She gave her husband's arm a squeeze. "We should listen to what he has to say."

Terence nodded slowly. "OK," he wheezed.

"Great," Christopher boomed. "Is there somewhere private we can talk? We've a lot to discuss and very little time — I'm due back in London tomorrow. Now," he said, taking their arms and leading them off into the forest, "how does a forty percent agent's fee appeal to you...?"

In the glade, Del was only sixteen lines away from the close of the play.

"'If we shadows have offended,

Think but this, and all is mended:

That you have but slumbered here

While these visions did appear.'"

"Two weeks," he was thinking. "Two short weeks but it feels like a lifetime."

"'And this weak and idle theme,

No more yielding but a dream,

Gentles, do not reprehend;

If you pardon, we will mend.'"

It had been an eventful fortnight. He recalled how uptight the Players had been when he arrived, the underlying friction, the laboriously straight version of the play they'd intended serving up.

"'And, as I am an honest Puck,

If we have unearned luck

Now to 'scape the serpent's tongue

We will make amends ere long.'"

Del had done them a favour. He'd scuppered any future outings, but he'd also freed them to live fuller, happier lives. They'd look back and laugh at the memory of these two weeks, point to them and say, "There's where the tide turned, where we learnt how to live."

"'Else the Puck a liar call.

So, good night unto you all.'"

But what about Del? Where could he go from here? Ordinary life would be a comedown after this. Could he return to plain reality? Inside, he shrugged. Of course he could. That was the great thing about bobbing along on the waves of chaos — there was always something new around the river's bend. Life would never again be this exciting, but it would be different. New people, new situations, new challenges. That would be enough. Right now he had this glorious moment when he was the centre of all in the world, and he intended to enjoy it.

"'Give me your hands, if we be friends,'" he shouted to the audience, spreading his arms and twirling slowly. They began to rise to their feet and clap even before he started the final line, and as he spun and spoke, the world itself seemed to be applauding. "'And Robin shall restore amends!'"

It was only as he left the glade, ears ringing with the sound of claps and cheers, that he realised he was crying like an undernourished baby.

EPILOGUE

∞ ∞ ∞

As the sun rose on what would be a cloudy day, Del Chapman squatted in the centre of a deserted glade and basked in the ghosts of memory. *There*, Felix and Nuala had made-up. *There*, Terence had attacked Finn. *There*, Ingmar had launched his final, surprisingly powerful offensive.

The glade had emptied many hours before. There was no group bow at the end, despite the whistles of the audience. Del and Finn had wanted to go out but most of the others couldn't be found or weren't interested. Eventually the crowd dispersed, marvelling that the Players were as modest as they were brilliant. The Americans buzzed about the play all the way back to their hotel (driven by a numb Shane Gallagher). Joan Casey stayed glued to her PC until dawn, trying to transfer into words the magic she'd experienced in the glade. Ferdy Frost sat meekly in the car as his mother drove him home, and said nothing disrespectful as she enthused about the show. And the fairies (a delighted Diarmid in tow) tromped back through the portal to Feyland, unaware of the Bard's impending announcement which would soon set their hearts exploding with fireworks of ecstasy.

Del couldn't detail all that had happened. He didn't know who the men with Kate, Terence and Anna were, or what had transpired between the twins, or where Ingmar and Don had disappeared to. But he didn't care. The success of the project was all that mattered. The fine print was for trivia buffs, not he.

Del had passed the intervening hours wandering the forest. He couldn't have slept, even if he'd wanted. The place was so alive. For the first time in his life he realised how busy the world was at night. Bats, owls, badgers, foxes, slugs — he marked the passage of them all, his senses temporarily heightened.

Finally, with dawn breaking, he returned to the glade. He walked around the grassy rectangle, stepping over chairs, smiling at the memories. Making his way to the centre, he crouched low and circled back to the questions which had plagued him earlier. What next? Where now?

He dwelt on the matter for moments only, before realising there was just one way to find answers. Coming to his feet, he strode across the meadow and slipped through the forest, never looking back, putting all thoughts of the past from his mind, facing forward, letting fate direct him as it pleased. Wherever he ended up — that would be where he was going. Whatever happened — that was what his future would entail. It was as simple and complex as that.

*

Two nights later, with the moon riding high in the sky, a brooding Del Chapman was shuffling along a narrow lane. He wasn't sure how he'd got here, or even where he was — the last two days were a blur.

As he exited whatever town he'd washed up in, and his feet guided him down a lonely road, a car pulled up and the driver honked his horn. Del thought about letting the car pass, but it was shaping up to be a damp night and he didn't want to spend it outdoors, beneath a bush.

"Thanks," he said as he sat in. "Where are you...?" He stopped as he made out the shape of an imp behind the wheel. "Puck!" he gasped.

Robin Goodfellow beamed at his passenger. "Pleased to see me?"

"Sure," Del grinned, "but why are you here?" He grew worried. "It's not about the Players, is it? Have they agreed to reform? Listen, if Oberon's sent you to drag me back, I'm not –"

"Nay," Puck laughed. "Even if they had reformed, 'twould make no difference to us good folk of Feyland — but I will tell you about that later. Right now, there is somebody I would like you to meet."

Puck nodded over his shoulder. When Del looked back, he realised they weren't alone in the car. A man – no, a *fairy* – was sprawled across the seat. The fairy in the rear wasn't bright and smiling like the fey folk Del was accustomed to. In fact, he looked dark and wretched.

"You are the Del Chapman I have been told about?" the stranger asked. "The one who split the Midsummer Players?"

Del nodded warily.

The troubled sprite smiled thinly, hopefully. "My name is Ariel," he said. "We have to talk…"

And as Ariel talked, Del smiled. And his smile soon gave way to thick, chaotic, anticipative laughter. And behind the wheel, a merry Puck drove. And outside, the moon shone. And beneath the moon, the world turned. And all was well.

THE END

this dream was spun between 26th june 1997 and 13th april 2018

Leabharlanna Poiblí Chathair Baile Átha Cliath

Dublin City Public Libraries

9 781717 200021